FOR CRYING OUT LOUD

J. PRESTON

For Crying Out Loud
Book 1 in the False Start Series

The moral right of J. Preston to be identified as the author of this work has been asserted by her in accordance with the Copyright, Designs and Patents Act 1988.
All the characters in this book are fictitious, and any resemblance to actual persons living or dead, is purely coincidental.

Copyright © 2021 by J. Preston

All rights reserved. No part of this publication may be reproduced in any form or by any electronic or mechanical means, including information storage and retrieval systems, or transmitted in any form or by any means without the prior permission in writing of the copyright owner, except for the use of quotation in book reviews.
To request permission, contact jo@authorjpreston.com.

Edited by: Adora Dillard
Cover Design: Ashley Santorro

Published by DIRTY TALK PUBLISHING LTD
www.dirtytalkpublishing.com

Contents

Author's Note	vii
Prologue	1
1. Remember Me?	9
2. What Just Happened?	25
3. Punishable By Strangulation	35
4. She Who Can Tame The Jerk	49
5. Edward Cullen Is Our Immortal Friend	63
6. In Need Of Divine Intervention	75
7. I'm Sexy And I Know It	85
8. Wiggle, Wiggle	97
9. I Sleep Naked	109
10. Totally Innocent	121
11. Wittle Kissy-Wissy	129
12. Temporary Insanity	143
13. Plenty More Fish	155
14. Horrible Kisser	165
15. Two Birds One Stone	175
16. Lonely Immortal Schmuck	187
17. Grow A Pair Pendejo	201
18. Basically Straddling Aiden	211
19. I'm A Lover	221
20. A Big Can Of Whoopass	229
21. Wonders Of The World	241
22. Cop A Feel	257
23. Nothing But Trouble	269
24. Pretty Hung Up On Someone Else	277
25. I Trusted You	285
26. Mr Perfect	293
27. You	301
28. Well, The Dogs Like Her	313

29. J To The Double N	325
30. Mile High Club	331
31. Sweet Cheeks	339
32. Sociopath	349
33. Hey, Beautiful	359
34. So Fucking Much	375
35. See Her Again	383
36. One Voicemail	389
37. Beep	393
38. Family	395
39. The End	407
Epilogue	413
For What It's Worth	421
For What It's Worth	429
About the Author	435
Acknowledgments	437
Also by J. Preston	439

To my husband.
Thank you for believing in me and supporting this dream of mine.

Author's Note

Thank you so much for picking up my novel and supporting me in this exciting new adventure. Your kind words and reviews are what keeps me motivated to write.

FOR CRYING OUT LOUD PLAYLIST
Music is a huge part of every book I write.

To listen head over to Spotify just scan or click the QR code

I hope you love these characters as much as I do.

Jo, xoxo

Prologue

Six years ago

For months, I've been basically stalking Jason's little sister in hopes of her noticing me. Now my time is up. This is her last week before she moves with her family again, and I am determined for her to finally see me.

I know her schedule by heart. In the next thirty seconds, she will walk through the main door and over to the swings. She'll drop her backpack on the ground, pull out one of her books, then read for the next half hour, swinging, while Jason finishes his football practice. He'll then come and pick her up, and they will walk home together like they do every Friday. The only difference is that this Friday they will start packing, and next week she'll be gone from my life forever.

Jenny Cowley is ridiculous.

Girls like her should not exist, purely for the fact of being so out of everyone's league.

Alas, she exists. She and her ridiculously blue eyes, the

eyes that are the colour of the sky in the Bahamas. Then there are those stupid, long, brown locks of hers. They can't decide whether they want to be straight or curly, so they are straight on the top and morph into the cutest curls below her chin.

She's always so quiet, sitting by herself reading her books, a complete opposite of her loud and popular brother, his presence demanding attention wherever he goes. Jenny turns heads too, not that she notices. God, last week a guy slipped on the floor of the cafeteria a few feet away from where she was reading. Food everywhere; a broken nose.

Jenny didn't look up once.

She just kept on reading, lost in her own world. I couldn't look away, my eyes drawn to her throughout the whole thing.

I've got it bad, I know. The whole thing is a bit pathetic, but it's not like anyone will actually comment on it. Not because I'm a loner. I get invited to all the parties and have a fair share of girls that seem to be interested in me. Thing is, I'm not tall or muscular or particularly handsome. One thing I've got going on for me?

My surname.

I'm Aiden Vaughn.

Yup, that Vaughn, from *the* Vaughn Industries. As in, my dad is one of the richest men in the UK, owning pretty much everything you can think of.

Because of my family name, I became 'the popular guy'. The guy who everyone wanted to be friends with. The guy who lives in a ten bedroom mansion in Kensington. The guy who threw the sickest pool parties, whose dad owned not one, not two, but ten Ferraris. Who even needs that many?

The guy whose parents were never there for him. The

guy surrounded by people: maids, staff, peers, so-called 'friends'.

The guy who was very...alone.

My dad's money made me popular, and I resented him for it.

Until this school year started. That's when everything changed.

It started with gossip.

All everyone was talking about was the two new kids, the siblings from the States.

I met Jase first. He walked into my English class, introduced himself, then sat down next to me, extending his hand and smiling from ear to ear.

Jason didn't have a clue who I was and was genuinely being friendly. It was a pleasant change from the leeches I had to deal with daily.

We ignored the teacher throughout the class and continued whispering about countries we've been to, cars, and football. By the end of that period, I was smiling for the first time in a while, happy to have finally met someone who didn't know who I was. Someone who was being himself around me.

Then came lunchtime.

I grabbed a sandwich and a packet of crisps, waving Jason over to come and sit with our group. He made his way to us, then stood next to the table, hovering. A short girl poked her head out from behind his back, smiling tentatively. The most beautiful blue eyes I've ever seen zeroed in on me as she waved awkwardly.

It hit me like a ton of bricks. She was gorgeous.

Her heart-shaped face had a few freckles scattered across her small nose, her full pink lips a stark contrast to her porcelain complexion, and those eyes, those ridiculously blue eyes, framed by long lashes.

When she noticed me staring at her but not waving back, she looked down, letting her long brown hair hide her face.

I never believed in love at first sight, but I was damn close to believing now. I wanted to touch her, make sure she was real.

"This is Jenny," Jason introduced her to everyone. She smiled again, and that was that. If she'd asked at that moment, I would have given her anything: my homework, my parent's money, my kidney. Just like that, I was a goner.

I'm not sure why, but that was the first and last time she ate with us. She was a year below and ate with a few girls from her year or by herself, reading a book.

I spent most of my time watching her in silence, like a shadow. Creepy and idiotic, I know. A year went by like that in a blink of an eye. Then, about a month ago, Jason told me his dad was changing stations again, and he and Jenny were going to have to move with him.

The first thought I had wasn't about my best friend moving away. It was about her, about not being able to see her again, not having the prospect of telling her how I felt.

When you're fourteen, things like that feel life-altering. The person you're in love with moving away? It ruins your life. I couldn't let her go without trying.

That's why I'm waiting.

I look at the entrance to the school, willing the doors to open. She should be out by now. My watch, an expensive gift from my father for a good grade on some stupid test, confirms she's late.

Nervously, I tap my foot, glancing around, then finally... the door opens.

Jenny walks out, her head tilted towards the sky, soaking up the sun. One of her white, knee-high socks has slipped down to her ankle. Her uniform peaks out from under the large, green military jacket she's wearing with the sleeves rolled up. Wrapped around her neck is a Gryffindor scarf; it's the first time I've seen it on her, and I swear I fall for her even more. Her chestnut hair moves, floating up with every gust of wind. She is spectacular.

Easily the most beautiful girl in the school; I've recently discovered that she doesn't even know it. She certainly never acts like it. Other girls would flip their hair, voices high pitched, laughing too loud, and lapping up all the attention.

Not Jenny.

I walk over to the pair of swings where she's heading, taking my time. When she sits down on one and opens her book, I sit down in the swing next to her and start rocking gently, drinking her in.

We're swinging like that for a couple of minutes, me studying her features while she's completely lost in her book. Her face first frowning at the words she's reading, then spreading into a wide smile. My heart is doing some serious acrobatics in my chest at the sight. The sun is shining on her hair, making her locks look like they're on fire. I can't hold it in anymore. I reach out my left hand and grab onto the chain of her swing.

Here goes nothing. "Hey," I breathe. Jenny frowns, as if irritated by the interruption, and then looks up from the book. Her gaze reaches my face, and the frown morphs into a bright smile.

"Hey, Aiden." She looks at me curiously, puts a marker on the page she was reading, and closes the book. It's *Life of*

Pi by Yann Martel; it's got a tiger in a boat on the cover, and I'm instantly intrigued.

"How's the book?" I ask as my mind goes completely blank. Her entire face lights up.

"It's amazing! You should definitely read it!" She says, grinning, and I can't help but grin back. Great, I'm so bloody obvious.

"Really? I'll check it out then," I say, shrugging my shoulders, and she smiles even wider.

"Here, take my copy and start as soon as you can." She thrusts her paperback at me. I hesitate, not wanting to take her copy away. "I've got another one at home. Dad bought two by mistake," she explains, nudging me with the book. I take it tentatively and put it in my lap.

"Thank you," I say, looking into her blue eyes. There are so many things I want to say at that moment, but words fail me. Instead, I dry my sweaty palm on my trousers and reach out, taking her hand in mine. It's small and soft and feels fragile.

"It's nothing," she replies, looking with confusion at our joined hands and blushing. Digging her shoe into the ground, she takes a big breath and looks away, fixating on something far away. I relax a little. She's nervous, like me.

"So you're leaving soon?" She looks up at my question and nods solemnly.

"Yeah...." she trails off. "Another year, another country..." She looks upset, so I pull our swings close, locking her knee between mine. We're facing each other, her nose inches away from mine.

"Don't be sad," I whisper, pulling her in for a hug. At first, she stiffens, but then quickly relaxes into me and puts her head on my shoulder, sighing. Her proximity makes the blood boil beneath my skin. Like a crack addict needing a fix, I inhale. Her hair smells like strawberries. My new favourite fruit.

"It's just that..." Her voice is muffled and upset, so I hug her tighter. "I hate moving. I hate new places, new people, having to constantly start over..." She pulls away and looks at me. There's determination in her eyes. "I just want to stay in one place for a change... I-I just want to be normal," she finishes in a barely audible mumble.

My heart hurts right along with the sorrow on her face, and I am sure. If I ever had any doubts, they're all gone now.

Making her happy is the one and only purpose of my existence.

I lean over, touching my lips to hers. Jenny gasps in shock, opening her mouth, and I decide to take the plunge and kiss her the way I've been dreaming of.

It's all I've been thinking about for the past year.

Kissing Jenny.

Jenny, whose lips are soft and vaguely taste of bubblegum, delicious. I close my eyes, slip my tongue inside her mouth, and wait.

Should I move it? I slowly drag it around her lips then slip it back inside her mouth.

She's not responding.

Shit, what if I'm doing it all wrong? I've kissed before, but never someone I really wanted to.

My tongue is producing copious amounts of saliva right at this very moment, even though every single time I've tried to talk to Jenny before, it dried with such speed, sound would have been like- *whaaaaat?*

Great.

I try to swallow some of the excess saliva, but it's tough when your tongue is hanging out in someone else's mouth.

Cracking open my left eye, I see Jenny's horror-filled

ones are wide open, and then... Then she punches me in my stomach.

What the-?

I pull my lips away, confused. She looks angry. Furious even. Her lips are wet, shiny, pink, and shoot me now, but I want to kiss them again, feel how soft they are, taste the bubblegum. My hand moves of its own accord, reaching for her face. She jerks away and wipes her mouth with the sleeve of her jacket, bends over to grab her bag, and runs away before I can process what happened.

Holding onto my stinging stomach, I touch my lips. My heart aches before my brain catches up.

Jenny doesn't like me; she hated the kiss. She hates me, she must hate me. That's the only explanation for why she'd punched me, right?

I squeeze my eyes and move my hand to my chest, which is now hurting a lot more than my stomach ever was.

Anger and frustration gather in my lungs with every breath I take.

No.

I will not let her humiliate me like this.

No.

I don't take rejection lightly.

No.

I will forget about her. I'm not in love. There's no way love hurts like that.

No, no, no.

Instead, I'll kiss all the girls and... I will tell the entire school that Jenny Cowley can't kiss! I'll make her last week in London hell on earth.

Yes!

That will stop my heart from hurting.

Maybe...

Chapter 1

Remember Me?

When life gives you lemons, throw them at life...
see if it'll make the same mistake again.
- Jenny

Every story must have a beginning. Something catchy to draw you in, something new. I'm not particularly fond of those — new beginnings. All that talk of second chances, being able to meet new people, make new friends, a fresh blank page to fill...

One.

Giant.

Lie.

How would you know, you may ask?

Well, let me explain.

I, Jenny Cowley, a nineteen-year-old who has only ever been kissed once and has a total of zero best friends, have lived in... Let me count. Oh, I don't know. Try fourteen different countries?

For I, my dear friends, possess the very rare ability to suck at starting over.

New beginnings. Huh.

Being a military brat did me no favours either. Since the ripe age of five, my dad dragged my brother and me all over this planet. Each year, we would live somewhere else. Paris, Warsaw, Sydney, Johannesburg, Berlin, London, Stockholm. You name it and we've probably lived there.

Wow, how amazing! I can hear you say.

Wrong!

Oh, so wrong.

Although I've picked up a few languages along the way, basically perfected British and Australian, and I got to see and live in some cool places, my childhood and teenage years were kinda lousy, actually.

An introverted, nerdy bookworm trying to make friends and not being able to stay anywhere for longer than a year doesn't quite go hand in hand. It's not like I was a hermit. I've tried, I really have, but none of my so-called friendships were strong enough to stick.

Hitting your teen years with no friends, no boyfriends, no prospects of said friends or boyfriends, and definitely no action is not a cakewalk. Trust me.

There are only so many things you can talk to your dad and older brother about. Periods not being one of them. Ha! Imagine that conversation.

Naturally, to save myself, and those dearest to me, the embarrassment, in times of need I'd turn to the Mother and Nanny of all — Google. I have learned many gross things from Google, like never looking up what a funny shaped mole might mean or why one has cold feet at night.

The answer will always be imminent death.

A result, which almost always leads to a heart attack or,

as the uneducated doctors of the world like to call it, a mild case of hyperventilation.

In time, my requests, no—downright demands—for a trip to the ER upon discovery of suspicious-looking discoloration on my toenail were met with laughter...

What can a teen do to survive such horrors except call upon child services? Well, this teen took matters into her own hands.

I studied hard, aced all my classes, got involved in extracurricular activities, and made it my goal in life to go back to the only place I ever called home.

I counted the years.

Months.

Days.

And now it's finally here, my last *new beginning*.

"Starwood, here I come!" I grin to myself, inhaling the crisp air as I walk out of the San Francisco International Airport and into the summer sun.

The eleven-hour flight from Amsterdam, where my dad is stationed at the moment, was a breeze. I fell asleep an hour into it and woke up with just enough time to change into shorts and a t-shirt in the small bathroom.

What wasn't a breeze was the turbulence halfway through my acrobatic changing clothes act. I may or may not have slipped and stuck my hand in the toilet... Let's just say I spent a good fifteen minutes scrubbing my left arm.

"Jenny!" A familiar voice calls out as I squint, looking around. My eyes are definitely not used to the brightness with which the Californian sun shines, so I reach into the back pocket of my shorts and pull out my Ray-Ban's.

Instantly, I spot the tall blonde dude standing to my left with a goofy grin and his arms wide open. Squealing with delight, I torpedo-style run into his embrace.

We're attracting quite a bit of attention, especially from girls standing in our vicinity, as he picks me up and twirls me around. Not the: *Awww, look at these two, so cute!* No, more like: *What the hell does he see in her?* kind... Nothing new there. I've had to put up with it most of my life. Jase, my older brother, and I look nothing alike. In fact, people always take a while to believe that we're actually related. When I was 7, Jase insisted that I was not his actual sister but a 'stray' Dad had picked up off the street and brought home one day.

I still think he may have been onto something there.

You see, Jason is gorgeous, objectively speaking, of course. He has that surfer-boy look, which he inherited from our dad. For some reason, girls seem to dig that, which makes him the ultimate chick magnet. His chiselled jaw, messy blond curls, and muscled arms make girls go 'ga-ga' for him. As if that wasn't enough, my brother was also born with a permanent tan and a 'tall' gene, which only adds to the things girls go crazy for when they see him.

I, on the other hand, am the exact opposite and a spitting image of our mom. 5'4 on my tiptoes and, on a good day, pale complexion with a heart-shaped face and long brown hair that's unbelievably hard to tame. The only similarity between us is our sky blue eye color. We both got that from our mom.

"Put me down!" I laugh out loud and wriggle in his arms.

"What? Too old to be seen hugging your brother?" Jase lifts his left eyebrow, hugging me tighter and pouting a little.

"No, you're suffocating me, you dork!" I chuckle as he lowers me to the ground.

"All right, all right!" He scoffs, still pouting. A girl to my left swoons a little. "Where are your bags, Squirt?"

I groan inwardly at his choice of endearment. I have avoided being called squirt for the past year, and that nickname is not making a comeback. Mark my words.

Pointing at Sully O'Sullivan, my monstrous blue suitcase, I lean down to pick up the tote bag I dropped while jumping into Jason's arms.

"Sooo, where is she?" I ask eagerly, looking around.

"Where is who?" My brother plays with the hem of his t-shirt, not fooling anyone.

"Come on, Jase! You know I'm talking about her. Where is she?"

"She's waiting in the parking lot..." Jason exhales in a huff and walks off, dragging my suitcase behind. Grumpy much? There's nothing else for me to do but to follow, so I bounce excitedly behind him.

Shit! The new me doesn't bounce!

I stop, clear my throat, and start my new way of walking, which I'm sure is akin to a runway walk. Gone are the old ways. I'm concentrating pretty hard, tongue out and all, when suddenly my head snaps up at the sound of my brother, the jerk, bellowing with laughter.

"Are you drunk? You're walking like Bambi on ice."

I glare his way and continue past him, reassuring myself that I can be a pro with enough practice.

Then...I spot her.

She's just as beautiful as I remembered.

Screaming with joy, I dart over to the blue 1964 Mustang Convertible I inherited from Nana. I hug her hood and coo. "Did you miss me, baby? I missed you. Look at you! Did you have a bath? Did Jasypoo give you a bath? He must have 'cause you're the shiniest baby here!" Jason snorts behind me, making me whirl around and narrow my eyes at his smug mug.

"Do you need some time alone, a fresh pair of underwear, maybe?" Innocently, I walk over to the comedy genius and, just when he least expects it, punch him in the gut.

Holy shit!

He doesn't falter, smirking at me instead! I cradle my right fist, Clyde in Bonnie, the left one, wishing I had an icepack on hand. Jason clearly has been working out this past year. "Anything else, Squirt?" I clench my teeth, the nickname fuelling my annoyance further.

"Nope, I'm good!" I make a conscious decision to hurt him later rather than further my own injuries at this very moment. I shake Clyde a little, then walk over to Kitt, looking at her adoringly.

Kitt has been Nana's pride and joy, second after me, of course. I named her that after discovering Nana's deep love for The Hoff and everything "Knight Rider". One of the few memories I have from my childhood is of us driving around Starwood, with the Knight Rider theme song blaring out of Kitt's speakers. I was five, and those were some of the best times I could ever remember. Shortly after my fifth birthday, though, Nana passed away. Dad was heartbroken, first losing his wife when I was born, then losing his mother.

We started moving around a few months after Nana's funeral...

I think Nana knew that no matter where life took us, Jason and I would always come back to Starwood, our home, and that's why she left us the house we grew up in. Kitt was always going to be mine.

"Earth to Jenny!" The devil incarnate dangles the car keys in front of my face, making me snap out of my thoughts. "Wanna drive, or can I have my last moment with her?" He asks.

Decisions, decisions, decisions. On one hand, I am

itching to hear the Mustang purr under my feet. On the other, I am totally the best sister ever since I know I should probably let them have this one last drive together. I decide on the latter.

"You go ahead." I smile at him, fishing my iPhone out of my bag. "I'm beat from the flight."

We slide into the car, and Jason puts Kitt's top down as he grins at me. I plug my phone into the upgraded sound system. The first notes of California by Phantom Planet blare out of the speakers as he wraps his right arm around me and hugs me to his chest, kissing the top of my head.

"Welcome home, Jenny." He says, and I sigh happily as we pull out of the airport.

The drive is pleasant and, sooner than expected, we arrive at our house on Columbia Street, just off campus. Stumbling out of the car, I trip over my legs and run to the porch, jumping on the same porch swing Jason and I used to swing on when we were kids. Sighing with content, I lean back, swinging with one foot and studying the swaying sky.

"Want to see your room, Squirt?" Jason asks as I move my gaze from the sky to his face. He's standing next to the swing, right where my leg is. Wrong move bro! I swing my leg out and kick him in the shin. Ha!

"Ouch! What was that for?" He asks, rubbing his shin.

"You should have learned by now that calling me Squirt comes with dire consequences, such as the wrath of Jen the Man!" I grin, hopping off the swing while Jason huffs.

As we walk into the house, I'm pleasantly surprised. Jason hasn't changed much apart from adding new sofas and putting up a sixty inch TV in the living room. I run to the bookshelves by the window and kneel over, digging into my old hiding spot. Soon enough, I find what I'm looking for. An old copy of *The Little Prince* by Antoine de Saint-Exupéry that Nana used to read to me every night before bed. I clutch the tattered paperback to my chest and follow Jason to my old room, hoping that he had the decency to change my old unicorn wallpaper.

To my surprise, we walked past my old door and headed towards the master bedroom.

"I thought you might prefer the big room." Jason smiles tentatively. My eyes widened with astonishment. This used to be Nana's old room. It looked completely different now. He painted the walls a warm hue of white and stripped the floors of the old, shaggy carpet, revealing dark stained wood. In the middle of the room there's a massive bed frame with two nightstands next to it. There's an enormous wardrobe, a chest of drawers in one corner of the room and a wide desk by the window, looking out into the backyard and pool. "It's the only one with its own bathroom," Jason continues as I look around in awe. All the furniture is painted soft, distressed white, giving it a French country style, and there are soft grey and pastel pink accents scattered around the room.

"You like?" Jason asks.

"I love!" I exclaim, realizing it's the same furniture that always used to be in this room, but no longer the awful poo-brown color. "Did you do it all yourself?"

"Aide helped me..."

"Aide?" I raise my eyebrow questioningly.

"I rented your old room," Jason exhales. "I was here all on my own, which wasn't fun, especially after my injury. Plus, it was nice to have the extra cash to run the house and buy groceries." I nod, not wanting to bring up what must have been one of the toughest years for my brother. After he broke his knee during a collision with a goalie, Jason's dream of becoming a professional soccer player was put on hold. He withdrew completely and made it clear that he was fine on his own. I'd missed him this past year, especially since I was so far away.

"I get it. Quite clever actually." I smile, mesmerised by my surroundings. Then it hits me. "My old room?" I chuckle, thinking of the unicorns.

"Calm down, the unicorns are gone." The mind reader answers.

"Shame. It would have been funny." Grinning, I slide past him towards the kitchen.

When I get in, I zero in on the fridge and open it in search of something to drink.

"Jason..." I groan. "Have you ever heard of this thing called food? You know you ingest it; it gives you energy then you poop it out?" I inquire mockingly. The fridge is empty, bar 15 cans of beer. Yup, boys live here. That much is clear. "We need to stop by a grocery store," I say, digging around the back of the fridge and fishing out a can of Cola. Score! "So who is this Aide guy, anyway?" I ask, turning around and closing the fridge. Jason is standing behind me with a stupid look on his face. So, basically looking like Jason.

"He's my friend from International Studies."

"Aaand?" I probe, opening the can and taking a large swig.

"You probably don't remember him, but he went to the same school we did when we were fourteen or something..."

"Cool," I say. Jason clearly isn't up to discussing our flatmate. Deep down inside, I am excited at the prospect of having someone else here. Jason is great, but too much of each other and things can turn brutal. "Do you want to go shopping then?" I change the subject. "We can get some food, and I want to get some stuff for the room. You know, bedding, curtains, cushions." I trail off, making a mental list.

"Aide should be here soon, let's wait for him and then we can all go together," Jason replies. I guess the two of them are attached at the hip.

"Fine, I'm going to unpack then. Let me know when he gets here so we can set off." I smile and turn around. As I walk to my room, I pull out the phone from my back pocket and send a quick text to Dad.

ME: *Arrived safe and sound. Jason picked me up from the airport. Kitt sends her love xx*

Before I can put my phone away, I get a reply.

DAD: *Glad to hear you're ok. I guess Jason managed not to burn the house down yet. Yay! Take care of him, munchkin, and be careful. XXX Dad*

ME: *I will. Need to unpack now, then going to get groceries. Miss you x*

DAD: *Miss you too. XXX Dad*

Setting the phone on my nightstand, I walk over to the large window and open it. The backyard and pool look so inviting that I briefly consider fishing out my bikini and going for a quick dive. But I decide against it, torture first, fun later.

I sigh and ogle Sully, which is leaning against the bed. Unpacking is the bane of my existence, and I toy with the idea of paying Jason twenty bucks to unpack it for me but quickly change my mind when I think of how he would make fun of my new clothes and underwear.

All my life I've been a bit of a tomboy. Not by choice, might I add. I was always in boys' clothes that were too big, courtesy of my brother, the giant. This last year, I invested in underwear that actually fit me—thank you, Victoria's Secret—and clothes that didn't make me look like a small boy. I was now in the possession of a few sundresses and a couple of jean skirts. Small steps.

Groaning, I unzip Sully and start pulling out my clothes, throwing them in random drawers. Some things never change, and I. Am. A. Mess. with a capital *M*.

Later, I'll sort them later, I decide as I zip Sully up.

I look at my handiwork, quite satisfied with the results, and proceed to stuff Sully under the bed, huffing on all fours, butt in the air, channeling my inner Grace Kelly with all that grace.

"You've got a killer arse." I startle at the British voice, banging my head on the bed in the process, and whirl around to face the offender. A tall guy is leaning on my door frame, smirking at me. He is hot, like seriously H.O.T. He must be at least 6'3, has messy brown hair and the most amazing green eyes I have ever seen.

I narrow my eyes. Killer ass? Is this a new way to greet strangers? I didn't get the memo. No matter how hot this guy is, he is not talking to me like that. No more miss nice and quiet Jenny.

"Keep staring and you can say bye-bye to your small balls," I sneer, eyeing him closer.

"Oooh, feisty. I forgot how entertaining you could be... sometimes." He smirks at me as the feeling of dread slowly creeps up on me. British accent... London... I clench my fists, trying to stop myself from pouncing on him and showing him just how feisty I can be.

"Who the hell are you?" I bark at him. He smirks and lazily looks me up and down. I silently pray. Not him!

Please God, not him. I'll give you my spleen, should you ever need it! Just. NOT. Him!

"Don't you remember me, Slobbery Jenny?" My jaw drops in horror. Only one person could call me this. Aiden.

The asshole who stole my first kiss back when I was thirteen, salivated all over my face, called me Slobbery Jenny, and told everyone that I was the one who couldn't kiss. Granted, I didn't know what I was doing, but he sure as hell didn't know either. I'm pretty sure he would have kept on traumatising me by drooling all over my face if I hadn't stopped him by punching him in the stomach and running away. Real brave, I know.

I look closer and sure enough, he looks familiar. He is much taller now, has muscles he definitely didn't have when he was fourteen, and has an aura of confidence about him which just spells 'jerk'. This is definitely Aiden Vaughn or Aiden Von Schmuck as I called him ever since *The Kiss*. He used to be skinny, gangly and as big a nerd as I was. He definitely changed. If I wasn't before, I am definitely, truly, madly pissed off now that I know who he is.

This dude stole my first kiss, did a shit job of it too, and now he is commenting on my ass? Oh, he is going to get sucker-punched again. I decided to give him a chance for an out.

"If I were you, I'd keep my sicko thoughts to myself and slowly walk away." I keep my voice level and take a deep breath, trying to control myself. I count to ten, real slow. One. Two. Three. Four...

"Oh, yeah?" He interrupts me. Dude has a death wish. I used to dream of this moment, you know? Finding him one day and punching the living shit out of him. Fair payment for all the hurt he caused me, right? I know that's not very mature, but I am certain that it will make me feel better. He was never this hot in my dreams, but that just made the stakes higher. I shall enjoy messing up that pretty face of his. "And what exactly will you do if I don't?"

There it is. That smirk. I wonder if he realizes it will cost him his pretty boy teeth. I smirk back.

"Meet my best friends asshole, Bonnie and Clyde," I growl, clenching my fists and literally jump on him, Bonnie and Clyde are ready to show him a good time. He doesn't expect the ferocity with which I lunge at him, and with an oomph escaping his chest, we end up on the floor in a pile. I quickly scramble up and start throwing punches at his chest. This should be more fun than the punching bag at the gym. As my fist connects with his stomach, we both wince in pain. Jesus effing Christ. Did Jason and this sad excuse for a guy live in the gym or something? His abs are so hard it feels like I'm punching the floor. I do not falter though and throw more punches his way, connecting with his shoulder, chest, and stomach. My aim is a bit off balance as the punches land all over the place.

"Ouch!" He winces. And I smile inwardly, happy that at least he feels some pain. "Stop it, you psycho! I was only joking!" he says through gritted teeth. His face ducks my punch, and he grabs my wrists, holding them tight to his chest.

I guess I am angrier with him than I thought since, in the heat of the fight, I yell, "You lied to the entire school about me!"

"What are you on about?" Oh hell. He doesn't remember? He ruined my first kiss, he ruined all kisses for the rest of eternity and he doesn't even have the decency to remember?

Shit. I am acting like a lunatic. Aren't I?

Hold your horses! I narrow my eyes at him. That lying piece of scum!

"You just called me Slobbery Jenny, you know exactly what I'm on about!" I snarl, trying to wriggle my wrists from the iron hold he has on them.

"All right, jeeez. Just calm down. I was only joking." Joking my ass! I'll show you joking! I take advantage of the position I am in and knee him in his jewels with all the force I have. He groans in pain, and I swear his eyes are tearing up. Ha! Eat this Hulk's prettier and less green brother!

"I hope it's the last time you joke about ruining kissing for me, asshole. Do you realize that after the disgusting kiss from you, I couldn't bring myself to let anyone kiss me ever again? It was *THAT* horrible and *THAT* traumatizing!" He stills, and his eyes grow wide. Shiiiiiiiiiit. Shit. Shit. Shit!

"I was your only kiss?" he whispers in astonishment, his forest green eyes searching mine for confirmation. I clench my jaw tight and look at a dark spot on a floor near his stupid ear. I've already said too much.

"What the hell?" Jason yells from behind. Arms wrap around me, pulling me off Aiden. Ok... So this might look sketchy from an innocent passersby perspective. "Jenny, why were you on top of Aide?"

"Errrr... No reason?" I ask, rather than state. My eyes dart around, looking for a lifeline. I obviously will not tell my brother the whole story.

"Yeah, no reason..." Aiden slowly gets up, his eyes stay fixed on me. "She slipped and I tried to catch her, but we both fell in the process?" He answers questioningly. So we are both terrible liars. No biggie. I'm sure Jason will buy it. Not.

"Right..." Jason slowly looks from me to Aiden, then back at me again. "Riiight."

"So shall we go to the store?" I ask innocently, changing the subject. Yup, I am that smooth. Sheer talent, ladies and gentlemen.

"That's why I sent Aiden to get you and say 'hi', actually." Oooh, so 'you've got a killer ass' does translate to 'hi'. Good to know.

"Let's go then. I'm driving!" I grin at Jason as if nothing is wrong and start for the front door.

"Actually, we're taking my jeep," Aiden interrupts my exit, and I turn around to glare at him. "We need the boot space, but you can ride up front and be in charge of the radio?" He looks at me apologetically. I stop glaring and try to figure out what his game is. I can take advantage of this situation.

"Fine," I smirk. I've got some torture music in mind. Maybe some N'sync, or better yet, yodelling! Short stick, you conniving little jerk. Short stick.

Chapter 2

What Just Happened?

I'm not clumsy! The floor hates me, the table and chairs are bullies and the walls get in my way...
- Jenny

Having the one guy you can't stand constantly by your side is infuriating. Ever since our fight on my first day in Starwood, Mr. Von Suck has been dancing around me like a puppet.

Jenny, would you like this? Jenny, are you warm enough? Jenny, your shoelaces are untied, you might trip and fall!

I did trip and fall, but that's beside the point.

I spent the last two weeks basically hiding from him. Where I went, there he'd be, making my life miserable. Whenever I'd be in a compromising situation, such as on my ass after falling down the porch steps, he'd be the first to help me. Coming out of nowhere, suddenly by my side, poof —like a freaking genie. All that was missing was a lamp.

I'm not quite sure what changed his attitude towards me, apart from growing a pair, but I am seriously not buying this goody-goody act. I suspect that, deep down inside, he is just coming up with a new way to humiliate me in front of everybody.

Jason is no help at all. It's like he is oblivious towards all the weirdness surrounding Aiden and me, or at least choosing to ignore it. As a result, I spend my days sitting in my room reading or in a general state of misery.

I tried sneaking out through the window once, but as luck would have it, Aiden was just coming out to the pool and witnessed my very graceful fall right into the rosebush. He had proceeded to drag me to the bathroom and insist on carefully cleaning all my scrapes. Brilliant. I'd made sure to look out for any poisonous concoctions in his bathroom, and I definitely did not stare at his bare chest...

After that incident, Aiden had taken up residence by the pool, sitting there all day and watching my window intently, waiting for God knows what. The sight isn't too bad, all shirtless, abs glistening from pool water. But there's only so much undercover ogling one can do before being discovered.

Consequently, my room turned into a den, the curtains drawn, doors closed. It's so dark in here it's giving me SAD. What's worse, the only time I get to use the pool is at about two am, when I am certain that both the guys are sleeping.

But no more!

Today is going to be different. I'm finally going to make it out the door. The weather is gorgeous and I just can't stand being inside anymore.

So here I am, dressed in a white sundress over my white bikini and wearing flip-flops. Armed with my purse and car keys, I will stealthily, ninja-style, make it out of the house. Just watch me!

I crack my door open and tentatively glance into the hallway, prepared to shut it immediately if I spot any males in the vicinity. The house is eerily quiet. There was no one by the pool when I checked earlier and my hopes skyrocket. Could this be? Not taking any chances, I tiptoe towards the kitchen and look out the window. Sure enough, the Jeep is gone! The Jeep is gone, people! Hallelujah!!!

With more confidence and a lot louder, I walk towards the fridge and grab a bottle of water before heading towards the front door.

In no time, I am outside, breathing the fresh air and soaking up the morning sun. Pure bliss. Just as I'm locking up, I hear a car coming down the street. Shitsticks! I'm not going down without a fight. I dart down the front steps and, like the mature person that I am, hide behind Kitt's back wheels just as Aiden's black Jeep turns in and parks in front of our house.

Three guys get out of the car. Jason, Aiden and Teen Wolf. Seriously, the guy looks like Derek Hale's hotter brother. He is beyond sexy.

Trying not to get caught crouching behind Kitt like an idiot, I quickly frog jump towards the side mirror and check my reflection.

"Whatcha doing?" I jump up, startled by the sudden discovery of my hiding place, and bash my head on the side mirror. Rubbing the sore spot on my head, I get up. Jason is leaning over Kitt's hood and looking at me with interest.

"Oh, I dropped my keys..." I say tentatively. Aiden and Teen Wolf walk over to us. No, Aiden walks. Teen Wolf? Well, he saunters, oozing hotness with every step. I blush and look at my neon orange toenails.

"Hey there, gorgeous." Aiden smiles at me.

"Love the white dress, Angel." Teen Wolf goes straight into pick up line mode as he looks me up and down. And although I can see through the cheesy line, heat still rushes to my cheeks. Stupid Teen Wolf.

Jason speaks up, saving me from standing there, blushing and wringing my hands, awkwardly.

"Dudes, small reminder here! That's my sister, so please wipe the drool off your faces before I puke." I hear throats clearing and man noises and look up at Jason, who is laughing.

"Jenny, this is my idiot friend, Carter. Carter, this is Jenny."

"Hey, nice to meet you." Carter grins as he walks over. "Where was Jason hiding you all last year?" he murmurs, leaning in to give me a hug. This would be totally okay, but being the nerd that I am, I have entirely misinterpreted his intentions and I stick my hand out to shake his, connecting with his package in the process. I squeak in horror and jump back as the grin on his face widens.

"You're mighty friendly." He winks at me. Dear Lord, please open the pits of Hell so the ground can swallow me whole. Thank you.

"Stop trying to corrupt my baby sister." My brother laughs at Carter.

"Hey, not my fault she finds me irresistible," Carter replies, putting his hands up in defence. Then he winks at me.

Again.

College boys... They're getting increasingly more irritating with every day. First Aiden, being all Aiden. Now this Carter dude thinks he hung the moon? I. Don't. Think. So.

My mouth opens and words come out before I have a chance to think. "Irresistible, eh? Sorry to burst your bubble, buddy. I prefer men to boys, so why don't you wait until puberty ends and call me then. Two years should be enough, right?" And there go my chances of having a boyfriend. Ever. Way to shoot down Teen Wolf.

"Ouch!" He puts a hand on his heart and winces, still smiling. In my peripheral vision, I see Aiden relax his fists. "I think I like you even more, now that I know you bite."

"Cut it out, Kennedy." Jason interrupts our brief exchange. "You're such a little manwhore."

"I might just change my ways for her," Carter retorts, not taking offence. His eyes are twinkling as he cocks his head to the side, looking at me. I bite my cheek, trying to stop myself from grinning. Is this flirting? I thought I was insulting him. But if this is flirting, I might actually stand a chance. I'm pretty great at insults. "I think she's special."

Jason snorts as he comes over and puts his large arm over my shoulder. "She's special all right." I kick him in the shin.

With my foot.

My foot, which is in a flip-flop. Holy Mother of broken toes!

But the pain is worth it because Teen Wolf smiles even wider and says, "I really like what I'm seeing, Jenny." Jason huffs and Aiden strolls over closer to us, barging into Carter's shoulder as he walks past him.

"Where are you going, beautiful?" he says, standing right in front of me, his green eyes focused. Ugh, I roll my eyes on the inside. What's with the compliments?

"I was going to go to the beach..."

"Which beach?"

"Wolf Cove." I narrow my eyes.

"Without a wetsuit? It's a surfer beach. Whatcha planning on doing there?" He cocks his head.

"Without a wetsuit, Dad. And I'll be beating the world record in holding breath underwater... I'm going swimming, obviously, what else?" I reply, smirking.

"You'll freeze your cute little butt if you go swimming without a wetsuit. There's a cold current in the bay."

"Watch me prove you wrong."

"With pleasure," Aiden replies, his eyes dancing with a smile. "Let me just go get my towel." What the hell?

"Are you serious? You're not coming with me!"

"Oooh. Are you scared I'll discover you're a little wimp?" He taunts.

Years of sibling rivalry kick in. "No way, Ponyboy!"

"Well then, it's sorted. I'm coming with you and bringing my stopwatch. We will see if you can last longer than ten minutes." What an absolute dork. Who even has a stopwatch?

"No problem, buddy, but what's in it for me?" I cross my arms over my chest.

"If you lose, you'll make me supper every night for a week—"

"And if I win, you'll do the same for me." I finish smiling sweetly.

"Fine."

"Deal," I say, already looking forward to having someone else do the cooking.

"Great." Aiden turns around and runs into the house.

"What did I just witness?" Jason asks, confused.

"We're all going to the beach?" Carter asks hopefully.

"No, mate, *we*'re watching the game. Stop staring at my sister like that!"

"Like what?" Carter smiles innocently. I smile back.

"Nothing," Jason grumbles as I smile even wider. I must look like a weirdo.

"Can I take you out to dinner?" Carter asks, and my jaw drops. He walks over to me, puts a finger under my jaw, and closes it gently.

I move my face away from his finger and clear my throat.

"Maybe," I say.

"Maybe?" he asks.

"Maybe?" Jason asks, perplexed.

"Maybe what?" Aiden asks, running back to us, towel in hand.

"Maybe." I shrug.

"What do I have to do to convince you to say yes?" Carter's eyes smoulder. Holy shit, that smoulder! My mouth goes dry and thoughts about breaking my self imposed Man Kiss Ban are crossing my mind. Surely it's time to wipe that awful first kiss from the memory.

"Maybe what?" Aiden, the terrible kisser, asks again, but louder and with a frantic tone to his voice.

"I don't know," I say to Carter, ignoring Aiden. "I'm not really into players."

"She's not into anyone," my brother pretend-coughs.

"Maybe what?" Aiden's voice is high pitched and practically shouting.

"Not for lack of trying." I scowl at Jason. "No one asked me out on a date before," I say before thinking. Ugh, now Teen Wolf knows I'm pathetic and will surely change his mind.

"How is this possible? You're beautiful and so—" Carter starts.

"If you lose, you go on a date with me!" Aiden shouts.

All eyes go to Von Schmuckattack and everyone goes

still. I look at him. Really look at him. He's pale and there's a light sheen of sweat on his temple. His knuckles are white as he's clutching his towel like it's a security blanket.

Somehow, jerkface stirred up a feeling akin to pity in me. I sigh. I really don't need to have any sort of feelings towards him.

"So now if I lose, I have to make dinners for a week AND go on a date with you?" He's dreaming if he thinks that's going to happen.

"Yes."

"What the fuck is going on, douchebags? Can we all agree to leave my little sister alone, please?" Jase interjects, he really needs to learn that telling me not to do something is a surefire way to ensure I'll be doing it.

"I can make my own decisions, thank you very much."

I look at Carter as he winks at me. AGAIN. Does he have something in his eye? A tick? God knows. He's clearly a player, but a hot one. And in all the books I read, the heroine always turns the bad boy all gooey. I fancy myself a gooey, sexy bad boy. "I might go out with you, but I want to make sure you're not a total ass first, so... How about we hangout some at first, and if you can keep it in your pants for the next couple of weeks, I'll grace you with my divine presence." His gaze is calculating, and he looks from me to Jason, who is shaking his head.

"I can," Carter replies. "But I'd be coming over and hanging out with you in the meantime. Since I'll be celibate, I can at least get to know you." I roll my eyes. What a jerk. But I need all the practice I can get.

"Great." I turn to look at Aiden. "If I lose," I start. "I'll do all those things and go on a date with you. If that happens though, and you ruin this first for me as well, I will find you and cut your balls off, capish? Also, since now we're adding things to the bet, if I win, you will do all the chores in the house, including scrubbing the toilets. Deal?" I say innocently.

"What other firsts did he ruin?" My brother and Carter ask in unison.

"None of your business." Aiden and I are in sync as we reply at the same time. He walks over to me and tucks a stray strand of my hair behind my ear, the back of his hand leaving a hot trail on my skin. I fight the urge to step back.

"Deal," he says and smiles at me.

"Jenny!" Jason growls at me. "What first?" He enunciated each word, furious. I can guess where his mind has wandered. The guy has no clue just how inept I am when it comes to men. Question is, though, should I save Aiden's butt? If you asked me a couple of weeks ago, I wouldn't have hesitated and would have handed his ass to Jason on a silver platter, but somehow I've grown to tolerate his presence. And honestly? I don't want his blood on my hands or his perfect, stupid face messed up. Don't judge me, he's nice to look at!

"Chill Jason. Just a kiss... My first kiss! He slobbered all over my face, it was disgusting."

Carter explodes into laughter as Aiden's face grows red. My brother wears a blank expression, then a small smile creeps up his face. It quickly disappears as realization dawns on him.

"You were the one who called Jenny that name?" He struts towards Aiden and punches him in the stomach. "You're an asshole. She cried for weeks after we left London!" Aiden bends over in pain. My face turns beet red, but I feel serious love for Jason right now.

"It's ok Jason, I'm long over it." I say coming over to him

and taking his hand. He is still pissed. And, let's be honest, I am not over it, but he doesn't have to know.

"I deserved that," Aiden says through clenched teeth.

"This is better than the Kardashians." Carter chimes in.

"Jason..." I say in a calming voice. "We talked it out and it's all good," I lie to my brother, and he relaxes a bit.

"Are you sure?" He asks, searching my face.

"Yes." I smile at him. "Now I need to go. I've got a bet to win," I say, kissing him on the cheek. "See you later, Carter." I look over at the Teen Wolf Casanova.

"Oh, you shall." He winks at me.

I walk over to Aiden and grab his hand. "Come on, moron, we've got to go," I mutter as I drag him over to my car. "Not sure if you realize, but I just saved your life. You owe me," I add quietly. He nods and squeezes my hand in reply. I like how it feels. My hand in his. Then I catch myself and take it back quickly. I should be shuddering in disgust, right?

I look back at Jason and Carter making their way into the house. Carter turns back and waves, flashing me a panty-melting grin.

How did this happen?

All my life not a single guy was ever interested in me, apart from that fateful day when Aiden kissed me, and suddenly I have two players asking me out... Weird.

I guess sundresses are magic. I wish I knew that earlier though. Would have saved me a lot of trouble.

Chapter 3

Punishable By Strangulation

Of course I'm an organ donor. Who wouldn't want a piece of this?
- Carter

Silence.

Ten minutes into the drive and we're both completely silent. As we reach 101, I can't take it anymore. There is, at least, another fifteen minutes of driving in front of us and silence is no longer on the menu. I switch the radio on and tap the first playlist on my phone.

"No more N'Sync, I beg you..." Aiden pleads, putting his face in his hands.

"Please!" I snort. "Like I didn't see you mouth along with the lyrics! Anyway, it was just the one time to screw with you."

From the corner of my eye, I see him staring at me incredulously, just as the first notes of Heat Waves play from the speakers.

"You know Glass Animals?" he instantly asks, puzzled.

"No, Sherlock," I reply, rolling my eyes. "I've got random stuff on my phone I never heard of, just for moments like these."

He clears his throat. "It's just that they're from Oxford."

"And?"

"Nothing, I love this song," he mutters, rubbing the scruff on his chin.

I sigh. "You know, up until a few weeks ago, I lived in Europe. It's not that crazy that I've heard of them. Stop being such a snob, Aide."

"I like it when you call me Aide." His mouth spread into a slow smile.

I exhale in exasperation. "Great. Now that we've got that sorted, why don't you tell me what you will be cooking for me when I win?"

"Not that you'll win, sunshine, but I'm a fantastic cook. Don't you worry about it."

I raise my eyebrow. He cooks? "Riiiight."

"I am!" he exclaims. "I'm basically a chef! I can even cook sushi!"

"By definition," I laugh. "You can't cook sushi, but ok MasterChef, I'll believe you... For now."

Aiden huffs but doesn't respond. We stay quiet for a few more minutes until I decide to break the silence between us. Again.

"Weather's been a bit of a downer," I say just as Aiden blurts, "Jenny, I'm really sorry."

"Huh?" I'm confused.

"Really? You want to talk about the weather?" Aiden looks at me in disbelief.

Well, what else did he want to talk about? My life story? No chance... Not because, since he ruined my life with that horrible kiss, I basically didn't have a life... Yeah, definitely not.

"What are you sorry about?" I glance his way.

Stay High comes on through the speakers and he closes his eyes and gently rocks his head to the music.

"What are you sorry about?" I ask again, frustrated.

"Apart from that N'Sync flop, I like your taste in music so far." He avoids my question.

"Awesome. I was awaiting your approval. Now I can die in peace," I say sarcastically. "Since we've gotten that out of the way, will you tell me what you are sorry about?" He looks out the window and then starts inspecting his cuticles.

"Aiden," I growl.

"I like this song. It reminds me of you." What. The. Hell? Did he just tell me that he thinks I can't get over him? I clench my right fist in anger, my face getting red. I'm two minutes from pulling over and letting Clyde say hello to his face.

"What?" I try to keep my voice calm. He clears his throat and rolls the window down, putting his arm out and making wave motions with his hand in the air.

"I mean," he clears his throat. "Never mind."

"Oh no, you don't! How does it remind you of me?"

"Well..." he starts again. "What I mean is... It's well... I can't keep you off my mind, no matter how hard I try."

My jaw drops all the way to the gas pedal and I swerve the car. Thank God there's barely anyone else on the highway. I collect myself, gripping the steering wheel tighter and chance a quick glance at him. His face is flushed, and he is looking out the window, gazing at the oh, so beautiful, industrial scenery. After a really long silence, he straightens himself up and looks over at me. I avert my eyes back to the road, pretending I wasn't looking at him at all. This, this is beyond confusing.

I hate him and he hates me. Is he saying he's trying to be indifferent? Although, I don't think I can honestly say I still hate him. He irritates the living shit out of me, but I don't hate him. I dislike him, and I still haven't forgiven him for what he did to me back in London... Which he has yet to apologize for!

How dare this asswipe tell me he can't get me out of his mind. What is that supposed to mean? And what the hell am I supposed to say to that? Guys...

Urgh! Idiot guys!

Deep breaths, Jenny. Deep freaking breaths.

"Look, forget it," he says just as I see our exit and indicate right, to get off the highway. I don't reply; I just drive and fume. Pissed as hell. The audacity!

Ok, so maybe I'm overreacting, but I am really, really upset that while he was off living his life, he unintentionally ruined mine and...well, now I have no experience with boys. Like zero experience, so how in the name of all that is holy am I supposed to know how to react to such statements? Cue my fury. In my head, that's the right way to react. Plain and simple.

The parking lot is empty. Swell! No one here to witness Aiden's gruesome murder! Thank God for small favors. I switch off the engine and jump out, rage propelling my movements.

Maybe I should have calmed down before jumping out. Maybe then my flip-flop wouldn't have gotten caught between the door and the seat. Maybe I wouldn't be flying onto my hands and knees now. Maybe. Who knows?

I land on my hands, scraping them on the asphalt, my

right foot still in the car, left on the ground, butt in the air, face inches from the ground. Ouch!

Within seconds, Aiden is by my side.

"Are you ok?" He panics, dislodging my foot. I whine, tears pooling in my eyes, the determination not to cry slowly diminishing. Aiden's eyes are glued to my butt. Butt, which is now fully exposed since my sundress flipped up over my hips... Fabulous.

"Will you stop looking at my killer ass and help me up?" I bark out, tired of his antics.

"It is spectacular. Truly, it should be framed and put up in Tate Modern for everyone to look at it in awe," he says wistfully, helping me up. "Then again, no, I wouldn't want anyone else looking at it." His eyes are dark and he is still looking at my butt, quite possessively. Someone, please write a manual on guys. I'm lost here. Who's the female equivalent of Neil Strauss? I need help!

My hands and knees are nowhere near as bad as I thought they would be, just a minor scratch on my left palm. Lucky. I make a move to pull my sundress down, then think better of it and take it off completely.

Aiden's eyes are wide as he is scanning my body in the white bikini. I smirk at him, throw my dress into the car, and stroll towards the water. Growing up a tomboy meant loads of sport and dangerous activities, which, in turn, meant a lot of scrapes and bruises, but also a body of which I am damn proud.

"Get your stopwatch ready, you're about to lose that bet," I say over my shoulder. I reach the water and kick off my flip-flops. Aiden is a few steps behind me, probably staring at my butt again. "Ready?" I turn around before walking into the water. Aiden nods, holding up the stopwatch and dropping the towel on the sand. He sits on the towel and waits, his eyes still roaming all over my body. I shiver as a chilly breeze touches my bare skin, take a deep breath, then turn back to the water and step forward.

"Son of a motherless goat!" I shriek. The water is freezing. So cold, the Baltic Sea in Europe can forget about its first place in my Coldest Bodies of Water in the World ranking.

"Cold?" Aiden laughs at me as I jump from one foot to another.

"Nope," I say in a high-pitched voice. "It's lovely, truly like bathwater." He bursts out laughing while I try to convince myself that getting into the water rather than turning around, walking over to Aiden, and strangling the smartass is a better option, or at least an option that will not end with a prison sentence. So far, I'm ankle-deep, and the prospects of going any further are looking slim. Maybe I should just run in?

"I need your shoulders submerged to start the timer," the keeper of time, also known as asshat, says mockingly. No, officer, I'm not guilty. He was being a major ass. You understand that's punishable by strangulation, don't you?

Goddamnit! I am not cooking for him! That's my new mantra, one that will drive me forward into the freezing water of San Francisco Bay. I take a couple more steps, goosebumps forming all over my body. I bounce on the balls of my feet and continue.

I am not cooking for him!

I walk further in the freezing water around my mid-thigh. Oh sweet baby Jesus! I jump from one foot to another, then in place. Then bounce parallel to the shoreline. I can do this!

I am not cooking for him! I am not cooking for him! I am not cooking for him!

I count to three and dunk!

"Aaaaaaaargh!" Someone screams. No, sorry. Not someone. I do. "Start the damn stopwatch!" I shout, then try to swim, but the water is too cold and my muscles are stiff. Nonetheless, I persevere and start swim-walking.

It appears I have found faith again as, between repeating my mantra, I prayed to anyone who'd listen for time to go faster.

"Thirty seconds." Aiden is standing on the shore, his toes barely touching the waterline. Smartass.

Thirty seconds?

Thirty seconds?!

How is that even possible? It feels like I've been submerged for hours! My toes are turning numb and I do not know how, but I am sweating in the water. Why am I doing this again? I can't remember. My teeth chatter and I try to walk the opposite way, but my muscles are really stiff, so I just stand there.

"One minute," Aiden is frowning, ankle-deep in the water. "Are you okay?"

"Peachy!" I reply, my voice hoarse and shaky. How the frak has it only been one minute? I feel so cold; I have to close my eyes and try really hard to breathe. Did I forget to mention that I am a major wimp when it comes to the cold? I'm the person always wrapped in three blankets while everyone else is sporting shorts and t-shirts. This might not have been my best idea.

"Jenny, if you're cold just get out of the water." His voice is pleading. I shake my head. If he thinks I'm quitting he's dumber than I thought he was. I'd rather die. "Jenny..."

"How long?" I interrupt, my voice with renewed power. No cooking, no cooking, no cooking! That was the mantra, wasn't it?

"Five minutes." Ha! Halfway. I close my eyes again, then open them instantly. What the hell was that? There was a shadow and I'm pretty sure it was a ginormous shark. The water is not so bad by now, probably cause I'm feeling numb. "Jenny please get out of the water, it's not worth it." I hear him say. Not worth it? Not worth it, my ass! Like hell, not worth it! Am I repeating myself? Why am I in the water again? I take a couple of steps forward, still fully submerged, but on bent knees, bent and really stiff. "That's it, love, just come out of the water." Huh?

Something slides over my leg and I shriek, losing balance.

"Jenny!"

I go underwater and the waves and stiffness of my joints are not helping. But the water actually feels okay now. My shaking body must have warmed it up. Friction and all that. Can you have friction with water? What happened to my brain? Oh my god, Jason's dumbness finally rubbed off!

Being completely submerged underwater actually feels much better than having my head out until the shark slithers against me again, and I open my mouth to scream. Water fills my lungs at the same time that a wave crashes into me. And everything goes blank.

Warm, strong arms wrap around me. I'm no longer in the water. The air is so cold that I whimper. Something fuzzy wraps around me and I bounce in someone's arms, Aiden's arms, as I'm being carried somewhere. I let my head fall on his warm shoulder and have a coughing fit, splattering water over his chest.

"I've got you." He whispers into my hair as he carries me for a while.

"Is she okay?" I hear a female voice.

"I don't know! Do you have showers here, can I use one to warm her up? She's freezing."

"Yeah, right this way." The voice is nasal and too loud.

Whatever was wrapped around me is ripped off, and I cling to Aiden like a shaking spider monkey when scolding hot water pours over my body. Like any sane person would, I scream.

My eyes fly open and I try to wriggle out of Aiden's grasp, but his hold on me is tight. He soothes me, stroking my hair and whispering into my ear. "It's okay, love, you'll be okay. You just got a bit cold."

I did not get a bit cold, goddamnit! A shark tried to eat me! But then he adjusts his hold on me, his hard chest pressing into my side and, for a minute, I forgot what I was going to say.

"I'm okay. Think I was just in shock," I murmur. The water feels tepid now that my body's adjusted to it. Aiden exhales in relief and reaches for the knob to increase the water temperature. I look up at him. He's not as bad as I thought. He saved my life from a shark attack, and it was an enormous one, Jaws size at least. I suppose he could have changed in the last few years. I wriggle in his arms again, but he is not letting go.

"Aide..." I say quietly, my voice hoarse. "Aide, I'm okay, you can put me down." His jaw twitches and his grip tightens. "You scared me to death." His eyes focus on mine. I want to look away, but I can't. His green eyes have me under some magical spell. They are dark, like emeralds, and it feels like they're looking straight into my soul. "If something had happened to you..." He starts again. "God, Jason would kill me." Is he seriously more concerned about what Jason would do than my near death?

"Well, you saved me from the shark, so you're good, you can put me down." He doesn't move, still looking at me. "Put. Me. Down!" I say, punctuating each word with a weak punch to his chest.

"Okay, okay. So violent." He puts me down, his arms still wrapped around me. I feel like a child next to him, he's so big and feels so strong. He reaches over, pushing a wet strand of hair behind my ear, his fingers tracing down my jawline then neck, leaving a hot trail. My breasts are pressed against the upper part of his abs, and I have to tilt my head up to look into his face.

Hold it!

MY BREASTS ARE PRESSED AGAINST HIS ABS.

We are both basically naked, bikini and swimming shorts excluded, and our bodies are touching. There is literally no space in between us for the water from the shower to get through.

This is the closest I have ever been to a boy! Scratch that, he does not feel like a boy. Aiden, all hard ridges and muscles, definitely feels like a man.

I must look like a deer caught in the headlights, because he lazily unwraps his right arm from around me and cups my face with his fingers, his thumb on my cheek, rubbing it gently.

"Don't ever scare me like this again. I just about had a heart attack when you stopped replying to me," he says gently, and my knees basically decide to stop working. If it wasn't for the fact that Aiden's left arm is still firmly holding my body, I'd be on the floor.

Melting into a puddle.

I take a deep breath to calm myself down, but, as luck would have it, I swallow some shower water and start choking. I'm a professional mood killer. I should put that on my resume, right after Microsoft Office Skills.

"Can we go home now?" I croak out. He nods and turns off the water, opening the shower door. There are a couple of fresh towels on the side. He grabs one of them and wraps it around me like a blanket, then reaches for the other one and puts it on top of my head, and the other towel. Not only do I feel like a small child, but by now I probably look like one too. Great.

He puts his arm around me and I start shivering again but don't dare speak for fear of having to go back into the shower with him again. I don't think I'd be able to survive another minute with him in there. As we walk outside, a pretty, young woman is waiting for us.

"Good, you're okay," she says looking at Aiden's bare chest. I grit my teeth, but make no sound.

"Yes, thank you for your help. We'd better get going though. Need to get this one somewhere warm," Aiden replies.

"Oh, sure..." She sounds disappointed. Then her face brightens. "Well if you ever need my help again," she says, reaching behind her desk, "here's my card." She hands Aiden what looks like a business card. "Call me anytime... If you need...anything..." She winks at him suggestively, and the urge to roll my eyes wins over my politeness.

"Sure... Thanks," Aiden replies and takes the card from her. Suddenly, I feel really irritated. I turn around and stomp outside in a huff while Aiden flirts with the woman. The sun is shining again, warming my still cold skin. I notice we're in the building next to the beach, probably a two-minute walk from where Kitt is parked.

Aiden walks out and drops something in the trash. My heart skips a beat as I realize that was the business card he got from the woman inside.

"I tried paying for the towels you're using, but Caroline insisted I just bring them back next time I'm here." He scrunches his face, still managing to look beautiful. "I'd rather not... Do you mind putting on some warm clothes so I can give them back to her straight away?" I nod, irritated that he knows her name, but relieved at the same time that he doesn't want to see her again. Caroline can suck it.

"I only have the sundress," I mutter.

"I think I've still got some workout stuff in your boot, from back in the winter." He smiles at me. "You'll need to take off that wet bikini." His smile grows bigger at the horror in my face. "Don't worry, I'll turn around." He winks at me then grabs my hand and walks me over to the car. I'm still shivering a little, but I guess that's a good sign. I hand him my keys and he pulls a duffel bag out of the trunk. From it, he takes out boxer shorts, grey sweatpants, a t-shirt, and a large hoodie.

"Now change," he orders, handing me the clothes. "Make sure you're properly dry before putting anything on." I nod and he turns around.

I guess I'm about to get naked in public. I look around and there is no one here except for Aiden and me. I rub my body with one of the towels then wrap myself with it, peeling the bikini bottoms off underneath it. I quickly put on the boxer shorts, then sweatpants. I then cover up my top and take off the bikini top. As I turn to grab the t-shirt that I put in the trunk, the towel slips and I squeal.

"Jenny, what's wrong?" I feel a hot breath on my neck. I quickly cover my boobs with my arms.

Turning red with embarrassment I say. "The towel slipped. Turn back around."

"Oh... Okay, not looking. I'm going to take the towels back. I'll be back in a sec," he says just as I pull the t-shirt over my head. I hand him the towels then reach for the hoodie, pulling it on and zipping it up. Bliss. "Oh and Jenny? I'm driving us back." I nod as he runs off. The sweatpants and hoodie are massive on me, so I roll them up so that they fit me. I find a pair of socks in the bag and put them on as well.

Finally I feel a bit warmer; the shivering has stopped. Relieved, I take a deep breath, which is when I smell it. I lift the top of the hoodie up to my nose and sniff again, just to make sure, and I have to sit down before I collapse in ecstasy. I could roll myself in this scent for the rest of my days! It is the most amazing thing I have ever smelled in my entire life, a mix of soap, citrus, and something earthy.

I take another deep breath then quickly open my eyes, making sure Aiden isn't back and witnessing my weirdness. He isn't. I close the trunk and slide into the passenger side of the car just as he jogs back, carrying my flip-flops. How did he remember my flip-flops? He gets into the car, turns it on, then wraps his arm around my shoulders pulling me in closer to his body.

"You need to be warm, just snuggle into me," he says when he realizes I stiffened. I relax a bit and put my head on his shoulder as we pull out of the parking lot. I take a deep breath and—oh my god—the scent that was lingering on the hoodie hits me full force, straight off of Aiden's body. I gasp and basically start drooling. "Are you okay?" he asks, getting back onto the highway. I try to say something, nod even, but I can't move or speak for fear of inhaling his scent again.

My brain turns into mush and my eyes are glassy, from lack of oxygen probably. How the hell have I not noticed his smell before? Do all guys smell this good? Because, if they do, I'm suddenly glad I've never had any social life.

I mean, how would I have ever graduated high school if I can't form even one coherent thought due to the smell of one stupid boy? This must be the near death experience talking. Yes, definitely.

"I have an idea!" Aiden interrupts my thoughts, hugging me closer. "Let's go get you something warm to eat. I know a great place just around the corner."

I manage a nod as we exit the highway.

Chapter 4

She Who Can Tame The Jerk

***When life gives you lemons, keep them...
because, hey free stuff.***
- Jason

"Here you go, sweetie." Mrs. Bloom puts a bowl of steaming hot soup in front of me and shoots Aiden a disapproving look. "Really Aiden, how could you let this happen? Look at the poor thing!" She pats my cheek, eyes full of concern. Aide's head hangs low in shame. Eat this sucker!

We arrived at 'The Cottage' B&B about ten minutes ago. As soon as we parked and my eyes fell on it, I fell in love with the white stone building, sloped roof, blue picket fence, and the massive apple tree by the main entrance. It looked just like an English cottage. A woman in her seventies ran out to greet us and, upon seeing Aiden, squealed with delight and started hugging him. Then she noticed me and the fuss started... She bombarded me with a million questions and hastily ushered us inside. After I recounted my near-death experience, *cough*, Mrs. Bloom, who turned out to be English, like Aiden, escorted us through a homely-looking kitchen to a dining area. Aiden and I sat down at a small wooden table and were told not to move until the food arrived. Between Aiden, Mrs. Bloom, and the whole cottage thing, I felt like I was back in England, thirteen again... Ahhh, memories... The rain, London, Big Ben, my old school, being slobbered all over by Aiden... Ew!

"Thank you so much for the soup, Mrs. Bloom," I say, smiling sweetly.

"Oh, please call me Jill, love. And dig in, you need to get warm from the inside." She looks back at Aiden sternly, making him cower. Huh. This is proving to be entertaining. Seems there are women immune to his charms. I should probably come here more often and take lessons in 'How to remain indifferent to hot guys'. Jill sighs loudly before walking away. I eat a spoonful of the warm soup and let out a moan of approval.

"So how do you know this place?" I ask Aiden once I've had a few mouthfuls.

He looks up at me, smiling. "I found it my first week in Starwood. I was feeling rather homesick, ready to pack up, go back to London, and I decided to go for a drive, clear my head. So I drove around until I stumbled upon this Bed and Breakfast. It looked like cottages back home and there was a sign that said 'We serve Full English Breakfast'. I was sold. Then I found out Jill was originally from Cotswold. We started talking, she fed me and...I've been coming here ever since. She's like a surrogate mother to me. Always asking me about my grades, if I'm dating anyone." He laughs. "That's probably why she interrogated you when we got here. She wanted to know as much about you as possible. Thanks for telling her about your 'near-death' experience." He makes quotation marks with his fingers. "And how it was my fault... I'm never going to live this down."

"Ease up, champ! It'll do your ego some good." I grin at him, trying to put on an English accent. I fail miserably, I guess, since Aiden chokes on his coke with laughter. Nevermind. I decided to change the topic. "So do you bring a lot of girls here?"

Aiden flashes me a smile. "Wouldn't you like to know?"

As a matter of fact, yes. I would. But I am definitely not going to let that slip, so I just shrug instead, taking another spoonful of the gloriously hot soup. Aiden's face falls a little, then that evil smirk of his appears on his face as he says, "Sure, lots and lots of girls."

I huff inwardly, obviously. On the outside, I am a pristine example of stoicism and indifference. I take another mouthful and bite off a large chunk of bread. Too large. I am now stuck chewing what feels like ten pieces of Hubba Bubba gum at once. Have you ever tried stuffing ten Hubba Bubba's into your mouth? No? Well, I did. Jason dared me to, and it was agony! Jason managed seventeen, which I'm pretty sure was because his brain is smaller, therefore he had more space. I made sure to share that opinion at the time, to his disdain.

My eyes begin to water as I try to breathe and chew at the same time. Pretty sure I'm looking like a hot version of a chipmunk. Doesn't bread get soggy with liquid, making it easier to swallow? Worth a try! I take another mouthful of the soup and let it just sit there, embracing the whole chipmunk thing as Aiden decides to speak.

"Listen... Jenny..." My ears perk up, and I try very hard to keep the bread and soup combo in my mouth rather than letting it trail down my chin as it's currently trying to do. "I think we should talk about what happened." He continues, oblivious to my struggles. I decide to let him talk. If he wants to talk about how I nearly died, I will not stop him. In fact, I'm pretty sure I will milk this for a long, long time. "I know you said to Jason that we've already spoken about this and it's all good, but we both know that was a lie..." I sit up straighter. Oh no. No, no, no, no, no. He is not trying to talk about that kiss, is he? I mean, does he want me dead? First the ocean, now the bread-soup currently lodged in my throat. My eyes bulge a little, but Aiden is not looking at me. He is examining his cuticles. What a girl... "So the thing is, I never explained what happened or said that I was sorry. Which I am, Jenny. I truly am sorry." He is what? Aiden looks up at me just as I graciously spit the contents of my mouth all over the table.

No, just take a second and imagine it. Projectile spit. Pieces of wet bread covered in soup scattered around. ALL. OVER. THE. TABLE.

Dumbfounded, I choke out the remnants of the food that was trying to kill me. Did he really just apologize to me? Aiden Vaughn just apologized... Well, color me surprised. Then again, what was he apologizing for? Kissing me? Doing a really shit job of kissing me? Traumatising me for life? Giving me a horrible nickname? Ruining my social life? Ruining any interest I might have had in the opposite sex? Although that last one has clearly backfired, as the interest has come back with the vengeance of a three-year-old who had their lollipop stolen...

I narrow my eyes at Aiden, wiping the drool off my face with the back of my hand, looking like a feral child, no doubt. Aiden looks horrified, grabbing napkins from the table next to us and cleaning up the mess.

"Are you ok?" He asks, panicked. I probably look like I

just had a stroke, mouth wide open, narrowed eyes, and disbelief and anger on my face. I rearrange my features into ones that do not resemble a weirdo and nod slowly.

"Sorry, choked," I say. "What are you apologizing for exactly?"

"Goodness me!" Jill appears out of nowhere, carrying a pot of tea. She sets it down on the table next to us and runs over to me, taking my hand in one of hers. "Are you okay, love?" She looks at me, concerned, then touches the back of her hand to my forehead as if to check my temperature. "What happened?" she asks, shooting Aiden a fierce look. I am about to speak when she whirls around to face him fully. "What have you done this time, Aiden?" She throws a cleaning cloth at him, and he starts wiping the table. "Honestly, look at the poor thing. She is horrified! Why would you scare the first girl you ever brought here? What have you said to her?" She yells at him. I look at Aiden, searching his face. Did she just say 'first girl' he's ever brought here? But he said... I mean... Lots of girls, no? I slump in my chair. Why would he lie to me? I'll never be able to understand guys.

"I'm really sorry Jill. I just swallowed the wrong way and Aiden surprised me and... I'm sorry," I say, deflated, looking at my lap. Aiden is still methodically wiping the table.

"Oh dear," Mrs. Bloom says. "It's all right, sweetie. Aiden will clean this up, don't you worry." She shoots Aiden another disapproving look, and he starts at the table with renewed fierceness. I think I might love this woman. She who can tame the jerk. "Would you like some tea? I've got some good old English Breakfast with milk for you." She smiles at me sweetly.

"I'd love some." I smile back as she hands me a cup.

Jill swiftly cleans up, then disappears, leaving us alone. We are sitting there in silence not looking at each other. Aiden is picking at his nails, acting all weird and nervous.

"Aiden," I sigh. His head shoots up. He zeroes in on me, his eyes big and hopeful and so freaking gorgeous and green I have to look away... When I look back at him, he is still gazing at me. I focus on a spot just above his left eye, hoping that it looks like I'm looking back at him rather than a major case of cross-eye.

"Jenny..." he says softly, his voice silky and deep. I'm suddenly glad that I'm already sitting because, man, can I just tell you, this voice would melt any girl into a puddle. And I'd go as far as to say it would probably make straight guys reconsider their orientation. I clear my throat and focus on the tip of his nose.

"Aiden." My voice is wobbly, so I clear my throat again. "Can we go back to before I nearly choked to death on bread and broccoli soup, please? I'd really like that."

"Sure." He smiles. I know that because my eyes wandered down to his lips. Treacherous eyes. I concentrate and move my gaze to one of his dimples. Isn't it annoying that he has dimples? It's like God knew all my weaknesses and decided to test me by putting them all in one person...

"Great, let's go back to what you were saying, then." I shake myself out of my daze and look him straight in the eyes. "You were apologizing." He instantly looks down at his hands.

"Yes." I hear his quiet voice. "I'm really, really sorry, Jenny." He looks back up at me and I can hear the sincerity in his voice. "I wanted to apologise so many times to you, but I was young and dumb, and so damn proud. I thought the world ended when you rejected me." He winces. "I'm so sorry for the rumour I spread around school. You hurt me and I just didn't understand... God, Jenny, I was an idiot. I'm sorry. Just really, really sorry."

I don't know what to say, so I keep on sitting here, quietly, just looking back at him. I'm not going to say that it's okay because, well, it's not okay. He fidgets a little, and when he notices I've got no intention of saying anything just yet, he starts talking again, his words coming out fast.

"Please Jenny, you have to understand. I was a stupid boy, still in school. I was an idiot and I just didn't realize—no—I didn't think of how my actions could affect you. God, when you said that I traumatised you and that it was the worst kiss ever... Well, it makes a guy really sober up, I guess. Have you really not kissed anyone since?" He looks up at me, and I blush like the inexperienced school girl that I am. I shake my head. "Damn!" he swears. "Jenny, I'm so sorry. Please forgive me?" He looks at me with his puppy dog eyes. Damn the man and his freaking eyes. I sigh.

"Here's the thing," I start. "What you did was a real jerk move, and it obviously impacted me in some way... But at least you're apologizing and trying to make amends. I can work with that, especially since we now live together. I mean, I have to see your face every day." I scrunch up my nose as if in disgust, and Aiden laughs, running his hand through his hair. What can I say, having to see his face every day is definitely not a chore; no, no, no. "I'll tell you what, let's just start over, ok?"

"I'd love that," he says with that silky smooth voice of his again, and he smiles at me. I decide to throw the guy a bone and smile back. This will be easy, right?

We arrive back at the house shortly after four. Carter and Jason are in the kitchen, chatting and drinking beer.

"Who won?" Jason looks up at me, then freezes. "Why the hell are you wearing Aiden's clothes?" He screams. Carter whips his head around, looking at me just as Aiden walks in. "What the hell, man? Why is she wearing your clothes?"

"Chill Jason," I step in front of Aiden, shielding him from my brother. "I was cold after my near-death experience. The clothes were in the trunk. I wore them to get warm, duh."

"Your what?" Jason's face goes white, and he stills. "Jesus, Jenny, what happened, are you ok?" He rushes over and hugs me.

"Oooh, I want to get in on that!" Carter says, then hops off the stool he was sitting on and runs over to Jason and me, still hugging. He launches himself at my brother and me, wrapping his arms around the both of us. "I love family moments like these," he sighs. "They make me feel so wholesome."

I laugh and wriggle myself free out from under them. They're still hugging.

"Don't worry," I say, grabbing my phone and quickly snapping a photo of the two of them, "I'm okay. I just got scared by a shark, that's all."

"Seaweed," Aiden coughs. I let it slide because, well, he's not wrong.

Jason pushes Carter away and sighs with relief. "Jesus, Jen. Don't scare me like that! So who won?"

"Who won what?" I ask.

"I did." I hear a person who's now dead to me whisper behind me, the adorable English accent suddenly annoying.

"Eh... What?" I whirl around.

"Well, I had to pull you out of the water at around the seventh minute—"

"Aha!" I point at him. "So you admit that you forcefully took me out of the water. I did not ask for it, nor did I agree to it!" Case closed.

"Jenny...you went underwater; you weren't coming back up. I didn't want you to drown."

"Still! I would have stayed in the water until the agreed time passed had you not dragged me out!"

Jason starts laughing. "Jen, I admire your spirit, but from what I am hearing, Superman over here might have saved your life. Least you can do is to cook for the man for one week."

"And go on a date with me, but we can do it later this week." Aiden's quickly whispered words were barely audible.

"Fine! You won. Happy?" I huff and stomp off to my room.

Once I slam my door, I turn and slide down to a sitting position. I thought that might happen, but after our heart-to-heart, I really believed he might let it slide. Would I let him off though if the roles were reversed? Nope, probably not. I sigh and jump into the shower.

After a twenty minute, steaming shower and at least five different interpretations of Aretha's "Natural Woman", I wrap my towel around my body, walk back into my room, and jump-squeal. You know, that thing you do, when you're startled and you scream and jump at the same time? Yup, that one. I did that.

Carter is lying on his back on my bed, his feet crossed and his arms behind his head.

"Did I scare you?" He arches his eyebrow, smiling up at

me. His eyes are twinkling. I compose myself then walk over to my dresser and pull out clothes I can put on.

"No, that's just how I usually greet highly annoying people. What are you doing in my room?"

"Waiting for you..."

"Why?"

"Just wanted to hang out."

"And you choose the moment I got into a shower to do so?"

"You were gone for a while... I thought you'd be done with your shower by now. Plus, I only got here two minutes ago, so I decided to wait for you. I knew you wouldn't be much longer and wanted to see your pretty face, and boy, am I glad I waited." His eyes are smoldering and I can feel my face getting red. He stands up, walks over to me, then reaches with his hand to pull a strand of wet hair behind my ear. I move my face to the side. When I speak, my voice is small and a bit too high for my liking.

"Well, could you please give me some privacy so I can get dressed?"

"I'd prefer to look, or better yet, for you to stay in that little towel, but I can turn around if you really want me to," he says theatrically.

I blush again because I want him to leave my room, but I also want him to stay. I take a couple of steps back, so I can catch my breath and think for a second, then make a quick decision.

"Do whatever." I say and walk back into the bathroom, locking the door behind me. Not taking any chances. I quickly dress in the shorts and t-shirt I pulled out of my dresser and towel dry my hair as best as I can. I look over my reflection in the steamed up mirror, then decide to pull my hair up into a high ponytail. That should stop him from touching it, I hope. When I walk back, Casanova is back on my bed, looking as comfortable as an old shoe. I stand in the doorway for a second too long.

"Come, sit down." He seductively pats the space next to him on the bed. His eyes are dark and hot, and something breaks in me. I laugh. Hard. So hard I can't stop for a good minute. "Did I say something funny?" Poor guy is looking confused but still trying to pull the sexy, dark, and dangerous thing.

"Man, you really like to try hard, huh?" Still laughing, I jump onto my bed by his feet and make myself comfortable, crossing my legs and pulling a pillow to my chest.

"I am not trying hard at all." He seductively smiles at me. "You don't want to see me try. You wouldn't be able to resist me." He sits up and moves just a little bit closer. My skin prickles.

"Oh please, try me." I say confidently. I am such a faker. Inside, I am shaking with anticipation...

"Very well." He moves closer to me. Once his knees are touching mine, he moves his hand to my wet ponytail and wraps it around his fingers. What is it with him and hair? "I love it when a girl puts her hair up, it's so sexy." He drawls the last word. "You look stunning like that. I can see your neck and that very kissable spot just behind your ear." His fingers, now wet from my ponytail, move to the side of my neck. My breath catches when they connect with my skin, and my heartbeat speeds up when he gently starts sliding them down my jawline. His face is getting closer to mine. My eyes connect with his dark ones. I can see the concentration behind them and something snaps. I start laughing. This time I fall face-first on the bed, thumping my fist into the duvet.

"Nothing?" Carter asks in disbelief.

"You almost had me," I gasp through laughter. "But I just don't think this," I point between us. "Is meant to be. I mean, you're super hot and everything, but, but, but..."

"I know!" He interrupts me. "There's just this friendly vibe between us, isn't there? Plus, I don't like to compete with my best bros."

"Exactly!" I exclaim. Wait, why would he be competing with Jason?

"Phew... I probably wouldn't have been able to just be focused on you anyway. You're superhot too, but a guy's got needs!" He laughs.

"Slut." I punch him in the shoulder and we start laughing again.

"See? We're besties already. This will work."

"Oh yes! We can braid each other's hair –" I start in a mock girly voice, but before I finish he starts laughing so hard that I can't help but join in.

Soon we're both lying on the bed giggling at each other. I'm holding onto my stomach, Carter's eyes are watering when I hear someone clear their throat.

"Wait, wait, wait." I laugh, putting my hand over Carter's mouth to quiet him down "Did you hear that?" He chooses that exact moment to lick my hand, making me squeal and laugh even harder. Someone clears their throat again.

Wiping my hand on Carter's t-shirt, I sit up to see who it is. And instantly stop laughing.

Aiden is standing in my door, his lips shut tight, forming a thin line, his eyes shooting daggers at Carter.

"Oh hey, bro!" Carter smiles at Aiden. "We were just getting to know each other," he says suggestively. I whip my head towards him and frown. What? Carter just winks at me, then drapes his arm over my shoulder and looks back up at Aiden.

"I can see that. I have eyes," Aiden says through clenched teeth. What is he so pissed off about?

"What's up, Aide?" I interrupt this weird exchange.

Aiden looks at me. "I was going to make myself a sandwich and wanted to know if you wanted anything to eat..." he starts, then looks over at Carter, whose arm is still around my shoulders. I try to shrug it off, but Carter is not budging. "But I just remembered, you're my cook." He finishes coldly. What happened to the guy who, not so long ago, was apologising to me? I thought we were going to try the friends thing... The guy in front of me looks bored and disinterested.

"Sure." I shrug, feeling a bit off. "What sandwich do you want?"

I can get through this.

Chapter 5

Edward Cullen Is Our Immortal Friend

When life gives you lemons, turn to life and say, "I didn't order this shit. Bring me the Oat milk Latte I asked for!"
- Jenny

The next day is not much better. Aide wakes me up, knocking loudly on my door and demanding breakfast.

I managed to wriggle myself out of making him a sandwich the night before by stating the deal doesn't officially start until the morning after the bet. Now, I'm clearly being punished for it. It's before six am on a Saturday, the last weekend before school starts, and I'm awake at this ungodly hour. I groan and drag myself towards the shower, before thinking better of it and stopping by the door to my bedroom on the way. I open it groggily only to see Aiden leaning on the wall, his arms crossed, his foot tapping impatiently. He is wearing surf shorts and a t-shirt with a Hula

Girl on it, and is basically looking fresh as a daisy, smelling of that citrusy, soapy mix that makes my knees weak. I, on the other hand, am in my tartan PJ shorts and an old Chelsea FC t-shirt that has seen better days. I definitely need a shower and a coffee before I can do anything.

"I'm just going to have a shower and then I'll make you breakfast," I say, pulling my hair out of the bun I slept in. It drops to my shoulders in a messy tangle. Great. That'll be at least half an hour of hard work.

Just as I'm about to turn and walk back to my bedroom, I look at Aiden and my lips turn into a half smile. He has ceased his highly annoying foot tapping, his hands dropped to his side and his mouth is slightly ajar. I cock my head to the side.

"I'll take your silence as agreement." I smile triumphantly and turn away.

"Wait." Aidan's voice is hoarse. I turn slowly. "I'm hungry now. Can you make me a sandwich and then have a shower?"

I groan. I'm about to protest, but the look in his eyes is so hungry, I don't.

"Fine," I huff. "Let me at least wash my face."

Aide nods then walks into my bedroom and sits on the bed, his gaze following my every move. I roll my eyes and walk into the bathroom. That's the second boy on my bed in as many days.

When I get back into the room, my bed is made and Aiden is flicking through my copy of *The Little Prince*. He looks relaxed, happy even, and like he belongs. I shake my head to get those thoughts out of my head just as Aide looks up at me, smiling from ear to ear, his dimples making my head spin, or maybe it was the head shaking? Yes, it was the shaking. Hundred per cent.

"Let's go then, oh master!" I say mockingly. Aiden just smiles wider and jumps off my bed.

He still hasn't told me what sort of sandwich he wants, so I decide on good old PB&J. I head towards the kitchen cupboards and pull out the jars, spotting some Wonder Bread. Yuck. But I'm not jumping through hoops for Mr. Grumpy Pants. I can feel his eyes following my every move. Suddenly, I'm aware of just how short my shorts are and how tattered and full of holes my favorite t-shirt is. I turn reluctantly, the bread in my hand, his gaze raising the hair on my arms.

Or is it cold in the kitchen? I should get to that shower fast, and the faster I can make that sandwich, the faster I can do it. I turn away from him, walk towards the kitchen island, and drop the bread on the counter.

"What do you think you're doing?" I hear Aiden's deep, smooth voice from behind me. I turn around, only to see him hovering close behind me. Too close. His breath hot on my neck.

"Making you a sandwich, wasn't that what you wanted?" I sigh. What a weirdo.

"Not with that crap, you're not! That loaf has been here since we moved in last year and looks exactly the same."

"Okay then." I move to throw the loaf in the garbage just as Jason, dressed in surf shorts and a t-shirt, comes into the kitchen and shrieks.

"What are you doing?! Leave Edward alone!" He grabs the loaf out of my hand and hugs it to his chest. Why the hell is he up this early?

"Edward?" I ask.

"What's happening to Edward? Did he finally go green? Did I win?" Carter runs into the kitchen, eyes wide, cheeks flushed. When did everyone start waking up at the freaking crack of dawn on Saturday mornings, and what is Carter doing here? I put my hand on my forehead. Do I really have to spend my time with these idiots?

"I thought you were going to wait in the car." Aiden narrows his eyes at Carter.

"Chill your pants, Aide. I was on the porch swing, listening to the birds and bees and all that, when I heard Edward's name, and we all know I've got money on this week." Carter replies, walking over to Jason, who is still cradling Edward in his arms, and gently prying it out, inspecting it. "Boo, no green." Carter makes a sad face then replaces Edward on the shelf I found him on.

"Do I even want to know?" I ask no one in particular.

"Edward is our immortal friend." Carter says, walking up to me and giving me a hug. This time I manage not to touch any offending body parts, I proudly notice. After a few seconds, he steps away, his arms on my shoulders appraising me.

"If that's how all the chicks in England dress in the morning, no wonder you English guys are into soccer." Carter grins at Aiden. "Isn't Chelsea your favorite team, *mate*?" Carter continues as Aiden turns red. "I thought so. Say Jenny, are you planning on putting something else on or shall we assume you're happy with our friend over there having blue balls while we're surfing?"

"Shut up, man!" Aiden growls as I wriggle from under Carter's grasp. Jason is deep in thought, looking at the loaf of bread, oblivious to the conversation going on in the room. I walk over to him, ignoring the other two males going alpha at each other like werewolves.

"Jason, Edward? Bread? Are you okay in the head?" I smile as I notice the rhyming. The two alphas in the corner look ready to grow fur. Edward... Immortal friend... Werewolves... Did they call the bread Edward after Twilight? It must be worse than I thought. Should I call psychiatric services or something? I thought I was the only one in the family that named everything, anyway. Jason sighed and looked up at me. "Edward? Like Twilight Edward?" I ask. Jason sighs again and nods solemnly.

"It was named by this chick I was seeing at the beginning of last year. I didn't have the heart to tell her that it sucked, and so the name just stuck. Now it's Edward, just get over it."

"Jeez, okay. So what's up with Edward then?" I gesture towards the loaf of bread. Jason sighs again, pulling a baguette from the cabinet and eggs from the fridge. "Since you're making breakfast, you might as well feed us all." He smiles, handing me a frying pan. I shrug and turn to the stove as he jumps up onto the counter and sits with his back leaning against the kitchen cabinets while I heat the pan and start slicing the baguette.

"So...?" I pull out plates, cutlery, and a large mixing bowl.

"So." Jason starts as I crack the eggs into the bowl. "Edward was here when we moved in—"

"What?" My jaw drops as my hand holding a pinch of salt stills above the eggy mixture. "You mean when I moved in a few weeks ago?"

"No, Jen, when I moved in last year!" He clarifies, passing me the pepper mill.

"That means it must have been here forever!" I exclaim, grabbing a whisk and fiercely beating the eggs, turning toward my brother with the bowl in one hand and whisk in the other. Jason narrows his eyes and looks above my right shoulder, shaking his head. I whirl around only to see Carter and Aiden sitting side by side, their heads cradled in their palms, elbows on the kitchen counter, making googly eyes like deranged boy scouts. "Knock it off!" I shoot in their direction, turning towards Jason. "But it felt fine..." I start.

"Exactly! It didn't have any mold, it felt as soft as the breads in the store. It looked and felt brand new!" Jason exclaims. "So we decided to keep it and see how long it lasts."

"You mean how much longer than about fourteen years?" I raise my eyebrow, pouring the eggy mixture into a pan.

"Yes, and then...we decided to make it more fun..."

"More fun than sitting and staring at a fourteen-year-old loaf of bread? Oh, do tell!" I say, but the sarcasm is lost on my brother, who just continues.

"Yes! We made bets on when it will start going green, you know, when it goes bad! So far we've got five grand worth of bets in the pot. You see, other people bet on it too. There is a whole website dedicated to Edward." He finishes proudly.

"Five thousand bucks?" I exclaim, stirring the eggs. "Website?"

"Yeah," Jason nods. "EdwardCullenGoesGreen.com. You can place your bets there and see updates and photos. Edward even has his own twitter account. Someone from Starwood set it up. It's a thing!"

I shake my head with disbelief, dividing the scrambled eggs onto four plates. "You guys need girlfriends."

"Aide has his eye on someone." Carter grins. My smile falters and my chest tightens. I must be really hungry.

"Well, you definitely need a life." I say, setting the plates on the kitchen island and grabbing a fork.

We eat in silence for a minute, bar a few noises of appreciation over my scrambled eggs.

"So anyway, why are you guys up this early? Carter, did you say you guys are going surfing?"

"Yes." Carter replies while chewing a piece of baguette.

"I hope you're taking wetsuits. I nearly froze to death yesterday," I say, looking at Aiden.

"Ah, you see my young padawan." Aiden smiles at me. "Our friend just opened an indoor surfing arena and we're going before it opens to the public. Wet suits we need not." I stifle a laugh. What a geek.

"In that case, may the force be with you," I say, getting up and clearing my plate.

"I'm in love... Seriously," I hear Carter whisper. "If you're too chicken to act, I'll make a move bro."

What the hell? I turn just in time to see Aiden punch Carter's shoulder.

"Ouch! That will bruise!" Carter exclaims, rubbing his shoulder and making a hurt face at me, trying to get some sympathy without a doubt.

"You can tell all the ladies you were in a fight. It'll gain you some street cred." I laugh at them.

"Marry me?" Carter says as I laugh, and Jason punches him in the other shoulder.

"Nope," I say.

"You halfwits better stay away from my sister!" Jason growls, and I smile.

"Do me a favor boys, clean up after breakfast, okay?"

They all nod in unison as I walk out towards my bedroom and the shower.

I spend most of the day by the pool soaking up the late summer sun and working hard on reapplying SPF onto my body.

By noon, I'm bored out of my mind and decide to hunt for something to read. I go into the living room and start digging through bookshelves when I hear a noise coming from the kitchen. I grab the thickest book I can see, *Gone With The Wind*, and tip toe towards the sound, the massive book above my head in both of my hands. The sucker is really heavy. With a loud and scary, at least in my opinion, shriek, I jump into the kitchen ready to fling the book at the intruder just as it slips from my grasp and falls to the floor.

Shit.

I bend over to snatch the book up just as Aiden turns around, holding a jug of lemonade and two glasses. I exhale loudly.

"I nearly killed you!" I say, grabbing the book from the floor and pressing it against my chest in hopes of covering my small red bikini.

"Riiight." He grins at me.

"Where's everyone else?" I enquire, eyeing the lemonade.

"You mean Jason? Him and Carter went to grab some food in town and meet up with some friends."

"And you didn't join them?"

"I didn't feel like it. Plus, I've got better things to do."

"Ah..." He is probably waiting for someone. I turn around, making my way back to the living room when Aiden speaks up again.

"You want some lemonade?"

"Yeah!" I grin. "I'd love some. You must have read my mind."

"Cool. I'll bring some outside in a second," he says, smiling at me, his green eyes sparkling.

"Okay." I nod and swallow loudly, slowly backing away into the living room. When he can't see me anymore, I turn around, put the book back in its place, and run to the patio, my heart hammering in my chest. What is going on? I must be having sunstroke or something, so to cool off I jump into the swimming pool. I manage to do one lap before Aiden steps onto the deck, two glasses full of lemonade in his hand. My mouth waters at the sight, and I reluctantly swim towards Aide's tan and muscly legs. He sets the glasses on the edge of the pool, sits down, and flings his feet into the cool water. I reach out and grab a glass, gulping the contents in three large swigs, making a satisfied noise at the end.

"Thanks!" I peer up at him, then look at the other glass, still full of lemonade. "I was really thirsty."

"You can have the other one." He smiles. I reach for it without hesitation and take a big gulp just as he starts taking off his t-shirt, resulting with me spitting up the lemonade onto the grass near the pool. Super sexy, I know.

Aiden raises his eyebrow. "Are you okay?"

"Yup." I cough. "Went down the wrong way." I croak out, still coughing, my eyes darting between the spot on which I hacked out my lemonade and his now bare chest.

Aiden slips into the pool next to me, and I stiffen for a second, but then I'm instantly relieved as his chest is now covered with water and only his head is sticking out.

"So," he starts. "Are you looking forward to the beginning of the school year?"

"I am actually." I reply tentatively. "For the first time in a long, long while."

"Oh?"

I swim away, not sure if I want to talk to enemy number

one about my deepest thoughts. I dive and swim the length of the swimming pool underwater. When I pop my head out, Aiden is still in the same place, his eyes squinting against the sun in my direction. I sigh and turn around, looking up at the sky. We're quiet for a moment until I can feel my skin prickle under water. It grows warmer and warmer until I can't stand it anymore and turn around to glance in Aiden's direction. He is mere inches away from me. His face, for once, on the same level as mine, his emerald eyes searching mine.

"You can tell me, Jenny. I will never use anything you tell me against you. I promise."

"You're asking me to trust you, but I'm scared," I say, hesitating. "All I know from you is hurt… It's only in the past few days that I have stopped hating you." I trail off. His face grows sad, and he swims even closer to me.

"Jenny," he says, taking my hand under water and pulling me towards the edge of the pool. He sits me down on the bottom steps so that my body is still submerged but my shoulders and face are out of the water. He kneels in front of me as I pull my legs to my chest. His body is touching mine and I shiver; there is an electric current running between us, and I look around for a toaster someone surely must have just chucked into the pool. "Jenny," he repeats softly. "I am so sorry for the pain that I have caused you." His large, warm hands cup my face, and I resist the urge to close my eyes and let him touch me and speak softly to me forever. "I can only apologise for the foolish, egotistical person I once was," he continues. "But I have changed, and I promise you with all my heart that I will do everything in my power for you to fully trust me again. I want to be your friend, someone you can confide in. I want to be there for you when you need a hug. I want to make sure that you smile every day for the rest of your life and that I'll never cause you to be sad or angry at me ever again." His eyes are peering into my soul, and my walls are crumbling with every heartbeat. Warmth radiates through his hands and flows down my body. I have never felt that way, and I am not sure what it is exactly that I'm feeling, but it's making me want to run. Run as far as I can go.

"You can't promise me that," I whisper.

"Why?" he asks.

"Not unless you're fully prepared to break your promise." He looks at me questioningly, and I smile despite the fact that I don't want to smile. I want to run either away from him or into his arms, which one I'm not sure. "You're a guy," I say. "You're bound to infuriate me and make me angry. Isn't that how things go?" He laughs then. It's the first time I have heard him laugh out loud, and the sound is amazing. It's deep and soft at the same time, and it instantly makes me want to laugh too, so, without thinking, I join in, and we laugh together. After a while, I stop and put my hands on his, gently prying them off my face.

"Okay," I say.

"Okay?"

"Okay, but you can't get angry at me for no reason, and you have to be totally open with me," I say, thinking of the previous evening he went completely cold towards me when I was laughing with Carter.

"I can do that, but Jenny?"

"Yes?"

"Can you please stay away from Carter? He is a great friend but not a good guy when it comes to girls..." His eyes are so sincere with concern that I decide to throw him a bone.

"Don't worry about Carter," I say. "We're just friends." I

smile and get up, walking out of the pool. When I reach my towel, Aiden is still sitting in the shallow bit, looking at his hands, deep in thought. "Do we have any more lemonade?" I ask as he looks up at me. He nods, gets up, and walks towards the house.

I sigh with relief. I was finding it really hard to breathe with him so close to me. How can I act normal around him when I'm beginning to realize that it's not the cold kitchen, not sunstroke or a toaster in the swimming pool? I might actually be into him. I might actually dig the guy who I blame for all the miserable things in my life.

Shit.

Chapter 6

In Need Of Divine Intervention

I'm not saying I'm Batman. I'm just saying no one has ever seen Batman and me in the same room together.
- Carter

I breathe deeply, trying to compose myself. How did I go from hating the guy to wanting to smell him until the end of days?

I sit on the sun lounger and put my head in my hands just as my phone buzzes. I reach for it, and a smile instantly spreads across my face when I see the name on the display. Then I burst out with laughter when I tap on the message.

CARTER: *HEY GRGS! WHATCHA WEARING?*

ME: *Hey there Casanova, how was surfing and lunch?*

CARTER: *BORING ENOUGH 4 ME TO ENQUIRE ABOUT UR OUTFIT. I BET UR IN A HOT RED BIKINI!*

I look up. What the hell? How did he know? I tentatively look around and then behind me. My phone buzzes again.

CARTER: *I KNOW EVERYTHING HOT STUFF! LIKE THAT UR BLUSHING RIGHT NOW. SOO MUCH RED MAKES LITTLE CARTER HAPPY*

ME: *You're disgusting. Do you have cameras in here or sthg? Oh God! If the answer is yes, you need serious help!*

I put my phone down and stand up just as the patio door slides open, and out comes Carter, grinning from ear to ear. He runs over to me and picks me up, twirling me around. And I can't help but laugh.

"I don't have cameras...yet!" Carter says, still holding me tight. "But I have to admit you've got some fantastic ideas and I shall look into that!" I shake my head; I should have known better, and try to pry myself out of his grasp to no avail. When my bare feet connect with his legs, I push as hard as I can. He finally lets go and I find myself propelled into the air and straight into the swimming pool, falling into it as gracefully as a sack of potatoes would. I stay under water devising my plan. When I resurface, my face is arranged into a painful grimace.

"Shit babe, are you ok?" I can hear the panic in his voice. Ha, sucker!

"Carter..." I moan in pain. His eyes are big and concerned as he runs over to the edge of the pool. "My leg." I whimper. He is now crouching by the edge, holding out his hand for me. I grasp it and pull it with all my might. Carter falls into the water with a loud splash and fairly loud roar. I laugh like a deranged psychopath when he emerges with a pissed off look on his face. Then, he slowly smiles at me.

"You know, if I was a chick, I'd have so many comebacks right now." He says, swimming over to me.

"What would Little C say if he heard all this blasphemy," I gasp.

"Little C?" He cocks his head to the side and his brown eyes look at me questioningly.

"Little Carter..." I say, not sure I should be having this conversation with Carter at all. He grins at me and, exasperated, I swim to the edge of the pool and propel myself out. Carter is right on my heels and jumps up, trapping me between his arms.

"I like the nickname you gave him, although I should probably warn you, Little Carter is anything but little." His voice is husky and his eyes are smouldering, and I sigh.

"Kennedy... We had this conversation. I mean, you're like a gay friend to me."

"I know, Cowley, but let's just get something straight. I am as far from gay as possible," he says while his face inches closer to mine. My heart hammers in my chest so loud I am sure the entire neighborhood can hear it. When I feel his minty breath on my lips, I decide enough is enough and take action by swiftly moving my right arm to the side and knocking his grip off balance, causing him to fall back into the water and bang his chin on my knee.

"Ouch!" I whimper, holding onto my knee as Carter comes back up from underwater gasping for air.

"Jesus, woman, be careful! This face is precious. You mess with the face, you mess with my chick magnet powers!" I get up, rub my knee, and walk over to the lounger, grabbing my towel and wrapping myself in it.

"Get over yourself, princess," I retort, sticking my tongue out at him. "You hurt my knee. It will bruise. In my book, we're even." Carter pouts, then flings himself out of the pool and onto the ground in one swift motion. How do guys do that? Make it so freaking graceful and easy looking...

"Gimme." He says, strolling my way.

"Huh?"

He sighs and rips the towel off of me in one quick motion, making me twirl out of it. My jaw drops. How the hell?

"I live to please. Those skills are essential in the bedroom, Grasshopper," he says knowingly while towelling himself off. "You're lucky only my wallet was in my pocket. If my phone was there I'd have to commandeer yours for entertainment."

"Oooh, he knows big words," I gasp mockingly. Carter just laughs and plops onto a lounger. "So how was lunch and the fake waves?" I ask.

"Okay, I guess... It got boring though, so I came here so you could entertain me instead, but you and I have different definitions of entertainment it appears," he says, winking. I sit down next to him and roll my eyes. I'm about to reply when Aiden comes back outside with two glasses in his hands. At the sight of Carter, his jaw tightens, but he keeps a pleasant expression and comes over to us, handing me a lemonade. I smile up at him and get a tight smile in return. At least he's trying to be nice...

"What are you doing here?" Aiden asks, sitting down on the lounger next to Carter.

"I was bored. Jason left with some chick soon after we sat down to eat, and I was left alone, so I decided to come join you guys rather than eat alone. Oh, thanks!" Carter replies, grabbing the glass from Aiden's hand. "Yum! Awesome work, Jen!"

"Errr, I didn't make it..." I replied quietly. Please don't bring the bet up, please don't!

"Aide?" Carter raises his brow. "I thought she was your slave cook at the moment.... I mean, if she was mine she'd be in a little French maid outfit," Carter says thoughtfully as I grow a deeper shade of red. "Little C would like that..." he mutters under his breath, and I kick him in the shin aghast!

"Dude!" I say. "Not cool!"

"Sorry," he grins. "You know I'm only messing with you, hot stuff." He pulls himself closer to me and messes my hair up. I groan.

"I'm gonna head out then." Aiden stands up, his fists in tight balls, and the muscle in his jaw pulsating, making the dimple in his right cheek appear and disappear.

"Oh... Really?" I say, getting up as well. Aiden nods, then turns around without saying goodbye and stomps off. I follow him tentatively for a few steps before stopping in my tracks. "Bye," I say quietly, waving at his retreating figure.

"Daaaamn girl, you've got it bad!" I hear Carter from behind me putting on his best gay-friend voice, but it ends up sounding more like Queen Latifah in The Beauty Shop. The guy needs to work on his impressions...

"Thanks for stating the obvious, Shaniqua," I say, dropping my head.

"All right little one, how about we go inside and watch some sports on ESPN, would that cheer you up?" He looks at me hopefully. I sigh, nod, and reach out for the two empty lemonade glasses. I hear the front door shut and my shoulders sag a little lower. "Fine, fine. We can watch Love Actually or something equally disgusting. Now put that frown upside down and let's go get us some Hugh Grant." This time his accent is spot on, and I smile a little. "That's it, babe." He beams at me, grabbing the towels from the loungers and wrapping his arm around me, guiding us back to the house.

"Right," Carter says as we get to the middle of the living room. "You choose the movie and I'll put these bad boys in the dryer and get some popcorn." I nod and look at him walking away as I find my shorts and t-shirt on the chair next to the patio door. Then I walk to my room, where I change out of my wet bikini.

By the time I'm back in the living room and on the sofa flipping through available movies, I can smell the popcorn and hear it cheerfully popping in the microwave. My mouth is watering well before I hear the 'ding'. Carter comes behind me and jumps over the back of the sofa, sliding into the seat next to me. He hands me a soda and the bowl full of popcorn, which I dive into instantly. If the world was ending now, I'd die a happy woman. No joke. Carter looks at me, hoovering up the popcorn like a cocaine addict getting his first fix in a month, and shakes his head slowly.

"What?" I exclaim, popcorn bits flying out of my mouth. I chew a bit more as Carter's jaw drops in disbelief. "What?" I repeat myself. "I've got an unhealthy relationship with popcorn," I say. "It's all take! Take! Take! Take!" I grin mischievously, then look over at Carter, scanning his face and hugging the bowl to my chest. "You want some?" I ask quietly, not really wanting to hear the response if it's a 'yes'.

"No," he shakes his head. "I wouldn't want to separate you two. You look like freaking Gollum…"

"My precioussss," I hiss, grinning a grin that is sure to have popcorn bits in my teeth, but who cares?

"Yup, definitely friends." Carter says.

"Hey! Are you saying that this is not attractive?" I enquire, stuffing an entire handful of popcorn in my face.

"Soo attractive Jen, so attractive..." He shakes his head, then grins at me. "Anyway Gollum, what are we watching?"

I swallow the half chewed popcorn in my mouth and press play on the tv. "The Notebook." I say in a hushed voice. "Have you seen it?"

"No," he whispers back. "And why are we whispering?"

"Shhhhh, you'll see. Just watch."

Two hours and four minutes later, we're both crying our eyes out. Carter's t-shirt is soggy with my tears and some of the soda I spilled while I wailed at the end of the movie.

"He reads to her every day..." Carter sniffles. "Even though she doesn't know..." He sniffles again. "I want to love someone like that!"

"I know! I want Ryan Gosling," I whine.

"Who doesn't, girlfriend?" Carter puts on a Southern accent and suddenly he is a lot more handsome than he was previously. "Who doesn't?"

I spend the rest of the weekend getting ready for the first day of school and hoping to bump into Aiden, even if that means being his cook, but to my dismay, he is MIA. On Sunday evening, I give up and decide to suck it up and knock on his door. I stand there, like an idiot, raising my hand to knock, then lowering it with a sigh at least fifteen times.

"Are you having fun, over there?" I jump at the sound of Aiden's voice, embarrassment washing over me.

"Yeah..." I reply, turning to face him. "I was just exercising my arm, you know?" I say, making circles with my right arm. His green eyes are playful and a small smile dances across his face, making the dimples come out as if on cue. "How long have you been standing there?"

"Long enough." He chuckles, walking over to me. Closer and closer. I take a step back until my back hits the doorframe and I have nowhere else to go. Aiden is so close the scent of soap and citrus and something earthy engulfs me and, no joke, my freaking knees wobble. Aiden leans down and reaches out with his hands, putting them on the wall on either side of my head. My breath wavers and that enticing scent is now filling my lungs. He smells wonderful. I try focusing on pinpointing what is the earthy part of it rather than on the proximity of Aiden's face.

"I... I just..." I stutter like a schoolgirl. "Wanted... Erm, wanted to know..." God, this will take me all day.

"Wanted to know what?" He asks, leaning closer into me, his nose in my neck. I stop breathing. Heat pools in my belly, and suddenly I'm aware of every single inch of my body. His left arm moves, and the door to his room opens. He leans away, a triumphant half-smile on his face, and I blush. The bastard knew exactly what he was doing.

"If you want anything to eat," I finish, crossing my arms and keeping my head high.

"Hmmmm..." The sound he makes is rough and low, and a shiver travels up and down my spine. He rakes his hand through his hair, his green eyes hungrily boring into mine. "I am hungry..."

"Great." I squeak out cheerfully, my voice high and raspy. "I'll be back in a second!" I walk out of that damn hallway as fast as I can. Who the hell turned the thermostat all the way up? Freaking goblins and fairies!

Too soon, I'm back in front of his door, which is now ajar, stepping from one foot to another trying to remember how did 'Hail Mary' go. I'll need divine intervention to survive this.

"Exercising your arm again?" Aiden's soft, deep voice comes from inside the room. *How the hell did he—?* I push the door open, my face a mask of indifference to his alluring presence and the power he clearly has over me. "Sit down," he says. And I sit. On the floor. Right on the spot I was standing. As if hypnotised. Way to keep it cool, Jenny.

"I meant here." He laughs, pointing at the spot on his bed next to where he's sitting, and I grow hot again, thinking of being in bed with Aiden. He stands up, pulls me up, and sits me on the bed, then sits right next to me.

I am yet to utter a word for fear of looking like an idiot. I mutter, "I brought you strawberries." Throwing the bowl filled with fresh strawberries at him. He looks at the strawberries, then at me, then back at the strawberries, licking his lips. I wriggle in my spot as he takes the bowl from me, looking up at my face. His emerald green eyes are on fire. Since when are strawberries sexual? Oh right, since always. Brilliant move, Jen...

"I haven't touched strawberries in six years..." Aiden says quietly, still staring at me.

"Why?" I ask, surprised.

"They reminded me of someone I wanted to forget."

"Oh."

"But." He pauses and licks his lips again as I fight the urge to bite mine. "I think I've waited long enough. I think I'd really like a strawberry." He says, picking one up and slowly bringing it to his mouth. I lose the battle and bite down on my lower lip to stop myself from drooling just as the strawberry reaches his lips. He bites it, closes his eyes, and hums with approval. "Delicious," he says, opening his eyes and looking straight at me. "Just as I remembered." For some reason, I feel like he's trying to say something else, but for the love of God, the meaning between the lines is lost on me as I'm trying not to pant like a dog in heat. "In fact," he continues, oblivious to the state he has me in. "I think you've convinced me. I think next, I might give bubblegum another try."

Chapter 7

I'm Sexy And I Know It

I'm really good at giving other people life advice but when it comes to my own life I have no idea what I'm doing.
- Aiden

After the whole strawberry incident in Aiden's room, I ran and hid in my bedroom like the inexperienced girl that I am. All night I've been tossing and turning, excitement about the first day in Starwood mixed with visions of green eyes, full lips, and plump strawberries keeping me up.

At five am, I give up the charade and get up, deciding to just get ready and make breakfast. After a long shower and my interpretation of Sky Ferreira's "Everything Is Embarrassing", I get dressed in my grey skinny jeans and an oversized, black, sleeveless Rolling Stones t-shirt. I even put in an extra effort and dry my hair so that it does not resemble a bird's nest. I nod at myself in the mirror with approval.

You're going to crush it today, Jenny. On my way out to the kitchen, I grab my phone only to notice a message from dad.

DAD: *Have an amazing first day in Starwood, pumpkin! Can't believe my little girl is in college! LOL, dad xxx*

I smile to myself. No matter how many times Jason and I try to explain, Dad still thinks lol means 'lots of love'... I quickly type a reply.

ME: *Thanks, daddy, I'm so excited! Miss you loads and lol back at you xxx*

I go to the kitchen and start preparing breakfast. I decided to make pancakes with bacon and maple syrup. My favourite. I'm almost done when sleepy Aiden walks in, wearing nothing but a pair of boxer shorts. My jaw drops as he dazedly heads to the fridge, opens it up, and pulls out a carton of orange juice, his muscular back to me. He closes the fridge, turns around, and freezes, noticing me staring at him like a starved child staring at a chocolate cake. He looks glorious, his face puffy from sleep, yet, somehow, still sexy. I lower my gaze to his chest, then his six-pack, and stop at the V starting above his boxer shorts. I'm positive I must be drooling. Clearing my throat, I smile at him, pretending his ripped body does not faze me.

"Morning," I say cheerfully.

"Morning," he replies, looking me up and down. His voice is hoarse with sleep. "What's for breakfast?"

"Pancakes," I reply, gesturing towards the stack to my right.

"Mmmm, delicious." Aiden's gaze travels up my body and stops on my lips. I clear my throat again and turn around back to the stove. I flip the remaining pancakes and fuss over the bacon. When I turn back around, Aiden is gone. I breathe a sigh of relief.

Half an hour later, what sounds like a herd of elephants comes down the hallway and stumbles into the kitchen.

"I smell pancakes!" Jason sing-songs, finishing off with jazz hands.

"Morning," I reply, laughing as he gives me a kiss on the cheek. "Get your ass over to the table."

"Best. Sis. Ever! This breakfast definitely beats our usual toast with butter!"

Aiden walks in, his hair wet and tousled, just as I put the plates on the table.

When we finish, the boys help me clean up the kitchen. By the time we're done it's half eight, and I grin like a dork. It's time to go to college! I run to my room, grab my bag, and run back to the kitchen. Both Jason and Aiden stand by the door waiting for me, their hands behind their backs, looking all suspicious.

"What's up?" I ask, stopping in my tracks.

"Well, sis." Jason takes a step towards me. I feel nervous. Is he going to jump on me and start tickling me like he used to when we were ten? "It's your first day in college today and, well, we've got something for you." He smiles from ear to ear as my eyes widen. I look from my brother to Aiden. Did they really do something so sweet? I cock my head to the side as Jason puts his hands in front of him. In one of them there's a silver bracelet. My hand shoots up to my mouth in astonishment.

"Oh my gosh!" I squeak as Jason pulls my hand away from my mouth and fastens the eyelet bracelet around my wrist. There is a single charm on it, a heart with the word 'sister' engraved on it. My jaw is on the floor as Aiden steps toward me, he takes my hand and attaches two more charms onto the bracelet. One is a book, *'Le Petit Prince'* engraved on it, and the other is just one word: GEEK. I look at both of them, my eyes filling with tears, and bring them both into a group hug. This is hard since they're both so much taller than me, but they just lean down and hug me back. "You guys are amazing." I sniffle. "You didn't have to, but I really love it. Thank you."

"It was Aiden's idea," Jason mutters into my hair, and I squeeze them both harder.

"It's perfect," I say, letting them out of my death grasp and smiling up at them. "Thank you, thank you, thank you!"

Aiden blushes and looks down at his shoes. "Ready? I thought we could drive together and I can guide you around campus." I raise my eyebrow at the hopeful look he's giving me..

"Please, Jenny! I really need Kitt. I'm supposed to pick up a friend for school today." I sigh and hand over the car keys to my brother, who is currently giving his best puppy dog eyes.

"Let's go then!" I smile, grabbing Aiden's arm and walking out of the house, still mesmerised by the wonder on my wrist. Was it really his idea? That's so thoughtful and sweet.

The drive to the campus is short, and I'm so excited that I can't stop chattering about everything. Aiden just smiles his dimpled smile and nods at appropriate moments, encouraging my incoherent ramblings.

"... So that's why I think monkeys should wear pants, you see," I finish as we park.

"Yes." He tries to contain his laughter. "Makes sense, Jenny."

"I know! Thank you!" I say, then close my mouth, looking around at the red brick building ahead of us. We walk through the gates in silence. I notice the Starwood Eagle Crest above the metal arc of the gate. I'm silent for once, drinking in every detail, the freshly cut grass, the two stone lions on each side of the steps to the main entrance, their paws resting on a stack of books.

I grin like a kid in a candy store. I can't believe I'm here!

Aiden chuckles beside me. "I've never seen anyone this excited to be in school. Come on, I'll show you around before your first lecture. What is it anyway?"

I go a deep shade of red. I was hoping I could avoid this topic. "Cell and molecular biology." I mutter under my breath. Aiden stops in his tracks.

"Jenny, I know you're studying Biomedical Science. You don't need to feel ashamed that you're a genius and will one day save all our lives with a cure for cancer or something equally incredible. Why do you think I got you the 'Geek' charm?" he asks. I look at my bracelet and start playing with the charm, then look back up at him and smile. He's right. I should just release my inner nerd.

After the extensive tour of the campus, Aiden walks me to my first class. We arranged to meet in the parking lot later, to drive home together. The lecture hall is almost empty, so I take my pick of seats and sit down in the third row, taking out my MacBook. There are five people in the room excluding me, all guys, all wearing glasses, checked shirts, and sleeveless pullovers. I look down at my Rolling Stones t-shirt. I'm going to blend in just fine... Not.

The room slowly fills up with more nerdy looking people, and I slide lower and lower in my seat, trying to make myself as small as possible. Five minutes before the start of the class someone plops, exhaling heavily, in the seat next to mine. I look to my right through a curtain of hair. A girl.

"Is it just me, or is everyone else but us an ultra-nerd in here?" I hear her whisper. I look over and see an Abercrombie model sitting next to me. Not kidding. She is gorgeous; she's got big brown eyes and is grinning her perfectly straight teeth at me. Her golden brown hair is falling onto her shoulders, she's wearing a crop top with 'I'm Sexy and I know It' written on it, dark skinny jeans, and neon orange Nikes.

I smile back at her. "Thank God, I thought I was the only one," I whisper back. "I'm Jenny Cowley."

"Hayley Scott. Loving your taste in mus-"

"Good morning everyone. My name is Professor Adam Granger," A deep voice interrupts us. The entire room instantly quiets down as focus shifts to the man up front. I hear whispers, and it's easy to figure out why Adam Granger is the youngest professor on the faculty and a Nobel laureate for his work in biomedicine. "Welcome to Cell and Molecular Biology. Look around you." We all turn our heads. "You probably know that this subject is no picnic. Half of you will be gone by the end of the semester, then only half of those left will make it to year two." I hear people snicker and see in my peripheral vision someone pointing at Hayley and me.

I slide down in my chair again, but Hayley just puffs up her chest and holds her head high. Following in Hayley's confident footsteps, I decide to Elle Woods the hell out of those nerds. I'm here for a reason and they can underestimate me all they want. The professor nods in our direction in acknowledgement and winks at us. "Looks can be deceiving," he continues. "I myself was in this room ten years ago in torn up jeans and an AC/DC t-shirt. My classmates had a bet on how long I'd last and here I am now."

Hayley and I smile at each other. "I like this guy already," she whispers to me, and I nod. It doesn't hurt that he's nice to look at too.

Back-to-back class and the following lab finish in a blink of an eye, and we're done for the day. I can't believe how many pages of material I have written down and how much we've gone through. This will definitely be one of the toughest subjects. As we walk out, Hayley grabs my hand.

"So Jenny, study buddy or even just a plain old buddy? I don't know anyone here!"

"Yes!" I exclaim, excited to make my first friend. We walk outside, arm in arm, chatting about classes and things we have in common when a girl walks past us barging my shoulder and making me drop my bag in the process.

"Sorry!" I mutter.

"Watch it, dykes!" I hear her taunt from behind me. Hayley lets go of my arm.

"Get off your high horse, bitch. You're the one who wasn't looking," she sneers back. I turn around and see a pissed off girl, her platinum blonde hair cropped to her chin. She's wearing a low cut top and a very short leather skirt with high-heeled boots, and she has a fake, orange tan glow about her. Way to bring classy to college...

"Well, well," the blonde bimbo narrows her eyes at us. "Look who we have here, Hayley Scott and her little minion." Hayley is visibly taken aback, so I decide to step in.

"At least I don't look like an Oompa Lumpa. Now skedaddle, mind your own business. What was it again? Torturing kittens and turning tricks for a dollar fifty each?" The girl's face turns red and I swear smoke is about to escape her ears. She looks royally pissed. I bend over, picking up my bag, and pull Hayley by her elbow before the chick starts throwing punches.

"C'mon Hayls, let's go." I look over at the girl again, she's clenching her fists. Her eyes, heavy with make-up, are now just slits. Who let the tacky in?

"You messed with the wrong bitch!" I hear her scream at us as we're walking away. Hayley and I look at each other and burst into laughter.

"Classy," Hayley says, and I nod through tears.

"Do you know her?" I enquire. Hayley doesn't strike me as someone who'd hang around with the Oompa Lumpa sort.

"I don't think so…" she trails off.

We walk through the green, chatting. I find out that Hayley used to be a model—duh—and that she is living in the dorms on the edge of campus, not too far from my house. We're almost by the main building when something hard hits me in the head, knocking me out.

I wake up on the grass. Shit, did the blonde bimbo attack me? I shouldn't have messed with her… I turn my head to the side and take a deep breath. The smell of freshly cut grass fills my nostrils, reminding me of Aiden. That must be the earthy ingredient in his smell! I open my eyes to Hayley kneeling above me.

"You okay, babe?" she asks.

"I'm so sorry. I did shout 'duck'," I hear someone say. I sit up to see a jock with a football in his hands, looking apologetic.

"It's okay," I say, rubbing the back of my head.

"Angel! Whatcha doing rolling in the grass without me?" I hear someone from behind me and I turn around, wincing from the pain, to see Carter strolling over to us.

"Who is that?" Hayley whispers, awestruck.

"Casanova." I smile up at him while Hayley helps me up.

"Carter, dude," the jock says. "I'm sorry. I didn't know this was your girl."

"What happened?" Carter growls, noticing my pain, and the jock takes a step back.

"I shouted 'duck'," he repeats himself, taking another step back. I grab Carter's arm.

"Kennedy, chill! It was an accident. You know I'm prone!" I say, pulling him towards me. His eyes land on my face and he folds me into his chest for a hug.

"You'll kill me one day, Angel," he mutters into my hair, kissing the top of my head. "Who do we have here?"

I push myself away and see Hayley turning bright red, and Carter strolling over to her.

"Kennedy, Carter Kennedy, and you are?" I roll my eyes. Hayley looks up, unsure on how to proceed.

"This is Hayley. She's my friend, so she's off limits, Casanova."

"Well, that's no fun." Carter pouts at me.

"Get over yourself, princess," I say, playfully punching his shoulder. "There's plenty more fish." I gesture around us as girls try to catch his attention, pulling their tops down, revealing cleavage and making 'sexy' faces at Carter. Why is it always me? I shake my head in disbelief.

"Aww, that's no way to talk to your favorite man on earth. You know I've only got eyes for you, sweetheart." He pats my head and I fight the urge not to punch him for that move. He grins at me, seeing me clench Bonnie and Clyde.

"I love it when you go all feisty on me! Just not in the jewels! My grandmother would never forgive you!" I roll my eyes at him again and turn to Hayley.

"Believe it or not he's my friend. You'll get used to his

obnoxious ways pretty soon." I stick my tongue out at Carter and start walking away, dragging Hayley behind me.

"Jenny!" I hear Carter shout behind me, and I stop to see him jogging up to us.

"What?"

"There's a party this weekend. Come with me?"

"What party?"

"It's at one of the frat houses. Please, pretty please with a cherry on top? Hayley, will you come too?"

"Fine," I reply.

"Not sure," Hayley says quietly.

"Yay!" Carter says cheerfully, kissing me on my cheek, then speeds off towards one of the buildings.

"He's so hot," Hayley states matter of factly.

"Yeah, he's also just a friend," I say.

"So you never told me you're friends with *the* Carter Kennedy. Next you'll tell me Jason Cowley is your brother." She pauses, looking at my mortified face. I'm trying hard not to burst out laughing. "Oh my god, he is, isn't he?"

"Yup," I say, popping the 'p.' "We are one big, happy family in our little house. By the way, you should come over sometime, we've got a pool and everything."

"Are you kidding? I'm so there, just name the time! You're so lucky..."

"I also live with Aiden Vaughn..." I add quietly, spotting his jeep in the parking lot. He's leaning against the hood, looking bored while some girl is attempting to flirt with him.

"You're killing me!" Hayley throws her hands in the air. "How do you end up with the three hottest guys on campus while I'm stuck in the smelly dorms?"

"I blame it all on Jason," I reply, grinning. "Plus, you're my friend now, so you'll be stuck with the three stooges as well. You're welcome." Hayley laughs out loud and gives me a hug.

"Right babe, I've got to go, but I'll call you tonight and see you in class tomorrow! So glad we met, I think we'll be the best of friends." She smiles at me genuinely, and I'm surprised to find I've got the same feeling for the first time in my life.

"See you tomorrow, sister from another mister!" I wave at her and turn towards Aiden and the flirting girl. Ugh.

As I get closer, Aiden spots me and smiles, standing up and walking towards me, the girl left behind forgotten mid sentence, with her mouth hanging open. I wave at him.

"Hey there, superstar," he greets me. "How was your first day? Did you find a cure for cancer yet?"

"It was great, thanks! No cure yet, but I'm working on it! How was your day?" He puts his arm over my shoulder and guides me back to his car.

"Aiden..." the girl whines as we get to the Jeep.

"Umm, Laura, was it?"

"Lauren..." she replies, pouting.

"Like I said, I don't want to be the student body president, but thanks for thinking of me. I'll see you around?"

"Yeah, that would be great," she purrs, and I scrunch up my face. Girls are ridiculous. Aiden opens the car door for me and I slide in.

"So Jenny, I've been meaning to ask you." He looks at me as he gets into the driver's seat and turns the ignition on.

"Ask away," I say cheerfully.

"There's the Beginning of The Year Party at one of the frat houses this weekend and I was wondering if you wanted to go?" I'm speechless. Is he asking me out? "I mean, you'll get to meet more people and stuff. You don't have to go with me..." he trails off.

"No," I interrupt him. "I mean, I've already agreed to go with Carter..." I look down at my hands.

"Oh." His voice is tight, and I look up at his face. The muscle in his jaw is pulsating, and suddenly I feel like somehow I just let him down.

We don't speak for the rest of the drive home, and when we get there he just goes straight to his room, leaving me behind in front of the house confused. Majorly confused... Was it something I said?

Chapter 8

Wiggle, Wiggle

Raisin cookies that look like chocolate chip cookies are the main reasons why I've got trust issues.
- Jason

First week of college is a blur of classes, caffeine, getting to know Hayley, and some more classes. By the time I realize, it's Friday already. The day of the party.

When my last class of the day finishes, I am beyond excited for the evening.

"Are you sure you don't want to come tonight?" I ask Hayley as we walk to Kitt.

"I'm not ready for a party just yet," she replies. "What I am ready for is to dress you up and make you up so that when Aiden sees you he won't be able to stop drooling." She winks at me, patting her massive bag full of clothes and makeup. Hayley had witnessed my inability to form coherent sentences when Aiden was around, and apparently his 'lustful' gaze whenever I walked into the room. Even though I told her he'd been avoiding me this past week, she decided to play cupid.

"You know he is the sole reason I've never had a boyfriend, right?" I decide it's time to burst her bubble.

"Was he this dreamy when you guys were in London?"

"Ha! No, he was geeky. Kind of adorable actually, but a horrible, horrible kisser."

"Jennifer Cowley!" Hayley steps in front of me, stopping me in the middle of the parking lot. "Are you telling me you have previously kissed Aiden Vaughn and haven't divulged all the details yet?"

"Shhhh." I try to quiet her down, she's practically shouting and people are starting to watch our little exchange. I fish out Kitt's keys from my pocket and take Hayley by the hand. "That's what I'm trying to do now, but you're making a scene. C'mon, let's get in the car and I'll tell you what exactly happened, and trust me, it was not exciting."

I tell Hayley the story of my last week in school when I was thirteen and the touchy subject of my first kiss.

"You mean to tell me you haven't kissed a guy since?" she asks, incredulous.

"Well, no..."

"But babe, not every kiss is the same. Plus, guys learn with age, and, from what I heard, Aiden has learned a whole lot, if that's where he started from."

"I don't know, Hayles. I've never actually talked to anyone about this, so it's been just eating me up from the inside, making me want to avoid guys altogether," I say solemnly.

"You mean you've never told any of your friends? Why?

It's nothing to be ashamed of! He was the one that fucked it up, not you," Hayley states bluntly.

"Errr... I mean... Ok, I'm just going to come out and say this, cause this is not going to sound any better with time... I never had a best friend, or even good friends..." I reply, focusing on the road intently.

"Well, that's ridiculous." Hayley rolls her eyes as I park in front of my house. "You're one of the coolest girls I know. It's impossible that you've never had a best friend."

"It's true. But hopefully, I do now..." I look up at her hesitantly.

"Oh, babe!" Her eyes are big as she lunges at me, enveloping me in a huge hug. "Of course you do! I mean, I've known you for a little less than a week and I'm already going all territorial on your ass. Of course I'm your best friend, and you're mine."

I smile and hug her back full force. "So there's one more thing I should probably tell you," I say once we break away. Hayley looks at me questioningly as we get out of the car. "You know the bet I lost with Aiden, the one where I had to cook for him? There was one more condition..."

"Spit it out, bestie," Hayley pokes me.

"If I lost, I also agreed to go on a date with him..."

"Oh my God! I knew it. You guys are so in looove! Your babies are going to be so beautiful!" She squeals as I wince.

"Calm down, chihuahua, he hasn't mentioned it since... Plus, that'd be my first date... Ever."

"Don't worry, Jenny," Hayley says, putting her arm over my shoulder and guiding me to the front door. "He won't be able to wait much longer. I'm sure he'll ask you about it soon." We get inside the house and go to my room. "And when he does, I'll dress you and do your makeup again! He will not be able to keep his hands to himself, yay!" she sing-songs as I put my head in my hands in resignation. "Oh..." She suddenly stops, flinging the clothes out of her bag onto my bed. "What about your date with Carter tonight?"

"What?" I burst out laughing. "What do you mean?"

"You're going on a date tonight, to the party..." she says, looking at the floor.

"Ewww, no! Did you think..? Eww! I told you, Carter and I are just friends. He's like Jason to me. I'm wingwomaning him. I fully expect to be abandoned once he finds his first target for the night."

"Really?" Hayley looks up. "I mean, you two are always so flirty..."

"Hayles, really? Flirting is how Carter speaks. You should see him having conversations with Jason, it's utterly weird... Wait a minute, do you like him or something?"

"No! Well, maybe. I don't know..." Hayley sits on my bed and sighs. "Honestly, it's confusing. Guys were the last thing on my mind when I worked my ass off to get into Starwood. Urrrgh. I just don't know. Let's just drop it for now and see how we get on with getting through this semester, okay?"

"Okay, but if, at any time, you change your mind and want to talk about guys...I'm here!" She clearly needs to figure this out first.

"Thanks, hon. Now let's get you made up, not that you need much work..."

"I don't know, Hayley, I never really wear makeup. Are you sure about this?"

"Trust me! I've picked up a few tricks along the way. I'll make you look irresistible, yet fairly natural. Don't worry, you will not look like an Oompa Lumpa."

"Speaking of, did you find out how she knows you?" I ask as Hayley puts a pile of clothes in my hands.

"Go try these on," she says, pushing me into the bathroom and closing the door behind me. I strip off and put on the first thing. It's a golden sequin, fitted dress; its collar is high; and it's got short sleeves, but the length of the dress has a lot to answer for. It barely covers my bum. "Yeah, I found out how she knows me. She was trying for a campaign they selected me for." Hayley continues through the bathroom door. "She must be holding a grudge or something."

"Oh... That explains how she knew your name and why she was being so bitchy," I say, walking outside.

"My, my." Hayley chuckles.

"What?" I ask. "Did I put it the wrong way around?"

"No hon, my top looks lovely on you. I clearly didn't think this through though..." She touches her finger to her chin.

"Not my fault I'm little." I pout.

"I know!" Hayley exclaims. She runs into the bathroom, grabs the pile of clothes from the floor, then runs back into the bedroom, dropping them on the bed. She then proceeds by fishing out a black garment and throwing it at me. "Try this."

I reluctantly go back into the bathroom and change into the black thing, which happens to be amazing. It's a black, sleeveless, fitted dress with a mesh neckline and back; the black material at the front of the dress is cut into a sort of sweetheart neckline but with a bit more edginess. It's gorgeous. It's sexy, but not too revealing, and it's just the right length, coming to my mid-thigh.

"Are you going to make me wait much longer?" Hayley asks impatiently. I open the door and step out. "Yeeeesssss!" A loud squeal comes out of my best friend's mouth, and I grin at her. "I love it! Do you love it?" She continues excitedly. "It's the shortest dress I own, and it's just amazing on you!"

"It's perfect!" I nod.

"Okay, shoes next. Show me what you've got." I take her to my closet and point at my small collection of Chuck Taylors and flip-flops. "All right, all right," Hayley nods to herself. "I can do this. We can find something... Yes! I'm on a pure genius streak today!" she exclaims, grabbing a pair of black high tops with skull print on them. "This will have to do, but we need to get you some heels asap! Here, put these on," she orders. When I'm done, she takes one of her silver cuffs and puts it around my wrist next to my charm bracelet. I look closer. It's got small skulls all around it. "It's Alexander McQueen," she says, seeing my confusion. "It'll make you fashionably casual with your converse and the hot dress, trust me. Now, to hair and makeup." She pushes me onto the bed and pulls out what looks like a suitcase full of brushes and powders and creams. I close my eyes and pray that I come out of this alive.

After what feels like days of having creams patted onto my face, powders carefully spread all over my eyes, and sprays and potions applied to my hair, Hayley finally steps away from me with a satisfied nod.

"Perfect." She nods to herself. "Have a look."

The girl looking back at me from the floor-length mirror in the corner of my room has me speechless. Hayley did exactly what she promised. My makeup is delicate but somehow makes my features defined. The black eyeliner around my eyes makes my blue eyes pop, and my lashes have never been this long before. I twirl around, amazed at how bouncy and healthy looking my hair is. Hayley pinned it to one side, making it drop over my right shoulder. I look incredible.

"How did you do this?" I ask, impressed.

"Well, you're gorgeous, honey, so I didn't actually have to do that much." She smiles at me. I run to her and give her a hug.

"Thank you! You're amazing! I look hot!"

"Babe, you're hot with or without makeup." She laughs. "Oh, before I forget, text me your shoe size and I'll see what I can do with your heels situation."

"You're like a fairy godmother." I look up at her in astonishment. "You're the best!" I definitely lucked out in the best friend department.

Carter arrives just as we're done packing up all of Hayley's stuff back into her ginormous bag.

"Hello there gorgeous and gorgeouser." He winks at Hayley as he saunters into the living room. Then he does a double take and checks me out, whistling. "Well, well, Gollum, you clean up hot!"

"Shut up, Kennedy," I say playfully, punching him on the arm. "Are the guys with you? I haven't seen them all day."

"No, hot stuff. They should be at the party when we get there. You guys ready? We'll go grab something to eat before the party."

"Actually," Hayley interrupts, "I'm not coming. But I'd really appreciate it if you could drop me off at my dorm."

"Nonsense, beautiful, you're coming with us," he says, fixing his gaze firmly on Hayley's face, and she looked over at me in panic with pleading eyes.

"Carter, when a lady says 'no' it means 'no'. Not 'let Carter convince you otherwise'," I say.

"Hmmm..." Carter pauses. "Fine, but come eat with us first? I can't let a lady go hungry."

"Okay," Hayley agrees weakly.

After a meal comprising of burgers and fries, we drop Hayley off at her dorm and make our way to the party, which is in full swing by the time we get there.

Masses of bodies are spilling out of the front door, and the music is pumping to the rhythm of my hammering heart. Carter takes my hand and guides me to the porch, veering around the bodies of the not-quite-sober people. I step to the side when a girl who is busy sucking some guy's face suddenly pulls away and begins throwing up in the nearby bush. The guy just leaves her behind and moves on to the next girl, who looks almost as drunk as the first one and is willing to grant him some tonsil hockey time.

"Yuck," I say as we cross the threshold.

"That's nothing, Grasshopper. It gets worse as the night goes on." He laughs at the disbelief on my face.

"But it's already ten," I state, like that means that the party is about to finish. Frankly, I don't know. This is my first party. Ever.

"That's what I mean," Carter shouts in my ear over the music as we step into the living room. "The party is just about to start. Do you want a drink?" I nod, then look behind me at the exit and remember the girl who was throwing up.

"Water, please!" I specify. Carter nods and walks towards what appears to be the kitchen area, still holding my hand. He lets go of me when we get there and walks over to the fridge, fist bumping with a few guys on the way. I take my alone time as an opportunity to look around. If this party is about to start, then what the hell do they call the state it is in now?

There are at least three couples sitting on the same couch basically dry humping side by side. In the middle of the living room, the makeshift dance floor is filled with bodies and, as I'm about to turn, a drunken girl is propelled onto somebody's shoulders. She squeals with laughter and pumps her fists in the air.

I turn back to the kitchen and see Carter doing a keg stand while everyone is cheering wildly. I start wondering if I'm only here to be his designated driver just as he somersaults off the keg and back on his two feet. He grabs the bottle of water, two red cups to his right, and walks over to me, his eyes still clear, albeit getting a bit glassy.

"Grasshopper! Did you see that?" he asks, handing me the bottle of water, downing the contents of one of the red cups then pouring my water into it.

"Yes, I did. Pretty impressive," I say, looking questioningly at the cup with an arched brow.

"Oh, this? People can get aggressively pushy when they notice you're not drinking alcohol. It's best to pretend," he says. It's kind of sweet that he's taking care of me. "C'mon, let's scout the area." We make rounds, and it's clear that Carter is one popular guy. Everyone is trying to chat with him and say 'hi'. He ignores some, says 'hi' back to maybe half of the people who try, and introduces me as 'Grasshopper' to a handful, which makes me roll my eyes. Does he really think he is my Mr. Miyagi?

When I look at my watch next, it's almost midnight, and the party is truly getting out of hand. Some people are snoozing on the floor, some girls are dancing on the tables, stripping their tops off, and most of the crowd is engaging in some form of snogging in the available spaces of every room.

I haven't seen Aiden or Jason all evening, and Carter is, by now, positively slurring his words.

"Jennyyyy, you're so prettyyyy." He lifts his hand to my hair but misses and pokes my chin instead. "Oops!" I laugh it off.

"C'mon big guy, let's find my brother," I say, taking his hand and starting for the living room.

"He'll be uppstrais. I mean uptsairs, up-stair-sss, yesss," he finishes triumphantly.

"Let's go then!" I say cheerily. I'm planning to dump the drunken mess on my brother and head home. When we get to the first floor, it takes a few tries and a few interrupted sessions of what looks like an exquisite drunken love making before we finally stumble upon a room with Jason in it. He sits in the middle like a king, with girls on either side of him forming a nice little circle.

"Jenny! Carter!" he exclaims. "We're playing truth or dare, come join us!"

"Yaaay!" Carter plops between the couple of the girls. "My turn, my turn!" I suppress the urge to laugh.

"I'm okay, Jason. I'm just going to head home." I smile at him.

"Do you have a ride? Aiden should be around. Ask him if you don't." He's around? I perk up.

"Ummm, no, I'll just get a taxi." I decide to play it cool and stumble around all the girls to give Jason a kiss on the cheek.

"What about me?" Carter whines, so I lean over and give him one too. He quickly wraps his large arms around my waist and pulls me on top of him, making me squeal. "That a girl!" he says, satisfied.

"Carter, bro. Let go of my sister." I hear Jason growl, and Carter's death grip on me loosens. I wriggle off of his lap, which he seems to be finding amusing since he starts singing Derulo. "Wiggle, wiggle, wiggle!"

"If you're about to sing 'You know what to do with that big fat butt', I'll punch you," I say, finally managing to stand up. Carter just makes a zipping, locking, and throwing away the key motion on his lips and smiles hugely with his mouth still closed. "Night you two, have fun," I say, leaving the room and closing the door behind me.

As I walk down the hallway, I spot what seems to be the only free bathroom in the house—score—and decide to make a pit stop before calling a cab. Frat parties are not my thing. Once I'm done, I make my way out of the bathroom and proceed down the hallway and towards the staircase. It's empty up here, the music still loudly pumping, but no one seems to be taking advantage of the breathing space. I notice there are socks hanging on doors. That's why. This is the official 'bang section' of the house. A door to my left opens and a drunk guy stumbles out, falling on top of me. He's taller than me and heavier, but I manage not to fall and just push him off me.

"Hey beautiful," he slurs. "What's your name?"

I hesitate. "Jenny. Are you ok?"

"Jenny... Pretty name for a pretty girl. I'm fine now that you're here." His eyes are dark and he is not swaying as much as he was just a second ago.

"Well, have a great night. It was nice meeting you." I say, turning around, but he grabs my arm and pulls me back to face him. His grip is tight, and it's starting to hurt.

"You're not leaving, are you?" he says steadily, none of the previous drunken slurring noticeable. I take a step back, but he's still holding my arm, so he follows me until my back is against the wall. "What's a pretty girl like you doing all alone upstairs?"

"I'm leaving." My voice is calm and strong, even though inside I am shaking like a whippet in a snowstorm. "I was dropping off a friend of mine. You're hurting my arm." He looks down at where his hand is tightly wrapped around my upper arm and releases his hold a little, but doesn't let go.

"And you were going to go without giving me a kiss goodnight? Now that's not nice, is it?" His voice is menacing as he leans over me and opens the door to a bedroom next to where we're standing. My eyes widen. "Let's have a little talk about manners," he says, towering over me.

"Hell no!" I growl and ready myself to knee him in the jewels when, suddenly, his body is flung away from me and into the opposite wall.

"What the fuck do you think you're you doing?" My saviour leans over the guy who is clearly knocked out. He turns around and takes my hand in his, and a warmth floods my body, all the fear and adrenaline leaving instantly. "Let's go, Jenny," Aiden says. I nod and follow him downstairs.

Chapter 9

I Sleep Naked

They should announce the sequel to Groundhog Day and then just re-release the original.
- Jenny

I see her as soon as she walks in, looking stunning in a black dress and, believe it or not, a pair of Converse. I get up from the armchair I was sitting in and walk towards her when I notice her hand in Carter's. She looks up at him and he leans over and whispers something in her ear, making her big blue eyes even bigger from shock. Then they smile at each other, like they share some sort of a secret.

Something in me breaks. I can't look at this shit. I am so fucking done with him, her, this stupid party. The music is blasting out of the speakers, fueling my rage. Someone cleverly decided to play Rage Against The Machine at the party. I turn around and make my way through sweaty bodies bouncing and screaming to the sound of Killing in the Name to the back garden and pick up a bottle of vodka on the way, taking a large swig as I step outside. The cool breeze hits my face, and I remember that I'm the designated driver tonight. Fuck! I throw the bottle, roaring for added effect, as far as I can, it shatters against a tree, breaking into million pieces, just like my heart did a minute ago.

I sit down on the steps and count to one hundred, taking a deep breath with every number. I'm overreacting, surely. She promised they are just friends, didn't she? She did.

I sigh and get up, stretching my arms and legs, deciding to go for a walk. I sneak out through the back gate.

She looked incredible, her body wrapped in the tight black dress, the sheer material covering her cleavage making it that much sexier, her hair swept to one side exposing the side of her long neck... Just thinking about it makes my mouth water and my dick harden. I need to snap out of it. I walk for what seems like an hour, and by the time I'm back at the frat house, the back garden is filled with people rolling in the grass, drinking and making out.

"Hey baby." A girl I vaguely recognise stops me with her hand on my chest. "Are you having fun?"

"Sure," I reply and gently take her hand off my chest.

"I can make it sooo much more fun for you," she purrs, leaning close to me. The smell of alcohol on her breath engulfs me. And when I look into her eyes, they're glassy and unfocused.

"Not interested," I say the truth. I'm not interested, haven't been interested in anyone since the day Jenny arrived, all cute and feisty like a kitten. And all my feelings came rushing back. I push past the drunken girl and walk off towards the house, but I catch a familiar name in someone's conversation, and I stop in my tracks to listen.

"Did you see the chick that's with Carter tonight? I'd

fuck her so hard she'd forget her own name," a drunken guy states, and I clench my fists.

"Forget about her man," another guy interjects, taking a large gulp from his red cup. "I'm pretty sure Logan wants to tap that." They both chuckle, and I start shaking from rage.

"Isn't he upstairs with that chick who wasn't too keen?" the first one speaks again.

"She's drunk enough to be keen now," the second one replies as my blood boils. Who the fuck do they think they are? I tear inside the house, scanning through the crowd of drunken faces. I run into the kitchen, then the living room. Where the hell is she? Then I see her, walking up the stairs, where the 'fuck rooms' are, holding Carter's hand and smiling at him.

I literally drop to my knees where I'm standing and bury my face in my hands. What the fuck happened for her to choose him, to go with him? Someone walks past me, kneeing me in the shoulder in the process. "Sorry, handsome," a girl says, smiling down at me. "Need help?" she says, extending her hand to me. I take it and get up. She seems sober and I welcome the change.

"Thanks," I mutter. "I'm Aide."

"I know who you are, silly." She laughs a throaty laugh, throwing her head back, her short blonde bob bouncing above her shoulders. "We met last year."

"We did?" I rack my brain.

"Yes, silly. I'm Chloe." I draw a blank.

"Oh, yeah, sure! I remember you. Chloe." I decided it's probably best to just go with it. "Thanks for helping me up. How have you been?"

"Good, thanks. Listen, have you seen Jason anywhere?" She asks, tilting her head to the side. I narrow my eyes. She could be just one of his groupies.

"No, sorry," I say, noticing a girl running down the stairs, crying straight into the arms of her friend.

"Logan is a douchebag." I hear the girl enveloping the crying girl in a hug say. "Thank God you came to your senses before anything happened." My ears perk up.

"Aiden?" I focus back on Chloe.

"Sorry," I mumble. "Got to go. It was nice seeing you again. Keep in touch." I rush my words as I walk away from Chloe, then run up the stairs two at a time.

I open a few doors, catching couples screwing. None of them are Carter and Jenny, and I sigh in relief.

I open another door and step into a dimly lit room with two very familiar faces grinning up at me.

"Where is she?" I ask, shutting the door loudly behind me. Both Jason and Carter have chicks wrapped around them just begging to be fucked. Jenny is not in here, not with Carter, not in his lap. Thank God. I would have broken his face if she was, and that would have been hard to explain.

"Aiden, my man!" Carter says drunkenly, and I try to resist the urge to punch him. How could they just leave her alone? "Come join us."

"No, thanks." I turn to Jason. "Where is your sister, Jason?"

"She's not with you? She wanted to leave, so I told her to find you for a ride. Oh wait, I remember, she's taking a cab." My blood boils at the stupidity of my two best friends, but I'm relieved that she is out of here and safely on her way home. I exhale loudly.

"Aiden, come sit with me!" a drunk girl in the corner exclaims excitedly. I ignore her.

"When did Jenny leave?" I ask Jason.

"Like a minute ago, I think. Maybe a bit longer..." he replies, and I resist the urge to shake him.

"Aideeeennn," the girl in the corner whines.

I turn to her. "Not interested," I say for the second time tonight and turn to the door. I still might have a chance of finding her and—I don't know—just making sure that she gets home, okay? Pathetic.

I reach for the doorknob.

"Where are you going?" Carter asks from the floor. The girl on his lap is currently licking his face.

"Out," I say, opening the door and heading into the dark hallway.

"... leaving," I hear someone say. That voice... Jenny? "I was dropping off a friend of mine. You're hurting my arm," she continues. What. The. Fuck. Is someone hurting her? I start toward the voices.

"And you were going to go without giving me a kiss goodnight. Now, that's not nice, is it?" a male voice says. My vision turns red. "Let's have a little talk about manners," he continues as I clench my fists and throw myself at the guy towering over Jenny.

"Hell no!" Jenny growls in her angry kitten voice, and as I fling the guy off of her. I am proud of the determination and the bravery and the fucking anger I hear in her voice. The bloke connects with a loud thump to the other wall, and I kick his body, not responsive, but I'm too enraged. I want to murder the fucker.

"What the fuck do you think you're doing?" I scream at him. Jenny is still in the place I left her; her eyes are huge and scared, and suddenly I don't care about the lowlife on the floor. All I want is to take her to safety, hold her, make sure she's okay.

I take her hand in mine. She visibly relaxes at the

contact. Her hold on my hand is tight and warm. Her touch feels so fucking good I almost shiver. Instead, I say, "Let's go home, Jenny." She nods, her huge eyes not leaving my face as I guide her downstairs and into my jeep.

My knuckles are white as I clench the steering wheel. I'm trying hard to shake off the anger, but I can't seem to calm down.

"You're shaking," Jenny says softly, touching my arm. Her warm touch grounds me just a smidge. "Are you angry with me?" Jesus, how could she think I am angry with her when she is the only thing I care about?

"It's not you I'm angry with," I say slowly.

"The muscle in your jaw is twitching. You're angry at something," she states as I park the Jeep in front of our house. I look at her and give the observant vixen a half smile.

"I'm angry at the shithead who tried to intimidate you. I was ready to murder him back there. God, if I hadn't shown up on time..." I trail off, clenching my fists again.

"I would have been fine," she juts her chin out proudly. "I can take care of myself." My jaw drops. She is the most adorable, yet clueless, thing I've ever seen. "But thanks for your help, I guess," she adds, barely audible as she slides out of the Jeep and starts for the house. Cheeky. I run after her. She can walk fast, I'll give her that.

"Pardon me?" I say, raising my eyebrow when I catch up with her.

"Nothing," she says, sticking her tongue out at me as she

opens the front door. I'd give my left kidney for that tongue in my mouth.

"Nothing? Are you sure?"

"Yup, I'm sure." She scoots to the living room, holding back laughter. I follow her before she ducks behind the couch.

"Oh, yeah?" I pounce at her, and we fall on the sofa. She squeals and starts pushing me off.

"Definitely!" she says, laughing. I grab her wrists and push them above her head, holding them there. Her mouth forms an 'o', and her eyes grow huge as I lean toward her. I'm tempted to kiss her, but now is not the right time. She swallows loudly, and I lick my lips. Lifting a corner of my mouth, I bring my free hand to the side of her body.

"You bastard!" she squeals as I tickle her. "Stop it! No! No!" she screams through laughter.

"What did you say earlier, then?"

"Aiden, stop it!"

"What was it?"

"Please!" She giggles uncontrollably.

"Say it." I pause the tickling for a second. She's breathing quickly, her chest heaving up and down, and for a brief second I wish we were in my bed. There goes my right kidney.

"Never," she whispers, kicking her legs, but she misses and I resume the tickling torture.

"Say it!"

"N-no!"

"Jenny..." I growl. Her hair is scattered around her face like a halo. She is grinning and laughing, her eyes closed. Never have I ever seen anyone so beautiful in my entire life. Tears start streaming down her cheeks.

"Fine, fine!" she shouts through laughter.

"Say it."

"Oh God, please stop, stop, stop!"

"Not until you say it." I laugh.

"Thank you, okay? Thank you, thank you, thank you!"

I stop, and she breathes a sigh of relief.

"Now that wasn't that hard, was it?" I say, leaning over her and kissing her on the forehead. She stills and relaxes only when I move away. I get up and pull her up to standing. "C'mon, kitten. Want to watch a movie or do you want to go to bed?" I say, praying for the former. She looks between the TV and the hallway leading to her bedroom, hesitating, then nods to herself.

"Movie," she says. "Let me get changed first. Let's have a pajama movie night." She smiles up at me, and I can't help myself.

"Oh, kitten..." I say, brushing a strand of hair off her face, anticipating her reaction. "I sleep naked." Her face turns red, and I fight the urge to bite my lip. She looks so fucking innocent and...it's all my fault. Fuck. I will work my ass off to make it better. "Don't worry, I'll make an exception tonight." I wink at her and walk to my room.

As I strip to my boxer shorts, I briefly consider the fact that after tonight I will most likely have to live with the biggest case of blue balls known to mankind. I pull a pair of sweats and a t-shirt on, then sit on my bed preparing myself for two hours of sitting next to the hottest woman on earth. I'll need a strategy.

Like a glass of water to spill on my crotch when shit gets too hard to cope with... Literally. Maybe I should just stuff a bag of ice cubes down my boxers? After deliberating for what feels like ages, I decide to just wing it and run for a cold shower if the situation gets out of hand.

I step outside of my room and go to the living room,

stopping by the kitchen where Jenny is leaning on the kitchen counter, her face propped on her arms, arms on the worktop, nose inches from the microwave, watching the contents intently. I run my hand through my hair, trying not to think of her bum, which is currently sticking out in my direction, basically waving 'hello' and enticing me to come over and take a bite. Shit.

"Hey," I say, my voice hoarser than it should be. Jenny jumps up with a squeak and turns to face me. She looks delicious in a white tank and tartan shorts. Her face is scrubbed clean, all traces of makeup gone.

"Damn it, Aiden! There are knives in here! Don't scare me like that, you could end up with a shitty circumcision job!" she exclaims, throwing her hands up, exasperated.

"Kitten, all the knives are in the drawer next to where I'm standing." I laugh.

"I'm fast! Like a ninja." She narrows her eyes at me.

"No, you're not." She gasps, aghast, then narrows her eyes into slits.

"Did you see me do that?"

"Do what?" I'm confused.

"Exactly!" She lifts her chin up, like she's just proven a point, and I burst out laughing just as the microwave dings.

Jenny takes the warm bag of popcorn out and starts for the living room. "FYI," she says, "I don't share." I bite my lip to stop myself from laughing. She is one of a kind.

"What do you want to watch?" I ask, sitting down on the couch next to her once I've calmed down.

"I dunno." She taps her chin in thought. "How about Star Wars? I want to re-watch them since the new one is coming out soon."

My jaw literally drops. "Which one?"

"Let's start from the beginning," she says. "I mean the

second one cause the first one sucks ass." And I have to physically stop myself from attacking her right here on the sofa...

I clear my throat, find the movie, and press play. As the music starts, I hear a quiet 'Yaaay!' from Jenny, and I wonder if it's at all possible to fall for someone any deeper than I am for Jenny at this moment. She gets herself comfortable, pulling her legs underneath her and leaning on me, covering herself with a blanket.

"Want some?" she asks, sticking the bag of popcorn in front of my nose.

"I thought you didn't share..."

"I don't, but I am willing to give you a small handful." She scoffs and I smile, picking up a few kernels.

"Thanks, kitten."

She shrugs, then settles deeper into the groove between my arm and my shoulder. She hasn't changed the shampoo she uses since the last time I smelled her hair. It still smells like strawberries. I move my arm, settling it around her shoulders, and pull her in closer. I briefly consider whether her lips still taste like bubble gum... I don't have any kidneys left to find that out.

Halfway through the movie, her phone chimes, and I see Carter's name. She pulls up the message and sighs loudly.

"What?" I ask. I'm dying to know what he said.

"Nothing..." she replies, and I stiffen. She looks up at me and her cheeks flush. "He's just being his usual annoying self. He says 'hi' and is asking if I'm still being your French maid, at least I think that's what it says. He clearly can't type when drunk." I smile with relief. I'm going to bring it up. Just suck it up and say it.

"Jenny..." I start, "about our bet." She pauses the movie and turns to face me, her face weary.

"You weren't serious about the French maid outfit, right? I know I didn't cook much, but you weren't here and..." She looks down at her phone and makes a face, then looks back up at me. I struggle not to laugh. Then I start to imagine her in a French maid outfit and laughing is the last thing on my mind. Where's that bag of ice when you need it?

"No... Although, that would certainly be..." Amazing? Hot as fuck? Incredible? Mind-blowing? Sexy? All of the above? "Interesting."

She exhales a relieved sigh.

"I was thinking about the part of the bet where you agreed to go on a date with me. A proper date," I say.

"Oh," her mouth drops open and her blue eyes get larger. "I mean, yes." She shakes her head, closing her mouth and biting her lower lip. I'm struggling to keep my hands to myself.

"I was thinking we could go next weekend, if you're free, that is."

"Let me check my schedule," she says, pausing. My shoulders sag. "Yep," she continues. "Just as I thought, wide open." She grins at me. I grin back, like a fourteen-year-old.

"Ok then." I say, pressing play on the movie while Jenny settles herself back on my shoulder. There's no way I can focus on what's happening to Anakin and Obi-Wan.

When the movie finishes, I switch the TV off. Jenny is not moving. Her eyes are closed and her face nuzzled in my neck. I have a serious cramp in my shoulder, but I don't give two shits about that. Instead, I gently move her, then slide my arms underneath her body, lifting her up and carrying her to her bedroom. I quietly open the door and set her on the covers, then pull a blanket over her small frame. She looks angelic, and I can't stop myself from pressing my lips to her forehead.

"Aiden," she mumbles, and I still mid-action. "Cuddle," she orders sleepily, and I chuckle.

"Are you sure, princess?"

"Mmm," she mumbles, grabbing my hand, her eyes still closed. I pull my t-shirt off but leave my sweats on. I need as many layers as possible between me and her. I slip under the covers, and she instantly moves in on me, putting her face on my chest and draping her leg over mine. Fuck, there's no way in hell I'll be able to sleep.

Chapter 10

Totally Innocent

I wonder what my dog named me...
- Aiden

The sun is hot on my skin. I stare straight at it until my vision blurs and dark spots appear. I close my eyes and savour the sensation of seeing the sun against the black of my eyelids, like an eclipse I saw when I was seventeen.

"Jenny..." Aiden's deep, soft voice surrounds me, making me shiver. "Jenny," he says again, and I open my eyes to see his beautiful face in front of me. I get up and walk over to him, propelled by courage I didn't know I possessed. "You are so beautiful," he says as I reach him. I put my hand on his bare chest and trace circles with my fingers. Aiden wraps his powerful arms around me and pulls me in closer.

I crane my head up and see him beaming down at me. Happy, I'm happy. "I want you," he whispers and pulls the strap of my top off my shoulders, leaning down and kissing where his fingers left a trail from my shoulder to my arm. He moves his lips back up to my shoulder and my neck, tracing little kisses down my collarbone. A guttural sound escapes me as he licks, then nips at my skin.

"Aiden..." I moan as his hand traces up my back and under my top. "Aiden..." As his kisses go from my collarbone down towards my breasts, his jaw brushing against my nipple.

"Aiden," I mumble through my sleep, waking up slowly. I'm hot. Hot from desire and the sleepy memory of his burning body against mine. I shut my eyes tighter and try to go back to my dream. Where was I? The side of my face presses against his chest and my hand is still tracing circles on his skin. My leg is wrapped around his midsection and I press myself against him, sighing with pleasure when I feel his erection against me. An arm snakes around me and holds me tighter. A hand strokes up and down my leg.

This feels so real, so vivid. I can smell him next to me. I can feel his chest rising up and down with every breath he draws. I open my right eye and nearly die of a heart attack. What the hell?

My dream seems to be reality. How did this happen? Aiden is in my bed, sleeping on his back, his arm wrapped around me while I'm happily drooling on his chest. Shit!

Am I drooling on his chest? I move my right arm and discreetly check his torso for any signs of wetness next to my face. As my hand connects with his hard, warm chest, I nearly moan.

How am I supposed to survive with the British God of hotness in my bed without attacking him like the inexperienced sucker that I am?

I move away, peeling my sticky leg off of his thigh and my head off his chest. He hums in protest, but lets me move and turns to his side, facing me. His left arm is still under my neck, and just as I am about to move, he wraps his right arm around me and pulls me into his chest, or rather pulls me in so that his face is in my chest...

"Mmmmm strawberries, you smell like strawberries," he mumbles through his sleep, sniffing my hair and nuzzling between my boobs. God, this feels too good.

"Aiden," I whisper.

"Jenny," he mumbles and pulls me in even closer, dropping sleepy little kisses on my collarbone, just like he did in my dream. What. The. Hell.

"Aiden." I try to pry myself gently out of his grasp, to no avail.

"Mmm, you're so damn sexy," he mumbles, burying his face in my chest again. His breath tickles my breasts and a shiver of pleasure runs up and down my body as he licks the top of my cleavage. Shit. The asshole better be sleeping.

"Aiden, wake up," I say quite loudly, patting the side of his body not so gently. I need to put a stop to this while I still can. Otherwise I'll be losing my virginity in the next ten minutes.

"Mmmm?" he mutters sleepily.

"Wake up, sleepyhead," I say, pinching his side.

"Aww, what's that for?" he mumbles, opening his eyes, his gaze landing straight on my boobs, since it's right in front of his nose. "Now that's a sight I wouldn't mind waking up to every day," he mutters.

"Stop staring and let me out of your death grip," I say, feigning annoyance. In reality, I'm quite pleased. I wouldn't mind sleeping next to this hunk of a man every night, either. Not that I'd ever voice that desire out loud. Like never. Ever.

Aiden reluctantly loosens his grip and lets me go.

"What the hell, Jenny!" My door bursts open and a pissed off Hayley storms in. I scream and jump away from Aiden like we were doing something I-wish-we-were-doing-but-would-never-have-the-guts-to-admit-it… "Oh shit!" Hayley's jaw drops to the floor.

"Morning," I say, my face crimson, putting as much distance between Aiden and me on the bed as possible.

"Now I get why you didn't text me back last night," she says, cocking her head to the side with a knowing smile. "I was worried I'd have to look for you in a ditch somewhere, but I can see you were being taken care of." She grins.

Aiden shoots up in the bed. "It's not what it looks like," he says groggily, and somehow my chest squeezes. Goddamnit! I wish it was exactly what it looked like. "We watched a movie and then we just fell asleep." In my bed… me straddling him and having dirty dreams. Yup. Totally innocent.

"Uh-huh." Hayley smirks.

"I've got to go, anyway. I'm supposed to be at the centre soon," Aiden says, yawning. What centre? Way to throw a poor excuse into this combo…

"Uh, okay. I'll see you later then," I say as he gets up smiling at me and starts walking out of my room, my gaze following his perfectly shaped backside all the way to the door. He stops next to Hayley, bends over, granting me a view I wish I could take a picture of to pick up his t-shirt off the floor, then leaves the bedroom, closing the door behind him.

I wipe the drool from my face.

"Well, well," Hayley says with her hands on her hips. "Well, well, well…."

"Nothing happened," I say.

"Nothing?" She asks with disbelief?

"Nothing," I admit, to my dismay.

"Then what do you call him sleeping in your bed?"

"A dream come true?" I make an innocent face.

"So you admit it then?"

"Admit what?" I decide to play dumb.

"You've got it bad for him. As I said before, there's a fine line between hate and love, babe. A fine line indeed." I sigh and nod. I don't want to admit it out loud, but I can acknowledge the fact that my feelings towards him have made a u-turn in the last few weeks. Damn it. "So how was last night?" Hayley asks, sitting next to me on the bed.

"I am pretty sure frat parties are not my thing," I disclose.

"You're preaching to the choir, sister!"

"Aiden finally asked me out," I say.

"What?! And you took all this time before you told me? Details, now!" she practically screams at me.

I tell her about last night's conversation with Aiden, and she once more nominates herself as my official stylist and makeup artist.

I go shower while she rummages through my closet in search of an outfit. When I get out, I find her sitting on my bed with a smug smile.

"I smell a trap," I laugh, putting my wet hair up in a bun. Hayley scoffs.

"Uh-uh, I found it," she says mysteriously.

"Well?"

"Ta-da!" She gestures to her left. I walk over to her side of the bed and gasp. How the hell did she do this?

"You're incredible..." I whisper; eyeing up the white, oversized, silk blouse; ripped, skinny blue jeans; and a red, suede belt I used to wear in high school.

"Which brings me to the next topic," she says with an

excited smile on her face. "I've got something for you." She reaches to her bag on the floor and pulls out what I can only describe as the most beautiful thing in the world.

It appears I've got a thing for high heels. I start jumping up and down, clapping my hands. Hayley just shakes her head and passes me a pair of gorgeous, red suede sandals from Jimmy Choo. They have an open toe and cut out details on the sides with a woven design running from one side to the other. I look at the zip fastening on the back of the heel and the ankle strap and gently caress the shoes in my hand, hugging them to my chest. Hayley laughs.

"Put them on," she says. "They've got a tiny platform which will add a bit more height. Plus the color goes perfectly with the belt, completing your outfit."

In what seems to be my Cinderella moment, I slip my feet into the otherworldly things and stand up straight, wobbling a little.

"You've got a week to practice walking," Hayley says, taking my hand and guiding my first Bambi-like steps around the room, giving me pointers. An hour later, I confidently stroll around my room, not holding onto Hayley or the walls. Although my feet are killing me, I am seriously considering staying in the shoes forever and pledging my undying love to Mr. Choo.

"Okay," Hayley says. "Time to take these bad boys off and let your feet rest for a bit. They're on loan from a stylist friend of mine, so I'll need them back at some point, but they're yours for now." I sit down and reluctantly take the shoes off. I gently stroke them and put them in my closet, waving at them before closing the door.

"Ladies!" My door flies open, and in comes Carter, wearing sunglasses and the same clothes he had on last night. Does anyone even knock these days? He starts taking his sunglasses off, then suddenly pushes them back up his nose with a small cry. "Jenny, what voltage do you have here? 2000? So bright, so fucking bright!"

I chuckle. "It's called daylight, genius. How was the rest of your night?"

"Good, I think. I woke up in your brother's warm embrace on the floor of his bedroom... Not quite sure how we got there. Thankfully, we were both fully clothed. Not sure what I'd do if we weren't, probably have nightmares for years to come." Hayley and I outright laugh. "Too loud!" Carter winces and covers his ears, which just makes us laugh louder and harder. "Stop with the incessant cackling, I beg you!"

When we finally calm down, Carter sighs with relief and walks towards my bed, jumping onto it and wrapping himself in my comforter. I raise my eyebrows at Hayley, who just shrugs at me in response.

"Do you mind if I snooze for a bit?" Carter asks, digging himself deeper into my pillows and sighing happily.

"Sure..." I answer like I have a choice. Which, clearly, I don't since I can hear quiet snoring coming from underneath the pillows.

Hayley and I exit the room, leaving Carter behind. The house is quiet, bar the loud snores coming from Jason's room.

"C'mon," I say. "Let's have some breakfast."

Chapter 11

Wittle Kissy-Wissy

I won't be impressed with technology until I can download food.
- Jason

The thing is, I was obviously half asleep while I basically motor-boated Jenny's chest. Not that it didn't feel like heaven. Thank God for small favours and Hayley walking in on us when she did. A minute later and I could not be held responsible for my own actions.

So I ran out of there like my ass was on fire and hiding a raging...ugh.

It's not a big deal. We just slept in the same bed.

NOT. A BIG. DEAL.

Fuck.

All I could do this week was think about her body wrapped around mine. Her fingers tracing a fiery pattern on my chest. Not necessarily a good thing. I couldn't focus in class or in the Youth Centre where I volunteered.

I wasn't sure how to act around Jenny, so I just did what any coward would. I made sure we didn't 'bump' into each other at home or in school.

But I watched her. I went back into my stalkery, high-schooly, pathetic ways. I knew her schedule, where she'd be, and...I watched her. Talking with Hayley on the green in front of the library. Catching up with Jason before one of her classes. Laughing with Carter by the gymnasium. I nearly ripped his head off that time he pinched her side, making her squeal. I seriously considered hiring a hitman. Someone who could just take him out quietly.

Not a big deal...

Who am I kidding? Jenny Cowley is a big deal; she is the real thing, and I am on a straight path to losing my mind. I need to shake out of it before I destroy my friendship with her, Jason, or Carter. I can't just let my emotions take over and wreak havoc, can I?

I sigh and look into the bathroom mirror, then down at my watch. Twenty minutes.

Twenty minutes until I go get Jenny and take her out for our date. I pour some cold water on my hands and run them through my hair, trying to get the fuckers to agree with what I have in mind. They seem to have a mind of their own, though.

A soft knock startles me. I turn and open the bathroom door hesitantly, revealing Jason. He pushes past me, then closes the door behind him, locking it and turning around. His arms crossed over his chest.

"Jason..." I start. How am I even going to explain to him what's going on in my head?

"No, man. You do not talk. I talk," he says, going all brother bear. I lean against the sink and nod for him to continue. "Don't do anything stupid. Just take her out to dinner, make some conversation, then bring her back home. No funny business. She's my sister, not some chick you pick up at a frat party."

"I know, Jason. You know I'd never do anything to hurt her."

"Is that so?" He narrows his eyes. "I seem to remember something different, like when you spread a rumour about her, making her retract into her shell. Ring any bells?"

"I'm sorry..." I hang my head. How do I even go about explaining it? "She punched me. I mean, I kissed her then, and she punched me. I was really hurt...and an idiot." Jason's mouth lifts in a half smile.

"You've got that right... At least it sounds like my little sis can take care of things when someone tries to take what's not theirs." His smile disappears, and he looks straight at me. "None of that shit tonight, capisce?" I take a deep breath and nod. I'll try. The truth of the matter is that I can't stop myself from thinking about her. "Good talk, man!" Jason lightens up and pats my back as he makes his way out of the bathroom. He turns around before opening the door. "I'll break your face if you so much as touch her without her permission. No—scratch that—she's off limits, period."

I watch the door close behind him, then look back up into the mirror. I splash cold water on my face and go back to my room, where I pull on a pair of black jeans and a white top. In the last ditch effort, I run my hand through my hair, but it just sticks out however it wants, so I let it go.

I go to Jenny's room and knock.

"I'll be out in a minute," she yells through the closed door. I lean against the wall, closing my eyes, taking another deep breath and giving myself an internal pep talk. It's not too late to go back to my room and forget about the whole thing. That would probably be the safest thing to do.

"Hi," she says, standing next to me. I didn't even hear her come outside. I turn to say 'hi' back, but no words come out. Instead, I just gape at her, mouth open and everything. She looks incredible, and I can't stop myself from checking her out. She's wearing these amazing red heels. Did she know I've got a thing for red heels? She seems taller, her head reaching my neck. Not good, not good at all. That much closer to lean over and kiss her plump lips.

"Hi," I finally croak out. Checking out her legs in the ripped skinny jeans she has on, my gaze goes higher, stopping at her waist where her blouse is half tucked into her jeans. I can see a glimpse of a red belt and I force myself to look higher up, lingering for a second too long on her chest, then moving to her neck and finally her beautiful face. Her chestnut brown hair is loose on her shoulders, twisting into waves here and there.

"Hi," she says again, looking down and blushing a little. She's probably as nervous as I am. The thought makes me relax.

"Ready?" I ask, smiling down at her.

"Would you put them away?" she mumbles, irritated.

"Pardon?" I ask, confused.

"The dimples, goddamnit. I can't think when you're unleashing them full force." She goes a deep shade of red, almost matching the amazing shoes she's got on, and I laugh.

"Sorry." I try hard not to smile, but the fact that my smile might affect her just made my day. "Let's go, kitten," I say, taking her hand and guiding her out of the house. We pass Jason, who is sitting on the couch.

"You kids have fun," he shouts at us. "Young man, make sure to bring her back home by midnight!" he finishes in his best 'dad' voice. He's wearing a pair of thick-rimmed glasses and has an unlit pipe in his mouth. God knows where he got the props from. Jenny laughs.

"Night, Jason," she says, as we walk outside.

"Don't do anything I wouldn't do!" Jason yells. "No wait, that's a lot of things! Just don't do anything!"

We walk to the Jeep and I open the passenger door for her. She smiles at me gratefully. I can't shake off the feeling of happiness, like what we're doing feels so fucking right, but in the back of my mind I keep remembering this is Jenny's official first date and, as much happiness as that thought brings me, I am also aware it's entirely my fault.

"Music?" I ask, getting into the driver's seat and pulling out of the driveway. Jenny distractedly presses the button for the radio and loud country music starts playing from the speakers.

"Mmmm," I start. "Big fan of country then?"

"Sorry," she mumbles, switching the radio off. "Can we just keep it off? I'm a bit nervous."

"Sure," I say, putting my hand on hers and squeezing it for reassurance. "What are you nervous about?"

She looks up at me, then quickly looks away. "I don't know," she says, biting her lip. "I guess I'm worried that I'll be a terrible date."

"Ah," I say, trying not to laugh. How could she ever think that? "What, with your shit chat and no sense of humour? Yes, I can see why you might be worried."

"Jerk," she punches me playfully on the shoulder.

"C'mon, kitten, you know you'll be great. Just relax." I smile at her. When we arrive at the restaurant, I squeeze her hand. "I'll make you a deal," I say. "Since it's your first proper date, I'll tell you some first date horror stories so you can see how lucky you are that your first date is with me." I flash her my best smile and run out to open her car door. She takes my hand and slips out of the car.

"Lucky that your big head fits through the entrance to the restaurant?" She giggles.

We follow the hostess to our table, and I pull out her chair for her, determined to make this the best date she'll ever have.

"May I get you something to drink?" the waiter asks. I raise my eyebrow questioningly at Jenny.

"Water is good with me," she breathes.

"As per the ladies' order, could we please have a bottle of Chateauneuf-du-Tap...and a bottle of Champagne?" I look at Jenny. She nods excitingly. The waiter smiles and walks away.

"Tell me about the horror stories," Jenny speaks, looking down at the menu.

"Some of them are less horror-y than others, and some of them are not mine, but I guess at least you'll see how a date can go downhill really fast." I take a deep breath and start, "I once took this girl out for drinks. She was really nice. When we got to the bar, she called her mum to join us...along with her mum's boyfriend." Jenny giggles. "I am sad to admit her mum was a lot more fun than she was."

"More!" Jenny smiles, lighting up the entire room.

"Okay... When I was seventeen, my mum tried to set me up with one of her friend's daughters. It was so awkward. Neither one of us spoke a word to each other except for 'hi'...and 'bye' thirty minutes later when we realised we had nothing to talk about." Jenny's eyes are huge and she's trying to hold back laughter. "I've got a better one. Last year, Jason went out with this really pretty girl. They were getting on like a house on fire. Drinks were flowing, and as she got increasingly more tipsy, she started to speak baby-talk to him, asking if he wanted a 'wittle kissy-wissy'."

"No!" Jenny bursts out laughing.

"That's not all," I continue. "When he excused himself to go to the bathroom, wanting to make a call for backup, she actually asked him if he needed help wiping!" Jenny gasps. "When he got to the toilet, the waitress serving them told him that the girl just placed a pacifier on his plate and that if he needs escape through the back door, she can help." Jenny shakes her head in disbelief. "He ended up dating the waitress for a month...so I guess something good came out of it."

"Typical Jason..."

"Yup, don't know why he wouldn't dig that girl. Baby-talk is soo sexy." I wink at her.

The waiter comes back to the table with our Champagne. He takes our orders and visibly checks Jenny out with appreciation. I clench my fists and try keeping it cool. I didn't think I was the jealous type but it's becoming evident that I am.

"What's wrong?" Jenny asks, gently touching my hand.

"Nothing." I relax and smile at her. I take the glass of Champagne and hold it up. "Cheers, kitten," I say.

"Cheers! To my first date." She beams, and I can't help myself.

"To our first date." I hold her gaze, then take a sip.

"So how does this work, anyway?" she asks. "What do you normally do on a first date?"

"You talk; you get to know each other," I reply. "You ask questions you'd like to know the answers to. For example, why were you excited about the first day of school for the first time in a long time?" Jenny looks surprised.

"Oh." She blushes. "You remembered that." I nod.

"Well, I guess I can tell you." She takes a big breath. "It's just that... You know all my life we would move around, each year a different place and I just...I hated it. I'd have to start over in a new school every year. Just as I made friends, we'd move again. It was so exhausting. So the prospect of the next few years in one place was exhilarating," she finishes in one quick torrent of words.

"That's understandable."

"Your turn," she says.

"Mmm?"

"Tell me about yourself. What was it like growing up, Aiden VonSchmuck?" she says, then covers her mouth in realisation. I laugh.

"Is that what you call me?"

"Used to... Old habits die hard, I guess." She grins, sticking her tongue out at me.

"I suppose I deserved that," I say, laughing. "And, to answer your question, my life growing up was peachy. Especially if you like fake friends who are only after your money and status and expensive presents from absentee parents," I finish. Jenny looks at me with sadness. She reaches out and takes my hand, squeezing it.

"I'm sorry," she says just as our food arrives. I kick myself for bringing the mood down as we dig into our dishes.

"So what do you want to do when you grow up?" Jenny asks me.

"Wow, imagine that."

"What?"

"You're the first person to ever ask me that..."

"Oh."

"Everyone just assumes that I will follow in my father's footsteps, get a business degree, go back to England, take over the company…" I say. "No one ever asked me what I want."

"And what do you want?" Jenny cocks her head to the side.

"I want to help people," I say, quietly.

"That's great," she says encouragingly. "So what's your major? Sociology?"

"I'm still undeclared," I wince.

"How come?"

"Ongoing battle with my father," I admit. "He wants me to do a business orientated course. I don't."

"Oh, that must suck. I'm sorry," she says. I'm about to shrug it off when a familiar girl strolls over to our table.

"Aiden, darling. How have you been?" She leans over and kisses me on both cheeks.

"I'm fine, thanks. How are you, uhhmm…"

"Chloe, silly!" she exclaims, shaking her blonde bob. Ah yes, that was her name. "I'm well, thank you. What are you doing here?" I look over at her, then at Jenny, who is fuming. What does it look like I'm doing? I'm about to reply when Jenny interjects.

"Long time no see, Oompa Lumpa." Chloe veers to look at Jenny.

"If anyone is a midget here, it's you," she says, then turns back to me.

"At least I'm not orange," Jenny mumbles under her breath.

"Sorry, I didn't realize you were with someone," Chloe continues, ignoring Jenny. "You looked so bored, I thought I'd come over to say 'hello'."

"Couldn't be more wrong," I reply, seeing the anger on Jenny's face. "I'm quite happy with the current company." Jenny looks up and throws daggers at Chloe's back with her eyes. I decide to take matters into my own hands. "We were actually about to leave," I say, getting up and taking Jenny by her hand.

"Oh, okay then. Don't be a stranger." Chloe pouts.

"Fat chance," Jenny mumbles, and I fight the smile threatening to break through. Kitten has claws.

We walk away and I pay the bill.

"Sorry that our date got cut short," I say as we get into the car. "Do you want to go anywhere else?"

She huffs.

"Jenny?"

"Home," she growls.

"Kitten..."

"Don't you kitten me! How do you know the she-devil?" Jenny narrows her eyes at me. She looks fiery and angry and... Fuck Jason! All I want to do is kiss her right now.

"I don't, really," I say with a half smile. Could Jenny be actually jealous? "I think she used to date Jason last year, or be one of his groupies. I'm not sure."

"Humph!" Jenny replies, crossing her arms and looking out the window.

"Kitten..." I say again.

"She's just so...so mean! I can't believe you'd hang out with someone like her." She turns to me. I smile and hold my hand out to her. She takes it reluctantly and I squeeze it.

"I don't, Jenny. Was she mean to you?"

"Doesn't matter. I'm just pissed off she messed up my first date," she says.

"Our first date," I correct her.

"Yeah." She relaxes. "Sorry, she just irritates the crap out of me. I'm messing this date up even more, aren't I?"

Her hand is still in mine and, honestly, the world could

end and I'd die with a happy smile on my face. She couldn't mess it up in a million years.

"It's not over just yet," I say, pulling into our driveway.

"But..." she says, confused. "We're home."

I get out of the car and open the door for her.

"I've got something for you," I say, taking her hand and closing the door behind her. I turn back to the house. It's dark.

"You do?"

"Uh-huh." I smile, reaching into my back pocket and handing her the small object. She takes it and looks at the silver charm.

"A strawberry..." she trails off.

"You smell just like one." I smile.

"Aiden, is it m-" I stop her, pressing my finger against her lips.

"Don't spoil this moment with questions you're not ready to hear the answers to." I look deep into her eyes. I'm laying it on thick, but I can't help myself. She's everything I want. The need to make her mine consumes me. I take the charm and attach it to her bracelet. "There, now you have two nicknames." She rolls her eyes.

"Thank you. It's very thoughtful of you." She smiles, then pulls my face down and kisses me on my cheek. I just about have a heart attack, then she walks past me towards the door. She turns halfway up the path. "Walk me to my door." I follow her like a puppy as we go inside.

When we stop outside her bedroom door, I take her hand.

"A good date should always have some dancing involved," I say.

"Is that so?" She smiles. I nod.

"May I have this dance?" I ask.

"There's no music..." she replies, confused.

I pull my phone out and scroll down, pressing play when I find the right song. I press the volume button up and put the phone back into my pocket, taking Jenny into my arms. She presses her head against my neck and we sway to the rhythm of the song. She's so close to me I can feel her heartbeat, the heat of her body.

I pull her in closer and inhale the scent of strawberries filling my nostrils. All I can think of is kissing her. All I can do is to hold her close and not let go. I need to make sure that she knows what a proper kiss is like. I need...

I need her.

When the lyrics start, I whisper the word into her hair. *'I think I might have inhaled you...'* *'You gotten into my bloodstream...'* She looks up at me and smiles. I decide there will never be a better moment.

"You know, there's another dating disaster story I wanted to tell you about," I say, looking into her blue eyes.

"Oh, yeah?" she asks playfully.

"Uh-huh. When I was fourteen, I was head over heels for this girl," I say. "She was my best friends' little sister and completely out of my league, plus I was a total coward, always too afraid to talk to her." Her eyes go huge, and I lift my hand to caress her cheek. "One day I found out that she'd be leaving forever and decided to just suck it up and tell her how I felt about her."

"I think I know this story," she whispers.

"I don't think you know my version..." I reply. "The next day when I found her, she was waiting for her older brother. I was terrified, but walked up to her anyway. We talked a little and then I kissed her. She was my first real kiss." Jenny gasps. "I thought it was the most amazing thing in the world, her lips on mine. Her lips tasted like bubble gum. I remember that... I often wonder if they still taste the same," I say, touching my finger to her lips. "But she must have thought differently," I sigh. "In fact, she must have thought the kiss was horrible since she punched me and ran away, leaving me heartbroken."

"Sorry." She mouths.

"Don't be, I did some stupid things after that... I'm sorry."

"I was your first real kiss?" she asks in disbelief. I nod.

"I need you to know..." I whisper, leaning down.

"Yes?" she whispers back.

"That I've learned how to kiss since then."

"Oh," she gasps as I brush my lips against hers.

I take her head between my hands and press my lips gently to hers. I don't expect the force in which she responds. She wraps her arms around my neck, pulling me down and pressing her body to mine. I nip at her lower lip, sucking on it gently, and she moans, making me growl. Her heady scent surrounds me. I'm so fucking crazy about her. I pull her up and hold her tight against me while she wraps her legs around my waist, her lips against mine, her hands in my hair.

She sneaks her tongue in between my lips and I can't take it anymore. Groaning, I attack her lips like they're the last drop of water in a desert. Praying for self-control.

I can't take this any further.

I can't.

She doesn't taste like bubble gum anymore, she tastes like strawberries. I pull her in, exploring, tasting, probing...

Our kiss becomes more and more frantic and I press her against the wall, leaving the comfort of her lips and burrowing my face in her neck, kissing and sucking her soft skin. Jenny moans and pulls me in tighter against her, rocking into me as she grabs my hair and pulls, ripping my head away from her neck.

Fuck, she's so hot, so demanding as she presses her lips against mine and passionately kisses me. I can't think straight anymore, there's just me and her and nobody fucking else counts.

Nobody.

"I take it you two had a good night then," Jason's pissed off voice breaks me out of my dream.

I reluctantly pull away from Jenny. We're both panting. Her face is flushed and her hair is a mess. She looks fucking glorious. I gently put her down.

"Hi, Jason." She blushes. "Yeah, it was really nice." She looks up at me and winks. I swear my knees weaken. She must know how sexy she is. "Thanks for the goodnight kiss, VonSchmuck." She stands on her tiptoes and pulls my head down, placing a kiss on my cheek. "Night boys, I'll see you tomorrow." She walks into her bedroom and closes the door behind her.

I turn around to face the music, and my eye connects with Jason's fist.

Chapter 12

Temporary Insanity

Kiss me if I'm wrong, but dinosaurs still exist, right?
– Carter

The memory of Aiden's hot lips lingers on mine for days after the kiss. I'd have never in a million years thought that kissing could be that amazing, well, at least not after the first time he kissed me...

The second first time? A whole different story.

It's like he lit a fire in me I never knew existed, and now I have serious hots for the boy. The kind that makes me want to dry hump him when I see him or think of him... And I think of him a lot. The problem is, I don't see him.

Aiden Vaughn has disappeared from the face of the Earth. After our incredible kiss, which was rudely interrupted by Jason, I went to my bedroom to take a cold shower before bed. As one would, when one is so incredibly turned on, one can't think straight... You get my drift.

When I woke up the next morning, the house was empty. Both Aiden and Jason were off somewhere. I thought little of it and just went about my day, meeting up with Hayley for a study session and an incredibly vivid description of the kiss I shared with a certain someone the night before. Let's just say catching up on lab work did not take precedence.

After unsuccessful attempts at studying, we finally parted ways. When I got home, Jason was back but Aiden was still MIA. Jason was behaving like a child, huffing in the corner and flicking through sports channels on TV, so I left him to his own devices to calm down.

He's been calming down for a week now... Seriously. My brother is full on avoiding my presence, and whenever I'm trying to talk to him about what he saw, he changes the subject and leaves the room. This would not bother me as much if it wasn't for the fact that Aiden has been gone all that time. He's not been in the house and he hasn't tried calling or texting me. Although, to be fair, I haven't either; but he should try contacting me first, right?

Jason's childish dodging attempts have quickly transformed from being entertaining to hurtful. I haven't done anything wrong, have I?

Well, I am about to find out. I storm into my brother's bedroom, pulling the covers off his body. I silently pray that he is alone in his bed. It seems that someone up there is looking down on me with a gracious eye since they answer my prayers. Phew. That could have been awkward.

"Lemme sleep," Jason mumbles.

"Wake up, wake up, wake up!" I shout at him. He springs up to a sitting position and rubs his eyes.

"Everything okay? What's going on?" he asks, looking around on high alert.

"No, everything is not okay!" I say, sitting down on his bed. "Why are you avoiding me?"

"What?" His shoulders slump. "Jenny…do we have to do this so early in the morning?"

"It's eleven, genius," I say, fighting the lump in my throat.

"Exactly. C'mon sis, let's talk later." He exhales.

"No!" I clench my fists. My voice is wavering and my eyes feel hot and prickly. "Jason, why are you not talking to me?"

"I am. We're talking right now, aren't we?" He sighs.

"Right, after I basically accosted you in your sleep. Awesome talk." I roll my eyes. "All week you have been avoiding me. You've barely spoken to me and…and… Have I done something so wrong to make you want to abandon me? I understand Aide would be all cowardly, but you're my brother…. Is it because I kissed Aiden?"

Jason's jaw clenches, and he looks away. "No Jenny, you did nothing wrong. I just didn't want you to get hurt. Again." He says. "I'm sorry. I haven't abandoned you; I was just…ashamed." His words hurt.

"Ashamed of me?" I ask incredulously.

"God, no!" He replies quickly, looking back at me. "When I saw you and Aiden, I got so angry. Earlier on, before your date, I told him not to take advantage of you, not to even touch you, not to do anything. I told him you were off limits. And then he kissed you and I lost it. I punched him."

"You did what?"

"I punched him." He hangs his head. "He didn't fight back. He didn't even block my punches, and I must have thrown at least three or four before I calmed down. It's like he knew he deserved it." My jaw drops.

"Did it ever occur to you that I might have wanted to kiss him? That he wasn't the one taking advantage of the situation?" I ask.

Jason winces. "I'd rather not think of that possibility."

"Well, you should, because it was fifty-fifty between us. It doesn't matter now anyway, it's not like he wants a repeat," I mumble.

"What are you talking about?"

"He's been gone this whole week and I haven't heard from him once."

"Urgh," Jason growls. "It might be partially my fault." He buries his face in his hands.

"Spill brother bear."

"Well... Shit. Okay, so," Jason stumbles on his words before taking a deep breath and collecting himself. "After I, errr, expressed my disappointment through the use of physical, uhmm, signs, I told him that if he values our friendship he'll leave you alone. He promised he would."

"He did?"

"Yeah, he agreed. Then about half an hour after our altercation, he received a phone call from his father. His grandmother is not well, so he took the earliest flight back home to be with his family. He's in London at the moment."

"And you're only telling me this now?" I ask with disbelief. "He's supposed to be my friend, too! He must have been so anxious about his grandma this past week, and I didn't even know to ask about it!"

"Jenny, please don't be mad at me. You know I'm a protective little shit. I love you, squirt, and I just want you to be happy."

"I guess at least I know he's alive and not ditched in the ocean by my overprotective brother... You know I'll eventually date and kiss someone anyway, right?"

"To be honest, as much as it pains me to admit it, if you were to date anyone, Aiden would probably be my first choice." His words ignite a spark of hope in me. Could Aiden and I ever be like that? Jason continues, oblivious to my inner turmoil. "But I want you to be sure that you want to be with him, that it's not just because he's the first guy you noticed that's shown interest in you. And most of all, I need him to be serious about you. You're my sister. Once he marries you he can kiss you all he wants... Otherwise, I'll kill him." I hug my brother, laughing.

"You are an overprotective little shit, aren't you?" He nods. "Thank you, for trying to protect my honor and being an amazing brother. Can I ask you for a favor, though?"

"Sure."

"I like Aiden." Jason scrunches his face up. "I don't know exactly how much or if it'll go anywhere, but I really like him and I would be so grateful if in the future you'd try not to meddle so much. I want to learn things on my own and, if I ever need my big brother-"

"I'm always here for you."

"I hoped you'd say that." I smile at him.

"Now can I please go back to sleep? I got home at four a.m."

"Work hard, play hard?"

"Play hard for sure." He grins at me.

"All right then." I say, getting up. "One more thing though..."

"Sure, what is it?" Jason plops his head on his pillows and sighs happily, closing his eyes.

"Don't tell Aiden we had this talk, okay?"

"No problem, squirt. I think that's definitely wise," he says on a yawn. "Plus, if he really wants to be with you, he'll fight for you no matter the repercussions. Men are like that."

"Thanks, Jasypoo."

As soon as I'm outside, I text Aiden. To hell with keeping it cool. I need to know if he's okay and if his family is okay. That's what any friend would do.

ME: *Hi, I just heard about your grandmother. I hope everything is ok.*

It should be afternoon in London, so hopefully he'll see it soon. As much as I want to bombard him with questions, he's got more important things to think about at the moment. I walk towards my room when my phone pings.

AIDEN: *Hi, thanks for your text. My grandma is absolutely fine. My dad used her as an excuse to lure me back home for board meetings.*

ME: *Wow, that's a low blow... Glad to hear your grandma was ok all along though! When are you back?*

Three dots appear and disappear for a couple of minutes. My heart speeds up. Finally, his text comes through.

AIDEN: *I'll be back next week. Can we please talk then? I wanted to apologise for my behaviour after the date.*

My fingers shake as I type a reply.

ME: *Sure, what do you mean?*

AIDEN: *I shouldn't have kissed you...*

I drop to my knees. Five little words. Twenty-three letters. That's all it takes to make my heart hurt. Why the hell is it hurting in the first place? I squeeze my eyes, ordering myself to keep it cool. Shakily, I type a reply.

ME: *Is this because Jason punched you?*

He texts back instantly.

AIDEN: *Jason was right to punch me. I'm really sorry.*

The phone slips through my fingers and falls to the floor. Men fight for what they want...

It's silly, really. At the back of my head, somewhere deep, behind a pair of heavy metal doors, I think I hoped that he wanted to be with me as much as I was starting to realize I want to be with him. I guess hell has a new pavement built just for me, one made out of hope rather than good intentions.

My phone pings again and I pick it up, thinking that maybe it's Aiden apologising for his last text, claiming temporary insanity. But hell just laughs in my face and, next to my pavement of hope, erects a cute little house with a white picket fence and a freaking dog in its backyard made out of wishful thinking.

The disappointment cuts me to the bone.

CARTER: *WHATCHA UP 2 GRSHPPR? WANNA HANG?*

I clench Bonnie to my chest, willing the hurt away and slowly get up. Last thing I need right now is to be alone and moping. There's not a guy on this planet, except Ryan Gosling, that deserves the tears of a woman. I will not let some guy, except Ryan Gosling, make me feel like I'm not worth a fight. Carter is exactly what I need right now. I grab my bag and car keys and jog outside.

ME: *I'll be at yours in 5.*

Not that I'm counting how long it's been since Aiden's rejection, but I'm outside of Carter's apartment in 4 minutes 20 seconds. I ring the bell and tap my foot impatiently, waiting for him to open the door. When he does, I fall into his arms, realizing just how much I need a hug and someone to tell me that everything will be okay.

"Grasshopper, what's wrong?" he asks, holding me tight and stroking my back. I take a deep breath and untangle myself from Carter's embrace, determined not to cry. Why would I cry anyway, it's not like I'm in love? I just... Really like him... And that kiss... I want more of that kiss...

"Aiden's a spineless piece of British crap," I blurt out.

Carter chuckles and pats my head, guiding me inside. "Tell me something I don't know. Wait here. In anticipation of your arrival, I got some tasty supplies." He sets me down on the couch.

"Please tell me it's Cookie Dough BJ," I whine. Carter stops in his tracks halfway to the kitchen, then walks backward, retracing his steps to me..

His eyes are huge. "Really? How do you even go about it? Do you just spread the cookie dough all over it?"

"Err no, you just stick the whole thing in the bowl, obviously."

"The whole thing?" He looks at me, then at his crotch, then back at me. I narrow my eyes.

"BJ, as in Ben & Jerry's, you perv!" I exclaim, laughing. I knew coming here was the right move.

"Oh... Oooooh, I get it. No, I don't have ice cream... I thought you were being awfully forward...propositioning me like that." He grins, making me groan. I throw a pillow at him, which he ducks then runs off to the kitchen, coming back with a bag of popcorn. He is certainly getting brownie points for that move.

"My hero!" I take the bag from him and rip it open, digging in and spilling some popcorn on the couch in the process.

"There she is!" Carter laughs, plopping down on the sofa next to me. "The Gollum has returned!" I just nod and swallow a large handful of popcorn, ladylike, of course. Maybe not. "So what's up little one? Why is Aiden on our naughty list?" I sigh, chew the popcorn, then swallow and sigh again.

"We kissed." Carter raises his eyebrows questioningly.

"Was it as bad as the last time? Did you run away again?" He laughs.

"Har-har, very funny. It was better this time around... No, that's an understatement; it was amazing."

"So what's wrong?"

"Jason punched him then told him to stay away. Now Aiden is in London and says the kiss was a mistake." I pout.

"Oh."

"Yeah, oh."

"Well, I know for a fact that Aiden is crazy about you."

"And I know for a fact that he doesn't want a repeat performance!"

"Are you sure?"

"Pretty sure." I sigh. "He basically said Jason was right to punch him and tell him to stay away..."

"Awww, grasshopper." Carter pulls me into his chest. "Could it be-" He stops mid sentence.

"What?" I ask.

"Nothing."

"Come on, Kennedy. Could it be what?"

"Well, could it be that you're a horrible kisser and he doesn't want to do it again?" I punch him.

"You can be such a dick!"

He raises his hands in surrender. "What?! I'm just saying, if you ever need to practice you know where to find me."

"As if!"

"Don't dismiss it before you try it. Plus, you were the one offering BJs earlier on... Just saying." I punch him again and we both start laughing.

"Ugh! What do I do, Carter?" I ask once we calm down. "I mean, what am I supposed to do with this shit?"

"Trust me, grasshopper, he won't be able to stay away for too long. You're too good for him anyway, and he knows it. If he's got even one brain cell in that empty British head of his, he'll fight for you."

"But Jason basically told him that if he ever touches me again their friendship is over."

"I'd just like to point out that he never said anything like that to me, so if you ever need a man." He wiggles his eyebrows. "I'm yours, as is Little C."

"Right." I smirk. "He's never said that to you cause you're not an actual threat."

"Ouch!" Carter puts his hand over his heart. "Straight through the heart, grasshopper, straight through the heart!"

"Honestly though, what do I do? You're a guy, you should know!"

"Well, you could dress in short skirts and revealing tops, for starters. That would benefit us all." I roll my eyes. "Jenny, just give him time and talk to him when he's back, but don't push it, just gauge what he's feeling. Guys are complicated, not that anyone cares..." I smile. "In the meantime, I'll devise a bulletproof plan to get him red hot jealous."

"Huh?"

"Oh my god, I can feel the super villain cogs in my brain turning already!"

"You've got a brain? That's new."

"Stop it, grasshopper, or I won't help you." He narrows his eyes at me.

"Sorry," I say sheepishly.

"You're forgiven." Carter nods graciously in my direction. "So it's decided, if you can't wait for little Aiden to take his time coming to terms with his feelings, we will make him jealous. I'll think of something awesome."

For Crying Out Loud

Why do I have a bad feeling about this?

Chapter 13

Plenty More Fish

When life gives you lemons, put them in your bra! It won't solve your problems, but the extra attention is nice.

- Jenny

The drive from the airport back to the house is pretty quick, considering it's Friday afternoon. The closer I get to Starwood, the quicker my heart beats in anticipation of seeing her again. Will she even want to look at me? We've had no contact since our exchange last weekend, where I apologised for the kiss, which doesn't surprise me. I was an asshole. Dismissing what we shared like it didn't mean a thing, like it was a mistake, like it wasn't the hottest damn kiss I've ever had. I wonder if she knows that the words I typed hurt me as much as they did her. If they hurt her at all, that is.

I press my foot harder against the accelerator, not really caring about speed limits, wanting to get to her as fast as possible. Minutes tick by as I get stuck in traffic, so close... It's infuriating knowing that if I just left my car in the middle of the road now, I could walk faster than the crawling speed I'm currently driving. The irritated drivers around me beep their horns like it'll help. It doesn't; it just makes everyone else that much more pissed off. When I finally arrive at the house, what feels like decades later, her car is parked outside. She's here.

I breathe in and look at my reflection in the small mirror. My bruises are almost gone, there's just a slight yellow tint around my eye and on the side of my jaw. My father nearly flipped out when I arrived in London, all beaten up. Serves him right for luring me down to attend board meetings pretending that Grandma was sick. When she found out he did that, she screamed at him for thirty minutes straight. I smile, remembering. Not that he was bothered.

"Have you declared your major yet, Aiden?" He kept on pestering me. "You're in your second year, you've got until Christmas to decide on a business degree. If you don't— Let's just say you'll be back in London before you know it." I clench my fists, remembering his words. Should I just suck it up and go for the stupid business degree, live the rest of my life unhappy and following in his footsteps?

And then there's Jenny.

I run my hand through my hair, exasperated. Jason has been my best friend for so long. He was so angry when he found Jenny and me kissing. That kiss. That Earth-fucking-shattering kiss... I can never repeat it. But I can relive it in my head over and over. I close my eyes, doing just so. The door to the house is unlocked and, when I walk in, the living room is empty, so I go to my room and drop my bag on the bed. I'm trying to figure out my next move when I hear laughter from Jenny's room and decide that it's probably for the best to get our 'talk' over with. Hoping that she'll be able to forgive me and still be my friend, I knock on her door. I need her in my life, even if it's just in a friend's capacity.

"Look who decided to grace us with their presence," Hayley mocks. I'm not even bothered. Instead I peer above her shoulder into the room, Jenny is sitting on the bed surrounded by books.

"Can I talk to Jenny?" I ask. She's avoiding looking my way and, at the sound of my voice, her fists clench.

"Jenny is busy," Hayley replies, narrowing her eyes at me.

"Right... When will she be free?" Hayley turns her head to look at her. Jenny sighs, gets up from the bed, and walks towards me. My heart skips a beat.

"I don't really have time for jerks these days," she says.

"Jenny, I'm so-"

"Don't," she interrupts me. "I've heard enough of your meaningless apologies in the last few months. You acted like a child." She crosses her arms over her chest; my eyes are instantly drawn to the area. Before I make an even bigger fool out of myself, I look back up at her face. "And I don't really want to talk to you right now. In fact, I don't even want to be around you. You need to figure out what you want."

She turns around and walks away.

"Kitten-" I start, but Hayley interrupts me.

"Babe, you want to stay at my place tonight?" she asks Jenny.

"That would be great, thanks," Jenny replies, gathering a few books from her bed and dropping them in her bag. There goes my plan of trying to talk to her later once she's alone and her Hayley-shaped bodyguard is gone.

They leave without a goodbye, and I can't help feeling responsible for the situation. I acted like a dick. As soon as I'm back in my room, moping, my door swings open and Jason strolls in.

"Get ready!" he says excitedly. "We're going out!"

"Hello to you too," I reply grimly.

"What's that sad face for?" Jason asks. "You still upset about having that conversation with my fists a few weeks ago? I'm over it if you are." I sigh. That's the thing about guys. We don't hold grudges. "C'mon, Aideypoo. Best way to not think about my sister is to go out and have a good time. Doctor Jason is in the house and he wrote you a prescription for fun times!" I shake my head at my best friend but get up reluctantly. He gives me a big hug. "You know, man, my sister might be off limits, but there's plenty more fish in the sea." I know that, but all the pretty fish look bland next to Jenny...

At eleven, we pick Carter up and all go to the Star, a local club where most of the students go. The fact that they are shit about checking IDs might have something to do with it. By the time we get there, most girls are already drunk. Jason will have a blast picking his arm candy for tonight. I, however, can't seem to focus on anyone in particular.

I go to the bar and down two shots of tequila. I hate that stuff, but it makes me relax pretty quickly, so it's my poison of choice.

"Hey stranger." Someone runs their finger down my arm. I turn around to see the blonde bob chick. The 'she-devil', as Jenny calls her. I smile, thinking of Jenny. The she-devil smiles back at me. Crap, she probably thought I was smiling at her...

"Hey yourself," I say, trying to remember her name.

"Forgot my name again?" She arches her brow at me.

I sheepishly run my hand through my hair. "Busted."

"Should I be offended?" She laughs.

"I'm sorry..." I scrunch my face apologetically.

"It's Chloe." She rolls her eyes and puts her highly manicured hand on my arm. Her long red nails look like talons covered in crimson blood. I shudder from under her touch. "I'll tell you what, if you buy me a shot I'll forget all about it." She smiles at me. What the hell, I might as well...

I buy a couple shots and two rounds of drinks. We down the shots, then the Mojito's.

"Why don't you get another round?" Chloe slurs a bit. The girl can't hold her drink for shit. "And I'll run to the ladies' room."

"Sure," I say, then turn to the bartender, ordering a drink for her. With a nice buzz already, I'm done drinking for tonight. It's good enough to keep me entertained, but not strong enough to be hungover tomorrow. I turn to the dance floor, and all my cheerful buzz disappears when I see Kitten, dressed in a gold sparkly dress—which is way too short even for her slight frame—and gold heels. She looks out of this world as she strolls towards me, her hands on her hips. She turns the heads of pretty much every single guy in the club, some girls too... She's fuming, her cheeks are red and she's breathing through her nose like she's ready to charge me. I love how I can still bring up emotion in her, even if it's anger. Passion often follows anger, I think hopefully.

"I thought you said that you don't hang out with Chloe!" she throws at me accusingly, and I revel in the fact that she's close to me, talking to me. If I can keep her here, shouting at me, at least I can be near her.

"Since you didn't want to talk to me, I had to find

someone else to keep me company." I smirk. Jenny is getting more and more aggravated.

"And you chose her?" she spits out.

"I didn't. I was by myself, minding my own business, when Chloe joined me. It seems some people like talking to me," I reply with a bite. If this was a cartoon, steam would be puffing out of her ears right about now. She looks furious. I bite my lip, trying to stop myself from smiling.

"You find this funny?" Jenny asks, exasperated. She drops her hands to her side and looks up at me in disbelief. I'm trying hard not to be obvious about how her striking beauty affects me. Her gold, sparkly dress shimmers in the dim lighting of the club, reminding me of a mid-day sun reflecting in the dark of the ocean.

"No, kitten," I say, the alcohol in my veins urging the words to come out. "You look iridescent tonight. You're like a vision. No other fish would ever compare…"

"Did you just call me a fish?" Jenny asks, scrunching her face, perplexed.

I'm about to reply, but I get interrupted.

"Grasshopper, fancy seeing you here! What are you up to?"

"Just catching up with this guy." Jenny nods in my direction.

"Hanging out with VonSchmuck?" Carter asks. I guess the nickname has spread. Great.

"Uh-huh. Asking him when he sold his soul to the devil." Jenny shakes her head.

"Kitten, she's just a friend," I try to appease her.

"Is that so?" Jenny narrows her eyes and takes a step closer to Carter, distancing herself from me. I feel her absence straight away. "Funny. You see, Carter is also just a friend," she says, smiling up at him, and the bastard snakes his arm around her waist, nodding. "He's a very good friend. In fact, say Carter, how about we drop off Hayley at her dorm and go to your place?" she asks innocently.

"Are you thinking what I'm thinking?" Carter looks down at her, his eyes searching hers. I have a bad feeling about this.

"How do you feel about BJ?" she asks, looking at him through her lashes. My heart stops. What. The. Fuck.

"You know I'd love to," Carter replies, holding her tighter and licking his lips. My hands are shaking. No, my whole body is shaking. Did I really just hear what I think I heard? "Later, Aiden," Carter throws over his shoulder as they turn to leave. It takes all the self-control I can muster not to jump at him and shred him to pieces. She's not mine. I had my chance, and I blew it. Fuck.

FUCK! FUCK! FUCK! FUCK!

"Have fun with your 'friend'," Jenny says as they walk away.

My world spins out of control. Round and round it goes like a carousel, only faster and with no protection to break my fall. And I fall. Fuck, do I fall. Right onto my egotistical arse.

"Two more tequilas," I shout at the barman, who nods and slides the shots towards me. I down one after another.

"Aiden, are you crying?" Chloe asks drunkenly when she gets back. I touch my face and notice the wetness around my eyes. Holy shit! What the fuck? Am I actually crying? No, it's probably the tequila. Some lime must have gotten into my eyes when I rubbed them after the shots. I don't fucking cry. Ever.

"No," I say steadily, not looking at Chloe.

"Sure," she drawls. "Smells like girl trouble to me." She

touches my arm again, and I fight with myself not to cringe away. "C'mon, Jason, you can tell me."

"Aiden," I correct her.

"Hmmm?"

"My name is Aiden."

"I know that, silly." She giggles drunkenly, downing her drink. I want to just walk away and leave her there, but the gentleman in me needs to make sure that she gets home safe. She reaches for her second drink and gulps it down. Soon, she'll become a liability. "Jason, I'm…" She starts.

"Aiden," I growl.

Chloe hiccups.

"C'mon, I'll take you home," I say, puffing the air out of my chest. So much for trying to forget about Jenny tonight. Images of her and Carter swirl around my head like locusts. What have I done? Chloe nods and gets up, unsteadily, to her feet with a triumphant smile. Hiccuping. Fan-fucking-tastic. She's clinging onto me as I guide us outside of the club and grab the first cab I see, pushing her gently inside. I walk around and slide in next to her. Chloe is leaning against the window snoring. Just my luck. I shake her gently. "Chloe, where do you live?"

"Home," she answers sleepily. I shake her again.

"Where is home?"

"Home!" she answers, irritated through her sleep.

"Where to?" the taxi driver asks impatiently. I sigh and give him my address. I can't just drop her off in front of the school, hoping that she'll find her way. Starwood can get shady at night, especially with drunken frat guys roaming the streets.

When we get to the house, Chloe is full on sleeping, so I pick her up and carry her inside. The house is empty and I'm half glad, half disappointed. Does that mean that Jenny is still with Carter doing god knows what? Chloe is so out of it that when I drop her on my bed and cover her with a blanket, she doesn't stir. I take a couple of pillows and settle down on the floor.

"Jason…" Chloe mumbles through her sleep. Shit. This is not good.

I try to make myself comfortable, but the floor is hard and my mind can't settle. Jenny's face looking up seductively at Carter appears every single time I close my eyes. After an hour, I give up and go to the kitchen to get some water. Chloe and I are still the only people here. If Jason gets lucky tonight, he most likely will stay at the girl's house since he doesn't like bringing them here. He says they get too attached, even the ones who swear they understand it's only a one-time thing.

I grab a glass and fill it to the brim with fresh water. Holding the cool glass against my face, I look around the moonlit kitchen. My gaze falls on a piece of paper attached to the fridge. I walk over to see it better; it's a shopping list, written in Jenny's handwriting. I scan through the items. Eggs, milk, orange juice, bread… My eyes stop at the bottom. Rocky Roadish BJ. What the hell is that? Some secret code to blow Kennedy? I wince. She wouldn't put that on the shopping list. Would she?

I pull my phone out of my pocket and google it. Relief at images of Ben & Jerry's ice cream makes me sit down on one of the stools. I take a deep breath of relief, a massive weight lifting off of my shoulders. I still have a chance with her. Walking back to my room, I decide to fix things tomorrow. Jason will just have to get over the fact that I'm in love with his sister. I will not mess up again. I slide back onto the floor and smile.

Chapter 14

Horrible Kisser

When we were fourteen, Jason said onions are the only food that makes you cry. I threw a coconut in his face.
- Aiden

After a satisfying session of Ben & Jerry's finest—also known as 'suck it diamonds, ice cream is the real girl's best friend'—Carter drove me back home. It's funny how that boy has proven over and over that he's got the biggest heart when all I used to think about him was that... Well, that he's a massive player. What I realize now is that beneath all that player persona and the incessant innuendos, he is truly a fantastic friend, one that I want to keep forever.

I toss and turn all night, unable to forget the image of Aiden and Chloe being cozy with each other. Chloe had her talons on Aiden's shoulder whenever I looked their way. She's like a harpy, that one. Once the harpy left him alone for a minute, I decided it was the time to confront him about hanging out with the spawn of Satan. I stalked towards him, ready to scream at him until his head fell off, but one look at his gorgeous green eyes and I had all but forgotten why I was in front of him in the first place. Until my gaze fell on his lips, and I saw that stupid smirk on his face. Then it was a free-for-all, and thank heavens that Carter showed up in time to make my exit that much more punchy.

It's the morning, and I feel a bit shitty about letting Aiden think that Carter and I are anything more than friends. Then again, he deserved it for hanging out with Hell's finest. Plus, he was the one who insisted that the kiss we shared was a mistake and not to be repeated. That kiss...

While washing my hair, I decide to do some squats. Girl's gotta work out, ya know? Turns out, that wasn't the brightest idea. I slip in the shower and bang my elbow on the floor. Will I ever learn? Not likely.

Once dressed, I head towards the kitchen, drooling at the thought of breakfast. I'm starving and can't wait to have some avo toast. Speaking of toast, I'm also quite curious to check up on Edward. Both Hayley and I bet on a couple of dates for The Day, and things are getting competitive. Maybe I could pierce the bag and let the air in? Nah, that'd be stooping too low.

The shower is on, and I figure Jason must be in it. The door to his room is closed, but Aiden's is ajar. My heart stops in its tracks, and I hesitate for a second but then decide it's probably a good idea to call a truce with the annoying Brit. She-devil aside, I want to talk about that kiss. That kiss...

Maybe I can persuade him to kiss me again? Just a little. No need for a big hoohaa about it. Teeny-tiny kiss. Like a goodbye one. That's all I'm asking. Who am I kidding? I'd never stop at just one if I had my way... Sigh.

I reach his door and softly knock. "Aiden?" His

bedsheets rustle, followed by a sound of soft footsteps. I must have woken him up. I brace myself for what must be a glorious view of his body... Didn't he say he sleeps naked? Oh, please let him be naked. I'll go to church every Sunday if he is, I swear! I lick my lips as the door opens and my jaw hits the floor.

In a stunned silence, I watch Oompa-Lumpa lean against the door jamb and sleepily look me up and down, appraising. She's wearing an oversized t-shirt, which I recognize immediately as one of Aiden's. It's got a dancing hula girl on it. Her hair is all over the place, messy and matted, her makeup smudged just a little. The word 'sex-hair' pops into my head. She narrows her puffy eyes at me when I reach them in my appraisal. Fuck my life.

"What are you doing here? Are you following me?" she growls.

"I live here." My voice sounds distant compared to the deafening sound of my breaking heart.

"Really?" She looks up at me quizzically.

"Yeah..." I slowly turn to walk back to my room.

"Aiden is in the shower." My head whips back at the sound of his name. Chloe is standing with her arms crossed and a triumphant smile on her face. "Now scoot little minion," she says as my shoulders sag. "We don't need the interruption. I'm hoping for round two when he gets back."

Shit. The. Bed.

I turn and storm into my bedroom, slamming the door behind me. No way in hell am I giving the two of them the satisfaction of seeing me upset about this. They both deserve each other—little conniving turds! I have not been this pissed since some asshole doctor pulled me out of my mother's vagina. Seriously.

Grabbing my car keys, I stalk to my window, anger

rippling down my body in waves. I tear the window open and jump in one swift motion out of my room, landing on both of my feet like a seasoned traceuse. Parkour, baby. Channeling my inner caveman, I inhale deeply through my nostrils then spring up and stalk to Kitt, crouching down underneath Aiden's window. I must look like a feral child right now, but honestly, I don't give two little, scrawny Aidens. Oh yes, I decided just now to officially swap in my dictionary the word 'shit' for the word 'Aiden'. It works. Trust me.

Either way, I would not walk past that room again in case I heard something that would turn me into a murderer. I'm too pretty to go to prison. I stalk toward Kitt and jump over the door inside, glad that I left the top down, making my escape that much easier. As I jam the keys into the ignition, I briefly consider the fact that I have become quite awesome at jumping out of and into things. I should put that 'Aiden' on my resume: 'Excellent at graceful jumps over hurdles; can land without injury'. I'd get a job as a stunt woman in a jiffy.

I plug my phone in and select the song that best depicts my current mood. Doesn't get better than STUPID by Ashnikko. I turn the volume to the max, press play, and rev the engine, pulling out like I'm a street race driver, screaming the lyrics along to the song.

'Stupid boy think that I need him.'

I inhale deeply, trying to calm my shaking hands. The song starts for the third time when I find myself outside of Carter's apartment, still heaving with anger. I walk up to his door and ring the bell. He opens straight away, like he was waiting on the other side all this time, and smiles at me.

"Well hello, grasshopper. Miss me already?"

I open my mouth, but nothing comes out. Carter looks

at me questioningly, drawing his eyebrows together. "Grasshopper?" He looks behind me and his eyes go huge. He probably noticed Kitt parked haphazardly on his lawn. I might have destroyed some of the greenery. There may be one bush overturned, but it was like that when I arrived! I swear! Adrenaline leaves my body at the same time that my legs decide to stop working. He catches me as I slide down to the ground. "Jenny! What's wrong?" He's panicking. I can see the fear in his eyes. Who wouldn't be afraid if a crazy woman arrived at their door, acted like a freaking goldfish gasping for water, and then decided to take a little nap on their doorstep? I open my mouth again and what comes out sounds a lot like a pterodactyl on drugs.

"Jenny, please talk to me." Carter takes both of my hands into his. We're sitting side by side on the steps. I turn towards him; blink twice; take a big, shaky breath; then open my mouth.

"He's the biggest asshole in the universe. He's worse than fucking Voldemort and Darth Vader combined," I state, managing to keep my voice steady.

"Okay, let's rewind. Last night you didn't want to talk about what got you angry, except for he-who-must-not-be-named, that is. Is today's crazy behavior also connected to him?"

I nod.

"Right..." Carter drops my hands. "I need details."

I breathe in deeply, then exhale. My hands are shaking without Carter holding them steady.

"Last night," I start, focusing my gaze on a leaf stuck to one of the steps below us. "Aiden was fraternizing with the enemy." I close my eyes. "It seems he's been fraternizing throughout the night and also this morning...in his bed." I clench my jaw. Carter puts his arm around me and pulls me into his chest. "I'm not heartbroken," I say in defence, opening my eyes and pushing him away. "I'm pissed off that out of all the girls he could choose to sleep with, he chose the one he knew is a bitch to me."

"Jenny." Carter's voice is soft.

"I don't need your pity. I just need someone who I can get angry with." My voice is robotic.

"Who's the enemy? Should we go TP her house?" He sighs.

My lips lift in a half smile.

"Her name is Chloe Price," I say, lifting my gaze to Carter's face. He looks shocked.

"Chloe Price? Are you sure?"

I cock my head to the side. "Yes, why? Do you know her?"

"I guess you can say that..."

I narrow my eyes. "Not in the mood for that. Spill."

"I think you'll be better off asking Jason for the full story," Carter starts, but, seeing my expression, rolls his eyes and continues. "I suppose I can tell you the bulk of it." I nod, curious. "Last year, Jason dated Chloe for about a month. She got obsessed and started stalking him when he dumped her. She'd place herself in situations where she knew he'd be; she'd barge in on him in the morning if he stayed over with another girl going all crazy-bitch, screaming and throwing things at him. Once, she even told Jason she had slept with me just to make him jealous. Needless to say, that never happened." She did what?!

"So the psycho-bitch is prone to lying?"

"Yes."

"That still doesn't explain what she was doing in Aiden's room this morning with bed head and nothing but his t-shirt on," I say.

"Oh."

"Oh indeed." I nod solemnly. I knew the whole situation didn't bode well.

"Well, not that I want to defend Aiden...but psychos often know how to get their way and make things appear a certain way. Trust me." Carter chooses his words carefully.

"Hmmm..."

"Just talk to him, let him explain first. It might be true, but it also might just be another Chloe scheme to get Jason jealous."

"Fine," I exhale. "It's just that...I confronted him about her last night, you know? And he still brought her back home, even though he must have known it would piss me off..."

"That's true, but don't forget we left together, making it look like we were up to no good..."

"I'm still pissed off," I say, crossing my arms. "Why are you even defending him?" I narrow my eyes at him.

"I'm not." Carter laughs. "It's just that I've been in a similar situation and don't like it when people are manipulated into thinking something is true when it isn't."

"I hate it when you make sense." I huff.

"I know, grasshopper. I'm not all good looks and a fantastic sense of humour."

I laugh. "Why would he bring her home though..." I trail off. "Shit... It's me, isn't it?"

"Huh?"

"I'm the horrible kisser! I was the one all along! He's trying to let me down gently."

"Somehow I don't think that's the case, Jenny..."

"How would you know? I'm sure that must be it. First he goes away without contact, now he brings other girls to the house. That must be it! He just doesn't know how to tell me that I'm a horrible kisser!" I exclaim.

"Jenny," Carter has a playful smile plastered across his face, "I don't think that's it." He gets up and extends his hand to me. I take it and he pulls me up. He looks into my eyes then gently pulls me into a hug, kissing the top of my head. I exhale loudly into his chest.

"Well I'm pretty sure that's it," I mumble into his shirt.

Carter's chest lifts up and down in a chuckle then goes still, stiff almost. After a second he relaxes and takes a small step back from me.

I look up at him questioningly as he brings his hand up, lifting my chin up. His eyes are focused and dark, looking down intently at me. His jaw is tight and it takes me a few seconds to comprehend that he is leaning down toward my face.

Instinctively, I close my eyes when his lips connect with mine. The pressure is gentle, as if he's unsure whether or not I'll kick him in the nuts for his action. When I don't, he presses his lips firmer to mine. I rest my arms around his waist, and it seems that was all the encouragement Carter needed. He moves his hand from under my chin and pulls me up so that I'm barely on my tiptoes. I move my arms to grab ahold of his neck, moving my lips to the rhythm he's dictating.

Carter leads this kiss, like a professional dancer leads his companion around the dance floor, skilfully and with a hint of determination. When he moves his tongue across my lips I melt a little. Where the hell is this coming from? This kiss is so different from the one I shared with Aiden. This kiss is gentle and giving and a bit hesitant, whereas Aiden's kisses were all need and passion and desire. I open my lips and let him sneak his tongue in between. I can taste the coffee he must have drank before my arrival. I move my tongue along to the rhythm he set. It's nice. Kissing Carter is nice, but is it enough to make me forget about kissing Aiden?

I gently move away and Carter leans himself further into me, unwilling to break the kiss before he realizes what's happening. Then he finally steps away.

"Fuck, grasshopper..." he says breathlessly, making me notice how breathless *I* am. His eyes are dark and his chest is rising up and down quickly. I take stock of myself. My cheeks are flushed, my breath is quick, and my knees are wobbly. It seems my body responded to the kiss even with my brain going for a walk around the neighborhood. "It's definitely not about the kissing," Carter finishes his sentence at last.

He turns away from me muttering curses under his breath.

"Carter?" I gently touch his shoulder.

"Yeah?" His voice is still hoarse, and his back stiffens at my touch.

"You ok?" I ask as he turns around.

"Yeah... I just," he sticks his hands in his pockets as if to keep them to himself, "wasn't expecting that."

Yeah, me neither...

Chapter 15

Two Birds One Stone

If we're not meant to have midnight snacks, why is there a light in the fridge?
- Jason

I wake up smiling even though my back is killing me. After spending the night on the floor, that's to be expected. Why do I even get myself into situations like this? Oh wait, my grandmother taught me manners, that's why. Chloe's gentle snores are coming from beneath the duvet, so quietly I sit up and stretch my aching muscles before standing up. I head out to the shower, hoping the hot water will ease the pain in my joints. As the water starts pelting on my back, my smile stretches from ear to ear. The thing is, I just can't stop thinking about her. It's impossible. I need to find her and tell her that no matter the consequences, I want to be with her. I need her. It's that simple.

Will she want the same thing? I imagine her nodding back at me, a playful smile forming on her lips. She would wrap her arms around me and press her lips to mine, first gently, then hungrily. I can see it so clearly. I reach out with my hand and place it on the wall of the shower, panting. The water droplets slide down my face as I imagine her jumping into my embrace, legs wrapped around me. She moans as she rocks into me, feeling me harden at the motion through her jean shorts. I wrap my fist around my cock and start stroking it up and down as my imagination continues the ride. In my head, I pull away from her and bend down, trailing kisses along her neckline to her breasts. She's not wearing a bra, so I take advantage, sucking her nipple through her thin, cotton shirt. She gasps, then arches into me, begging for more. I abide, moving to the other nipple, biting and sucking through the flimsy material until Jenny moans loudly and starts rocking against me frantically. The hand on my cock pumps faster as, in my head, my mouth goes back to her neck, then back to her lips. I fuck her with my tongue like I want to fuck her with my cock, my hand sliding down into her shorts, reaching her clit and rubbing it through her panties until she writhes beneath me, whining for release. When she comes, it's loud and sexy and takes me over the edge. I grunt, spilling into my hand, my breath unsteady. Shit.

I soap up and rinse off, then turn the water cold. I nearly cry out as the freezing torrent hits my skin, but the wide grin on my face stays. She'll be mine.

Everything is going so smoothly this morning, even my hair surprisingly looks okay, like it knows it'll be a big day. I smile at my reflection. You've got this dude. All it takes is courage, just put yourself out there.

There's just one more thing, or a person to be exact, I need to take care of. I walk back into my room to see Chloe sitting on my bed wearing one of my favourite t-shirts. What the fuck?

"What are you doing in my t-shirt?" I ask, grabbing clothes from my closet.

"Sorry. I woke up halfway through the night in that tight dress that I was wearing last night and... Shit. Sorry... I thought you wouldn't mind..." she says sheepishly, a small blush spreading on her cheeks.

I wave my hand at her dismissively. "Get dressed. I'll drop you off at your place," I say, making my way back to the bathroom to change into my clothes. I look back for confirmation that she's heard me but, to be honest, I don't care. I'd drag her to my car while she's wearing my t-shirt and drop her off wherever as long as we can make it fast. The sooner this is over, the sooner I can talk to Jenny.

Nothing can spoil my mood right now.

Nothing.

I walk back into the bedroom and see that Chloe is wearing her own clothes. She's holding her heels in her hand and swinging them back and forth. She's ready, that's good. When she sees me, she starts stepping from one foot to another as if the floor is burning her soles. "Do you need to use the toilet or something?" I ask, squinting at her. She shakes her head. "What is it then?"

She drops her shoulders and looks down. Quietly, she replies, "Uhhhh, your little friend stopped by." Okaaay... Jason? Carter? "The one from the restaurant," she clarifies, seeing my confusion. My heart stops beating. Jenny was here. She saw Chloe. Was Chloe in her own clothes? Was she mid-change? Oh shit, what if Jenny thought—

"When? What did she say?" I ask. The panic in my voice is obvious.

"When you were in the shower." Without a word, I turn on my heels and run towards Jenny's room.

"Jenny!" I roar, opening her door. The room is empty, the window is wide open, the curtains dancing with the wind. I run to the window and look out, but Jenny is obviously not there.

I turn around and, trying to keep it cool, quickly walk back to where Chloe is. she hasn't moved an inch. "What did you say to her?" I ask through clenched teeth, taking her by her elbow and gently guiding her to the front door. She doesn't protest, she just silently walks next to me. Why the hell is she not answering? "What did you say to her?" I repeat calmly, trying to relax. I don't want to scare her; it's not like she knows she just might have messed everything up.

"I said you were in the shower. Then she ran off, slamming her door," Chloe finally says as we walk outside. She's studying my face intently, gauging my reaction as the world crumbles around me.

Fuuuuuuuuuuuck...

Of course Jenny would come to some awful conclusion. What was I thinking bringing Chloe back to the house? I could have just left her at the club...and do what? The voice of my grandma mocks me. Let her drunkenly try to find her own way home? Damn it, grandma!

I look at my car, then at Chloe. I'm going to have to be a dick. I need to find kitten and explain.

"Call yourself an Uber," I say, running towards my car. "Sorry."

"But Aiden..." Chloe whines as I jump inside the jeep and speed away. I feel a bit guilty for leaving her stranded, but not guilty enough to stay and listen to what she wants to say.

Now, where the hell could Jenny be? She must be pissed off at me for bringing Chloe and letting her stay over. God knows, she probably wants to scratch my eyes out if she thinks anything more than that happened... I rack my brain as I run red light after red light. She's either at Hayley's or Carter's. Those are my two best bets. Carter's is closer, so I drive there first. I make an illegal u-turn and speed towards his apartment. I see them as soon as I'm on his street. Slowing down, I strain my eyes. I think...I think Carter is embracing Jenny, hugging her tight and kissing the top of her head. My knuckles are white from gripping the steering wheel tightly. I breathe slowly, it's just a hug. I'm almost at his place when Carter puts his hand under Jenny's chin, lifting her face up to his.

I stop breathing when his lips connect with hers.

Agape, I sit in my car in a trance, not wanting to believe what unfolds in front of my eyes. But it's hard, especially when Jenny doesn't push him away. Instead, she wraps her arms around his neck as he pulls her closer to him, lifting her up onto her tiptoes.

I don't notice that my foot pushes down on the accelerator. I don't notice that I'm on the wrong side of the road. I don't notice the cars parked around me.

I don't notice anything.

All I can see in front of my eyes is the image I'm focusing on in my rear-view mirror. I take the first right, skidding on the corner and drive away as fast as I can. I fail to notice that I'm driving over the speed limit in the residential area, and I fail to notice the brown dog in the middle of the road, at least not until it's too late.

I break like a maniac, pushing my foot to the ground and turning the wheel to the right. The car swerves and I'm driving into someone's yard and over their pristine rose bushes. My hands shake and my heart thumps, all because of the nagging feeling at the back of my mind.

I felt the dull thump on the front bumper.

I heard the yelp.

Oh God, please let the dog be okay.

I run out of the car and onto the street.

The dog is there. Lying in the middle of the road, not moving but breathing steadily. I kneel and hear him whimper as he notices me next to him. His head lifts and soulful brown eyes gaze into my eyes. He is magnificent. A medium-sized boy with shaggy brown fur. He looks like he has seen it all, done it all, lived a happy doggy life. Until I came along hell bent on destroying it all. My heart breaks and my eyes fill with tears. Emotions swirl inside as breathing gets harder and harder.

"I'm so sorry, little buddy," I whisper. A passer-by stops and gawks at us. "Do you know whose dog this is?" I shout at the man, trying to figure out what to do next.

He shrugs. "It's a stray. He's been running around here for the past two weeks. Serves him right for trying to screw my Minnie." Rage fills me, and the only thing that stops me from getting up and beating the guy to a pulp are the eyes of the mutt in front of me. They are still intently looking into mine, filled with pain and trust. I need to get him to the vet. I need to do everything in my power to make sure he'll be ok.

"Minnie is probably as stupid as her owner," I whisper to him. I stroke his dark brown fur and he moves his head to lick my palm. He is laying it on thick. I'm already half in love with the thing, and everything he does just makes my heart swell even more.

"Hold on, buddy," I say, ripping my jacket off and wrapping it around his body. Trying to move him as little as possible, I lift the dog up and take him to my car. He whimpers in pain as I set him down on my back seat.

After googling the nearest vet, I drive there, very, very carefully. The last thing I want is to cause the little guy any more pain. I snag a parking spot right outside the entrance and run into their reception, shouting at the first person I see to help me. I must look like a lunatic, but the receptionist is not phased and follows me to my car where I point inside. Her whole demeanour changes and she rushes back inside to get help. After what seems like way too long, they finally manage to move the dog into their examination room. Only when I see him disappear into an examination room do I dare to wipe the tears off my face. I stand like a loser in front of the door, too scared to move. The same receptionist who helped me earlier takes me by the hand and sits me down in the waiting room, handing me a glass of water. She pats my shoulder and says something to me, but I can't hear her behind the buzzing in my ears. My gaze focused on those damn double doors. Finally, a man wearing scrubs comes out. I'm back on my feet before I notice.

"Is the brown dog yours? Did you fill out the insurance paperwork?" His voice sounds urgent, and a heavy weight settles over my chest.

"He's not. I bumped him though. I think he's a stray," I reply. His face falls, and I can hear the whoosh of blood in my ears.

"I'm sorry, but if that's the case we cannot help him here, his injur-"

"He's mine!" I interrupt him too loudly. "He's mine. I don't have any insurance, but I'll pay for whatever you need to do."

"Thank you," the guy nods at me, relief palpable in his

voice. "I'll charge you only the absolute minimum. I won't charge my fees."

I nod in agreement as he walks away.

"Wait," I stop him, my heart beating loudly in my chest. "Is he going to be okay?"

"He's got a couple of broken bones, which we need to set. We're taking x-rays to check if his lungs are punctured since he's wheezing a little, but I think he'll be okay. Come back in a couple of hours." The vet disappears behind the same door he came out of. I pace for a while, then go to the reception to leave my details. My father won't even notice the charge on the credit card. Instead of leaving, I stay in my spot in the corner, not daring to leave the reception area in case the vet comes back with any news, my gaze not wavering from the door. I wait. And wait.

And wait...

Two hours go by and finally the door opens. I get up from my seat and look at him hopefully, praying that the brown dog is ok. The guy nods at me, smiling, and my shoulders relax a little.

"Is he okay?" I ask.

"We set the broken bones in his leg. Fortunately, there were no further injuries. You're very lucky. He's in shock, so you'll need to be extra careful," he says. "He's going to wake up soon, then I'd like to observe him for the rest of the day." A puff of air leaves my lungs in relief. I didn't realise I was holding my breath. "I'll make sure he gets all the required vaccinations. In the meantime, why don't you go get supplies? You'll need a bed, food, and a leash."

"I'll do that," I say, nodding. That'll give me something else to do except for just sitting here and slowly going crazy.

"You'll also need a name for him." The vet smiles at me kindly. I guess The Brown Fur Ball is not acceptable.

"Come back at five. He should be ready to go home with you then. I'll have his antibiotics and pain meds ready for you."

I go back to my car and sit there aimlessly before starting the engine. Not really sure where I'm going, I drive around until I find myself in front of Carter's house. No one's outside, so I walk up to the front door and ring the bell.

Kennedy opens with a smug look on his face. "Came back for mo-"

I shut him up with my fist.

"Shit! Ouch! Hello to you too, Aiden," Carter mumbles, holding the side of his jaw. "Come on in, we need to talk." He opens the door further to let me in, then walks to the fridge/freezer in the corner and fishes out a bag of frozen peas, putting it to his face.

"What the fuck was that?" I ask.

"I'm assuming you're referring to the fact that you slept with Chloe Price, while grasshopper was in the room next to you?" the bastard has the audacity to ask.

"What the hell? No!"

"Aaah. Okay, well, that's not what Chloe said to Jenny this morning..."

"Are you kidding me?"

"Nope," Carter replies, sitting down on his couch. I follow behind.

"Shit..."

"Yes. Jenny was royally pissed, to say the least," he continues. I can just imagine, but it didn't take her long to seek comfort with Carter...

"And you took advantage of that?" I narrow my eyes at him.

"Well...no. You were being a sad asshole who couldn't

make up his mind about her. You told her that you two can't be more than friends, kissed her, then told her it was a mistake. I needed to show you that you can't stand seeing her with anyone else, and that was the only way I could think of."

"What are you saying, that this was all for my benefit? How was I supposed to find out?"

Carter shrugs his shoulders. "You saw us, didn't you?"

"You knew I saw you?"

"Who else drives a black Jeep like a maniac in a residential area?"

"So the kiss..." I wince, remembering it vividly, too vividly.

"Jenny was horrified that she's a bad kisser and that you moved on to the next girl, so I killed two birds with one stone. She's a great kisser."

"She thought that she was a bad... Wait! What did you just say?"

"You need to stop being a self-centred prick and go find her, talk to her. I know you like her, you know you like her. Hell, everyone knows you like her. Go do something about it."

"You're right." I nod.

"Oh, and if she doesn't want your sorry ass anymore, send her my way please. That girl is something else." Carter looks down at his hands.

"What the hell, man?"

"Nothing, nothing," he mutters. "You know what? Not nothing. Jenny is incredible! She's funny, she's clever, and for some unbeknownst reason she likes you for the time being. But if she ever changes her mind... Aiden, I will fight for her. I mean it. So get your ass out of here and go set things straight while you still have a chance."

For Crying Out Loud

Nodding, I dart out of Carter's. He's right. He's so damn right.

I drive back, carefully this time, to our house. Jenny's car is parked up front. I park next to hers, then run up the porch steps and into the house. I scan the living room first, then the kitchen, and finally make my way to her room.

I don't knock, I just open the door and go into her bedroom. She's in the bathroom having a shower, so I settle myself on her bed and wait.

Chapter 16

Lonely Immortal Schmuck

Using your laptop to research buying a new one is like asking it to dig its own grave.
- Carter

What the hell?

How did I just go from crazy-angry to...well, kissing Carter?

This is ridiculous.

"Right..." I say. "I'm gonna go then. Forgot to feed the fish, you know?"

"You don't have any fish." Carter cocks his head to the side. His eyes are dark and intense, and I have the distinct feeling that I need to get out of here before I do something stupid. Like get closer to him and kiss him again.

"Huh?" What did he just say? I should be paying attention, not admiring the way his t-shirt hugs his chest.

"What fish, Jenny?" His lips form a smile. Shit, he's

right. Couldn't I say a cat or something? Oh wait, I don't own one either...

"Fish... The ones in the pond... In the park... Where the ducks are!" Well done, Jenny, you will make a great spy one day. Just not today.

"Right."

"Okay then, well I'll see you soon. Bye!" I blurt out, then run back to my car.

Holy shit. I mean HOLY SHIT! Carter just kissed me. I kissed him back and... Oh man, I kinda liked it.

Like I need more confusion in my life...

Let's get something straight. Carter Kennedy is a great kisser. And judging by his reaction, I am not too bad either. But even though I found the kiss, errr, let's call it pleasurable, it can NOT happen again.

Carter is a friend. No, he's been like a best friend, and I can't jeopardize that, no matter how confused I am in this moment. Then there's Jason. If he flipped out about me kissing Aiden, he'd outright murder Carter... And then there's also the minor matter of Aiden... And the She-Devil.

I drive back home, constantly checking my reflection in the rearview mirror, the expression of shock firmly plastered all over my face all the way until I park in the driveway. I notice Aiden's car is gone from outside of our house, so I deem the environment safe enough to go through the front door. Hoping that both Chloe and Aiden are not banging in his room, having just disguised his car somewhere in a bush to trick me, I tiptoe down the hallway. The door to Aiden's room is fully open and his room is empty. I breathe a sigh of relief.

Walking into my room, I can finally relax. Guys are so confusing. I should talk to Mrs. Bloom, she seemed to have a good grasp on how to get them trained. I also needed someone with whom I could discuss all the stuff that went down this morning.

Oh crap.

I swallowed the large lump, which appeared in my throat. I forgot about the one person I should have been thinking about all along. Whipping my phone out of my bag, I dial.

"Hey, bestie," she answers on the first ring.

"Hayley?"

"Jenny, what's wrong?" She must have picked up the panic in my voice.

"Hayley, I'm so sorry. It just happened and I wasn't thinking. God, I'm an awful friend," I blurt out, my voice cracking.

"Babe," she interrupts me. "Slow down. I don't know what you're talking about. Start from the beginning. What's wrong?"

I take a deep breath and recount the events from this morning, starting with She-Devil in Aiden's room and finishing with Carter kissing me. Hayley listens without interrupting until I'm done with the story.

"So, you and Carter, do you like like each other?" she finally asks.

"No, I don't think so." Fact is, I'm still totally into Aiden...

"Okay."

"I mean, Carter is a great kisser, one that can make you question your ability to stand upright. But he's also one of my best friends, and, to be honest, he only kissed me to check if I wasn't a horrible kisser, I think," I blurt.

"Okay."

"Are you mad at me? I'm an awful friend, aren't I? I

shouldn't have even let him kiss me... God... Hayley, please forgive me."

"Jenny..." Hayley takes a big breath. "It's fine. You've done nothing wrong. I never said I like him. I just think he's hot."

"Are you sure now?"

"Am I sure what?"

"Whether or not you like him?" I ask.

"I'm sure," Hayley slowly replies. "I like him as a friend. Like I said, I don't want guys to interfere with my studies. I'm on a self-imposed relationship ban, anyway. It all worked out for the best."

"I'm so sorry." My eyes fill with tears at the thought that I could have hurt my best friend.

"It's okay, really. I promise," she says, softly.

"Okay." I sniffle.

"C'mon girl, don't get upset over this." I nod, not that she can see me. "So Aiden and Chloe..." Hayls starts. "Are you sure?"

"Well, Chloe outright insinuated that something happened."

"Hmmmm, I've heard quite a few things about Chloe Price in our dorms, and honesty is not one of her qualities. Maybe you should talk with Aiden first. Not that I'm defending him."

"Maybe," I hesitate. "I just don't know what to think."

"It'll all be okay, babe. Maybe you and Aiden need to cool it for a bit?"

"Yeah, I guess." The thought of going back to being just friends makes me want to punch things, but Hayley might be right. Potentially, it could be good for us.

"Don't worry, Jenny, it'll all work out. You'll see." I can hear Hayley's smile through the phone.

"Thanks. I'm just tired of the whole situation. You're right, I think, going back to the start would be best." I walk to my bed and lie down, feeling deflated.

"Let's meet later. I've got a couple of things I need to do now, but I'll come over in the evening, okay?"

"That would be great, Hayley, thank you."

"See you soon then, hon." Her voice sounds normal, and I hope to God I did not screw up the first friendship I have had in years.

"Bye."

I turn the phone off and look at the ceiling. How on earth has it come to this? Should I just move to a different university and start anew? Away from all this drama. I close my eyes and try not to think of Aiden or Carter. I can still feel Carter's body heat around me. I squeeze my eyes shut, hoping it'll block the image of the two boys that have me so messed up.

When I wake up a couple of hours later, I feel groggy and disoriented. I sit up in my crumpled clothes, oblivious for the briefest of moments, then memories flood me. Chloe, Aiden, Carter, the kiss. Rubbing my face roughly, I try to wipe away traces of my thoughts, put them away in a vault somewhere, but it doesn't work. Instead, my skin starts to hurt. I sigh and make my way to the shower. I don't sing this time. My mood is as black as a starless night. I stand for what feels like an hour under the stream of hot water until my skin turns all wrinkly and the whole bathroom is so steamy I can't even see my toes.

I turn the water off and take a step, but my head spins from the heat and steam. I hold on to the wall and press my forehead against the cool tiles. After a minute, I wrap a towel around my body and take a few steps towards the bathroom door.

My hand reaches for the doorknob when the world begins to spin again. I manage to turn it and push the door before everything goes black and my body falls slack on the floor.

"You're okay, kitten." I hear a soothing voice far away. When I open my eyes, black spots are dotting my vision, and all I can hear is a loud ringing in my head. I'm no longer on the floor but in Aiden's strong arms. He gently lays me down on the bed and slides his arms from underneath me. "I'll get you some water. Wait here." What a genius. I obviously was going to go for a walk in my towel and not be able to stand properly... Duh.

I try sitting up, touching my hand to the bump on the back of my head, which has started to throb.

When Aiden walks back into my room, he's holding a glass of cool water and a wet cloth. Sitting down next to me, he gently presses the cool cloth to my forehead and hands me the glass of water, his eyes filled with concern, melting the ice around my heart. The coolness on my forehead feels glorious, and I move my head to my hand, trying to take a sip, but the throbbing gets worse and I just end up wincing and spilling some water on myself. He gently puts his hand behind my back and props me up, steadily guiding my hand that's holding the glass towards my mouth. I take a sip, then stop, suddenly hyperaware of Aiden's proximity and the fact that all I have on is a meager towel.

"Hi." I clear my throat.

"You scared me." He stares at me, his eyes dark, searching. I flush with embarrassment. Great. "You've got a habit of doing that."

I clear my throat again. "Mind if I put some clothes on?" He shakes his head. "In privacy?" I motion with my head towards the door.

"Oh... Right... Are you sure you're okay, though? You're not going to faint again, are you?" He gives me an already too familiar look of concern. He's right. I seem to be more accident prone than usual lately. I blame it on all the hormones.

"I'll be sure to call you as soon as I do." I smile innocently. He nods at me, then moves towards the door.

"I'm just on the other side. You have one minute, then I'm coming back in to make sure you're okay." I roll my eyes as he walks outside and closes the door behind him. Slipping into my yoga pants, a tank, and an oversized grey sweater with Mickey Mouse on it, I go in search of a hair tie. I'm in the process of tying my crazy hair into a messy bun when Aiden strolls back into my room. I grab my black Converse from the closet and slip them on, then, with a racing heart, I turn back around only to see Aiden sitting on my bed, looking as comfy as one can be.

"So..." I say, walking over to him.

"So..." he says, looking back at me.

"You and Chloe?" I ask quietly.

"You and Carter?" he asks, looking into my eyes. Shit.

"I asked first." I decided to play the first grader card. Aiden sighs.

"Chloe was really drunk, too drunk to make her own way home. I was raised as a gentleman..."

"So you took her home to bang her?" Bang her? Who even says bang out loud these days? I could just slap myself. Aiden draws his eyebrows together.

"No, kitten... I'd never... Do you really think I'd do such a thing?" I look down at my shoes. The tips are scuffed and the black material is faded. They're *super* interesting. "She slept in my bed and I slept on the floor," he finishes softly.

"You might want to update her on that." I look up at him. "That's not what she said…"

"Well, it's true, Jenny. Believe me."

"Okay." I slowly nod. I have no reason not to believe him; it's not like he's ever lied to me before, and he's being calm and open. Unless he's a master liar and all my friends are idiots, he might actually be telling the truth. Damn. This sucks. I really wanted to have the upper hand here.

"What about you and Carter?" Aiden asks, staring at me. His back is straight and his shoulders are tight. I look back down at my interesting shoes, smelling a trap. Maybe I could put some glitter on them? Draw on some smiley faces or monkeys? I look back up at Aiden; he's still expecting an answer. Damn.

"We're just friends," I drawl as Aiden raises his eyebrow at me. "The thing is, Aide, you're awfully confusing these days. First you pursue me, then you say you want to be friends, then you kiss me, then you don't want me. It's just too much." I blow air out of my lungs. "I don't know what to think…" I decide to just throw it right in his face and see his reaction. "Carter and I kissed this morning."

"I know." His jaw tightens. Oh.

"You do? How?" This is what I mean when I say he confuses the hell out of me. How on earth would he know, and why is he not bashing things? I mean, I destroyed at least four bushes when I thought about him and Oompa Lumpa…

"I saw you…"

What the hell?

"What the hell?" Aiden looks down at his hands. His cuticles are incredibly tidy. I quickly take a peek at mine and decide my scuffed shoes are way better to look at. "I was trying to find you. I wanted to talk to you and didn't want you to get the wrong idea about Chloe and I. I went to look for you and I guess I found you, only...you were kissing Carter." Well shit. The muscle in his jaw twitches, making that dimple in his right cheek appear, then disappear. I fight the urge to reach out and touch it.

"Aiden, I... I'm confused as to what you want me to say." I'm definitely not going to apologize, even though I feel like I want to. But I did nothing wrong. It's not like Aiden ever said he wanted to be with me.

"Nothing, I guess... I think I blew it, didn't I?" He looks up at me, his emerald eyes big and hopeful. What the hell is that supposed to mean? Blew what?

"What do you mean?"

"I want to try... Us."

"Oh." Jaw. On. The. Floor.

"I guess, I took too long to realize that." I narrow my eyes at him. Is he toying with me? Is he saying all this just because he saw me kiss Carter? What about him playing hot and cold with my feelings? What about Jason?

"No..." I start, trying as best as I can to gather my thoughts. "It's just that this shouldn't be this hard, should it? I mean, we seem to want the same thing, but every time something or someone gets in the way..." I pull my knees to my chest. "I think..." Oh God, am I really doing this? "I think that maybe we should take a step back and be friends for a little while," I finally blurt out. My heart is hammering in my chest. "See how that's going and take it from there."

Aiden has a solemn look on his face. "If that's what you want," he says, his puppy dog eyes staring right into my soul. I extend my hand towards him and put it on his shoulder. All I want to do is to reach higher, touch his face, pull him closer to me, comfort him, but I have to be strong about this.

"I don't really... But I think it's best to establish that we are sure what we both want first." I take a deep breath. "So, friends?"

"Friends." Aiden nods and puts his rough hand over mine, squeezing it. His hand is warm, his touch giving me shivers, and I wish I could take back those damned words and just pull him on top of me. This is for the best, I tell myself. "Well, friend." Aiden smiles a small smile at me, drawing my gaze to his lips and those sexy dimples of his. "I was wondering if you could help me out with something."

"Sure, what is it?" Please say you need mouth to mouth, please say 'mouth to mouth'. Moooouth tooo moooouth.

"Well," he runs his hand through his hair, looking sheepish. "I guess it's best to just come out and say it." Holy crap, is he going to come out to me or something? Ask me to help him find a boyfriend now that we're friends? Does that mean I'll never be able to lick him? Damn. "I may have hit a stray dog while I was driving—"

"What?" I exclaim.

"He's okay! He's okay. I guess, I kind of adopted him and need to go pick him up soon. Would you come with me?"

"How...? What...? When...? How much....?" Goldfish face makes an appearance again. "I mean, yes. Are you okay? What happened to the dog?"

"I am, but the little buddy has a couple of broken bones. You'll love him." He smiles up at me. "Also, you'll need to help me convince Jason that we need a dog in the house."

I laugh. That will not be a problem. Jason is a sucker for anything with four legs and fur. He once tried to bring home a skunk. He named him Stinky. Wonder why...

We spend the next couple of hours shopping for essentials for the pup, and when five o'clock comes around, I find myself in front of the vet's with Aide standing right next to me, smiling. Apparently I'm excited about the prospect of having a dog in the house, since my heart is trying to get out of my chest and my palms are sweaty. Aiden opens the door for me and I walk into the sterile office. A middle-aged man greets us and shakes Aiden's hand.

"Ah, you're here!" He smiles warmly at Aiden. "He's ready for you. Come back later this week so we can register him properly. But, for now, I'll let you both get to know each other first." He looks over at me and smiles as the double door behind him opens and a brown ball of fur comes out limping, a purple cast on his back leg. "I've got some antibiotics and pain medicine for him. You'll need to monitor him, but he should be fine." The man continues.

The ball of fur looks at me and Aiden with its large brown eyes, then hobbles over timidly. There's a line where the fur has been shaved off above the cast, revealing a skinny leg. I'm in love.

I kneel and stretch my hand out. "Hey you," I say softly as the ball of fur gets closer and starts sniffing at it. The tail wags three times before the dog whimpers happily and greets me, placing kisses on my arms and hair. I laugh. "Oh boy, do I hope you didn't have poo for breakfast!" I stroke his brown fur.

Aiden leans down, mirth in his eyes, pats the dog, and laughs. The dog starts going crazy for him, whimpering and licking and wagging its tail like a, well, a happy dog.

Once both the dog and I calm down a little, Aiden exchanges a few more sentences with the vet and then we all pile into the Jeep.

I insist on sitting in the backseat next to the dog and scratching him behind his ear throughout the journey. He's got his face on my lap and is breathing heavily but contently.

When we arrive at the house, Aide helps the dog out of the car, then grabs all his supplies. I've already opened the bag of treats and fed a couple to the pup, bribing him to love me more, of course. I know how this works.

We walk into the house. Jason is on the sofa watching football.

"Jason?" I say, smiling as the brown fur ball limps over towards him.

"Mmmm?" Jason mumbles. The fur ball is now by the side of the sofa and putting his nose on the edge, licking Jason's hand, the one that's holding the remote. "Aaaah!" Jason shrieks, startling me and the dog. "OhmyGod! OhmyGodohmyGodohmyGod! It's a dog! Can we keep it?"

I laugh and look over at Aiden. "I told you this would be easy."

"Yeah." Aiden walks over to the couch. "We can keep him. We need to name him first though," he says, setting the dog bed on the floor. Fur ball makes himself comfortable on it instantly.

"Dibs!" Jason shouts. "I'm amazing at naming animals. Ask Jenny." He's shit... But I'll let him off since we're keeping the dog. "I shall name you...Jacob Black! You'll keep Edward some much needed company. He was getting lonely, that poor immortal schmuck." I roll my eyes.

"Seriously?" Aiden asks with disbelief. "You want to name our dog Jacob Black?" Jason nods.

"How about Jake?" I interject. "We can shorten Jacob to Jake." Jason nods excitedly, and the dog barks happily.

"You see? Jake likes his new name, don't you Jake?" Jason leans over and lets Jake lick his face. I decide not to mention the poo eating. Let the boy have his fun. Both of the boys...

Aiden sits down on the sofa and pats Jake on his head. I join them, plopping on the coffee table. Jake quickly leaves Jason alone and tries climbing on my lap. I help him up. It looks ridiculous because I'm small and Jake is, well, a medium sized dog. But I'm happy and so is Jake.

"Look, he's a ladies man," Jason notices just as Jake buries his nose in my cleavage. I laugh and scratch behind his ear.

"I wish girls did that whenever I put my face in their boobs..." Jason trails off.

"Me too," Aiden agrees.

I roll my eyes and hug Jake closer to my body. It's been a while since I felt this happy.

Chapter 17

Grow A Pair Pendejo

I'd have a longer attention span if there weren't so many shiny things.
- Jenny

Jake slept in Jenny's bed throughout the night... Oh, how I envy the furry bastard. The smug look on his brown face said it all when I fed him in the morning. He knows exactly that we're both fighting for her affection; he's miles ahead and he's not afraid to play dirty.

I sigh.

"So she likes you more," I say, looking at him. "Stop rubbing it in or I won't take you for a walk," I gripe. Jake just cocks his head to the side and smiles wider, sticking his tongue out at me. "Fine, I'll take you for a walk. But you need to be careful. No running or jumping." Seems Jake managed to wrap every single person in the house around his paw, me included. "Want to come to the Centre? Meet my little brother, Benny?" I ask him. Jake wags his tail in response. "Let's go then, bud," I say, grabbing his lead and heading outside.

Jake hobbles next to me, never straying further than two steps behind. I smile at him, opening the door to the back seat and helping him up. He sits patiently while I walk to the driver's seat and settle in. It dawns on me that the bloody dog is allowed to sleep in Jenny's bed while I'm not. There should be a house rule, no dogs in bedrooms. I am the only male who should ever be allowed to sleep in Jenny's bed while she's there.

Shit, that makes me sound like a territorial asshat...

I think back to the night before. How she looked in that Mickey Mouse sweater and those damn yoga pants that made her butt just so edible. I wasn't joking the first day I saw her again or that time at the beach. Her arse is killer and there isn't anything I wouldn't do just to take a bite.

Shaking my head, I try to concentrate on the drive to the Youth Centre, which is conveniently only a block away from campus. The autumn day is perfect for a walk in the park; it's sunny with warm gusts of wind and there are golden leaves scattered beneath the balding trees.

When I park, I spot Benny straight away, he's sitting on the stone steps outside the main entrance. His slight frame is unmistakable, there's no other thirteen-year-old like him. He'll grow into a heartbreaker one day, no doubt about it. At the moment, he's long and awkward, but his face is angelic and his messy, dark brown hair paired with his long, black lashes and olive skin already make the girls notice him. He's looking around, shading his brown eyes from the sun with one of his hands. I notice he looks tired and anxious, but he relaxes as soon as he spots my Jeep. I start to feel anxious. Why would he be so cautious? Is something wrong? I start feeling shitty for not seeing him these past few weeks while

I was in London. I haven't even had a chance to properly speak to him on the phone since my father made sure I was constantly busy, and now I have that distinct feeling in the pit of my stomach, like something is wrong.

"Hey, bandito." I wave at him as I get out. My little brother is currently learning Spanish, so I like to throw in a few words here and there, as limited as my Spanish is.

"Aiden!" Benny runs towards me. "I thought you were going to bail on me again!" he says, stopping in front of me and playfully punching me in the arm. My heart squeezes for him, but I pretend like everything is just dandy.

"Ouch, man! You getting stronger or something?" I say. "Show me the muscles!" Benny grins at me and flexes his small bicep. The scars on his lower arm glow in the sunlight as the sleeve of his shirt rolls up on his skinny arm. "Nice!" I say as he consciously pulls the sleeves down. He's grown to be a lot more relaxed around me, but still gets wary about the scars in public.

"Who's that?" Benny asks, peering behind me and pointing at the dog. I turn around and look at Jake, who's currently licking his balls on the backseat. He is talented. I open the door to the car and lean over to help him out. I notice writing in a red marker pen on Jake's cast. *Jenny+Jake 4eva* and a small heart. My vision narrows to those small red letters, written in Jenny's handwriting, and a red haze consumes me. I clench my fists until I suddenly realise that I'm jealous. And it seems I'm jealous of a dog. That's new.

"This is Jake," I say, shaking myself out of the feeling. "I was thinking we could take him to the park for a walk and you could tell me what you've been up to these past few weeks?"

"Sure," Benny replies quietly and, as I set Jake on the ground, Benny leans over and pats his head, an action met with licking attempts. My phone buzzes, and I quickly check the caller ID. My father. I let it go to voicemail like I did the other five calls from him this morning. "Ignoring your Dad's calls will not make him go away, hermano." Benny looks up at me. He's right, but I seriously can't take another call about electing my major.

"Since when do they make thirteen-year-old's so clever, huh?" I shove him playfully.

Benny sighs. "Since I found out that most twenty-year-old's have shit for brains." He sticks his tongue out at me. I'd reciprocate, but the boy's got a point. I've been acting like a brainless idiot these past couple of months all because of a certain short girl with the bluest eyes, long brown hair, and the most amazing arse situated right on top of toned legs. Legs I can't help but imagine wrapped around me... Yup, shit for brains. I exhale and follow the smartarse.

When we get to the park, we walk around for a little while, catching up on the basics and admiring the beautiful scenery. At one point, Jake gets overly interested in a certain lady poodle, so I decide it's time for us to choose a bench to sit on and extract ourselves from the female doggie population in the park before he fathers any pups. God knows he's willing...

"So, what else have you been up to? How's school? How are your grades?" I ask. I like to ask him about school. The boy is practically a genius, and the topic always makes him smile.

"Grades are good. School is easy." Benny grins, but his smile doesn't reach his eyes. Instead, he quickly looks down and starts wringing his hands. "I've been staying at the Youth Centre this past week though..." he breathes.

That's new. Why wouldn't he be at home? I look at him

questioningly. He takes a deep breath, rubs his neck, then looks straight into my eyes. "My cousin is out on parole."

I stiffen, cold dread seeping into my bones. "Has he tried to contact or find you?" I ask him. "You know you can stay with me, right?" I try as hard as I can to mask the panic in my voice.

"Yeah, I'm good for now, I guess. He doesn't know about the Centre." He looks down at the ground.

"Benny, does your mum know?"

"You know her. She thinks my cousin can do no wrong. I left last weekend as soon as I heard he's out, and she hasn't even tried to contact me." I clench my fists, seeing the sadness in his big brown eyes.

"My door is always open for you, bud, okay?" I put my hand on his shoulder.

"Yeah, sure." He shrugs me off. "Thanks."

He's not going to take me up on my offer. He never does.

"Tell me, what's up with you? Did you get that chick you've been pining over?" Benny asks, smoothly changing the subject. I get it though. It's a tough subject for both of us, and pressuring him to talk is the worst possible thing I can do.

"Pining over? Really?" I laugh. "We are...friends," I say. Jake starts barking at something hiding in the nearby bush.

"Friends, huh?" Benny says, kicking a stone on the ground. "Did you tell her how you feel? I mean, you've got love written all over your face." He makes a heart shape with his fingers in the air, then makes googly eyes and kissing noises at me. I shake my head. "You need to grow a pair, pendejo, and tell her she's the one. Chicks love that stuff."

"Oh, do they?" I look at him playfully.

"Yes." He nods knowingly.

"And you know this how?"

"I just know, trust me." The little shit grins at me.

"Well, I told her. But she wants to be friends for now. What should I do with that?" I raise my eyebrow at him.

"Be her friend. Be the best friend she could ever have, and when she least expects it...BAM! You make it happen! Easy." Benny shrugs his shoulders. The boy's got a point. I see merit behind that plan. Plan 'Get Jenny Back.'

"Right." I laugh. "How about you? How're the ladies?"

"You know my heart belongs only to Miss Fernandez." Benny puts a hand over his chest. "That woman could make algebra interesting. She's incredible." He trails off wistfully. "Hey!" Benny suddenly shouts and breaks into a run. "Jake!" he yells. I look around and see Jake limp-running towards the edge of the park.

"Jake!" I scream and run after Benny. When we finally get to where Jake disappeared, I look around frantically. Where the hell is he? It's not like he can or should run far with his back leg in a cast.

The laughter trickles in from behind the trees that separate the park from the pavement. Happy dog yelps follow soon after. I'd know that laugh anywhere. My heart picks up its pace.

"What are you doing here all by yourself?" I see her rubbing Jake's belly. He's on the pavement on his back, all four legs in the air.

"Hey," Benny says in his flirty voice. "That's Jake. I'm Benny, and this is my big brother, Aiden."

"Big brother?" Jenny shields her eyes to look closely at Benny. She's probably trying to pinpoint any similarities between the little dude and me. I smile at her, getting a confused expression in return. I'm not surprised. Benny has more mixed blood in him than most people. His father was half Italian, half Guatemalan; and his mother is a quarter Mexican, quarter Vietnamese, and half American. That's a strong mix.

"Little Brother-Big Brother program at the Youth Centre," I clarify.

Jenny smiles and gets up, getting a disapproving sneeze from Jake. "Hi, I'm Jenny," she says, walking over to Benny and shaking his hand. The little shit just stares at her boobs, mesmerised. Can't really blame him for that, they are pretty awesome.

"Miss Fernandez, forgive me," he whispers. I burst out laughing.

"Benny, this is Jenny, Jason's little sister and my roommate," I say, grabbing Jake and attaching the leash onto his collar.

"Ooooh." Benny's eyes widen. "So this is Jenny... Nice!" He winks at me.

Jenny laughs. "Thanks. I'll take that as a compliment. So, what are you guys up to except not taking good care of Jakey, here?" She leans over the dog and pats his head, giving me a glorious view of her cleavage.

"Just catching up," I reply, putting my arm over Benny's shoulder and pulling him into me as soon as I notice he's been staring at the exact same spot.

"Which reminds me." Benny wriggles out from beneath my arm. "I've got some homework to do."

"I'll walk you back," I say.

"May I join you?" Jenny asks hesitantly.

"Sure," Benny exclaims. "Maybe after, Aiden can give you a lift home, or you could go for a coffee, or a romantic dinner. Wouldn't that be nice?" Jenny blushes and I shoot an annoyed look at the irritating cupid.

"There's this nice diner around the corner," Benny continues, ignoring my death stare. "Their burgers are to die for, Jenny. You have to try them!" he exclaims, flinging his hands in the air.

"Well, if I have to, I guess I've got no other choice, do I?" She smiles at Benny sweetly. Did the little devil just score me a date?

"Let's go then," I say, shaking my head.

Benny takes Jake's leash from me and walks off ahead of us. I take a good look at Jenny. She's wearing grey jeans and a large, pink tank with 'Nobody puts baby in the corner' written in sparkly letters on it. I can see the strap and the side of her pink bra underneath it. And when she bends over and picks up her bag, which looks heavy, I get another look at her cleavage. My jeans tighten and I curse myself silently. Like a gentleman, I walk over to her and take the bag out of her hands, trying to forget about the ever growing hard-on I'm currently sporting, courtesy of the sexiest woman alive. The bag weighs a ton. What the hell does she keep in there? Bricks?

"Thanks," she mutters gratefully, pushing her hair out of her face. She's got freckles now and a bit of a glow to her skin. The sun reflects in her eyes, making them impossibly blue. California looks good on her.

"C'mon, kitten, let's go before Benny steals our dog," I say, liking the taste the word 'our' leaves on my tongue. Like me and Jenny are together and have things that belong to us and only us. Like we're a couple, like we've got a future together. I peer at her from the corner of my eye. "Are you parked around here?" I ask.

She shakes her head. "I walked to the library. The day is so gorgeous." She smiles, tilting her face up, soaking in the last of the autumn sun.

"So, do you want to grab something to eat?"

"Sure," she says, shoving her hands in the pockets of her jeans. She shivers a little, so I take off my hoodie and put it around her shoulders. She smiles and, for a second, I think she's sniffing it, but then I realise that can't be right. We're just friends. Right? Too soon, we are back at the Youth Centre. We say goodbye to Benny, and I help Jake into the car. Jenny settles herself in the passenger seat, and I can't help gaping at her. The sun behind her head makes her look ethereal.

"Everything ok?" she asks.

It would be if you were mine, I think, but nod instead.

Chapter 18

Basically Straddling Aiden

When life gives you lemons... Ah fuck it, I'm done with these.
- Aiden

"So you work at the Centre," I say, remembering that I thought Aiden used it as a poor excuse the morning after the frat party. He slips into the dimly lit booth opposite me, folds his hands on top of the table, and starts fidgeting with a paper napkin, not looking at me at all. The booth is half moon shaped with a small, scratched, round table in the middle that has seen better days. It would sit three people at most. There are two of us, and I find myself wishing he chose to sit closer to me. I inch a bit towards the middle, pretending that I need more space, but all I really crave is his proximity.

He nods and looks down at his menu. He's been awfully quiet ever since Benny left the two of us alone and we dropped Jake off with Jason. I self-consciously sniff my hair.

Do I smell? All I can smell is that glorious scent coming off of his hoodie. I notice Aiden's playful gaze on me. Shit. He must have seen me.

"Smelling the strawberries?" he asks, arching his perfect brow. Damn the Brits and their ability to produce hunks like the fine specimen in front of me. I blush and quickly drop my hands to my lap. My fingers automatically go to the bracelet and the little strawberry charm attached to it.

"So, how long have you been Benny's Big Brother?" I ask, changing the subject like a champ.

"Just over a year now," Aiden trails off, his eyes going a shade darker. There's something I can't exactly pinpoint behind them. Anguish? Sadness? Whatever it is, it's prompting me to dig deeper, making me want to know more. I lose the battle between nosiness and courtesy and decide to just dive in head first with the question that's been on my mind since I first saw them together.

"Can you...tell me more about him?" I stumble on my words, having the distinct feeling that I'm touching on a difficult subject. Aiden's shoulders rise and fall steadily to the rhythm of his breathing, and, for a few heartbeats, I think he's not going to reply. Then he lifts his heavy gaze and fixes it on me.

"Yes," he starts. "When I first met Benny, I didn't know anything about the Youth Centre or the work they do. It was a chance meeting, actually. The little shit was twelve and tried to steal my car." He smiles a half smile.

"He did?" I ask with disbelief. The boy I met today did not look like a GTA mastermind. He looked like a young boy with his whole life ahead of him. Skillful young boy. I mean, he waltzed his way into my heart like a pro.

Aiden nods. "Some neighbourhoods in Starwood are worse than others. Not everything around here is all Ivy

League College Town. There are tough areas, ones you wouldn't think existed in a place like Starwood, ones where kids as young as ten know how to use a gun," Aiden says through clenched teeth. I lift my head up and look at him; he's staring at the table between us. The napkin he was playing with was in shreds.

I throw all caution to the wind and slide around the booth, sitting right next to him, taking his hand in mine and squeezing it reassuringly. Aiden radiates heat, warming my whole body without even knowing it. His rough fingers wrap around my small hand and he squeezes it back, looking into my eyes. No. In that moment, his emerald green eyes are gazing into my soul, asking it to let him in, melting me from the inside out. I shiver and Aiden puts his other hand on my arm, rubbing it up and down for warmth in a tender gesture. With every upward movement of his hand, I burn. And every time he brings it down, my heart melts for him a little more. I'm far, far away from being cold.

He inhales deeply. "Benny is from one of those neighbourhoods," he continues, unaware that my resolve to be just friends is evaporating with every shaky breath I take. "He had a tough life. His father died when he was five in a street shooting, and his only male role model was his cousin. His cousin who was the leader of a small gang." Aiden hangs his head. "Benny joined his cousin's gang when he was ten, started off doing minor jobs, like delivering messages, warning them when the police were coming. Little things, you know? Soon, though, his cousin saw the potential and started teaching him how to use guns and break into places." I cover my mouth to hide the gasp. "Benny started stealing cars soon after. He was their favourite toy." Aiden takes his hand from mine and rubs the back of his neck, closing his eyes. His lips are a thin line, and I have to fight myself not to touch him, comfort him. As much as I'm afraid of what the rest of the story brings, I know I need to let him finish. "When I met him, he was a shadow of the boy you met today. He was skinny, desperate, and had no regard for his own life." He stops and looks around the diner. "I don't know. I guess I saw something in him that made me want to help. I think it was the look in his eyes, like he wanted to get caught, like he couldn't take it anymore. So, instead of reporting him to the police, I took him out for a meal and just talked to him like a normal kid. Told him that if he wants a friend to talk to and another meal, I'll be at the same place, same time the next day, and the day after that...and every day until he's ready.

"It took him a week to come see me. As promised, I showed up at the diner every day at the same time. Sometimes I saw him hiding and checking if I was inside. Sometimes I didn't even catch a glimpse of him. But a week later, he finally came into the diner and sat opposite me. He was all sharp edges and attitude, and he was very, very apprehensive at first..." Aiden's lips give into a small smile. "I guess he must have thought I was going to rat him out to the cops at the first opportunity I got or something. It took him a month of free meals to start trusting me. But once he did, he told me about his situation." Aiden's body goes rigid.

I rub his arm for comfort and inch a bit closer.

"He said he wanted to get out." Aiden picks another napkin off the table and starts scrunching it with his free hand. "So we started planning... We found the Youth Centre, we made plans, we found a good foster family..." He takes a deep breath. "Somehow, his cousin found out and..." His voice breaks. "The day we had it all planned for, I was meant to pick up Benny from our usual spot, but he didn't show. I waited for a couple of hours. I kept on getting this bad feeling about him being late. So, finally, I decided to drive down the route Benny usually took to come see me. It was getting dark and I could feel my chance of spotting him on the street slipping away. I don't know what made me park my car where I did. Shit, kitten, I don't even want to think about what could have happened if I didn't." I can see that talking about this is causing him pain, so I slide myself even closer and put my head on his shoulder, hoping that my proximity will make it easier to talk. Aiden just wraps his arm around me, pulling me into an embrace and kissing the top of my head. He's holding me so close I can feel his heartbeat.

"I found him there, by the bins, you know? He was bruised and had deep cuts all over his body, arms slashed and bleeding..." His voice hitches. "I took him to the hospital, and they barely managed to save his life. A week later, his cousin went to jail for some puny crime, and by the time Benny got better he decided he wanted to go back home to his mum, try going straight without his cousin pressuring him."

"That's great," I say softly.

"Yeah..." Aiden says into my hair. "Except his cousin has been out on parole for the past week..."

This time, I'm not able to stop the gasp escaping my lips.

"What will you do?" I ask, a big lump lodged in my throat.

"I'll go back to the Centre this evening and meet with the social workers. We'll try to find a safe place for Benny. Somewhere he can stay without a threat on his life." His voice is full of desperation, and the lump in my throat grows.

"I'm so sorry," I say as tears start rolling down my

cheeks, emotions swirling inside me. The sadness I feel for Benny not being able to go home to his mother; the need to help; the need to make sure both Aiden and Benny will be ok. I don't understand what's happening to me. Aiden lifts my chin, looking into my eyes, and gently wipes away the tears with his thumbs.

"Shhhh," he soothes. "We'll figure this out. Don't worry." The words he says are reassuring, but the expression on his face is grim. I can't believe I ever entertained the idea that Aiden is shallow or only thinks about himself. I'm beginning to understand him more, know him more, and I really, really like that person. My heart swells for him and his altruistic need to help others. Suddenly, I find myself wanting—no—needing to be as close to him as possible. I wrap my hands around his neck and pull him closer to me, enveloping him in a hug. It's a bit awkward in the small space, but he puts his arms around me and pulls me onto his lap, hugging me close to him and rubbing my back.

"How can I help?" I ask through tears that are freely falling right now.

"Kitten..." Aiden says softly, brushing my hair behind my ear.

"Aiden, I want to help," I say, trying hard to calm my emotions. I realize that being an emotional wreck is not very helpful. It feels selfish in this situation, actually. But I can't help the despair I'm feeling.

"You could start volunteering with me at the Centre..." he mumbles.

"Done," I say, nodding for added effect. "What else?" The tears stop now that I'm in action mode.

"You could also..." He lifts my head away from his chest. His t-shirt is wet with my tears, but he doesn't seem to mind. Instead, he just puts his soft, large hand on my face and tilts it so that all I can see is his large, green eyes. "Fuck, kitten, I need you to get off my lap." He groans. Holy shit, he's right. I'm acting like a lunatic. "Unless you're going to kiss me," he finishes, his voice husky. A thrilling sensation starts at the back of my spine. I'm not breathing, he's not breathing. I take stock of the whole situation. Here I am, an emotional wreck, basically straddling Aiden, my arms wrapped tightly around his neck. Before my brain registers my actions, I adjust my body and my face moves towards his. I can smell his minty fresh breath, feel the heat of his body. My lips are an inch away from his and getting closer, closer... I close my eyes in anticipation.

Something in his pocket vibrates, and I jump. What the hell am I thinking? We're supposed to take it slow, be friends, no kissing business. Although, would a little bit of kissing business be that bad? I mean, how bad could it be?

I look at Aiden. He's breathing fast and his eyes are black as coal.

Bad.

Bad, bad, bad.

I scramble off of his lap, muttering, "Sorry." Aiden's heated gaze follows my every move. "Your phone," I squeak, pointing at his crotch. My gaze follows my hand and my eyes widen at the large bulge I'm greeted with. I swallow loudly and clear my throat, looking back up. Safe place. Think of a safe place; calm seas, little Aiden—I mean island! Shit, little island! "I think your phone is buzzing," I blurt out.

Aiden's gaze is still on me. The phone stops. Aiden licks his lips. I lick mine in response.

The buzzing starts again.

I shake my head to clear my mind from the haze.

"Are you going to answer it?" I ask. Aiden doesn't drop

his eyes while he shakes his head. "Please answer it." I plead.

Still holding my gaze, Aiden pulls his phone out of his pocket and lifts it to his ear. I'm in a trance; I can't move or avert my eyes. All I can do is watch him intently.

"Hello?" His voice is silky smooth and deep, and it makes my body shiver with pleasure in places I didn't realize could shiver. "Oh, hello, father." He looks away, the spell broken. I move back to the opposite side of the booth, putting as much distance as possible between myself and the hottest Brit on earth, shakily letting out the breath I was holding in my lungs. "Yes," Aiden says bitterly into his phone. "No, I will not be coming in November." He pauses. "Exams," he says, irritated. I strain to listen to the other side of the conversation, but the diner is too loud for that. "I haven't decided yet, Dad." Aiden exhales loudly, then rakes his hand through his hair, looking up at the ceiling with despair. "Fine," he growls into the receiver. "I'll be home for Christmas. We can talk then." He snaps, then chucks the phone onto the seat next to him, groaning loudly.

"Want to talk about it?" I ask.

"Not really," he huffs. "Just the usual crap..." He bites his bottom lip, making me lean toward him.

"So..." I start tentatively. "You said you're going home for Christmas? To London?" He nods like it's the last thing he wants to do. I chew on my lower lip, trying to figure out how to broach the subject. Aiden's lips part, and he refocuses his gaze on my mouth. "Jason and I are meeting up with Dad in London for Christmas this year too," I say, not quite sure where I'm going with that. I guess I'm just trying to take his mind off the conversation he just had with his dad and his eyes off my lips, not that I'm complaining.

Aiden's head snaps to attention. His green eyes meet

mine. "You are?" he asks. I nod, not really trusting my voice. Truth be told, Aiden's proximity, even with the table between us, affects me a lot. A lot, a lot. Like, rip the table out of the way, straddle him to infinity a lot... "That's cool." He smiles at me with those damn dimples. "Maybe we could all do something together then?"

"Maybe..." I reply, looking at a 'very interesting' scuff mark on the table. Inside, I'm doing an Irish dance from happiness. I'll be seeing Aiden over Christmas!

Chapter 19

I'm A Lover

Sometimes I write "drink coffee" on my to-do list just to feel like I've accomplished something.
- Jason

Being Jenny's friend, just her friend, is proving to be a lot harder than I expected. I find myself struggling to keep my hands to myself. Especially when she prances around the house in really tight yoga pants and barely there tops. Seriously, it's torture. Therefore, I resolve to spend most of my time away from the house.

I go to the park with Jake, I go to the Youth Centre to see Benny, I study in the library. Actually, these past two weeks I've been to the library more than I have my entire last semester. This might have something to do with the fact that my workload, at the moment, is almost unbearable. Since I still haven't declared my major, I'm taking a whole load of extra classes. The worst part is that I might not even end up needing them. Specifically, if Dad pulls me out of Starwood after Christmas like he's been threatening. He calls me almost every day; leaving voicemails about how a business degree is the best option for my career; how the entire world relies on Finance and Economics; how if I don't choose soon, he'll make the decision for me... Insert my daily eye roll here.

I huff and annoyingly shut the heavy Psychology book I've been studying. It slides off the open Econometrics book underneath. So I shut that one as well, narrowing my eyes at the massive volume. I stretch my arms out and yawn, looking around. It's the last Friday afternoon before Thanksgiving, and there are not that many people left in the library. I turn to my left and see a familiar face. Deciding it's time for a break, I get up and drop both the Psychology and the Econometrics tomes on the librarian's trolley.

"Hey," I whisper, sliding into the chair next to Hayley.

She lifts her head up disoriented, then smiles up at me. "Hey yourself, stranger."

"Fancy a coffee break? I'm pretty sure my brain died an hour ago. I need a reboot."

Hayley looks down at her book and notes, then back up at me. She nods, then closes her book and gathers the rest of her things into her bag. "Sure," she whispers back. "I think I'm done for today anyway. I've been reading the same paragraph about viral genomes for the past twenty minutes."

We leave together and I take her bag from her, surprised again at the weight.

"What do you girls carry in those things?" I can't help but mutter. Hayley laughs out loud and pulls a hair band off her wrist. Tying her straight brown hair into a high ponytail, she replies, "Everything that's necessary to have at any given time. It's like," she thinks for a second, "Mary Poppins! Remember her bag? I might not have a hat stand in mine, but I do have a lot of useful things!" she exclaims with delight! I grin back at her and open the door to the coffee shop. "Actually, I was going to go over to your house to see Jenny after the library. Are you done with studying?" she asks once we place our orders.

"Ummm...sure. I guess I can drive you there... If you want, that is?" It's probably about time I faced Jenny, anyway.

"What's up with you?" Hayley narrows her brown eyes at me, leaning on the counter as we wait for our drinks.

"What do you mean?" I play dumb.

She smirks at me. "Huh, so you do like her. I was beginning to think your avoidance tactics might be because you don't." I swear my face flames red, and I rub the back of my neck to...I don't know, clearly not to mask my embarrassment since that gesture is obvious. I drop my arm to my side. "Don't worry, I'm pretty sure you guys will work everything out. To be honest, I think you both should just lose your clothes and have sex already. It's so obvious you two want each other." My jaw drops and my face feels a hundred degrees hotter. It's not that I haven't thought about it. God knows I've been thinking about it too much. "Gotcha!" Hayley grins.

"Irshbshjuswannbfrnds," I mumble.

"Huh?" She looks confused. The barista hands us our coffees.

"I wish, but she just wants to be friends," I say quietly.

"Honestly? Do you want to know a secret?" Hayley asks, blowing at the hot drink while we walk to the car. The air had been chilly, and steam rose up in smoky clouds off our drinks. I nod at Hayley, opening the car door for her.

"You're like a lost puppy." She rolls her eyes. "It's kinda adorable. Okay. Jenny is confused. You can't play hot and cold with a girl and not mess her head up. I think your current tactic needs a rework. If you keep on staying away from her, nothing will change. You should try being around her and, soon enough, you'll see, she'll break her resolve. She's into you, Aiden. Just have patience."

"She is?" I look at her hopefully, starting the engine.

"Seriously, lost puppy... Yes, she is. But to let her come to terms with that, you need to be there. The less you're there the longer she'll deliberate and, by looking at your love stricken expression, you'd probably prefer if she'd make that decision sooner rather than later, yes?" I nod.

We drive in silence. I'm thinking about all the times that Jenny and I were in the same room, the way she looked at me, the blush on her cheeks every single time my hand brushed hers. Could this be? Could she actually want to be with me? All I've been doing is stalling and letting my ego get in the way, thinking that I've been rejected.

Is that what you want, to be friends? I remember asking her. *Not really*, she replied... What if, once again, I screwed up by not fighting for her? Was I right to give her space or was I supposed to just suck it up? A million scenarios run around my head like a bunch of drunken horses, racing. They are bouncing off each other, confusing and in complete chaos. When we arrive, Hayley jumps out of the car and goes straight for the door to the house, not waiting for me. I'm glad. I need to think of a strategy here. Being just friends with Jenny is hard, but that doesn't mean I can't do it; and while I'm being just friends, I can always try to get closer at the same time. I've got until Christmas to change her mind; that's a month. Unless. Jenny and Jason are coming to London too.

For Crying Out Loud

I get out of the car and rush into the house. Jenny and Hayley are sitting on the kitchen counter. They both wave at me, and Jenny blushes. I'm about to run past her when I decide Phase One of the Jenny Project is officially in action. I skid to a full stop, then turn and walk to her, embracing her in a hug, catching a whiff of strawberries when my nose connects with her hair. She's shocked and doesn't react. For a second, I'm mortified. I've done the wrong thing, then she wraps her arms around me and squeezes me gently.

"Hey, beautiful," I say, giving her a peck on her left cheek. "Feels like I haven't seen you in forever!" I exaggerate, letting her go and moving out of the hug. Her hands stay outstretched for a second too long before she catches herself and puts them next to her on the counter. "All good with you?" She nods, her cheeks turning red. I smile, hoping that my dimples show. C'mon little bastards, work to my advantage! Kitten's eyes grow wide, and she bites her lower lip. "I'll talk to you later about volunteering. Benny's been asking about you." I smile wider. Jenny nods again and Hayley crosses her arms, laughing silently and shaking her head. I turn around and stroll confidently out of the kitchen. I pat myself on the back. That was a good first step; now step two. I run to my room. Jake has made himself comfortable on my bed. I scratch him behind his ear, jolting him awake. I guess the no sleeping in beds unless it's me in Jenny's rule never really stuck. I grab my laptop then run into Jason's room.

I open the door shielding my eyes. "Cover yourself if you're indecent. Also, oink if you've got company." Jason bursts into laughter.

"Oink, oink, asshole." He laughs, and I take a step back. "Just kidding. It's just me and my ultra large penis here. He's like a separate dude, that one."

"Really, man?" I scrunch my face in disgust, taking my hand away from my eyes. Jason is sitting on his bed with his laptop on his lap and, thankfully, dressed.

"What?" he asks innocently. "You asked..." He grins at me.

"Yeah, I'm sorry I did... Anyway!" I change the subject to what's on my mind. "Jenny mentioned a couple of weeks ago that you guys are going to London for Christmas."

"Oh yeah! I've been meaning to ask you if you've booked your tickets already, completely slipped my mind." Jason replies. "Wanna take the same flight?"

"Exactly what I was thinking. I haven't booked mine yet, have you?"

"No. I always leave stuff like that to the last minute. Jenny will kill me..."

"Okay, let's book now," I say and bring up the airline's website.

We skim through flight options and decide to fly out in the morning a couple of days before Christmas and return just before New Year's Eve. The prices are steep, so I tell Jason to just transfer me money for the economy class and I'll book straight away. He seems legitimately relieved that he doesn't have to think about it anymore.

I go back into my room and change our flights to First Class, making sure Jenny's seat is next to mine and Jason's is as far away as possible on both flights. Proud of myself, I purchase the flights and text my dad the details. I also text Carter asking if he'd take care of Jake while we're away. As I press send, I hear a booming voice coming from the living room.

"Ladies, drop your pants. Gentlemen, pull yours up and walk away. Carter is here to serve your needs, my dears!" Jake's head goes up. He barks once, then hops off the bed and runs out of my room. I follow him, meeting Jason in the hallway.

"I guess Kennedy came by." Jason shrugs.

"I guess so," I agree.

Carter is spread eagle on the floor when we walk into the living room, Jake on top of him, licking the living shit out of him.

"No, please!" Carter giggles like a child. "It's ticklish!" I let Jake torture him for a couple of minutes longer before calling him. Jake looks at me judgingly, like I've just interrupted him in his favourite play time, which I suppose I did. He does calm down, however, and comes to sit by my leg, wagging his tail and looking at Carter, who's trying to catch his breath on the floor.

"What an entrance," Jenny laughs and helps him up.

"That dog," Carter looks at Jake lovingly, "is the best damn thing that happened on this side of the Atlantic. Aren't you?" He leans down, baby-talking to Jake, who yelps with happy appreciation, wagging his tail madly.

"Yes, you are," Carter continues, oblivious to how ridiculous he looks. His shirt is covered in brown fur and slobber, his precious hair all messed up. And half his face is covered in doggy saliva. "If I could, I'd take you away and never give you back," he says to Jake, then makes kissing noises at him.

Hayley bursts out laughing, unable to keep herself together. Jenny follows soon after.

"Oh. Hi Hayley, didn't see you there." Carter's voice suddenly goes deep. He straightens his back and runs his fingers through his hair. It doesn't help, now his hair sticks out in two directions, making him look like he's got horns on each side of his head.

"Hi," Hayley squeezes out when she and Jenny calm

down. "So you're a dog lover, huh?" She smiles at him, and I swear to God I think Carter blushes for a microsecond.

"I'm a lover," he winks at her, but Hayley just rolls her eyes, unaffected by his charm. Carter clears his throat, confused, then gestures around to all of us. "Since the entire gang is here," he starts, "I have come to cordially invite you to Thanksgiving dinner at the Kennedy household." He bows as he finishes.

"Really?" Jenny asks, excited. "A proper Thanksgiving with your family?"

"If you can call them a family, they're more like a herd of animals," Carter mutters.

"Oh, my god!" Jenny exclaims, jumping up and down. "Jason, our first Thanksgiving in America in years! And we're all going to be together!" She runs up to Jason and jumps into his arms. He twirls her around, his deep laughter bouncing off the walls. I can't help but smile. She looks so happy, so excited... A twinge of jealousy shoots through me when I look over at Carter. His expression is full of admiration as he follows Jenny's twirls.

Jake joins in on the excitement and starts barking happily and jumping up and down.

"You're invited too." Carter leans down and pats his head. "And you too, don't think you're getting out of this one!" he says, straightening up, looking Hayley straight in the eyes and wiggling his eyebrows.

"Oh..." She blushes, not quite as immune to Carter's charm as I thought. "I'm sorry, but I promised my family I'd go to see them." She gestures apologetically.

The funny thing is, Carter genuinely looks disappointed.

Huh, wonder what that's about?

Chapter 20

A Big Can Of Whoopass

I love children, but I don't think I can eat a whole one.
- Carter

"I can't believe you're all going to Carter's for Thanksgiving tonight. The whole female population of Starwood is jealous of you!" Hayley throws her hands up in the air for the umpteenth time. I just smile at her and continue walking towards her dorm.

"You know, you were invited too. You can still change your mind and come."

"No, Jen, it really is for the best if I just stay here. Please don't tell the guys I lied about going home." Sadness laces her words, but she catches herself quickly and tries to mask it with a smile. I can see right through it. This is the exact smile she puts on when she wants to appear like everything is okay: her 'professional' smile. Hayley has recently admitted to me that she's not going to see her family for

Thanksgiving. In fact, she hasn't seen her 'family' in years. I cried when she told me the whole story and swore to keep it a secret. As tough as it has been for her to tell me, I felt honored that she trusted me enough to confide in.

"Of course I won't." I give her a small hug. "It's your story to tell. I just wish you'd at least come with me to London for Christmas."

She wraps her arm around me as we walk into her building. Her room is on the third floor and the lift is out of order, so we climb the stairs.

"I wish I could, but even though I'm doing as many modelling gigs as possible during the school year without them getting in the way of studying. Holidays are the only time I really have to work, and you know I only have a partial scholarship so..." she trails off, opening the door to her room. Her lips are in a thin line and her eyes are sad and fixated on the poster above her bed. It's a white canvas with a big block 'You Go Glen Coco' on it. It makes me giggle every single time I see it. I love it.

"I know, I know... Sorry, I just wish you didn't have to do it..." I say, slipping under her arm and landing my butt straight on her bed in one swift jump.

"Me too. Anyway, let's not talk about this now!" she says, clapping her hands and turning around to her closet. In two long steps she's in front of it, opening the door and diving head first into what I call my personal paradise, filled with all the shoes, bags, and clothes I'm allowed to borrow.

For the next half hour, I get clothes thrown at me every few minutes. I sort them into three piles. Maybe, No, and I'm dying to try this on. Once we go through the clothes, Hayley insists I try them all, disregarding my oh so well thought out sorting system. We end up playing dress up for about an hour before choosing a couple of dressy, black dresses and one red. I fold them carefully and put them in my bag. Getting up, I gather my things and get ready to go home, the gruesome task of packing ahead of me. Seems I've only got a couple hours left before we're supposed to set off.

I hug Hayley goodbye and promise to call and take loads of pictures, so that she doesn't feel like she's missing out. Before we know it, we've wasted another half an hour, and I'm really starting to panic about not having enough time to get ready.

I run out of Hayley's room and down the two flights of stairs, patting myself on the back for not breaking my neck in the process. As I cross the green towards the parking lot, I hear someone shout my name.

"Jenny, wait up!" I look around. Did I forget something? But it's not Hayley. Instead, I see a thin girl with a short blonde bob and an unhealthy-looking tan approaching me. "Thank God you stopped! I thought I'd have to run to catch up with you, and, trust me, these shoes," she points at her extremely high heeled ankle boots, "are not made for running." I find myself nodding. The shoes, indeed, look dangerous if not mouthwateringly so.

"Chloe," I say tensely, once I stop drooling over the grey suede beauties on the dragon's feet.

"Hi," she smiles timidly at me.

"Did you need something from me?" I'm totally confused. Chloe looks approachable, apologetic even. Who knew the She-Devil had any other looks apart from the 'Die little worm, die' and the 'I'll rip your heart out with my dragon claws, then slowly eat it while you're looking at its diminishing heartbeat'...

"Well, yeah," Chloe replies, looking down at her feet. I follow her gaze and ogle the boots one more time. They must be about five inches high. If I had them on, they'd basically make me five feet nine. I'd be able to reach things from the top shelves and everything. As it stands, my converse did nothing to help my gnome-like height, especially in comparison to Chloe, who's towering like a giant above me. She's almost as tall as Aiden in those shoes, but not quite. She could probably reach his mouth with hers without having to climb him like a koala bear trying to summit a freaking bamboo. I cross my arms in front of my chest and huff with dismay at the unfair reality of my situation.

"Listen." Chloe looks down at me kindly. Kindly? What the hell is going on? Am I dying? Is it some sort of Make A Wish Thing? Damnit, who's in charge? This is not my wish! I want full access to Jimmy Choo's store! "I know we started off on the wrong foot and everything..." You think?

"You think?" My mouth runs faster than my brain. Chloe clutches her Chanel bag to her side and nods at me, her long earrings bumping on her shoulders with each movement of her head. "I just... I wanted to apologize."

I nearly choke on the chewing gum I've been chewing. "Y-y-you what?" The disbelief is making me stutter.

"I wanted to apologize for everything," she says in a small voice. "I've been behaving like a total bitc—not a nice person..."

"You don't say," I mutter, stunned.

"Yeah," she agrees earnestly. "I guess I owe you an explanation. Well, I don't owe you anything, but I wanted to explain myself anyway." Ah, there she is! For a second, I thought the reincarnation of Lillith might have actually gone back to hell for a bit, and a normal human being took her place. But I suppose that was just wishful thinking.

"Okay." I look up at her expectantly.

"Where do I start? I guess you might find this hard to believe, but I'm not a horrible person and I actually have feelings and... The thing is, Jason, your brother, he...he broke my heart," she blurts out. Thanks to Carter, this does not come as a total shock.

"Carter mentioned that you and Jason used to date."

She looks surprised but continues on. "Are you going somewhere? We can walk and talk, if you want to? Actually, it might be easier for me to say all this to you if I don't have to...you know, look at you? Sorry, that sounds bad, but it still hurts when I talk about it."

I nod and, in silence, we set off towards the parking lot, the jingling of Chloe's bracelets the only sound.

"So?" I prompt her.

"We dated for the better part of last year, did you know that?" I shake my head. I thought Carter said it was a month. "Well, it was almost eight months. I was in love. And so happy. I couldn't believe that he'd want to be with me. Then the rumours started, that Jason wasn't faithful." She clenches her fists, surely drawing blood with her sharp nails. "I never believed them. Most rumours are just that, rumours. But then I started seeing him around campus with other girls and..."

She stops in her tracks. "He didn't even have the decency to break up with me. He just phased me out. Stopped texting me, stopped answering my calls... Didn't even officially break up with me before I found him in another girl's bed." Chloe's voice hitches and her hand flies to her mouth, covering it. I can see the anger and betrayal in her eyes, clear as day. She's either an amazing actress or Jason really hurt her.

"I didn't know."

"Eight months and not even a text, Jenny! He just ghosted me," she exclaims, and my hand automatically goes out to her, landing on her arm, squeezing it.

"I'm sorry, Chloe. That's no way to treat a girl."

"Yeah." She nods, a single tear escaping her eye. She quickly wipes it away and turns to face away from me. "It can make a girl go a bit crazy, you know?" She laughs bitterly and resumes walking.

"I get it. I didn't realize Jason was playing mind games. It doesn't explain, however, why you've been such a bitch to me from the start," I deadpan.

Chloe sucks in a breath. Her head whips my way. "Wow, you really have bigger balls than most guys in Starwood, don't ya?" She smiles at me. I'm not buying it just yet but give her a short smile back. "Is it so hard to understand? I felt threatened," she says. I narrow my eyes. What is she on about? Why would she feel threatened by me out of all people?

"Huh?"

"You don't even know it, do you?" She smiles knowingly at me.

"What are you talking about?" I ask, exasperated.

"Jenny, you're gorgeous, and you were hanging out with models, Carter and Aiden. Driving the car Jason drove all last year. Then you were there at Jason's house—"

"My house and my car!" I interject.

"Yeah. Your house, your car." She smiles. "I thought for sure you have an agenda, then I found out you're Jason's little sister rather than someone who came out of his bedroom. I'm ashamed to say…I lied, hoping that Jason would find out and be jealous. I'm so sorry."

I have a distinct feeling that I must look a lot like a gremlin right about now. My eyes are large and glassy, my mouth is agape, and the thoughts in my head are causing havoc.

"Okay…." I drawl.

"I don't want to be that girl," Chloe says, grabbing my hand. We've been standing in front of Kitt for a while now, and I feel the need to lean on the hood before I collapse from confusion. "I don't want to lie and scheme just because some guy broke my heart last year. I might still hold a torch for him, but I'm not going to stoop that low."

I slowly nod.

"Will you forgive me? Can we please start over?" she asks excitedly.

"I guess," I mutter. "Thank you for telling me the truth."

"Oh, Jenny!" Chloe claps her hands and bends over to give me a hug. It's awkward, and I give her a stiff pat on the back, trying not to breathe in the cloud of Angel by Thierry Mugler that I just got assaulted with. My eyes start to water from lack of oxygen when Chloe finally breaks the hug and steps away from me. I take a lungful of fresh, gorgeous air, and exhale slowly. "I'm so glad I confided in you." She smiles at me.

"Yeah," I say. "It definitely took guts, especially since I'm his sister." Maybe she's not that bad in the end. Maybe her soul was not forged in the pits of hell. Who knows? If I went a bit psycho because of Aiden, who am I to judge another person who spent eight months in love with a jerk. My brother, the jerk. That boy is gonna get a big can of whoop ass next time I see him. She-Devil or not, no girl should be treated like he treated Chloe. I sigh.

I will have to give both him and Carter lessons on how to efficiently break up with girls. I'll probably need to Google that first since I've got no experience in that department whatsoever. Like zero. Zilch.

I obviously will not give any of these lessons to Aiden since he's going to marry me and I'll have his beautiful British babies.

HOLD UP!!

What?

This is what I'm talking about when I say that it's quite normal for a girl to go crazy because of a guy. I mean. Marry him. Ha.

Haha.

Hahahah!

Have his babies...

Hahahahaha...

Although they would be pretty... I wonder if they'd be tall like him or short like me? Would they have my blue eyes or his green? I hope green. And dimples. I'd return them if they didn't have his dimples. I'd be like nuh-uh! Go back into my uterus and bake some dimples right now, you little—

"Jenny?" Chloe pulls me out of my mind walkabout in la-la land. Shit, was she talking to me all this time?

"Yes," I say. I mean, it's fifty-fifty anyway. Might as well try to save face.

"So you do like him? I'm really sorry I made you think I slept with him. It was a shit thing to do."

What the...?

"What?" I guess my fifty-fifty did not pay off, cause I've got a peculiar feeling that I just replied 'yes' to something I'd never admit to. Ever. Not in a million years. At least not out loud. "Sorry, my mind wandered there for a bit and I'm not a hundred percent sure what I just admitted to..." I say sheepishly. Chloe giggles in her high-pitched voice, and I congratulate myself for not wincing at the sound.

"Oh. I was asking if you liked Aiden."

"Right. Aiden and I are just friends, but I still accept your apology. Even if we are just friends, it was not a cool thing to do," I say.

Chloe nods. "Yes, that's why I was saying I'm sorry..."

"No worries." I smile at her. "But listen, I do have to go or I'm going to be late." I glance down at my watch. Damn, another half an hour gone. I'm cutting it awfully close!

"Oh, yes!" Chloe claps her hands again! This might just be her most annoying habit yet. "You're all going to Kennedy's for Thanksgiving, aren't you? The whole campus is buzzing about it."

Gossip travels fast in Starwood. It's only been a week since we made the plan, and half of the school is already gone for the holiday. The half still left behind seem to have nothing better to do than to talk about my group of friends. I briefly remind myself that at least I have friends now, ones that would stand by me and stand up for me. That's a lot more than I had most of my life. I shouldn't complain.

"Yes. We are all friends, and this seemed like a conventional thing friends would do. You know, hang out on Thanksgiving together?"

"Well, have fun," Chloe says, fluffing her blonde bob. "I need to get back to the dorms. I've got a plane to catch." She gives me another awkward hug and a peck on the cheek. "So glad we had this talk." She grins at me with her pearly white teeth and turns on her gorgeous heels to walk away. I considered taking a quick snap of the boots but decided against it.

Rubbing the red lipstick stain she left on my cheek, I slide into Kitt and speed dial Hayley. I tell her all about my talk with Chloe while I drive back to the house, silently thanking Jason for installing hands-free in Kitt.

"I don't know, babe, she just doesn't seem like the person who does things out of the goodness of their heart."

"I know," I reply. "But she seemed genuine, and it really

sounds like Jason screwed her over, so maybe we should give her a chance?"

"Maybe," Hayley says just as I park in front of the house.

"Okay babe, well, I'm home now, so I'll text you later. I've got half an hour to get ready and pack!" I start to panic.

"Calm down, you'll be fine." She laughs through my speakers.

And she's right. I am fine. I even find myself with 30 seconds to spare. When Carter arrives, I'm already in the living room, my bag by my feet, Jake sitting with his head on my lap, and patiently waiting.

"You guys ready for some 90210, where the kids are pretty and the housewives have nothing better to do than drink mimosas at brunch?" Carter screeches excitedly, walking in through the front door. Jake barks once in response, tapping his tail twice on the floor, then puts his head right back onto my lap, looking at me adoringly. I love that dog so much it's ridiculous. I give him a kiss on the forehead and turn to Carter.

"Afternoon, Mr. Miyagi." I tip my invisible hat.

"Afternoon, grasshopper," he replies, bowing. "Looking like a vision, as usual." He smiles full force at me, and I have the urge to put sunglasses on to stop him from blinding me with his eagerness. "Where are the guys?" He arches his perfectly shaped eyebrow at me. I make a mental note to enquire about it later. Does he wax or thread?

"Still getting ready." I smile triumphantly, just as both Jason and Aiden walk into the living room.

"Beaten by a girl! You guys are a disgrace to men everywhere." Carter crosses his hands over his chest.

"In my defence," Aiden says. "I had to pack for two."

"You pregnant? Who's the father?" I smirk.

"Har-har, very funny. I also had to pack all the stuff for Jake."

Jason starts making kissing noises at Jake, and Jake trots over to him for some love. I roll my eyes. I'm pretty sure Jason packs his pockets full of treats just to make sure Jake follows him around.

"Enough of this chit-chat," Carter interrupts the Kodak moment. "Let's get going. I flew back home last weekend to pick up the Audi Q7 so we can road trip the hell out of this!"

We follow Carter outside and pack our bags into the trunk. Jake goes in the last row, and I sit by the window in the middle one. The door on the opposite side opens, and Aiden leans over, flashing his dimples at me. I tense up. Damn, this will be one long trip.

"Mind if I sit here?" he asks.

"Not at all," I reply, my voice a lot higher than I'd like it to be. Aiden smiles brighter and settles himself in. There is a seat in between us, but I can feel the heat radiate off his body even from this far. I glance over at him and blush when I see that he's been blatantly looking at me all this time.

"Oh, hell no!" Jason says from the front seat, looking at the both of us. He crawls over the console and sits in the middle seat right between Aiden and I. I'm, once again, able to breathe.

"Guys, I'm not your chauffeur. Someone sit next to me and entertain me. Eeeny-meaany-minyyy-mo—grasshopper, you've been chosen," he says, his finger trained on me all throughout his little speech.

"You were pointing at me all along," I grumble, but move over to the front.

"What's the point of choosing the navigator and the

radio controller if you can't choose who you want? Of course I was pointing at you," Carter explains, as if it all makes sense.

I get settled in the front seat, and we set off for the drive. During our road trip, I learn two things:

1. Carter Kennedy has an amazing singing voice. Seriously, when he belted out Wind Beneath My Wings, we were all stunned into silence. That boy is wasting away studying politics.

2. When Jake is fed too many treats by Jason...he farts.

Chapter 21

Wonders Of The World

Life isn't about finding yourself. It's mostly about chocolate.
- Jenny

Jake farts non-stop, making Jason giggle with giddiness like an immature schoolgirl at a 1D concert. I roll my eyes and lean my head further out of the window, breathing in the air that's whooshing at me at high speed.

Carter is driving way faster than the recommended speed limit, disregarding the signs and our safety. At least we're making good time, and it seems like the road we've chosen is fairly empty. We've been driving for about two hours, and we've just passed Santa Margarita. I quickly do the math in my head; that's about eighty-five miles per hour speed average.

Kitten chats with Kennedy up front in hushed whispers. They're both stealing glances at Jason and I every so often, and trying hard to hide their excited bursts of laughter. I'm about to look down at my phone, wanting to check where we are when Jenny turns around in her seat, grinning.

"Gum?" she asks innocently, raising her eyebrows and holding her hand up with Hubba Bubba in it. She waves it back and forth in front of our faces a couple of times, and Carter chuckles excitedly in the driver's seat. They're totally up to something.

"Thanks!" Jason reaches out and snatches the packet out of Jenny's hand. He pops a piece into his mouth and starts chewing fiercely, handing the packet over to me. I narrow my eyes at my grinning kitten in the front seat and grab a piece. It's the bubblegum flavour I remember from our first kiss. My eyes are instantly drawn to Jenny's lips, the memory of how they tasted on mine when I kissed her years ago so vivid. Almost as vivid as the massive failure the kiss had turned out to be. Jenny leans over to Carter and whispers something in his ear, making him guffaw and fist pump triumphantly.

Jake farts again, and I stick my face further out the open window. Jason giggles and hands him another treat.

"C'mon man, you're just making him fart more..." I groan.

"It's called conditioning," Jason explains. "He gets a treat every time he farts. I'm teaching him to fart on command." He sounds extremely proud of himself.

"Dude, the treats are what makes him fart, not your conditioning." I groan, but he doesn't seem to care. Instead, he leans over and pats Jake on the head adoringly. I gaze out at the passing scenery, trying to focus on something less annoying than the two of them, like the lack of fauna or flora and the city sign we just passed. "Why are we going into San Luis Obispo?" I ask no one in particular, yawning.

"Ooooh..." Carter replies quickly. Too quickly. "Jenny needs to use the toilet, so we're just going downtown." We passed a gas station a few minutes ago, so that excuse smells of deceit. I decide to let it go since both Jenny and Carter seem really excited about the prospect of a toilet in downtown San Luis Obispo...

"Did you get it?" Jenny whispers to Carter. He nods and points at the glove compartment on her side. She opens it and digs around, pulling out something small and shiny and stuffing it under her seat. What the hell is going on? "Oh yeah," she stage-talks, turning to me. "I really need to pee. I can barely hold it together." She scrunches her face as if in pain. I fight the urge to burst into laughter. She'll never be an actress or a spy. That girl can't lie at all. It's one of her more adorable traits, the complete inability to spin a lie. That, and the way she scrunches her nose when she thinks something is gross, and the way her eyes twinkle when she's up to no good... Down boy.

Carter turns off the 101 and veers through small streets until we stop outside of a place called Mother's Tavern. He kills the engine, and both Jenny and him turn their heads to face us, grinning.

"We can't have a road trip without visiting one of the Wonders of The World!" Carter exclaims excitedly, and Jenny nods in agreement. Jason looks intrigued and slowly gets out of the car. I follow suit, stretching my back once my legs hit the pavement. I lean back inside and grab Jake. He sniffs around happily, finding a fire hydrant to pee on. He's so cliche.

"C'mon! What are you waiting for?" Jenny grabs my hand and starts pulling me behind her. I bask in the warmth spreading through me at the touch of her hand and entwine my fingers with hers before she gets to protest, following her into a small alley. "Ta-da!" Jenny grins at Jason and me while Carter throws his hands up expectantly.

"Wonder of the World, huh?" I ask, looking around and raising my eyebrows.

"This is awesome!" Jason whispers, his mouth agape.

"Welcome to the Bubble Gum Alley!" Jenny jumps up and down.

"It's a bit disgusting," I say, looking at the walls covered in discarded chewing gum. Some people even wrote messages with chewed gum.

"But awesome," Carter finishes.

"Soooo awesome," Jason chimes in.

"I know!" Jenny nods. To my dismay, she drops my hand to pull the black, shiny thing she took out of the glove compartment. She sticks her phone into a small frame on one side, then extends the little handle into a long one. "Carter even got this selfie stick so we can immortalize this moment."

She orders everyone around, positioning us in front of one of the walls and planting herself in the middle, sticking the selfie stick out so that we're all in the frame, including Jake. "Okay! Now blow!" she orders and puffs her cheeks until a small bubble is formed out of her gum. We all follow suit, and she snaps a million photos. She then spells Hayley's name with chewing gum, explaining that she wants Hayley to feel like she was here with us. We help and take a few more snaps, smiling and pointing at the name on the wall. Finally, Carter and Jenny decide they had enough fun, and it's time to resume our road trip. With at least three more hours of driving still ahead of us, I couldn't agree more. We spend the rest of the trip arguing over music and taking photos of everything with the selfie stick. At one point, Carter belts out a tune like nobody's business, which

Jenny promptly records on her phone, staring at him with her jaw slack. And because I can't stand her looking at him like that, I lean over and pinch her side, making her jump in her seat and glare at me.

At least she's giving me her full attention again. As childish as that is, I call it a win.

It's late afternoon when we finally arrive at what can only be called, The Kennedy Mansion. There are round shrubberies surrounding the driveway and a fountain in front of the house. Oh yeah, there's a fountain. There's even a pair of grizzly bear topiaries on the sides of the entrance, very disturbing. Carter's mum waves at us excitedly from the front door as we roll down the gravel.

"Carter, darling!" she exclaims, launching herself down the steps and straight on top of Carter. She is the exact opposite of what you'd expect by looking at her. Her pristine Chanel jacket and skirt; her perfect hair and flawless makeup do not match her personality at all. She is friendly and loud and outright great, basically a stark opposite of my own mother. "And these must be your friends! Jason, Jenny, and Aiden! So pleased to meet you." She gives each of us a warm hug. "And you must be Jake! I've heard so much about you! You'll be spending Christmas with us, won't you?" She leans down to Jake who just a second ago was peeing on the beautiful rose bush next to where we're standing. He's got the sense to pretend like he didn't do it and, instead, wags his tail at Mrs. Kennedy. "Aren't you just adorable?" Jake must agree as he starts yelping happily and lies down on his back, asking for belly rubs. "Reagan is going to love you!"

"Is she here?" Carter pokes his head out from the boot. I go to help him with our bags, reluctant to leave Jenny's side.

"She went to meet some school friends. You know how

that is. They must celebrate everything as their 'last', since they're seniors." Mrs. Kennedy rolls her eyes. "She should be back soon. Your Great Aunt Berta is here, though. She's having a nap." We grab our bags and are about to walk inside when a black, sports Tesla speeds down the gravel towards us. It skids to a stop right next to our parked car, making gravel fly in the air.

Whoever sits behind the tinted windows likes a good entrance. I'll give them that.

"Rey-rey!" Carter exclaims, dropping his bag and running towards the car just as the driver door opens and a blonde girl wearing a white polo shirt and a short, tartan skirt jumps out straight into his arms.

"Corky!" She laughs as they embrace.

"Corky, like in the 'Life Goes On'?" Jenny mutters.

"Oh no! Like cute and dorky! When Reagan was little," Mrs. Kennedy whispers, "she couldn't say Carter's name. She kept on coming up with Corker, so we shortened it to Corky: cute and dorky."

"Oh, man." Jenny chuckles quietly. "This is ammunition for years to come."

Carter finally lets go of his sister and stomps proudly in our direction. "Everyone," he raises his voice, "this is Reagan, my little sister. She's amazing, so just get on with it. Rey, these are the idiots I hang out with." He gestures at us. "Apart from grasshopper. She's clever; she'll be able to make me that bionic arm I've wanted ever since I was five once she's done at Starwood."

"Hi." Reagan waves at us timidly. We all wave back in unison, like the idiots Carter introduced us as. Jenny goes over to her and gives her a hug. They quickly start chatting in hushed voices and laugh.

"Well, let's not stand outside. You all must be so tired

after the journey. I'm sure you'd like to freshen up before dinner," Mrs. Kennedy interjects. "Everything should be ready in a couple of hours. The turkey has been in the oven for the better part of the day, so hopefully it should all turn out delicious." Carter and Reagan exchange a glance and burst out laughing. "Now, now," Mrs. Kennedy puts her hands on her hips, "I remembered to defrost it this year. Stop laughing and get inside."

We all grab our bags and follow her inside where we're swiftly shown our rooms. I contemplate having a nap but decide against it and just shower quickly, then change. I decide on black jeans, a white shirt, and a skinny black tie, hoping that I will not be under or overdressed.

When I get back downstairs, Mrs. Kennedy is running around the kitchen like crazy, hopping over Jake, who's asleep in the middle of the room.

"Is there anything I can help you with?" I ask.

"Oh God. Yes, please!" She looks up at me flustered, her eyes darting from one pot to another, calculating. "I don't know why every single year I decide it'll be a great idea to cook Thanksgiving dinner all by myself..." She shakes her head. "Don't tell anyone, but I'm a terrible cook. I just exploded the yams!" She points at the stove. There's a glass pan with orange mush all over it; some of it got on the kitchen wall as well.

"How did that happen?" I ask, grabbing the pan and putting it next to the sink.

"I took the pan out of the oven and put it on the stove. I didn't realize the burner was on!" She drops her hands, resignation evident.

"Let's make....rustic, crushed sweet potatoes out of it," I say, rolling my sleeves up. "Did you roast any garlic and do you have pecans?" Mrs. Kennedy nods, then runs off, coming back with the items I requested. We mash the sweet potatoes with a little butter and garlic, then sprinkle the crushed pecans on top. "There," I say, looking at our creation.

"Amazing!" she exclaims, giving me a hug. "You saved Thanksgiving!"

"It was nothing." I dismiss my limited cooking skills.

"I'll let you in on a secret...Aunt Berta made her famous cherry pie." She looks at me expectantly.

"Delicious?" I say.

"If you want to lose your teeth. She never figured out which cans of cherries are the pitted ones." She smiles at me, taking the turkey out of the oven and setting it to rest on the counter. "Now, you just rest here until it's carving time," she speaks softly to the bird, I hope. "So Aiden." She turns on me, and I have a feeling I'm about to be interrogated. "You and Jenny, have you been dating long?"

"What? No! We're just friends!" I loudly stumble through excuses, raking my hand through my hair. But Mrs. Kennedy just looks at me like she knows very well that that's exactly what they are, excuses.

"Hi." I hear a timid voice from behind me, and the blood drains from my face.

"Hi, Jenny. Come to help? Aiden already saved the day in the kitchen, but you could help me with the table. I just want to make sure that everything is perfect." Mrs. Kennedy smiles. I slowly turn around to see kitten standing next to the kitchen table, her fists clenched and her eyes narrowed in my direction.

"I'd love to help out." Jenny nods, her features soften as she directs her gaze at Carter's mom. Time stops, and I stare at Jenny for what seems like a lifetime, not daring to blink for the fear of her disappearing. She looks beautiful. She's wearing a black dress with little bows on the sleeves, her hair cascading down her shoulders in waves, and the lip gloss she put on drawing my eyes to her already plump and inviting lips. I lick my own and, subconsciously, take a step forward. Her lips part a little, a blush forming on her cheeks. Involuntarily, I take another small step.

"Aiden, would you please grab Carter and everyone else? Dinner should be ready in 20 minutes," Mrs. Kennedy interrupts me. I shake my head and tear my gaze away from Jenny.

"Sure, no problem," I say hoarsely, trying hard not to look in the direction of the world's biggest seductress. I mean, seriously, did she study under Mata Hari? What powers does she possess to render me incapable of a single thought that isn't about her? She's a witch. That must be it.

I walk out of the kitchen and towards our rooms, trying to concentrate on anything other than what my body is currently wanting me to do, which is turn around, go back, grab kitten's hand and drag her into my bedroom for some serious getting to know you time. You know, the one that involves slowly undressing her and kissing every single inch of her body. That one.

I round the corner and stop, stunned. What unfolds in front of my eyes is Instagram worthy, if you're into that sort of thing...

Jason is flat against the wall. His eyes are enormous and focused on the fork in Carter's hand, which is dangerously close to Jason's face.

"I will gouge your eyeball out with this fork if you so much as even smile in her direction," Carter growls. "Rey is off limits. You understand me, horn dog?"

"What's going on?" I ask slowly, approaching my two best friends.

"Just having a little best friend-to-best friend chat with Jason," Carter replies, not taking his narrowed eyes off of Jason.

"Dude," Jason starts. "Get that fork away from my face!"

I walk over to the both of them and grab Carter's forked wrist. "What's going on?" I repeat, pulling the fork out of Kennedy's hand.

"Jason was looking at Rey like she's edible," Carter grumbles. I look from him to Jason.

"Just looking, man. Couldn't help it. Your sister is pretty!" Carter starts struggling away from my grip and charging towards Jason.

"You take that back!" he screams as I hold him tighter.

"Wow, double standards if I've ever seen them..." I mutter under my breath. They both still then turn to look at me.

"What do you mean?" Jason asks, cocking his head to the side.

"Well, for starters, this." I exhale, pointing at Carter. "Is exactly how you react when anyone even looks in Jenny's direction."

"So?" Jason grumbles.

"So try to understand where Carter is coming from," I continue.

"And you!" I point at my other traitorous best friend. "Trying to blind Jason just because he looked at Reagan while you went behind his back and kissed my kitten," I spit out, remembering the rage I felt when I witnessed that event.

"You did what?" Jason screeches. And suddenly I find myself dropping Carter and pushing Jason away and back against the wall.

"What are you guys doing? Is it some sort of boy on boy action? I could be into that." I hear a female voice from behind me. When I turn my head, Reagan is playfully looking at the three of us.

"Jason just found out that I kissed grasshopper this one time I wanted Aiden to realize he's in love with her," Carter stage-whispers.

"Ooooh," Reagan replies in an equally staged whisper. "Somebody call Kerry Washington cause we've got ourselves a scandal!" I blink a couple of times at her, then burst into laughter.

"Did you see that?" Jason mumbles at me, relaxing. I nod, not sure what he's referring to. I saw Carter Kennedy's little clone. "She's just...awesome," he says, and I laugh, realising that Jason might just have a little crush on the female version of Carter.

"Oh please. Like I need your approval." Reagan scoffs, rolling her eyes and flipping him the bird. He swoons. He literally swoons in my arms, unused to anyone rejecting him. Ever.

"Anywaaaaay." I let go of Jason. "Your mum says Thanksgiving dinner is ready," I say and start shuffling everyone into the general direction of where the delicious food aromas are coming from.

As we near the grand dining room, a middle-aged man comes out from around the corner and stops next to us, smiling. He's wearing a waistcoat, a dark velvet smoking jacket, and painfully red corduroy trousers with peacocks embroidered on them. He's got a pair of thickly framed glasses on, and an unlit pipe in his mouth, his thick, salt and pepper hair combed to the side. On his feet are bunny slippers...

"Daddy." Reagan smiles and hugs his side. "These are Carter's friends from college." She points in our direction.

"Nice to meet you all," he says in a deep voice and smiles, then looks into the distance, sniffing. "The food doesn't smell too bad this year. I wonder if it's edible this time..." he muses. "Have you seen Bertie?"

We shake our heads and follow him to where dinner is being served. A thin, elderly woman sits in one of the chairs; her hands folded in her lap pristinely; her old, wrinkled face hidden behind large, seventies style glasses. And I swear I see a smirk on her face before she notices us walk in.

"Bertie!" Mr. Kennedy booms, and the poor, old woman jumps in her seat a little, as if startled.

"That's our Great Aunt Berta," Carter says. "Jason, you go sit next to her. She likes them pretty boys." Jason rolls his eyes but starts walking towards the elderly woman. At his approach, her smirk turns into a larger one, and her hands move a tiny bit like she's rubbing them together. She's probably cold, like most elderly people. I look around for a blanket to hand to her.

"Aiden!" Jenny runs into the dining room, skidding to a stop. "Oh, hello." She blushes and curtsies to Mr. Kennedy. She fucking curtsies, and I have to hold on to the chair I'm standing next to to stop myself from running to her and scooping her into my arms and devouring her blushing face right then and there.

"I already paid them," Great Aunt Berta says, looking towards Jenny. "Why? Did the bookie say I still owe him?"

"Bertie can't hear well," Mr. Kennedy explains. Everyone nods in understanding, but my eyes, which are still on Bertie, notice the smirk on her face grow into a half smile. "She probably misunderstood you. What's the matter, darling?"

"Mrs. Kennedy has asked if Aiden could help in the

kitchen, it seems..." She looks down at her hands. "It seems that the bird is missing."

"Who is pissing?" Bertie says loudly. "Is it Carter? That boy really needs to be potty trained." We stand in stunned silence for a few seconds before Jenny bursts out laughing, and everyone follows suit. Bertie, once again, has a satisfied look on her face, like she knows exactly what she just "misunderstood."

"Missing!" Carter screams at Great Aunt Berta. "The bird is M-I-S-S-I-N-G!"

"You're kissing poultry?" Aunt Berta exclaims, then settles down. "Well...to each their own."

"What bird?" Mr. Kennedy says, wiping away the tears from under his glasses.

"The turkey! It's gone." Jenny says somberly, then grabs my hand and pulls me towards the kitchen.

"Aiden, thank God!" Mrs. Kennedy exclaims upon our entrance. "Where did I put the turkey? I swear I took it out of the oven!"

"What's going on, darling?" Mr. Kennedy walks into the kitchen, slipping on something on the floor and nearly losing his balance.

"Wilson," Mrs. Kennedy says, trying to hold it together. "I tried. I really did." Her eyes are brimming with tears. "I don't know how one could lose a giant turkey, but I did." The corners of her mouth turn down, and her bottom lip starts to tremble. In a few short strides, Mr. Kennedy is by her side, embracing her.

"It's all right," he soothes.

"It was there." She sniffles, pointing at the empty casserole dish on the counter. Something glistening catches my eye. I walk over to the countertop and notice the slithering trail of oily droplets. I follow it to the spot where, a few seconds ago, Mr. Kennedy slipped. Then to the corner of the kitchen, right where the pantry door is. I gently push it inward onto shelves full of jars...and Jake.

Jake is happily sleeping next to a half-eaten turkey carcass. Shit.

"What's in there?" Jenny says and slips under my arm to stand next to me. She gasps and covers her mouth with her hand. "Mrs. Kennedy... That ham you said you made 'just in case'? Let's just serve that, okay?" she says, her hands trembling.

"What? Why?" Mrs. Kennedy blinks at us and takes a step away from Mr. Kennedy's arms and towards Jenny and me and the pristine example of gluttony that is my dog. Jenny's whole body screams 'NO', so I intervene.

"Before you have a look, we found the bird, or what's left of it. You see, Jake—" Mrs. Kennedy pushes past me with the strength of ten women and barges into the pantry. I get myself ready for screams and Jake being thrown out of the house for misbehaving. Instead, I hear cooing.

"Oh, you poor baby, did you eat too much? Is your tummy hurting now?" I turn, astounded, only to see Mrs. Kennedy on all fours rubbing Jake's belly in circular motion as he whimpers.

Jenny and I look at each other, trying to hold back the laughter.

"I'll take the ham through to the dining room then," Jenny says and motions for me to follow. We quickly transport all the food to the table, Mr. and Mrs. Kennedy joining us along the way.

When we all finally sit down and start eating, I'm exhausted. But, fortunately, I'm sitting right next to Jenny. Not so fortunately, Jason is sitting opposite us. I peer sideways at kitten and grab her hand under the table, squeezing it. "Thanks for helping out with the dinner," I say quietly. She squeezes my hand back and smiles at me, her body tilted towards mine, inviting. I take the cue and lean over, placing a kiss on her cheek. My lips tingled as I pull away.

A fork drops, cluttering loudly on the plate, and both Jenny and I jump in our seats. I turn to look at Jason and am greeted with his shocked and terrified face. I open my mouth to say something, to try and explain why my lips were fused to his sister's cheek just a second ago, but he beats me to it and starts speaking first.

"Reagan," he says very loudly, but with an eerie calmness to his voice. A cold sweat starts to gather at the nape of my neck, and I feel Jenny's hand squeeze mine tighter. "Please tell me that this hand is yours." I'm confused. I look at Jenny, who shrugs at me and turns back to Jason.

We all look at Reagan, who's sitting on Jason's right side. Her right hand is holding a fork, frozen midair on the way to her mouth. Her left hand is resting on the table. We all turn to Aunt Bertie on Jason's left. She's oddly leaning towards Jason, both her hands hidden under the tablecloth and a satisfied grin on her face.

"Not again, Bertie!" Mr. Kennedy exclaims just as Jason shrieks loudly.

Chapter 22

Cop A Feel

Is it sexy in here or is it just me?
- Jason

Thanksgiving dinner was an entertaining affair. No small thanks to Great Aunt Bertie, who not only managed to cop a feel under the table but also, at one point, took her false teeth out and asked an already traumatized Jason to chew her food and feed it back to her like a mama bird would to a baby.

I swear that old lady has caused a lifetime of damage to my poor brother, damage that only expensive therapy will be able to fix.

I giggle, remembering the events and how wonderfully they unfolded throughout the evening. How, in the first instance, I thought the dropped fork was because Jason saw Aiden getting close to me. But, fortunately for me, it was just Aunt Bertie taking advantage of him.

I smile, thinking how Aiden and I burst out laughing, how Aiden's hand grazed my thigh while he held my hand, how I shivered when he leaned over to whisper in my ear, how his breath tickled my neck. My room's temperature is going up just thinking about the green-eyed devil that has been occupying my thoughts for the better part of the past few months in both the 'frenemy' and the 'super hot I-wanna-jump-your-bones' capacity...

I yawn. This is what my whole night has been like, not a freaking wink, just getting hot and bothered over a guy that isn't even in the same room. At about six in the morning, I give up on sleep and just take a shower, hoping that the warm water will lull me back to sleep. No dice.

I get up from my bed, where I have been daydreaming about Aiden all morning, and snatch my phone, scrolling through the photos of last night's events. I quickly choose the one where Aunt Bertie is licking Jason's arm and send it to Hayley with a note that I miss her.

I sigh and pull on a large, knitted cardigan over my tank top. I put my messy hair up in a high ponytail and decide to go explore the wonders of the Kennedy's gardens. There are some distressing topiaries up front, and I'm just itching to find out what's hiding in their well manicured back garden. The possibilities are endless.

The house is eerily quiet. It's fairly early, and it seems like everyone else is still asleep.

I slip out through the glass door and look at the exquisite landscape, breathtaking. Have you ever read that book, The Secret Garden? Well, what's in front of my eyes is exactly what I always imagined the elegant and vibrant garden would look like. It's mesmerising. I pull out my phone and stick my headphones in. There's only one song worthy of listening to when one is subjected to such beauty. I press play on Springsteen's Secret Garden.

Walking down the steps, I listen to the music and take in the abundance of vivid colors, the flowers, the weeping willow on the side surrounded by a sea of delicate white petals. I don't know the names of the plants that pepper the garden in white, orange, violet, and blue. I didn't even realize plants could bloom this late in fall. But suddenly, I'm overwhelmed with the want—no—need to learn more, to find out the names of the delicate and beautiful things that surround me.

I walk down the stone pathway, deeper into what I can only call a wonderland, overcome with emotions thanks to the crooning voice and teary music of Bruce. During the next half an hour, I walk around the garden in awe, listening to the same song on repeat and smelling different flowers, touching the delicate petals and the hard bark of the trees. I go back to the weeping willow I saw when I first stepped into the garden and lie down in the sea of white flowers.

I close my eyes and inhale the sweet scent. A touch of it reminds me of Aiden's smell; the earthy, citrusy fragrance of his body. I've recently discovered that Jake's fur, the spot just behind his ear where Aiden scratches him, smells a little bit like Aiden himself, and now, every opportunity I get, I bury my nose in that crook near Jake's face. He doesn't complain, and it's better than going around sniffing Aiden. If I did that, they'd commit me for sure.

Something wet drops on my cheek, and I reluctantly open my eyes to discover the brown face smiling at me with his canine smile.

"Hey trouble," I say, pulling my headphones out and giving him a hug. Jake licks my ear, making me laugh.

"Hey yourself." I hear a very sexy voice, one that has a British accent, and an even sexier owner. I sit up and smile.

"I see your stalking ways haven't changed?" I grin.

"What? No... What are you on about?" Aiden replies, rubbing the back of his neck. His face goes a bit red and his eyes dart to the patch of blue flowers to his left. Interesting.

"I'm joking." Half true. He's clearly hiding something, and if we're being honest, the first two weeks after I got to Starwood, the boy was stalking the crap out of me!

"Haha, yeah... Me too." He nods, then plops next to me. His proximity makes the air shift around us, and I seriously make a mental note to go see a doctor about these hot flashes. Could I have early onset menopause?

"So..." I say, swinging my feet from side to side until they touch in the middle, making a tapping sound. Jake looks in their direction, then crawls over and starts licking my shoe laces.

"Jake needed to pee," Aiden explains. Wow.

"I figured." I try to contain my laughter. Is Aiden Vaughn, the hottest guy on campus, nervous? It can't be. "I was thinking about yesterday evening," I start again, my eyes drawn to his large hands. My fingertips move on the ground towards his, drawn by a magnetic force that seems to be between us.

"Yeah..." Aiden nods solemnly. "I thought he was totally going to scream at me, you know, when I kissed your cheek." He looks away, back onto the patch of those damned blue flowers. How can they be so blue, anyway? And what the hell does he mean, anyway? Is he back to being uncertain about what he wants from me?

"Well, he was being assaulted by Aunt Bertie." I huff, blowing a stray strand off my face. I have the urge to cross my arms and stomp my feet, but decide against it. Partly because that's immature, and partly because Jake is happily chomping on my shoelaces and I don't want to disturb him. "Plus, I can make my own decisions. Jason needs to deal with it."

"I know, kitten. That's not what I meant." He takes my hand, the one that has been steadily inching towards him, and strokes the inside of it, his rough fingers making a pattern I can feel right down to my core. I fight the urge to moan. "It just took me by surprise, that's all." He smiles at me. The only reason I know this is because he puts his free hand on my chin and turns my head to face him. I scowl at him full force, and his lip twitches into a half grin, his dimples popping out. I force my head away from his grasp and turn it away from him, unable to hold in the smile. Bastard knows tricks.

"Unbelievable," he mutters under his breath.

"What?" I scoff, still not looking.

"You see the patch of those blue flowers?" He points at the incredibly deep blue flowers his eyes keep stopping on. I nod. "Your eyes," he starts. "Your eyes change colour depending on your mood. Sometimes they're like the sky on a sunny day, and sometimes, when I say something that makes you blush...they're exactly that color," he says, forcing me to look at him. "Just like right now. Incredible."

I start moving my feet again, blushing furiously and boring my eyes into my converse that are being licked clean by the fur ball at my feet.

"Did you notice the family name thing or is it just me?" Aiden swiftly changes the subject, cocking his head to the side as I turn back to look at him.

"Uh-oh. You mean how they're all named after presidents? Carter, Reagan, Wilson and even Aunt Berta!" I exclaim.

"Aunt Berta, really? After whom?"

"Hoover." I nod knowingly. To be honest, I don't know shit, but Herbert is the closest thing to Berta I've got, so I'm just gonna go with it and see if the Englishman bites.

"Herbie? Really... I guess that could work."

"I wonder what his mom's name is," I muse.

"Tyler, George?" he suggests.

"Bush?" I say the first thing that pops into my head. I blame the gardeny surroundings and the George in Aiden's suggestion.

"If Bush is her first name, her parents must have really hated her..." He chuckles.

"What about Rutherford or Fillmore?" I ask, looking at my nails, feigning disinterest.

"Oh well, if we're going in that direction how about Ulysses?" Aiden raises his left eyebrow at me. He must go to the same place Carter does, cause I'm telling you, his eyebrows are equally perfect.

"Nah, that will be the name of Carter's first born. Fact," I reply smugly. "I guess we'll just have to live without the knowledge of what his mother's name is."

"Or we could ask him?"

"As if! You know Kennedy, he'll never tell!" I laugh as Aiden tickles my side. I love how close we've gotten over the past week. His phone chimes and Aiden's face falls, his lips forming a thin line.

"What's wrong?" I ask, folding my legs under me and facing Aiden properly, making Jake yelp, displeased at taking away his chew toy, aka my shoelaces. Aiden's fists are tight and his knuckles are white.

"It's nothing, kitten," he says, but his eyes tell me a

different story. Jake walks over to him, but Aiden doesn't respond. I swear the dog looks at me judgingly, like he's trying to say 'do something' before he turns away, walking into the shade and settling down for a nap.

"Is it your dad?" I ask on a hunch, hoping that if I'm right, he'll open up. "You know you can talk to me," I say, putting my hand on his forearm. "Aide," I coax softly.

His head turns to me, and his eyes land on my lips. Everything in my power. That's what it takes to prevent the loud sucking in of my breath when his dark, forest green eyes meet mine.

"Yes," he says, and, thankfully, looks down at my hand on his arm. I start pulling it away self-consciously, but he puts his hand over mine, preventing it from moving.

"Is it about Christmas?" I ask, remembering the snippets of the conversation he had with his father over the phone when we were in the diner.

"You are an inquisitive little minx, aren't you?" he asks playfully, focusing his eyes back on mine. His lips twitch into a little smirk, and I shrug, pretending that he doesn't affect me. "It's not about Christmas, kitten," he exhales loudly, looking up at the sky then back at me. "I'm still undeclared."

His eyes bore into mine, gauging my response, but I'm confused. "Undeclared, as in your major? But how?" Starwood is an Ivy League School and I just don't see how this would be possible in a second year of study.

"Let's just say that I'm studying Economics and Psychology and Law and Social Studies. My advisor keeps telling me that the workload is too much, and my dad is pressuring me to choose one major. Economics, but—"

"But you want to help people," I finish for him, understanding the turmoil he must be going through. "So your father is pushing you towards Economics?"

Aiden nods. "Or anything else business oriented, anything that will help me become the next CEO of his company and rule the Vaughn empire once he retires."

"That's a lot of pressure. Especially if you don't want to follow in his footsteps…"

"Which I don't."

"What if," I start, an idea forming in my head.

"What?" He looks up, hopeful.

"You said you're taking classes in Economics, Psychology, Social Sciences, and Law, right?" He nods. "What if you declared your major as Law? That would be something that your father would deem approvable, no?"

"Yes, but I don't want to work for my father."

"I know, so you declare your major in Law, you go at it full time, your father gets off your case, and once you're done, you become a human rights lawyer! You still help people!" I exclaim, elated by my brilliance.

"That's doable." Aiden taps his finger to his chin, and I kid you not, if it wasn't for the fact that he's wearing clothes—a fact that displeases me—he'd be a spitting image of the statue of The Thinker. Just more muscular, and hotter, waaaay hotter. "I'd have to take more classes, but if I unload Economics, I'd have more time," he muses as I drink in his body. The t-shirt he's wearing is tight, just enough to pinch his torso in a way that shows off his defined muscles. I lick my lips, certain that I'm drooling. "And it would give me time to convince my father that me running his company is the last thing he wants. How did I not think about this before?" He looks up at me. "Kitten, you're brilliant!" he exclaims and launches himself at me, pulling me into his lap and enveloping me in a hug.

I suppose if he wasn't wearing that tight t-shirt and if I hadn't been drooling over him non-stop for the past twenty-four hours, I wouldn't have done what I did...I suppose.

As things are, just as Aiden's arms wrap around me, I move my head up and lift my face to his, ending up face to face with him, my legs wrapped around his middle and my hands fisting his tight t-shirt. My breathing is ragged and I know, God, I know there's no escape from this, from him, from us. Not now and not anytime soon. I silently pray that he has made up his mind about us and lift my face to his, fusing our lips together in what, from this day forth, will be known as the most epic kiss I have ever received.

Aiden reacts instantly, groaning into my lips, making them tingle. His hands move from around me; one twisting into my hair, messing up my ponytail, the other moving down my side, over my ribcage, and towards my hip as he lays me down on the grass. I moan and snake my tongue around his lower lip, nipping at it when he presses into me with approval. Hot flashes run up and down my body, and my chest moves with a speed I didn't know was possible. I run my hands over his hard chest, wishing the stupid material of his t-shirt away, whimpering. Whimpering! I didn't even know I could make sounds like this, but this boy and his tongue have magical powers. He moves his supernatural tongue slowly in and out of my mouth, teasing, drawing out the kiss, making me whimper more and arch my back, pressing myself into him.

He moans, and the sound reverberates from my mouth all the way down to the tips of my toes, like a delicious echo. I pull his t-shirt up and my hands finally connect with his hard, smooth chest, making me sigh with relief. Then he pulls away, and I'm about to protest when he slowly starts teasing my lips with his tongue, driving me crazy with the anticipation of the tingling sensation his lips cause when they connect with mine.

I tighten the grip my legs have on him, pulling him closer to me, my fingers digging into his back as he rocks against me with a loud groan in response. His lips descend on my neck, kissing and teasing and nipping and licking all the way to my cleavage, where he starts sucking like a hungry caveman. My treacherous body arches into him again, eager for more, wanting the full on connection I have only read about in trashy romance novels. I whimper his name, rocking against him, chasing the feeling that's just within my reach. His hand climbs back up and pulls at my collar, exposing my breast. With a satisfied moan, his mouth closes on my nipple and, as he sucks, I see stars. A pleasure builds in me as my body grinds into him, rubbing against his hard cock through my flimsy yoga pants. Faster and faster, moaning his name as he grips my ass and pushes against me with fervor. I come unexpectedly, shuddering, with his name on my lips. My body trembles as ecstasy courses through my body. I can't believe I just had my first orgasm. With Aiden, no less. And it was exquisite, earth shattering, and—God, forgive me—I want to feel this again and again. I pull his head back to my lips and kiss him feverishly, sneaking my hand down to his jeans, reaching for his zipper. I want to touch him, hold him, make him feel as good as he just made me feel.

"Kitten, wait," he says hoarsely. His eyes are pure onyx as he hungrily rakes them over my body. "Jason," he mutters, looking back towards the house.

What the hell? I literally want to punch him, like I did six years ago. Punch him, then straddle him, pin him to the ground, rip his shirt off, and lick him.

I need serious help...

For Crying Out Loud

"Oh, for crying out loud, Aiden!" I shove him away. Have I not just served myself to him on a silver platter? What is his problem? My brain seems to be winning the war with my hormones, this time. "I honestly can't do this thing anymore." I motion between him and me. "You can't kiss me one minute then suddenly remember that you shouldn't. Make your damn mind up." I grit through my teeth, jumping up to my feet.

My hair is a mess and my cheeks are flushed, and somehow, I manage to convince myself that this is all his fault, even though I was the one who couldn't keep my hands off him. Pissed as hell, I turn around and stomp off. That boy deserves a kick in the nuts.

"Jenny... It's not what—" he starts explaining, but I just stick my headphones in and run faster.

I smirk. His expression when I was shouting at him was priceless. I no longer have any doubts. I AM A GREAT KISSER if the fire in his eyes, his quick breathing, and his moans were any indication.

I walk into the house, bumping into Carter.

"Hey Miyagi," I say.

"Good morning to you too," he grumbles. "Ooh, have you been hopping in the grass?" He plucks a grass strand from my hair.

"Yeah, yeah and all the other pleasantries. Say Carter, what's your mom's first name?" I ask, my inquisitive nature winning over my annoyance with Aiden.

"Why?"

"Just wondering," I reply innocently.

"Bella," he replies, narrowing his eyes.

"Thanks!" I turn around and run to my room, trying not to laugh. I wish I could turn back, run outside, and share that piece of information with Aiden. He'd love to know that it's Bella and not some pompous name. I'd love to see his face when he finds out.

But I will not.

Aiden is like that plant I tried to keep alive in fifth grade and failed. Even though I may have just truly realized that I'm falling for the fucker, Aiden Vaughn is dead to me.

Chapter 23

Nothing But Trouble

If it has tires or testicles, it's gonna give you trouble.
- Jenny

Why the hell did I open my mouth? Why?

Kitten avoided me the rest of the day and flew back to San Francisco the next day instead of driving back down with us, under the pretence of an urgent study meeting. Urgent study meeting my arse.

I could kick myself. All because of my stupid mouth. But was it wrong that I wanted to give my best friend a head's up? To tell him that all I want is to be with his sister and that I will spend a lifetime making sure that she is happy? Because that was the reason behind my stopping her. I can't believe I made her come. Her body was so responsive to my touch. For a minute I felt on top of the world, and then her hand reached for my cock. I nearly died. If I didn't have this innate need to speak to my best friend first, I would have started taking her clothes off right then and there, showing her how many other ways I could pleasure her. And I didn't want to do that.

Well, okay, I did. But as much as I wanted her, as much as that was the best moment of my life, as much as the garden in the back of Kennedy mansion was beautiful, it was also not the right place to strip her naked and devour her. I wanted to do it. God as my witness, I've been wanting to do it since the first day she came back into my life. Just not then and there.

Jenny deserves the whole world, she deserves so much more than some arsehole taking advantage of her in the tall grass at the back of her friend's garden. She deserves to be cherished; she deserves scented candles and foot massages; she deserves someone who would build her a fucking Taj Mahal. And it's clearer now than it has ever been, I want to be that someone to her.

I just need to make sure that she knows that, and that a groping session in the garden, no matter how beautiful the surroundings, is not the way to communicate my feelings for her. I want to do this thing right. I want to do everything right by her.

Stupid. I'm so fucking stupid!

She was so angry and hurt... I can't blame her. I acted like a prick, even if my intentions were good. But Jenny is like fireworks, short fused and spectacular. So she walked away without giving me the time to explain myself after I so cleverly spoke Jason's name in the middle of our kiss. Let's just say I blame that little blunder on the fact that, in that moment, not much blood was left in my brain...

And now, sitting in my room, trying to study for finals, I can't focus on anything else but her legs wrapped around my waist and the way she moved against me, the way she felt under my body, the way she moaned my name as she came, the way her lips felt against mine, how her soft body responded to my touch.

I'm getting hard just thinking about it, and thinking about it is all I can do because kitten is avoiding the hell out of me, making it impossible for me to explain why I stopped her and said Jason's name in the first place.

God, even when he wasn't around, Jason seemed to hold his title of the 'ultimate cockblocker'. Making sure he's in my head every single time I get close to Jenny while he goes around getting lucky left, right, and centre; all he has to do is smile in their direction. He'll have a field day tomorrow at the End of Term party or, as most of the Starwood population calls it, the ET Party. People even dress up. Don't ask.

I try studying again, staring at my Civil Law textbook and reading the same sentence for the fifteenth time. My eyes are watering, so I look away for a minute, yawning and stretching my arms above my head. My last exam is tomorrow. I glance at the clock; it's still early, so no excuses.

Once again, I thank my lucky stars and...well, kitten. Thanks to her, I was able to drop subjects I had no interest in, like Economics and Finance, and focus properly on the exams I had ahead of me. Not to mention the elation both my advisor and my father must have felt upon hearing that I finally chose my major. My father was particularly pleased since I went ahead with his requirement, like the good little son that I was, choosing a major that would tie in nicely with his empire.

I hate myself for needing to please him in any way, but at least he's off my back for now, which gives me time to convince him that I am not the right person for his business.

For the next hour, my mind drifts back and forth between the text in front of me and the memory of Jenny's lips on mine. I keep on trying to figure out how I can get her alone. I need to explain myself and, in order to do that, I need her to stop for a minute and listen to me. Maybe tomorrow, at the party. Or, if worst comes to worst, on the plane to London, the day after the party. She'll have to talk to me then, confined space and all. She'll have nowhere to run.

I sigh and look down at the textbook again, resigning and closing it with a loud thump. There's not much concentration left for me to squeeze out of my brain, so I get up from my desk and position myself on top of the covers on my bed. Closing my eyes, I try to fathom how on earth I got to this point and how it's even possible that the sexiest girl on earth, one that is also amazingly clever, even gave me the time of day? Because she did. She was the one who kissed me in the garden and, for a second, it seemed quite possible that she wanted me—wanted us—as much as I did. Or at least she did before I ruined everything...

I fall asleep with Jenny's face on my mind and the memory of her soft skin on my fingertips.

Friday is a blur of last-minute studying, exam sitting, and coffee—lots of coffee. By the time I'm done I am exhausted, and partying is the last thing on my mind. But Jason assured me that 'anyone who's anyone', including Hayley and Jenny, are going. So I force myself into the shower. I'm packed and ready for our flight tomorrow, so I can just relax and have fun tonight, as soon as I talk to kitten, that is. I don't anticipate much drinking anyway. Flying with a hangover is a bitch, and I'd never put myself through that...again.

By the time we get to the venue, the party is in full swing. I look around, trying to find Jenny, but all I see in the strobe light is a mass of gyrating bodies dressed in metallic, alien-looking costumes. I feel like an alien myself, out of place and not really sure what to do, so I make rounds saying 'hi' to people I barely know but seem to think we know each other well enough for them to slap my back. When I finally spot Kennedy and Jason, they seem to be busy chatting up a group of blondes.

I start walking towards them when, from the corner of my eye, I notice Chloe waving at me. She's standing to the side of the dance floor and is surrounded by what can only be described as her clones. I wave back but keep going towards my friends. That's when I finally see kitten. I stop in my tracks just to drink her in. She's wearing a silver, metallic dress and a glittery headband with a couple of silver ball poppers that bounce with every movement of her head, making her look like a cute character straight out of Roswell High. She is laughing, and as I take a step forward to go and say hello to her, to finally put the silly misunderstanding behind us, I feel a hand wrap around my bicep. I look down at my arm, then up toward Carter's face.

"What?" I mouth at him. The music is so loud that even if I tried shouting, he wouldn't hear me. He shakes his head at me as if saying I should leave Jenny alone. I frown, not sure why he'd stop me. I slowly look back towards kitten, who's leaning against the wall. God, I wish her smile was meant for me. That's when I notice she's not alone. Next to her is some guy I've never seen before. He's leaning into her and smiling. He reaches out with his hand towards her face and takes a strand of her hair, wrapping it around his fingers, playing with it. Jenny doesn't push him away. She rolls her eyes as he leans closer to her mouth. I can't look, but like a trainwreck, I can't look away. I start walking their way, getting ready to beat the crap out of this douche canoe, or at least get him away from her, but Carter stops me. He pulls my arm and whirls me around just as the prick's face connects with Jenny's. I blink once, twice, the image of his mouth closing in on Jenny's on repeat in my head like an annoying gif you can't stop, but let play over and over.

I don't see anything else. All I can see is red with the image repeating itself. All I want to do is punch something. How the hell is this happening to me? Again! Carter pulls me towards the bar and pours two shots of tequila down my throat when we get there. I have two more, for good measure, as soon as the first two stop burning my esophagus. When I have two more, Carter says something to me then turns to walk away, leaving me alone, but I can't hear him over the rush of blood in my head and the loud music.

Maybe that's how it's supposed to be? Me alone, forever. I motion the bartender for another two shots. I'm swaying a little and can't properly focus on much, but that's ok. At least kitten is no longer the main focus; staying upright and getting hammered is. Downing my seventh shot of the night, I nearly fall off the stool I'm sitting on. So maybe I should slow down.

"Are you okay?" I see two Chloe's in front of me and I am suddenly glad I'm not alone. I shake my head to clear it then nod, putting my elbow on the bar for balance. But I miss and slump ungracefully. I clear my throat and reach for the last shot in front of me. Chloe pulls it out of my hand. "Let me take that. You seem like you've had enough," she says, then downs my shot. I frown at her. Who the hell does she think she is? Drinking my only comfort. I motion for the bartender and another two shots appear on the bar in front of us. Chloe rolls her eyes and shakes her head, then takes one of the shots and drinks with me. I'm glad to have a companion, actually. Getting drunk by yourself is overrated. "So tell me what's wrong?" she asks. Again, I frown and try my hardest to focus on her chin.

"She kissssed ssssome guy, or he kisssed her. Whooo the ffffuck knowssss," I slur, slumping in my chair and leaning on Chloe.

"Hon, do you mean Jenny?" She asks. I nod drunkenly into her armpit. She doesn't smell of sweat, unlike most of the people around us, which is a welcomed change. "Are you sure? I mean, you two seemed pretty hung up on each other." Oh, I'm sure! I nod again. "Shit..." she murmurs, shaking her head. "C'mon. You're pretty drunk, let's go get some fresh air and talk this through."

She grabs me by the waist and hoists me down off the stool and towards the door. I feel drunker than I thought I was, so I'm glad I've got someone to guide me out. I want out of this place and as far away from everyone as possible. Chloe is surprisingly strong, keeping me up while I lean on her. Why does kitten hate her? Chloe is nice, like now, for example. While Jenny is off snogging some bastard, Chloe is the one making sure I'm okay. Jenny... That girl seems to be nothing but trouble.

We get outside and the fresh air hits my face, enticing the tequila to flow around in my veins like they're on some sort of a racetrack. I'm trashed; that's a fact I've decided to accept, so I sit down on the concrete with Chloe standing above me. The whole world is spinning around, and I suddenly have the urge to lie down and close my eyes.

So I do just that.

When I wake up, it's morning and I'm in a room I don't

recognise. My head is pounding, the room spinning. I groan and put my hand to my forehead, pulling the duvet off my chest. My whole body is burning up and I feel like a frog died in my mouth. I sit up slowly, noticing I'm not wearing anything. What the hell?

Chapter 24

Pretty Hung Up On Someone Else

When life gives you melons, you might be dyslexic
- Carter

I see him as soon as he walks in, my eyes are drawn to him like a moth to a flame. He doesn't notice me, so it just gives me the opportunity to observe him as he makes rounds. He looks so handsome my chest aches. He's wearing a black t-shirt that is tight in all the right places, letting my imagination run wild, back to the time when my hands ran over his hard chest. Back to the time when, like a dream come true, we kissed in the garden under a willow tree.

It's just great, isn't it? The first guy I fall for ends up being a spineless piece of British poop... Can't stand up for himself in front of my stupid brother; the same stupid brother who, just a second ago, was busy getting his face sucked by some blonde. Why is he allowed face sucking time and I am not? Why?

I place my hand above my heart, taking a breath and following Aiden's movements. The club is full of students, the loud music pumping to the rhythm of my broken heart. And every time I see him smile at someone else, my chest squeezes as the feeling of rejection stabs my soul.

"What do you say, Jenny? Want to get that drink?" I move my eyes towards Derek, or Dylan, or David with the posh accent. I'm not sure what his name is. I wasn't really listening to him all the time he droned on about his fraternity. He's close to me, too close, but I welcome the distraction from the useless Brit who has been constantly on my mind ever since that kiss. My eyes dart back around the club at the thought of Aiden, but I lost him in the crowd of sweaty bodies. I look back up at Derek, Dylan, or David and try to smile. It comes out a little forced, but he doesn't seem to notice.

"A drink would be nice, but I don't want to lead you on..." I start slowly. His head cocks to the side and he flashes me a smile. He's handsome, I'll give him that. Tall and slim but muscular, and he's got those high cheekbones some people pay good money for. And a boyish charm about him that you so often see in designer advertisements in magazines. He could easily be a model. His eyes look me up and down mischievously.

"And why would you be leading me on?" he asks.

"I'm pretty hung up on someone else," I say resignedly. Derek, Dylan, or David glances around the club, searching. "Even if he doesn't want me," I add, mumbling.

"Is he here?" he asks. I nod, forcing my gaze not to wander around the club again in search of the boy who's determined to make my life a living hell. "Well, he's pretty dumb, in my opinion."

I arch my eyebrow, smiling. I agree, Aiden is pretty dumb. "And why is that?"

"To reject a gorgeous girl like you, he must be pretty stupid!" I laugh.

"Right," I say, blushing a little and silently thanking whoever manages this place for their choice in crappy lighting.

"In fact," he says, taking a strand of my hair into his hand and slowly twirling it around his fingers, "I think he must be a class-A idiot to let a girl like you pass him by." I laugh, throwing my head back and just letting his words sink in. It's nice having his full attention on me, and the feeling of being desired tickles my lower belly. At least with this guy I know where I stand. I know he likes what he sees, and the knowledge makes me brave.

"You know what?" I smile at him playfully. "I absolutely agree with you! I'm a catch!"

He grins at me. I notice he doesn't have dimples, and for some reason my heart sinks a little, but I don't let that interrupt our little moment too much.

He leans down towards me and whispers conspicuously. "You definitely are. You're so gorgeous, you know?"

I don't move, spellbound by his words as his face keeps leaning closer to mine, his eyes on my mouth, and the corner of his lips twitch into a little smile. I can feel his breath brush against my cheeks. It smells of whiskey. For a moment, I consider what it would be like to kiss him. I close my eyes and try to envision his lips touching mine, but all I can see is Aiden's dimpled smile and his emerald eyes looking into mine with something so deep behind them that I almost whimper, forgetting that it's just my imagination. When Derek's, Dylan's, or David's lips connect with the corner of mine, I'm not surprised. To hell with it, I think. To hell with Aiden!

But my body seems to think differently and, as my hands press against Derek's, Dylan's, or David's chest, I feel myself push him away. He's not him, and that's enough for me to shut him down.

"Sorry," he says, still smiling. "I just couldn't help myself."

I smile back at him and shake my head. "It's fine," I mumble. I spot Hayley from the corner of my eye. Her hands are on her hips and she's looking at me like I've done something wrong. "I've got to go," I say, pushing myself away from the wall and leaving Derek, Dylan, or David behind. His mouth forms a small 'o' and his brow furrows in confusion. I don't care. I really, really don't care. What has Aiden done to me?

"What?" I ask my best friend, standing in front of her and crossing my arms defensively.

"I didn't say anything..."

"You look like you want to, though." I huff.

"Not my business, hon," she says. But after seeing my expression, she exhales. "Fine. It's just, it sure looked like you were kissing a total stranger."

"I wasn't!" I all but shout. "I pushed him away. I wouldn't... I-I couldn't... He's not him." My arms drop and I can feel the corners of my lips turn down. Hayley's face softens, and she puts her arm around me.

"It looked like you were kissing that guy. And the him you're speaking of? He saw it all go down..." Shit.

No! Hold on. Why would he care anyway? It's not like he wants anything from me, does he? A twinge of hope tugs at my heart, but I try really hard to ignore it.

"He looked," Hayley continues, "fairly devastated. Carter had to drag him off to the bar."

"Oh?" I look up, searching for Aiden's broad shoulders and messy brown hair in the crowd gathered around the bar. I find him easily. First thing my eyes focus on, actually. It's like he stands out from everyone else around him. I smile a small smile and take a step forward in his direction. He has this magnetic pull on me that my body can't resist, no matter how much my brain screams at it.

I see Aiden down a shot and slam the empty shot glass on the bar, smiling a drunken, lopsided smile at someone to his left. My gaze momentarily darts to the person next to him, and my heart stops in my chest.

Chloe.

It's okay, she's kind of a friend now, isn't she? I try to breathe evenly. I can feel Hayley's hand wrap around my arm.

"You okay?" she says. I can barely hear her over the music. I nod my head in Aiden's direction, and her hand squeezes my arm harder. "Shit." I hear her muffled voice.

My gaze is trained on the twosome at the bar as they take another shot. Chloe's gaze darts around the club and stops on me. She winks in my direction then says something to Aiden, putting her arm around him and helping him up off the stool. He seems drunk, more drunk than I've ever seen him before.

My blood turns to ice when she leads him towards the exit. He's leaning heavily on her shoulder, as if he's finding it hard to walk. The room begins to spin as soon as their backs disappear behind the double doors to the outside. I can feel cold sweat gather beneath my hairline at the back of my neck as I stare, dumbfounded, at the closed door.

"Jenny." Hayley whirls me around to face her. "I'm sure

it's fine," she says. The loud music and the screaming people around us drowns her voice out. The room is still spinning, so I shake my head from left to right in an attempt to make it stop.

"Hello little sister, and little sister from another mister!" Jason swoops in, shouting at us above the music, grinning. I try to smile, but I'm sure my smile resembles a weird lip twitch. My eyes land on the double doors again, and I find myself unable to look away. "What's wrong with her?" I hear Jason's voice to my side. I shrug, not sure who he's talking about. Hayley's hand grips my arm so hard I'm sure she's drawing blood, and, if not, I'm certainly going to find bruises in the morning.

"Hey," Jason says softly, standing in front of me, his face blocking the view I had of the door. "Want me to take you home?" I must have nodded because I'm being gently guided by Hayley and Jason towards the exit and the double doors my eyes are fixated on. My heart speeds up. Will they be outside?

The question is answered as soon as the cool air hits me. There's a long line of club goers waiting for their turn to be let in, a few couples hugging and groping each other, but no Aiden and definitely no Chloe.

Jason pulls me into Aiden's Jeep and buckles me up. I lean my head into the headrest and close my eyes, inhaling the surrounding air that smells just like the guy I want so badly. The guy I want to want me back.

"I'm the designated driver tonight," Jason explains after Hayley questions him about drinking. She huffs and gets into the back of the Jeep.

I'm not sure how long we're driving for. My eyes are closed and my fingers trace the plastic of the console, tracing the pattern Aiden's fingers must have made. At some point, we drop Hayley off at the dorm. She gives me a hug and kiss on the cheek, instructing me to keep in touch over the Christmas break. I just nod and try to smile at her. I completely forgot we're flying to London tomorrow.

When we get home, Jason guides me into my room and sits me down on my bed, placing himself next to me and wrapping his arm around me, pulling me into his chest.

"Want to talk?" he asks.

I don't say anything. Frankly, I'm trying to gather my thoughts. I don't understand why my reactions are so intense. I mean, they only left together. That doesn't mean anything, does it? Why am I acting like it's the end of the world and the whole of the human race has been wiped?

"I don't know..." I breathe.

"C'mon, JJ," he says, using my old nickname. "You know you can tell me anything." I hide my face in his t-shirt.

"I think..." I mumble into his chest. He pulls my face away from his chest so that he can hear me properly. I close my eyes and let out a long breath, saying what I've been trying to avoid admitting to myself for the past two months. "I'm in love with Aiden."

Jason is quiet. To his credit, his breathing is steady and he doesn't blow up at me. Instead, he squeezes me harder.

"Yeah," he says slowly. "I thought that might be the case." I nod, feeling a bit better at having spoken my feelings out loud. "I guess I can live with my best friend...and my little sister. Nope! Ewwww!" I smile a small smile and swat at him. "There she is!" he exclaims, tickling my side. "I thought I lost you there for a minute in that brooding pile of frizzy hair!" He ruffles my hair as I push him away. "So, what's the problem? Why are you so upset?" he asks seriously, once he had enough of messing with me.

"I don't know, I just... Eurgh! I guess I thought he liked

me back; like, really liked me back. But all signs point to no." I huff.

"What signs?" Jason enquires.

"Well," I start telling him about how Aiden broke our make-out session the other day but decide it's probably best not to mention that to my brother. "He got drunk tonight and left with this girl..." I decide the most recent development is probably the best one to talk about.

"They could be just friends," Jason starts. "Aiden doesn't get drunk anyway; he's a golden boy." He winks at me.

"Maybe they are. And I can assure you he was plastered." I frown, remembering who he left with. "Actually, he left with your ex."

"Oh?" Jase seems surprised.

"Chloe Price?"

Jason's jaw tightens, and his whole frame stiffens. He seems agitated. This is weird since he's the most laid back and easy-going person I know.

"Are you sure?" he asks through his teeth. I nod, and he lets out a breath, closing his eyes and clenching his fist. "Right."

I touch his shoulder, not quite sure what to do. "I'm sure it's fine..." I say.

"Oh, it will be," he replies, a muscle in his jaw twitching. "Don't worry, squirt. I'll take care of this."

Chapter 25

I Trusted You

Nothing sucks more than that moment during an argument when you realise you're wrong.
- Aiden

My head is pounding, and the room is spinning; a room I don't recognise. The early morning light seeps in through the half closed, pinkish curtains, and I rub my eyes. But that doesn't quite stop the spinning. How much did I drink last night? Must have been a lot, I think, judging by the horrid taste in my mouth. It's like I've eaten roadkill or something equally horrid. I slowly sit up.

Oh right. Tequila.

Why the hell did I drink so much? I meant to talk to kitten and... kitten... She was kissing someone else. The memories from last night come back to me all at once, making my head spin more. I press my hand against my forehead in hopes that the pounding subsides.

I look around again. This is definitely a chick's room,

there's too much pink. I squint, trying to recognise the faces on one of the photos attached to the wall just as a hand snakes around my bare torso and a head pops from under the covers.

I turn my head to the side, then down as a feeling of dread slowly sets in my stomach.

"Hey, sleepy head," Chloe says, each word makes my heart sink lower and lower.

"Uhm, hi," I reply, my voice gravelly. I'm trying hard to remember what happened last night, but the last thing I can remember is Chloe stealing a shot from me. "Sooo..." I start, not sure how to broach the subject. I need to find out what exactly went on.

"Yeah..." She smiles at me timidly, sitting up. She's holding the thin sheet to her chest with one hand, and I realise she's not wearing anything underneath. "So, that was unexpected."

I don't say anything. My brain is working overtime trying to figure out if Chloe and I had sex last night, but for the life of me, I can't remember anything. I reach with my hand to my thigh and almost sigh with relief when I feel the thin material of my boxer shorts beneath my fingers. Although, I could have slipped them on at some point during the night...

"Chloe..." I whisper. She looks up at me, her eyes huge, almost looking comical, kind of like a manga character. I swallow hard. "So, umm. What exactly happened last night?"

Her lower lip trembles. Shit, I have no idea what to do when girls get upset. I'm pretty sure that patting her on the head and saying 'there, there, good girl' is not the best idea. Only because last time I did that I got punched and screamed at. Not my fault my only experience with upset females is with my dogs back in England!

"A-are, are you saying you don't remember?" she says, squeezing the sheet to her chest. Think Aiden, think!

"No, no!" Yes, yes! I have no bloody clue! "It's just... some bits are hazy." Good work! Her lower lip trembles even more. For fuck's sake! Is there anything my mouth can't ruin? "I mean, just little bits, you know? I remember all the big bits!" I waffle on, like a man sentenced to death trying his last bit of luck at an appeal.

"The big bits?" The corner of her mouth lifts in a small smile and her eyes trail down from my face to my crotch. "The big bits were definitely memorable." She winks at me. I have the urge to pass out, but I fight it, because I need to hear this. I need confirmation of what she's just implied.

"Yeah." I nod encouragingly, hoping that it's enough to make her talk. I'm pretty sure I'm white as the sheet she's holding onto. Side effects of the tequila from the night before, no doubt, but also the dread that's running through my veins at the thought of what might have happened in this room.

It's not like kitten and I are a couple, but I still feel like I've cheated on her. My stomach churns at the thought of being with anyone but her. Chloe looks at me through her lashes, pouting her lips at me. She looks like a sleepy duck. The bile rises in my throat. I fight hard to force it back down.

"I had so much fun..." She blinks rapidly at me. Does she have something stuck in her eye? "I never do this, but I'm really glad we did." Do what? We did what?

I think strategically. How can I pry the information out of her? My brain is shutting down slowly in a hungover haze. "You never do this?"

Chloe looks shocked. "Of course not!" she exclaims. "Who do you take me for? I don't just sleep with guys I haven't been going out with!" She seems offended, but frankly, I don't care. I got all the information I needed. My hand is in my hair, pulling at it before I even realise, my eyes stinging, and I want to punch something, but I try to keep a cool exterior.

There's just no way in hell that kitten will ever forgive me. I've ruined all my chances. How the hell am I going to fix this?

It's not like this one is a small one. I can't even say that it was an accident. I mean, you don't just trip and fall with your dick first in someone's vagina, do you?

"I had a really great time," Chloe continues. I don't know what to say, so I just silently stare at a small fleck of fluff on the bed sheet. Chloe touches my arm gently, making me flinch away. I move my head up to look into her eyes. "Did you?"

Did I what? I'm desperately racking my brain trying to figure out what she's asking me about. I fail miserably. All I can process is that I've royally screwed up. I feel sick. "Huh?" Chloe narrows her eyes at me.

"Did you have a good time?" she asks, frowning. The urge to lie crosses my mind. Sparing her feelings might be the decent thing to do, but I'm not a liar and I don't want to play pretend.

"Honestly Chloe? I'm really sorry, but I was too drunk. I don't actually remember us doing anything. I'm really, really sorry. I must sound like such a prick."

Her face falls and her eyes start to water. "But, but...last night you told me...you told me I was special. You told me you'd never met a girl like me. You told me you'd make me forget about Jason..." A tear rolls down her cheek. I can't believe I said those things to her. Was it the alcohol? Did I think she was Jenny? Chloe sniffles. "And... And...you did!" Her lips turn down as another tear follows the first one. "I thought this meant something. I trusted you!" She spits out.

"I'm really sorry. I didn't mean to hurt you," I say quietly, shaking my head, realising that I'm being utterly selfish thinking about how this situation will impact me when there are other people concerned, people who have feelings. I can be such a dick. I lift my arm and touch Chloe's bare shoulder, but she shrugs me off straight away.

"Get out!" she says through her teeth.

"I hope you can forgive me. I know I messed up. I'm really sorry. Can we still be friends?" I say, getting out of the bed and pulling my jeans on. I find my t-shirt and shoes and my right sock; the left is MIA.

"Friends?" she spits out. "Last night you said that you don't want to be just friends! You said you wanted more! I can't believe I bought your crap!" Tears are streaming down her face. I feel like she just slapped me with her words. Shame fills me. I've become the arsehole I always despised. You know the dude, the one who'd say anything to get a girl to sleep with him...

I walk over to Chloe's side of the bed and sit next to her, pulling her to my chest.

"I'm so sorry," I say, hugging her. She's stiff and tries to struggle, but I plough on through with my speech. "I promise you, if I was sober..."

"Then what? You'd never touch me?" she cries, and my heart breaks a little for the insecure girl in my arms.

"Chloe, I'd have never used you like that. I feel like shit about what happened. Not because I'd never touch you. You're amazing and beautiful, and a good friend, and I'm an asshole," I reply.

"I am?" She pulls her teary eyes away from my t-shirt and looks up at me, hope shining in her eyes.

"Of course!" I say, brushing a strand of her hair away from her face. Chloe's hand reaches to my face, and she pulls my face down towards her.

I pull away. "I'm sorry, I can't." She reacts instantly, pushing me away, her fists weakly punching me in the chest. I get off the bed, sighing. "I'm in love with her, Chloe," I say quietly, backing away towards the exit.

"You two deserve each other. You'll regret this, I swear!" she growls as my hand reaches the door knob. I already do, Chloe, I already do. It's still early when I get home. I tiptoe towards my room as quietly as possible. I really need a Nurofen or Tylenol, or a hammer to the head. Either would do.

Jason's door opens when I pass it by.

"You're up early," he says, looking me up and down. "Can I talk to you?" He steps aside, letting me into his room. I want to go get a shower, wash the night away, but I step inside. This will not end well, I just know it. Then again, I need to talk to someone or I'll explode.

"Tough night?" Jason asks, closing the door behind him.

"You could say that," I reply, rubbing my neck. Jason sits down on the chair in the corner of the room, his measuring stare not wavering in the dim light of the morning.

"Look man..." I start.

"What's up with you and Jenny?" he interrupts me, getting straight to the point. I guess there's no avoiding the subject. Plus, didn't I want to talk to him about Jenny, anyway? Yes, yes, I did. Just not straight after I have slept with his ex... Shit.

"I know you said she's off limits..." I say while Jason makes a circling motion with his hand, hurrying me up to get to the point. "I'm in love with her, so fucking in love." I sigh, hanging my head. "I've been in love with her since we were fourteen. I'm sorry, man... " Jason is silent for a long while. I lift my head up slowly, wincing, expecting him to shove me and tell me to get over it.

"Well, well, well..." he says from his chair in his best villain voice, stroking the imaginary cat in his lap. "Not sure what to say to that. Apart from that, it's obvious." He wiggles his eyebrows at me.

"And you're fine with that?" I say tentatively.

"As fine as one can be when their best friend has dirty thoughts about said person's little sister. But I can live with it as long as your intentions are honorable and you'll treat her right."

"Of course!" I almost smile, but then I remember what I did last night.

"If you don't... Let's just say you'll never be able to have children, or sex. Anything to do with your nether region," he motions towards my crotch, still stroking the bloody cat, "will be out of action after I'm done with you. Want to know why?"

"Not really," I reply, sure whatever he has planned will not be pleasant.

"Fine." He huffs, like I've just spoiled the best part of the story. "Let's get to the good stuff then. A little birdy told me that you left the club with Chloe last night." It's not a question, so I don't reply. "Want to elaborate on that story?"

Let's just take a minute to consider my options.

If I lie to him my 'nether region' is sure to pay for it. If I tell him straight away, there's a chance he might let it slide— Aaah who am I kidding? Third option anyone? Bueller? Bueller? Bueller?

I take a large breath in and decide to just tell him the

truth. It takes me about half an hour to spit it all out and, when I'm done, Jason is no longer sitting in his chair with his imaginary evil cat. He hasn't said a thing throughout my whole story. Somehow, the combination of the two things seems ominous.

Rightfully so, since not even thirty seconds after I think this, I get punched in the face.

Deja vu?

Chapter 26

Mr Perfect

I am currently unsupervised. It freaks me out, too, but the possibilities are endless.
- Jason

Sully is filled with presents for Dad to the point that I needed to flat out jump on it to close the monstrous thing. There are Twinkies and those disgusting 'Pancakes & Sausage on a Stick' things Dad is so fond of, amongst other 'American' things. Not that I'm trying to send him subliminal messages, like 'come back to America'. 'Let's stay here forever'. Noo, not at all.

When I'm done zipping up the blue monster, there's still some time left before we need to leave for the airport. Carter should be coming soon to pick up Jake, so I decide to go play with the brown fur ball before I'm separated from him for the next two and a half weeks.

Strolling down the corridor and dragging Sully behind me, I stumble into a full stop in front of Aiden's open bedroom door. Graceful it is not, but hey, I'm lugging at least two hundred pounds worth of crap in my suitcases. Okay, that might be a slight exaggeration, but you get my point. The thing is heavy!

Aiden is sitting on his bed, his suitcase by his leg and Jake sitting next to it, looking up at Mr. Perfect. And Mr. Perfect is exactly what Aiden should be called when he's sitting in nothing but his jeans, his hair wet and dripping droplets down his magical torso. Magical, because it's got me hypnotised. No joke. My eyes are glued to it and all I can think about is going over and touching it, maybe giving it a little lick. I have to dig my fingers into his door jamb to stop myself from looking like a fool in front of him and following through with what my brain is making me want to do. Naughty things. It makes me want to do naughty things.

Aiden is looking down at Jake and sighs, sticking his perfect hand attached to his perfectly muscled arm into his perfect hair. Ugh! I hate perfect! Not really, but I honestly wish this boy had a fault. Nothing major. Just a long nose, a missing finger, or a cross eye would do. Anything to make us, mere mortals, feel normal in his presence rather than get the distinctive feeling I currently have: that next to him I must look like a Blobfish. Google it.

"Stop judging me!" His voice startles me, and I jump in my stance like someone who just got caught ogling a forbidden cookie. I could never understand all that craze about fruit, cookies on the other hand? A chocolate chip one? Now that would have been worth getting rid of the whole Garden of Eden thing. All I'm saying is, that snake would have to honestly rethink its strategy if I were Eve. Imagine if we had chocolate chip cookies growing on trees, or Oreos... Oh my god, I'd probably have died and gone to heaven. I assume they'd have a chocolate chip tree in heaven, otherwise the whole thing is a scam! I digress.

"S-sorry," I struggle through the word, blushing furiously. "I-I wasn't, I swear!"

Aiden's head whips to me and, in seconds, he's on his feet and in front of me, his hands on my shoulders.

"Jenny," he breathes, his voice barely audible and his beautiful eyes boring into mine, making me melt in response, all the things he ever did to annoy me all but forgotten. Then I notice it, the dark circle around his right eye. My hand reaches out to touch it before my brain processes what I'm doing. When my fingers connect with his bruised flesh, Aiden sucks in a breath but doesn't move his head away. Instead, he closes his eyes and leans into my fingers. "I was talking to Jake," he says quietly, and it takes my brain too long to realize he is referring to the comment he made while I was watching him.

"What happened?" I ask quietly while he puts his hand over mine and spreads my fingers to the side of his face, his stubble rough on my palm.

He smiles a half smile, his eyes open and turned to mine, leaving me confused about what it was I was asking. "I had a little conversation with your brother." My jaw drops to the floor. Did Jason mess Aiden's pretty face up because I told him I was in love with him? Or was it worse? Did Aiden say that he doesn't want anything to do with me and Jason just defended my feelings? I'm about to take a step back when Aiden speaks again. "It's okay, kitten, we talked things through and everything's okay now." He smiles full force now, his dimples enticing me to stick my fingers in them to see if they're real.

"Oh," I reply cleverly, because, you know, I'm basically

a member of MENSA. They'd never say 'no' if they'd heard my conversational skills.

"Well," he says, pushing a stray strand of my hair behind my ear. "Almost everything is okay, but I'm planning to make sure it will be. We've got two and a half weeks for that."

I'm lost. I'm not sure what he's talking about anymore... Me or Jason? But I really hope he's talking about me, and I plan to use the next two weeks wisely. I'll either avoid him like the plague or I'll... I'm not sure, but it will definitely involve fewer clothes than he's currently wearing. My lips form a smile at the thought and I catch myself in the daydream, realizing that I'm actually daydreaming about Aiden in front of Aiden...

I clear my throat, taking a step away from him. Jake's head whips from me to Aiden, and his tail taps the hardwood floor a few times.

"Okay then," I say, confirming my status as a woman of few words. There's a first for everything.

"Helloooooo!" Carter sing-songs from the living room.

"When will we learn to lock the front door?" Aiden mutters, shaking his head. I take another step back while Jake runs to the living room to greet his favourite human. Second favorite, actually.

I turn on my heel and stomp into Jason's room, leaving Sully behind. Sucker can make its own way to the airport. Okay, I'm hoping Aiden will lug it for me. Seeing as he's got all the pretty-looking muscles, he might as well use them.

"What the hell?" I huff, putting my hands on my hips.

"Good morning, grumpy," Jason replies unimpressed by my show of displeasure.

"You punched Aiden!" I say accusingly.

"Yeah, well, we had a minor disagreement. We talked after and it's all good now," he replies lazily.

"It is?" I narrow my eyes. Could this mean that there's a slight chance my brother might be ok with Aiden and me dating?

"Yes!" he says, exasperated.

"Oh, okay then," I say, backing out of his room. "We leave in fifteen. I hope you're ready."

We're not leaving in fifteen minutes. In fact, we have another forty minutes before we need to start rushing, but my brother is that person. You know the one, the one who's always late to everything. That boy would be late to his own funeral, honestly...

With a bounce in my step, I walk to the living room. I'm excited for our trip, excited to see Dad. I've started to really miss him in the past couple of months. Phone calls a few times a week are just not enough. My scheming ways of convincing him he misses all the American ways better pay off!

When I enter the room, Carter and Aiden talk in hushed voices.

"What the hell were you thinking, man? Staying over at hers last night?" Carter's quiet voice makes me freeze mid step.

"I was obviously hammered, thanks to you, so I wasn't thinking," Aiden replies before Carter notices me and stops him, nodding in my direction.

I unfreeze myself and pretend I didn't hear any of their conversation, but as I walk, smiling, towards the two guys, my head is spinning. So Aiden stayed over at Chloe's. There's not really any other option or any other 'her' Carter could be referring to.

"Morning, grasshopper." Carter gives me a side hug.

"Corky," I reply, nodding at him. "What were you guys talking about?" I ask, deciding that beating around the bush will not help the situation in any way.

"Uhh, I got pretty wasted last night." Aiden says sheepishly. "We were just talking about how tequila and I are no longer friends."

Aiden outright omitting the truth hurts more than I thought possible. As awkwardness dawns upon us, I turn around, my eyes stinging, and busy myself with straightening up the skewed cushions on the sofa. I'm not going to cry, but I wish Aiden was man enough to admit to me he stayed over at Chloe's. I mean, it's not like he belongs to me, as much as I'd want him to. He's got every right to sleep wherever he wants. I just wish he wanted to sleep in my bed.

Carter leaves with Jake and, to my dismay, Aiden puts a shirt on. Rude. Once Jason finally emerges from his room, we pile into a taxi and drive to the airport. In silence. The ride is awkward as I sit in the backseat next to Aiden, who keeps throwing sideway glances my way. I'm determined not to react and stubbornly fixate on the scenery outside my window until we get to the airport. I shoot Hayley one last text and switch my phone off.

"Mr. Vaughn," a suited man in his late thirties says, addressing Jason. Jason raises his eyebrow at the man and looks over at Aiden, who's busy trying to pull Sully out of the taxi, nodding in his direction. The man clears his throat curtly and turns to Aiden. "Mr. Vaughn, please let me help," he says to Aiden this time. Aiden doesn't even look in his direction, he just grunts at him. The man moves to the trunk of the taxi, and the two of them successfully move Sully onto a cart. "Is the whole of your party here?" the man inquires.

"Who are you?" Aiden rudely asks the man who so kindly helped him just a second ago move the world's heaviest suitcase. Jason and I silently watch the exchange.

"Oh." The man clears his throat. "I do apologize. My name is Simon and I work for your father. He has asked me to ensure you have a pleasant send off this side of the Atlantic," he says and, I kid you not, clicks his heels. Dorothy. I shall name him Dorothy.

"You can tell my father that I don't need a glorified babysitter. We're fine on our own," Aiden barks. Disappointed, I start walking toward the trolley and consider just sitting on top of the suitcases and convincing one of the boys to drive me around the airport.

"I'm afraid I have to do this," Dorothy Simon replies. "Unless you're happy for me to lose my job…"

Aiden sighs and growls a curt, "Fine."

Dorothy Simon takes the trolley before I have a chance to put my plan into action and guides us through the express check-in and security checks, straight into the First Class lounge. I look around at the abundance of unnecessary things: the cushy sofas, the amount of food that's on display, the alcohol on tap and in decanters. Aiden's jaw is tight, and his leg twitches while we wait for our departure. Dorothy Simon settles himself on the sofa opposite us and sits up straight and unmoving, like a statue or one of the vampires from Twilight. I bump Jason's shoulder and motion my head towards him, chuckling. My brother, as if on cue, throws a grape at Simon. He misses miserably, but it still makes me laugh uncontrollably. The awkwardness from before, gone.

I look over at Aiden, his eyes laughing as he's trying his hardest to keep his lips from smiling. When it's time to get on the plane, I'm no longer mad at him. There's no point.

The only thing I can do is to try to convince him that it's me he wants, not Chloe. I've got two and a half weeks to do that.

My luck has no limit when I discover that I'm sitting right next to Aiden while Jason is in a different section altogether, way behind us. He grumbles for a bit, of course. But since, somehow, we've all been magically upgraded to First Class, he soon quiets down and settles himself in his comfy seat.

I do the same and thank whomever was in charge of random upgrades for sitting me right next to Aiden.

In First Class.

Where food is free.

Because, with all the excitement of the day, I forgot to eat breakfast, and when I'm starving my brain forgets to function. It makes me do stupid things.

Like pretend that I'm scared of flying just so that Aiden holds my hand.

Chapter 27

You

***I don't expect everything to be handed to me.
Just set it down wherever.***
- *Carter*

I look down, trying hard to believe my eyes. Jenny is squeezing my hand frantically. My eyes trace back up to her face, searching. Hers are shut tight and her lips tremble.

"Are you scared of flying?" I ask quietly, looking over my shoulder. Jason is snoring quietly, his seat reclined fully.

Could have something to do with the Benadryl I slipped into his juice when we were in the lounge...

I know what you're thinking: *Oh My God, did he just drug his best friend?!*

Please, hugs not drugs!

But well...

Yes and No.

It's best if I explain.

Jason hates flying—that's not right. He's okay once we're

up in the air, but at take off? A whole different story. Some sort of instinct kicks in and he outright panics, a trait I pray his sister does not possess. And, looking at her white knuckles wrapped tightly around my fingers, one can only hope. Ever since we started flying together, Jason and I have had a deal. This has a lot to do with a certain incident following one of said panic attacks. I slip something into his drink that will make him fall asleep. He sleeps happily throughout the flight. We don't get kicked off the plane. We don't get thrown into a small holding cell for suspicious behaviour. He doesn't get strip-searched. I don't get strip-searched. Simple.

Why would I need to slip him something? You see, Jason doesn't like to swallow pills. Seriously. He makes a massive deal out of it, like someone should build a shrine to him when he manages to get one of the little things down his throat. I kid you not, his eyes are watering, arms flailing, weird animal noises come out of his throat, and he does this thing with his neck, throwing it back and forth violently. I call it the 'chicken dance', which he doesn't appreciate. I stand by my opinion that that is exactly what it looks like.

So since we want to avoid the show every time we fly, we have a deal. I slip him something when he isn't looking. He unknowingly takes it, then falls asleep. Everyone is happy and everyone stays dressed and retains their dignity.

I look back at kitten. Her breathing is shallow and the hand that's not gripping mine is digging into her armrest.

"Jenny," I soothe, pulling her small frame towards me. "Don't be scared. I'm here. I would never let anything happen to you."

Her head whips in my direction, her whole body shifting to angle towards me. She lets go of the armrest and her free hand shoots towards my chest, fisting my shirt. Her huge eyes look desperate.

"How can you say that, how can you promise me such a thing?" she whispers. Her voice is shaky, and I wonder if she means more than just the flight.

"I promise," I reply. "I will keep you safe. I'll never let anyone hurt you." My words carry so much weight behind them. I, for sure, am making a much larger promise altogether, one that I will fight hard not to break.

"What about you?" she whispers, her breathing steadying a little. That's it, kitten, stop thinking about the flight and relax, I think as the plane rolls down the runway.

I take a deep breath. I've already hurt her so many times. "Kitten..." I start, my voice coming out needy and pleading at the same time. "I've already hurt you so much..." I drop my eyes. "Last night I—I—"

"Last night was a mistake, the whole thing was a mistake," she interrupts me quickly. "You did something stupid. Things happened." Her words are rushed. "It's not like you belong to me."

You belong to me... How I want her to say those words instead...

"I saw you kissing that guy and I went crazy," I try to explain as best as I can. "I didn't realise how drunk I got... And when I woke up this morning...."

"You woke up in Chloe's bed. I know," she finishes quietly. "Wait, kissing what guy? I didn't kiss anyone."

"I saw you..." I start and play the scene I saw the night before once again in my head. Could I have imagined it all? "He leaned down to kiss you..." I say tentatively.

"And I pushed him away. I didn't want him to kiss me," she says as hope makes a happy dance in my chest. "I don't ever want to kiss anyone..." Her voice is back to a low whisper. My breath hitches in my throat as my heart breaks in half. I'm the cause of that. I'm the reason behind her words. Me and the awful kiss I subjected her to when we were younger.

"I'm so sorry." I hang my head. "It seems all I do is hurt you..."

Jenny's soft fingers touch my chin, and she pushes my face up until our eyes connect.

"True, but—" she says, her lips forming a half smile.

"All this dancing around..." I shake my head, interrupting her. "I screwed up, didn't I? You'll never be mine."

"Yours," Jenny says the word slowly, and my heart flutters at the sound. "So do you like Chloe?" she asks out of nowhere.

"What? No, it was a drunken mistake! Kitten, if I could, I'd erase it all. All I want is—" I stop. Am I really doing this, putting my balls and my ego on a plate and handing it over to her so she could just stomp all over it? I am. "You," I finish without hesitation.

Her eyes don't waiver from mine and her breath doesn't hitch. She's silent for what seems like eons. Her one hand is still gripping mine while the other drops from my chin and rests on her lap. I notice we're in the air already. At least I'm a good distraction. Jenny takes a breath, and I ready myself for the blow. Here we go, she's going to say I'm just not the person she wants or needs, that I've screwed up over and over, and that, frankly, I'm just embarrassing myself with my confessions.

"I want you. I want to be with you. I always have. I always will, Jenny. You're the one for me." Words spill out. I guess, somewhere along the way, I decided more embarrassing confessions are needed, and I might just add my heart to the mix on that plate above which her foot is currently hovering.

"You never answered my question..." Jenny says, completely off the subject, startling me. What question? I guess I should be happy she didn't just outright reject me; although, isn't deflection basically a rejection?

"Question?" I ask.

"Will you hurt me?" she says quietly, blushing and dropping her gaze. It's my turn to lift her chin up to force her to look at me. I want her to see the sincerity of what I'm about to say.

"Never," I say, all the conviction I can muster behind my words. "And if you'll let me...I'll show you. I'll do everything in my power to never hurt you again. Ever." She's quiet once again, and I count my heartbeats, willing my aching heart to keep on beating.

"When I said I don't want anyone to ever kiss me again," she says, and I wince involuntarily, looking away from her as the world crumbles around me. "No, wait, let me finish," she rushes, seeing my expression. I force my head to face her again. She's so beautiful it hurts to even look at her. Especially knowing that she'll never be with me. I squeeze my eyes. I can feel her shift in her seat; she's much closer to me now. "Aiden," she sighs, her breath tickling my cheek just to the left of my lips. Her strawberry scent fills my nostrils, and I try not to inhale too deeply. I try not to think that this could very well be the last time we're this close to each other.

Why would someone do this to me? Create my ideal woman, parade her in front of me, then pull her away from me with one quick movement. "Aiden. Stop being stubborn and look at me." Her hand connects with my cheek. I open my eyes to see her smiling down at me. She's kneeling in her seat, facing me completely. Her hips within easy reach and her body radiating heat that warms me on the inside. "There, not too hard, was it? Now can I please finish what I started saying?" I nod for fear that if I open my mouth, I'll say something even more embarrassing.

"When I said that I don't want anyone to ever kiss me again," she says as my heart stops beating, waiting for her to just slide a dagger straight into it. I'll welcome the pain, I deserve it. "I meant, I don't want anyone to ever kiss me... but you." Her voice is barely audible, and I have to focus, replay her words in my head, process what I've just heard.

Thump.

My heart starts up again slowly, tentative but conscious of itself.

Thump, thump.

She said 'anyone but you'.

Thump, Thump. Thump, Thump.

Blood rushes around my veins freely, happily, because I think what kitten just said was exactly the opposite of what I was expecting.

"You mean," I say, my voice hoarse, staring at her. The corners of my mouth slowly lift into a small smile.

"I want...you," she replies simply, shrugging her shoulders.

I grin then, dimples and all, and pull her to me, hugging her.

"Kitten..." I murmur into her hair. She pushes me away and runs a hand through her hair, which I messed up with my exuberant show of affection.

"We need to get things straight first," she says, crossing her arms over her chest. I nod. I'd agree to anything she'd ask of me right now because she wants me.

She wants...me!

"Go on," I grin.

"This," she motions between us, "starts from the beginning, and properly this time. No dancing around, no playing hot and cold."

I nod eagerly. "I'll take you out on dates. And all the misunderstandings from before..." I hold my breath.

"We start from a clean slate," she says. "But that also means I need to trust you again. You can't keep things from me. We're friends first and foremost."

"Of course." I reach out my hand and touch her shoulder, giddy with the thought that this whole thing is happening. She puts her hand on top of mine.

"Great." She smiles. "Now, I've got the rest of Star Wars on my laptop. Want to watch them all?" I grin at the perfect woman in front of me and nod, leaning over to kiss her on the lips, because I can.

The kiss is chaste and sweet, maybe a few seconds too short. When I pull away, kitten is beaming at me. I pull her onto my lap and cover us with a blanket as we settle to watch the best movies ever made. The rest of the flight is too short for my liking. We talk, we sleep, we watch a movie and fall asleep again.

When a jolt wakes me up, I realise we've touched down, arriving in London. I pull Jenny closer to my chest, inhaling her scent, one that I'll hopefully get to smell every day If I play this right.

"Wake up, beautiful," I murmur into her hair and lean over to kiss her lips as she huffs disapprovingly. That's when I decide that I want to wake her up that way every day for the rest of my life. I am never letting this girl go. She kisses me back, then suddenly pushes me away. "Jenny, what's wrong?" I ask quickly as she puts her hand over her mouth, her eyes huge.

"Morning breath!" she mumbles through her fingers, making me burst into laughter. I stop as soon as I see her pissed off expression.

"I don't care about that, I just want to kiss—" I start but am interrupted when a shadow looms over us.

"You guys ready?" Jason yawns from behind me. "I slept like a beast!" he beams groggily. We nod in response and grab our things, getting off the plane and slowly walking down the long corridors of Heathrow Airport.

After a long while, we're finally through passport control and getting our bags. Jenny slips on one of her warm jumpers, and we all put scarves and jackets on. December in London can be brutal even though we hardly ever get snow.

When we go through to arrivals, I look around for John, my family's driver, but, instead, I'm surprised to see my father standing to the left leaning on the wall, too busy to pay attention as he furiously types into his Blackberry.

I walk over to him, confused by his presence. "Father? What are you doing here?"

"Aiden!" He looks up briefly from his phone before looking back down. "How's my lawyer son doing?" I wince at that comment, but it's not like he can see it, not looking at me and all. "I just flew in from Zurich and decided to surprise you. John is waiting in the car."

"Well, I'm certainly surprised," I reply.

"Aiden?" I hear Jenny's voice from behind me and I turn to her. "Our dad should be here in a couple of minutes, if you need to go."

"Great," my father mutters, looking up again. "Have you got all your luggage? Let's go then. I've got a meeting I need to be at in a couple of hours." He doesn't even look at Jenny or Jason.

"Father, this is Jennifer and Jason Cowley, my friends from University. You met them when I was in Grammar School, remember?" My father's head lifts up again, away from his Blackberry, and he slowly looks them up and down. I can see the instant judgement forming behind his eyes. "Jennifer is the one who talked me into studying law," I blurt out.

"Jennifer?" Jenny mouths, confused. I just shake my head at her and continue to watch my father's face. As soon as he hears my last words, his whole demeanour changes. He instantly smiles at Jenny and reaches out with his hand, taking hers into his large one and shaking it vigorously.

"Jennifer," he booms, smiling. "James Vaughn. So pleased to meet the voice of reason in my son's life."

Jenny seems a little confused, but does a good job of covering it with a smile. "Pleased to meet you, sir."

"Please! Sir, makes me sound so old. Call me James." Well, that's new. My father never lets any of my friends be this familiar with him. He turns towards my best friend. "You must be Jason. Are the two of you siblings?" Jason nods and shakes my father's hand. Wise move. Best not to speak in front of my father.

"They're here for Christmas, visiting with their father," I interject this abnormal behaviour. I'm starting to sweat a little. Fortunately, my father's phone rings and he steps away from us, excusing himself. "That was weird..." I say, patting Jason on the back and turning to Jenny to say goodbye.

"He seems..." Jenny starts, scrunching her face a little. "Nice?"

I chuckle. "Trust me, my father is anything but nice." I envelop her in a hug, inhaling her scent one more time. "I'll see you tomorrow, kitten?" I ask hopefully, pulling myself away from her and looking into her eyes.

"And the day after," she replies, winking at me. My heart skips a beat.

"And the one after that. I'm going to show you that I meant every word." Jason makes vomiting noises behind us. I wave him off.

"I can't wait," she says, smiling. I lean down and place a kiss on her lips.

"Until tomorrow then."

As I reluctantly pull away, my father makes another appearance, his gaze drifting between Jenny and I.

"Jennifer, Jason," he says, looking only at Jenny. "It seems I should probably try to get to know the both of you better. Why don't you come down for dinner on Boxing Day?" he asks, authority ringing through his words. He will not take 'no' for an answer. Shit.

"That's very kind," Jenny says quietly. "But we're here with our father and we wish to spend as much time as possible with him. We don't get to see him enough."

"Obviously, he is invited too. That's sorted then. The three of you shall join our family for a small get together on Boxing Day." He nods to himself. "Perfect." He turns on his heel and starts for the exit. "Aiden, please hurry. I'm on a tight schedule here."

I look apologetically at both Jason and Jenny and mouth 'sorry' before placing a kiss on Jenny's cheek and running after my father.

He's quiet throughout our drive, typing away on his phone. His jaw is set and I can see a muscle twitch in his left cheek.

"Son, I'm not against you dating anyone, but I wish for

you to focus on your studies. I don't want any distractions for you," he says finally.

I take my time forming a reply. This is a delicate subject.

"She's not a distraction," I finally say. "To the contrary, she makes everything come into focus."

My father nods once. "We can discuss this later."

I breathe steadily. I'm not going to let him destroy what I have only just put back together.

"You'll just have to come to terms with this, Father. She's clever, driven, and very, very important to me," I say through clenched teeth.

"So it seems," he replies as his lips form a small, barely visible smile.

Chapter 28

Well, The Dogs Like Her

A blank is the only thing I draw well.
- Aiden

The truth of the matter is, if I was a fourteen-year-old girl with a diary, my entries would look something like this:

Dear Diary,

I'm in love.

The city of London is seriously one of the most beautiful places I've ever been to!

Aiden is not too bad either, what with all his broodiness and muscles...

Joking, joking!

Aiden has been nothing but attentive, thoughtful, and amazing. It's weird, thinking about us as a couple. Because that's what we are now, a couple. The thought alone makes me smile every single time it comes to the forefront of my mind.

This trip has been close to perfection. Each day, the boy of my dreams shows up in our hotel with a bunch of flowers —Dad says my room smells like an expensive florist shop— then whisks me away to a different part of London. At times, Jason and Dad join us, and we do the touristy stuff we never got to do when we lived here. It helps that Dad actually loves Aiden. It's like Jason infected him with their bromance disease. The three of them are so awkward sometimes that I feel like I should just step aside and let them date. I don't. Instead, I just revel in the idea that my dad and my boyfriend get along.

My boyfriend... Eeep!

Who would have thought? Well, me. I mean, I hoped. A lot. But I never thought that it would become a reality and, now that it has, it's kind of better than what I imagined. The other day, Aide, Jason, Dad, and I went to South Bank to see the Thames all lit up with Christmas lights and visit the Christmas Market there. My boyfriend (Eeep!) secretly hired out one of the pods in the London Eye and surprised us with 'a flight'/ride out of the blue. The views were amazing! Sometimes in the hustle and bustle of busy London life, you can forget how incredible this city actually is.

One look at the skyline basked in the fading sunlight can take your breath away. Especially when Aide's strong arms are wrapped around you, pressing your body into his, and when he's nuzzling your hair muttering incoherent things about strawberries. Makes a girl's knees go weak, you know?

Aiden says that London during the Christmas season is his favorite, and I might have to agree with him, although I think London with Aiden holding my hand is my actual favorite. No, that's a lie. London, with Aiden's lips on mine, is the real winner.

The weeks go by too quickly. Aiden and I get closer and closer, so much so that I have to fight myself every minute we're together not to just blurt out that I have flat out fallen for him. Because, the truth is, I'm head over heels for that boy.

The moments we're alone are too few and too short with either my dad or Jason bursting into my hotel room, interrupting any devious plans I might have had of getting Aiden to lose any item of clothing. Not that Aiden is eager either. It's like I have to rip everything off of him and pray his newly acquired chastity belt has somehow fallen off.

For now, I am limited to kissing, not that I'm complaining. Aiden is a master in that discipline. His tongue is so skilled in the art of making me go gooey that each time we kiss I have to hold on to my clothes for fear of them just dropping off my body.

"You need to stop this." Aiden's deep voice brings me back from my musings.

He arrived in my hotel room a few minutes ago, a half an hour before the scheduled time, buying us a full thirty minutes of making out. Minutes which I was currently wasting ogling his body. The problem is that he surprised me as well! I was in the process of walking out of the shower, hair wet and nothing but the fluffy hotel bathrobe on, when he knocked on my door.

I was hoping for room service with my pre-ordered slice of chocolate cake, but Aiden was certainly a good replacement.

"Stop what?" I ask innocently, looking him up and down. The truth is, I've been staring at him hungrily all the while I was replaying those past two weeks in my head.

"Looking at me like that, and making those noises." His voice goes husky and his eyes turn to dark emerald. He takes a few steps towards me, and I turn away from him, looking out the window, his gaze on me so hot, for a second, I am worried it might incinerate the bathrobe. Not that I'd mind.

"It's hard not to look at you like that. Have you seen yourself in the mirror lately?" I smirk. My breath hitches when I feel his hot breath on my neck. Goosebumps rise all over my body, and I turn in one swift motion, making eye contact with him. He doesn't answer my question; instead, he leans down and covers my mouth with his. I moan with pleasure. I don't think I'll ever get used to his hot lips on mine and how they make me feel.

I wrap my arms around his neck and take a step backwards, a part of my 'Get Aiden and I into a horizontal position' campaign. Aiden growls and moves his face away from mine, making me frown. I don't know what he's made of, but it must be steel, because he's been seriously so chaste with me that it's infuriating.

"Kitten," he whispers. I move away from him and settle myself on the bed, positioning my bathrobe just so, in hopes of him following me. It's then I notice the small package in his hands.

"What's that?" I nod towards the box. My 'shiny things' antenna is working overtime. Aiden's cheeks go a bit red.

"I know we exchanged Christmas gifts yesterday, but I had one more for you, one I wanted to give you when it was just the two of us," he says, coming towards me and sitting on the bed. Score one, Jenny! Aiden is on the bed, everyone. I repeat, ON THE BED.

I look at the small blue box in his hands, remembering how, yesterday, Aiden joined Dad, Jason, and I in our

Christmas celebrations. How Dad's face lit up at all the American food I wrapped up for him. How Jason decided, after finishing a bottle of wine, that Christmas karaoke was the best way to celebrate Christmas, whether or not there was any music, and how we had to endure a full hour of Jason singing Last Christmas by Wham! Over and over... and over. How we Skyped Jake and Carter, and how Carter encouraged my untalented brother to sing more, all while laughing his butt off.

Ahhh, Christmas. The time you want your family exterminated. What I wouldn't give for one little Dalek yesterday.

"You got me another present?" I perk up, shifting from my 'sultry' position into one that is full on 'gimme, gimme, gimme!' Aiden's dimples make an appearance as his gaze drops down to my chest. I expect one of my boobs is half exposed. I let it slide since the boy came bearing gifts.

"Just a little one," he replies, handing me a small, greenish-blue box. I rip the white ribbon away with one strong movement and carefully lift the cover to reveal a delicate necklace with an infinity symbol pendant. I look back up at Aiden, my hands shaking as he takes the box away from me and lifts the chain out. "This is so that you know," he says, putting the chain around my neck, fastening it, "that I'm here for the long haul." He lets his hands drop to my shoulders.

"Thank you. It's beautiful," I say, putting my hand over the infinity symbol now resting on top of my collarbone.

Aiden smiles at me with his cute little half smile, and I all but lose it. Having had enough of the chit chat and wanting to express just how much I like the chain, I climb on his lap, straddling him and wrapping my arms around his neck. Before he can protest, I fuse my lips with his. To my surprise and utter delight, he doesn't protest. Instead, his arms drop from my shoulders and snake around me, causing my body to light up like a Christmas Tree. Through my incoherent jumble of thoughts, I can barely notice that his hands are touching the skin on my back.

His hands.

On my bare skin.

A feeling I'd need a Masters Degree in English to be able to even begin to describe.

I mewl with pleasure, ripping the tie of my bathrobe open. I don't think. There's nothing I want more than to feel what his body feels like on mine. And the fact that he hasn't stopped us yet propels me to pull his shirt up and press myself against him.

This time, Aiden is the one to groan. His fiery kisses are becoming frantic, and his hands now move all over my body, causing me to shiver. From the small of my back to my hips to my bottom, touching, squeezing, kneading. I break our kiss to pull his shirt over his head and thank the heavens and all that is holy he lets me. He pulls me against him, and the feeling of my erect nipples against his hard chest sends me into a frenzy. How can this feel so good? Aiden skillfully moves his lips from mine and down to my earlobe, nipping at it before moving lower and sucking at my neck, while his rough hand finds my nipple and tweaks it. I cry out in pleasure.

"Fuck, kitten, so responsive," he mumbles into my throat as his hand trails down, down, down over my belly button, caressing my skin and inching towards my pussy. When his fingers connect with my slit, he swears. "So wet. So fucking wet," he moans. "You're so beautiful, so ready for me." I moan in reply, and thank God he knows exactly what I mean by it, because he starts rubbing small circles around my clit while sucking my nipple. I rock against his hand, desperate for more friction.

"Aiden..." I moan.

"Yes, baby," his hoarse voice sends shivers down my spine. "Tell me what you want."

I'd blush, but I'm in too deep. I'm consumed by need; need for something. To feel him inside me, anyway I can. "I need you."

"Not now, kitten," he groans. "But I'll make you feel good. You want that?" He continues rubbing my clit as he speaks.

"Yes!" I exclaim as his finger slides down and plunges into me. "Yes, please."

"Please, what?" he growls, slowly stroking me while his thumb continues its assault on my clit. I can't think, I can only feel as I lift my hips in unison to his movement. This feels so amazing, right until he stops. "Please what, kitten?" he demands, biting my nipple.

"Please Aiden, make me come." I writhe against him as his fingers start up again, pumping into me with renewed vigor. I'm so close, I can see the edge, and when his lips connect with mine, I fall. I fall hard. His name on my lips.

He kisses me gently and starts pulling away, so I grab his neck and press my lips against his fervently, wanting to make him feel as good as he just made me feel.

I reach for his zipper and...that's when Mr. Chastity Belt decides to make an appearance. Seriously? How does he have control?

"Jenny." His voice is pained. "We have to stop."

"Don't you want me? Don't you want this?" I gesture to my body in all its disrobed glory.

"Fuuuuck," Aiden mutters under his breath, looking his fill greedily at my body before closing the robe and sitting up. I can see he's hard through his jeans, and he's straining to regain control. "I want you. More than anything," he says, his eyes dark and focused on my lips. "But I will not take your virginity in some shoddy hotel room, with your father and brother in the room next to us," he says, leaning over and placing a delicate kiss on my collarbone where the chain he gave me is resting. "There's no hurry. I can wait for you to be ready. And, when we do it, which, trust me, we will, I will need a lot longer than half an hour. I'll devour you over and over with my mouth until you forget everything and all that's left on your lips is my name. That's when I'll take you. Slowly, delicately, and lovingly because that's the way you should be made love to."

I all but lose my mind on the spot. Did I just hear him right? Because, if I did, I am so freaking ready to have that happen right now!

"Uh-huh," I manage incoherently before getting up and zooming to the bathroom to splash some cold water on my face. I take my time untangling my hair, which dried into a very pretty knot, then put on the dress I had hanging on the bathroom door.

When I get back to the room, I no longer experience hot flashes every single time I think about Aiden's mouth.

"You look beautiful." Aiden smiles at me from the armchair he's sitting on. I'm about to thank him for the compliment when my eyes land on the empty plate on the coffee table next to him, one with dark chocolate crumbs on it.

He wouldn't, would he?

I move my eyes to his mouth and whaddya know? There are chocolate stains in the corners of his mouth. Just like that, all my gooey feelings are gone.

Bastard ate my chocolate cake!

I am about to walk over to the chocolate cake thief and strangle the living crap out of him when the door to my room bursts open.

"A-ha!" Jason jumps in, spreading his legs into a wide stance and pointing his finger at the empty bed. I raise my eyebrows at him as he collects himself and starts picking at non existing flecks on his shirt, pretending like his grand entrance never happened. "Hey man," he nods to Aiden, who's still splayed out in the armchair. "I thought you might be here already."

"Just got here," Aiden replies, getting up and brushing crumbs off of his lap. They greet each other in an awkward fist pump, hug motion I never got the hang of while I go back to the bathroom to put on some makeup.

When I emerge back into the room, I'm greeted by the sight of Jason, Aiden, and my dad grunting and circling each other like three male gorillas. If it wasn't for the random burst of laughter, I'd have thought... Frankly, I have no idea what, but I'm glad I interrupted that bit of male bonding.

"You guys ready?" I ask, slipping my feet into a pair of black pumps. As if on cue, all three of them turn around to face me, grinning.

It's weird.

I decide to ignore them and grab my coat and bag and head for the door, hoping that they'll just follow me outside. They do.

We pile into one of London's iconic black cabs and ride the short distance to Aiden's house in the heart of Kensington. Before long, we pull up in front of a white, high, wooden gate. You can just about see the white brick house set behind the green line of trees obscuring the view of what's inside. When Aiden opens the gate, three brown

Labradors run towards us wagging their tails and their whole bodies.

"This is Fisher, Becker, and Buchanan," Aiden says, pointing at the excited dogs.

I burst out laughing. "Named after the Economists I presume?" I lean down to pat Becker on his head. "You're the best out of the three anyway, aren't you boy? Family economics is the way to go." I wink at Becker as he wags his tail in response, licking my hand.

"She's a girl," Aiden's dad says from the front steps of the house, making me straighten up.

"Sorry," I mutter apologetically.

"Don't be. It's refreshing knowing a young lady who can appreciate Economics." He smiles at me. "Jennifer, Jason, it's good to see you again. And you must be Robert?" He extends his hand to my dad, who stiffly shakes it.

We're quickly ushered inside and down the grand entrance into the reception room. Becker, Fisher, and Buchanan decide to follow my every move and slobber all over me, not that I mind.

Huh.

You think they learned that from Aiden?

Most likely.

Aiden's dad is constantly in and out of the room, glued to his blackberry, and his mum makes an appearance just as we're about to sit down for dinner. She's overly friendly. The type of friendliness that's hard to trust.

Slowly, I begin to understand why Aiden doesn't like to talk about home or his childhood. It becomes more and more evident that even though he never lacked clothes, books, or lavish gifts, attention from his parents was sparse to say the least.

There's a chill in the air when we settle for dessert in

the drawing room, and I find myself wishing I brought my cardigan with me. Aiden's mum and dad bombard me with questions in between undermining Aiden's grades, and I feel like I'm in some sort of a weird interview.

Aiden sits stiffly next to me, giving only short answers. His pocket keeps on buzzing and, with every vibration of a text or call, he gets more and more agitated.

I don't recognise the boy next to me. So, in between the questioning, I busy myself by petting the three dogs who positioned themselves around me.

"Well, the dogs like her," Aiden's mum brings me out of my thoughts, "and she's a good influence on Aiden," she continues as I watch my dad's face knot into one of disapproval. "I approve." She gets up and walks over to me, giving me a stiff and distant hug while Aide's dad grunts something incoherent.

So it *was* an interview.

When she pulls away, I look over at Aiden, who is staring at the screen of his phone.

His face is paper white and his eyes are wide.

Chapter 29

J To The Double N

When life gives you lemons, ask life if you can trade them for grapes; because wine is better than lemonade.
- Jason

As we settle into the drawing room for dessert, my phone vibrates with another text message. I sigh with frustration. This has to stop. I've been getting these texts since we left for London, and, as much as I'm trying to ignore them, it's hard.

I look over at Jenny; the dogs are lying at her feet. I don't blame them for that instant love. If I were a dog, I'd be gazing lovingly at her too. My chest squeezes at that thought, and I start thinking about Jake. Poor bastard is probably getting smothered at Casa del Uncle Carter. I didn't come up with that creepy name, Kennedy did. I decide to check in on the beast and text Carter to see how the two of them are doing. Jake had his cast taken off last week, so I'm worried. A reply comes back almost instantly.

CARTER: *DUDE!!!!!! HOW DARE YOU! It's sooo early and your loud text is making my morning headache even worse!! STOP this torture RIGHT NOW!*

I stifle a laugh. Morning headache, right... 'Morning headache' are just pretty words for a hangover in his ever-so-confusing language.

My phone buzzes with incoming texts, so I glance down at what Carter could possibly come up with this time. Instead, I see an onslaught of new messages.

Sighing, I leave the phone face down on my lap and move to hold Jenny's hand, gently squeezing it just as another text vibrates. Jason snatches the phone off my lap and, without changing his expression, scrolls through it. Without meeting my eye, he puts the phone in his pocket.

When we get back to the hotel, Jason pulls me to the side. "What the fuck?"

"What?" I meet his gaze.

"Why the hell didn't you tell me about all these texts from Chloe? There's like a hundred of them."

"What's there to tell?" I mutter.

"How long has she been texting you?"

I hesitate. "Ever since that night... The one I got sloshed," I clarify.

Jason snickers. "Still can't believe that our Golden Boy got shitfaced."

I shake my head. "I should be worried, shouldn't I?"

"Yes. Chloe can be...a bit obsessive. Last year, she

stalked me for over eight months after I broke things off with her. I'm telling you, never bring chicks to your place. Oh wait, you live with your chick...psych!" He grins.

"You know it's your sister you're talking about, right?" I shake my head. Jason's mischievous expression falls while he thinks through his previous statement. "I admit the whole Chloe thing is getting out of hand. I'm seriously starting to think she might have lied about what exactly happened. Apparently, it wouldn't be the first time either..."

"Nope, she's done it before. Trust me. Have you talked to J to the double N about what happened that night?"

"I tried, but we never actually discussed it. She said she wanted to wipe the slate clean."

"Well, in this case, I think you should. And soon. Shit like that is bound to come back to haunt you." He's right. Probably for the first time in his life. "Look, I'll take care of her. I'll text her or something, try getting her off your back."

"You'd do that?" I whip my head up to look at my best friend.

"I guess I just want my sister to be happy, and you seem to make her happy, so...I'll take one for the team." He exhales. I'm almost ready to jump on him and hug the living shit out of him in gratitude. Almost. But Jenny comes over and slips her hand into mine.

"All good?" she asks as Jason busies himself by tapping away on his phone. His tongue is sticking out in concentration.

I nod.

"I'm going up to my room. This lobby is so cold that one more minute out here and my nuts are going to freeze. And since I want to have children one day... You get my drift." Jason walks into the open lift, then stops in his tracks with his hand on the button. He slowly turns around and looks at

Jenny and I. "I'm going to get sloshed and see if my father would like to partake in the sloshing." He grins like an idiot just as the door closes on him.

Jenny asks. "What was that about?"

"Jason being Jason."

"Are you up for a walk? I want to show you something." She nods. I wrap her scarf tighter and pull her hat on, then take her hand and lead her out of the hotel. We walk a couple of streets before she speaks. "I saw Chloe texted you."

My heart speeds up. "You did?"

"Yeah." She nods, her voice barely above a whisper. "I didn't look. I just saw her name pop up on your screen."

"Jenny, about that night—" I start as we turn a corner.

"I'm not sure I want to know," she interrupts me. "I think it's better if I don't, you know?" She sniffles. "It hurts even thinking about it."

I don't want her to hurt. I want to protect her, tell her that everything will be okay and that...I love her. "Kitten—"

"Meow," she replies, making light of the conversation.

"Oh, wow," she gasps as we reach our destination. "It looks so much smaller now. It used to feel so big, didn't it?" She takes a step forward to the playground in front of our old school.

I guide her to the two swings I used to despise after that day. They look unassuming now. Jenny sits on one of the swings as I sit on the other.

"You know," Jenny whispers conspiratorially, "I carved my name on the bottom of the one you're sitting on."

I gasp in mock horror. "Vandal!"

"Not such a goody two shoes now, am I?"

"Never thought you were." I smile. "Wanna check if it's still there?"

"Yes!" she exclaims, excited.

My heart hammering in my chest, I grab the wooden seat and slowly turn it as Jenny claps her hands. Her eyes search the wood for less than a second before she sees the carving. She frowns.

"Aiden, I don't understand," she says, looking from the carving to me, then back to the carving. I look down. Her name is still visible. She did a good job carving it.

JENNY C., it says.

Right underneath her name there's a small '+' sign, and under it a neatly carved AIDEN V.

Both names wrapped in a wonky heart.

"What can I say? I wasn't a very good artist." I smile.

"When did you—"

"The same day you carved your name. I saw you, got intrigued, and when you left, came to examine."

"But that was halfway through the school year...months before you even talked to me." I can see the confusion on her face, and I take a step towards her.

"I carved my name next to yours in hopes that you'd look at your handiwork again, see it, and realise that I was in love with you and...I don't know, throw me a bone? Talk to me?" I smile.

"You what?" she chokes out.

"Silly, silly, kitten." I put my hand on her cheek to draw her in closer to me. "I said, I was in love with you. But that's not right, is it? I've never stopped being in love with you. From the first day I saw you, I was smitten, and it only grew. Even when you broke my heart, I still loved you. I hated you, but I loved you."

"Aiden... I— I—"

"I love you, Jennifer Elisabeth Cowley. I have never loved anyone else." I capture her lips in mine, and she folds into me, responsive and warm and so damn inviting. It starts to drizzle, but she doesn't seem to notice. I want to stay like this forever, but I'm worried she'll catch a cold, so I pull away. She smiles at me dizzily, and I brush my thumb against her swollen lips.

"Let's go back." I take her hand and turn back towards the street.

"Wait." Her voice is hoarse and her cheeks are flushed.

"You want to—"

"I love you too." She pulls my face back to hers, kissing me so hard I'm pretty sure there's steam rising from both of our bodies.

Chapter 30

Mile High Club

I never make the same mistake twice. I make it five or six times just to be sure.
- Aiden

"First thing I did when I got back to the hotel after that magical afternoon was text Hayley and Carter, obviously. I mean, saying the 'L' word to each other is major news, and they deserved to be the first to know. Besides, I only ever said it to my family and Jake before. When Aiden said that he loved me, the rush I felt was incomparable to anything I've ever experienced before. Suddenly, all the colors were brighter, all the sounds clearer, and everything seemed...just...so...good. And happy! I finally understood the meaning of the song lyrics to all the love songs. They all make sense now...you know?"

"Hayley was obviously ecstatic for me. We spent hours on Skype analyzing every single detail, probably over-analyzing. But that's what girls do. It's totally normal. Trust me. Anyway, Carter is the one I'm worried about. Normally, I can't swat the guy away with a fly swatter thingy for the life of me! This time...it took him hours to reply to me and all he said was, 'That's great, Jenny. I'm happy for you.' No emojis, no exclamation marks, no sexual innuendos, no making fun of me, and most disturbingly of all, he called me JENNY. He never calls me that. EVER!"

"I guess what I'm trying to say, or ask, is why do you think he would act like that?" I turn my face to the guy sitting next to me by the bar on the transatlantic flight. His expression is bored as he twirls a glass drink stirrer around in his martini glass. I look at him expectantly, clutching my empty champagne glass like my life depends on it.

The guy shrugs his shoulders.

"Oh, come on! You must have some insight!" I exclaim.

"Lady—"

"Jenny," I interrupt him.

"Jenny," he starts again. "I don't know. I just want to peacefully have a drink before I land and have to see my family again. I've got my own problems. My wife is divorcing me, my sixteen year old daughter just decided she wants to drop out of school and pursue a career in street dancing, and my brother's wife made a move on me this Christmas," he spits out in one breath. My jaw drops. Okay, dude has his issues. "Last thing I want to do is listen to a teenage drama about why your boyfriend hasn't texted you back sooner."

"Not my boyfriend." I cross my arms. "My best friend! You need to learn to listen." I shake my head. If you ask me, that's probably reason number one why his wife is divorcing him. I wave my empty glass at the lady behind the bar. She comes over and looks at me directly.

"Maybe he's got a thing for you?" she says.

"Him?" I whisper, motioning to the guy sitting beside me, the one whose life is in pieces. Same one who needs lessons in listening etiquette.

"Your best friend," she corrects me. "Sorry, I couldn't help but overhear."

"No, no, it's okay! Any input is good, but you couldn't be more wrong. My best friend is the biggest Casanova out there. I mean, he's better at chasing tail than Jake!"

"Jake? Is that your boyfriend?"

"My dog. He's amazing. Well, he's actually my boyfriend's dog, the hunk of a man sleeping so peacefully over there." I point in the general direction behind me. "My stupid brother named him after Jacob Black. I mean the dog, not the boyfriend. He wanted to continue the Twilight theme, you see. All because we've got this bread he called Edward...but I digress. That's definitely not the reason for his silence. There's absolutely no way Carter likes me that way."

The woman looks me up and down, then takes my empty glass away, handing me a glass of water instead. Oh well.

She leans on the counter. "Maybe he was busy then, chasing tail, as you've nicely put it."

"Hmmm, maybe. But why would he call me Jenny?"

"That is your name, no? Jenny?"

"Well...yes, but—"

"Look," she interrupts me. "Guys are simple. Don't read into things. Most likely he was tired from all that 'tail chasing' and just typed your name for lack of better ideas."

I consider that for a moment. It's quite plausible, I guess. I open my mouth to speak when the woman's eyes grow large and her pupils dilate. Uh-oh. Here comes trouble.

"Please tell me this hunk of a man is not your boyfriend," she whispers, motioning her head to someone behind me. I turn to take a look.

"Nope." I say, smiling while she exhales, opening the top button of her blouse. Jason comes over and slides into a seat next to me. He looks sleepy, like he's just woken up. His hair spikes in all different directions and there's a rumpled, pillow-shaped indent on his right cheek. I guess the woman likes what she sees, because she leans over towards him, exposing her prominent cleavage even more.

"Hi," she purrs. "How can I help you?" she finishes the sentence suggestively. Eeew.

I sigh. "Jason, this is..." I nod to her expectantly.

"Mary."

"Mary. Mary, this is Jason, my brother." God help her. Jason's eyes focus on her boobs, and he licks his lips in approval.

"Hi Mary." He takes her hand, flashing her a grin and turning her hand to kiss the top of it, lingering for way too long, in my humble opinion. I decide to break it up. I seriously don't need to be witness to the circus that's about to happen.

"And this is my friend..." I nudge the guy to my left who has just finished his drink. "John? Stan? Bob? Ludlum? Darth Vader?"

"Mark," he sighs.

"Mark," I exclaim happily. "Mark has had it pretty rough lately." I nod my head solemnly. "Go easy on him," I say, getting up and making my way back to where I can see Aiden, who's just waking up.

Mark huffs and pushes past me back to his seat. Rude!

I jump and land on Aiden's lap, covering his face with sloppy, energetic kisses, making him laugh in response.

"Kitten," he chuckles. "Please stop. I just woke up and I totally need to use the toilet!" Whoa, whoa, whoa! Are we at this stage of our relationship already? Can I burp in front of him? Are we sharing things like that?

Aiden grabs a hold of my waist and lifts me up, placing me right next to him. He gets up, kisses my forehead, then whispers, "Don't move. I'll be back in a sec." I squeeze his bum in agreement as he walks away.

A second it is not.

I inspect my fingernails, check my hair for split ends, pick fluff off of my t-shirt. Finally, mister, who definitely needed number two rather than number one, makes an appearance. His face is red, and he is holding back a laugh.

"What?" I ask, curious.

"You'll never believe," he shakes his head, "why I took so long."

"Number two?" I mutter.

"Huh? No." He smirks. "Jason."

"You locked yourself in the toilet with Jason?" I gasp, aghast. Joining the mile high club might just be on my bucket list, and this news is a mood killer.

"What? No! Jason was in the toilet...."

"Oh yeah, his bowel movements are unpredictable when flying. His stomach gets dodgy at high altitude," I reply knowingly.

Aiden bursts out laughing. Ha! I knew I was hilarious.

"God, kitten, you've got it all wrong. You're just too innocent," he chuckles.

Hell no! Innocent is the last thing I want him to think of me. Not when, as soon as the wheels of this plane hit the tarmac and we get back home, I want him naked in my bedroom.

"Vagina!" I blurt out quickly, making him spit out the almond he just popped into his mouth. Ha!

"What?" His eyes are wild as he looks around, checking if anyone heard my outburst.

"Nothing." I grin. "Not so innocent now, am I? Now tell me, what did Jason do?"

But before Aiden has a chance to reply, I spot Jason, kissing and groping...Mary! And it all clicks into place. All those times when we flew and Jason disappeared in the toilet, coming back disheveled and claiming a dodgy stomach. That little whore!

Jason saunters back towards us, looking all kinds of satisfied I do not want to know about.

"Dodgy stomach?" I ask, narrowing my eyes. Jason looks at me, confused. I can basically see a freaking lightbulb lighting up above his head.

Finally, he replies, holding his stomach. "Oh yes, you know me. Flying just makes it...reeeaaaally bad." He nods gravely.

Bastard is lying. Damn him and me for eating up his lies all these years!

Not fair!

It wouldn't be so bad if it wasn't for the fact that my boyfriend was hell bent on wearing his iron chastity belt. Locked with twenty bloody padlocks... Keys thrown away... In the moat of Edinburgh castle... Or something like that.

That's it.

I don't see any other way out of this. I am going to convince him to lose the freaking belt no matter what. I'll use a chainsaw if I have to!

Forgetting all about Jason, I yank Aiden to me and kiss him hard, running my hands under his shirt, nibbling his lower lip, and pulling his body closer to mine. He instantly responds, sneaking his skillful tongue in and out of my mouth, letting out a little growl. I can feel his reaction through his sweats, and it takes everything I have in me not to moan like a grade-A porn star at the magical sensation that erupts in my belly.

"Guys, ewww! Please, stop! This is disgusting. You're making me sick!" my brother exclaims. "Dodgy stomach over here."

I break away from the Deity that is my boyfriend—seriously, I'm two minutes away from building a shrine for him—and look at Jason. He's pointing expectantly at his stomach.

"Dodgy stomach." I shake my head in disbelief. "Can't believe I ate that shit up all these years..."

Jason just grins and shrugs. I'm about to punch the smug monkey when the seatbelt sign lights up and the pilot's voice booms through the PA system, telling us that we're about to land.

Brilliant! All the closer to home, to my bed. The sooner we get there, the sooner I can make my 'Take advantage of Aiden' plan a reality, and this time I'm not taking 'no' for an answer.

And if he thinks that I'm rushing again...well, tough. I'm not. Even through the ups and downs, my heart has been his for a long time. There's no one else for me and, more than anything, I want him to know that. I want him to know that I am sure of us, of how strong our love is. He's my 'one' and I just don't want to wait any longer.

I sit in my seat and buckle myself up, masterfully plotting in my head all the steps I'm going to take to seduce my boyfriend. Gah...I sound so desperate!

"Are you okay?" Aiden takes a hold of my hand and

squeezes it. What? Of course I am. I'm just planning how to get you out of your clothes, silly.

Then it hits me. I'm 'supposed to be afraid of flying'. Damn it, Jenny! Sloppy! So sloppy... I knew I was forgetting something. I squeeze his hand, hard.

"Mmm-hmm." And the Oscar goes to...

"It's okay," he says, kissing my hand. "Just breathe, it'll be over soon."

But breathing is hard when his emerald eyes are focused on me.

When we land, I text my dad to let him know that we landed safely and make my way over to sit on the plastic chairs in the baggage claim area. I spot Jason and Aide talking, and I smile. Who would have thought that my life would turn out like this? Not me.

This boy makes me so happy it's unreal.

I smile again, even though, for some reason, a sick feeling starts up in my stomach. Jason's and Aiden's movements are animated. I squint in their direction and notice Aiden is clutching his phone in his hand, looking down at it and then at Jason. I hope everything is okay...

That sick feeling grows, but I ignore it.

Jason takes the phone away from Aiden and looks at the screen. I can see it from here. His face loses all color and his eyes are ready to bulge out of his sockets.

I stand up just as Jason leans over and whispers something in Aiden's ear.

They both look at me.

The sick feeling grows and grows, and I squish it.

I'm sure it's nothing.

I take another step towards the guys.

The thing is...when you're this ridiculously happy, something is bound to hit the fan eventually, right?

Chapter 31

Sweet Cheeks

***Some people just need a high five…in the face…
with a hammer.***
- Carter

The ride back from the airport is downright uncomfortable. Both of the boys are acting weird, their movements are rigid, and conversation is reduced to 'yes/no' answers. You know you've lost the battle when both your brother and your boyfriend reply 'yes', in unison, to whether they'd prefer to get pizza or Chinese for dinner. Seriously?

I try not to read too much into it, even though the scene from the airport keeps playing on repeat in my head. What the hell could have happened to make both of them behave so strangely?

I can't take the weird silence and blank stares anymore. "Is everything okay?" I finally ask as we pull into our driveway. Jason looks at me in panic, then at Aiden, and shoots out of the car like his butt crack is on fire.

"Thanks, man," Aiden mutters to no one in particular before turning to me in the car. He sighs. "Kitten..."

"Helloooooo!" A high pitched, highly annoying, sing-song voice interrupts him while a hand taps on my door window. I turn to see Carter grinning from ear to ear, waving at me from behind the door. I screech and push the door open, throwing myself at my best friend, holding him in a tight embrace, just like a koala bear would hold its favorite, long lost eucalyptus tree.

"Carter!" I exclaim. He's here! He doesn't hate me! He's here!

"Welcome back, grasshopper," he says as my heart swells. He called me grasshopper, not Jenny! Grasshopper! Carter gently pries me off of his person and looks me over. "You've grown," he states, patting my head.

"No, I haven't," I shake my head in dismay, squirming from under his large palm. To be honest, I wish I had grown, but unfortunately, that book has been shut since I was twelve. Not even half an inch since then! Instead, I'm still very much in the hobbit-like height bracket.

Both Jason and Aiden murmur 'hi' at Carter, then grab our bags and make their way to the house. They're definitely avoiding something. Longingly, I look into the distance. If only I went to Hogwarts; I could unpack my suitcase magically, with one wave of a wand, Wanda the wand. I daydream for a few seconds about what could be, then look back at the front door behind which Aiden disappeared a second ago, dragging Sully behind him. I'm going to have to unpack that mother of suitcases without Wanda goddamnit. I should probably do it sooner rather than later.

"Want to go for a walk?" Carter startles me out of my

misery. Yes! I nod eagerly at the welcome distraction before I let my face fall. Sully will not unpack magically by itself, Wanda or no-Wanda.

"I need to unpack," I whine.

"I'll help you." Carter smiles.

"Really?" The hope in my voice is unmistakable. I latch onto it like a tapeworm to the wall of an intestine.

"For a price, of course." Of course.

"What do you want?" I ask, expecting the worst. Like having to piggyback him to campus for a week or shine all his shoes or... Or... Or taste-test all his food for poison. Although that last one wouldn't be so bad. Corky gets most of his meals delivered from nearby restaurants, so as long as it's not that oyster place, I'm game.

"I'll help you..." Carter starts out slowly, visibly still deliberating. "If..." He taps his chin. "If you tell everyone that you think I'm sexy." His finger silences my response. "But, in a natural way," he finishes, proud of himself.

I narrow my eyes and draw in a big breath, about to laugh and tell him to go stuff it, but something stops me. Something shaped like a massive blue suitcase named Sully. Why did God not think it wise to equip me with basic unpacking skills, why?

"Fine," I say with resignation. "Now, how about that walk? I want to hear all about your Christmas and all the girls you led astray. How many hearts did you break this season?" I look at my best friend with playfulness.

Without saying a word, he puts his large arm around me and guides me away from the house. I try to fill the silence with mindless chatter about Aiden's dogs, but Carter is somewhere far, far away, not really listening.

"Miyagi?" I ask.

"Hmm?" He looks at me absently.

I touch his shoulder. "Is everything okay?"

"Sure, little one." He smiles, looking down at me. "So you had a nice break, eh? Professed undying love for each other with Ady-wady?"

"Yeah, something like that." I smile back at him. "My break was pretty good, except it was missing one suuuper special ingredient."

"Aah. Well, yes, that's right. Everyone knows that the C. Kennedy component is necessary for good times. It must have been...tough... Sooo tough." He shakes his head at me with pity.

"Extremely." I nod sarcastically in agreement, my lips in a thin line. I change the subject back to him. "So what did you and Jake get up to?"

"Oh, you know...not much," he says, rubbing the back of his neck. "Went back home, heard your big news, went out a couple of times. Nothing special. All the special I get up to is reserved for my little grasshopper, of course." His smile feels disingenuous. I look away, not sure how to get him to spit out whatever's the matter.

"Sounds like fun." I take a deep breath. "Carter—"

"Jenny—" he says at the same time. We both laugh. "You first," he says, nudging me.

"I just... Is everything okay? I mean, between us. You seem different...distant." I look up at him in time to see his face fall momentarily just a second before he rearranges it back to his usual smirking one.

"Of course, grasshopper!" he says, pulling me into a hug. "I'm sorry if I seem distant. I just have a lot on my mind." He kisses the top of my head and pushes a strand of my hair behind my ear.

"Are you sure?"

"Three hundred and fifty six percent sure," he replies,

playfully touching his finger to my nose. I scramble out of his grasp.

"That number doesn't exist." I sigh. "But I'll take it." He grins at me with triumph in his eyes. "So if it's not me, what's wrong? What's on your mind?"

Carter retracts into himself for the second time today. He turns around and starts walking back towards the house. His gait is so quick I have to run to catch up. "Kennedy!" I grab his arm to slow him down. He does, just a little, ever so reluctant. "C'mon, you can talk to me."

"Not about this," he mutters so incoherently I almost miss it.

"About what?" I pull on his sleeve. He looks at me in a panic and starts walking even faster. I run after him when suddenly he stops in his tracks and turns to me. His features soften and his hand reaches out, touching the side of my face and cupping my cheek. He closes his eyes and exhales.

"Jenny..." he whispers. My heart is beating fast from all that running and I breathe in harshly, trying to steady the crazy rhythm. Carter's thumb gently rubs my cheek, and I'm no longer sure that my galloping heart is due to that running. My breath catches, and I dare not exhale.

"We're heading out to get some food!" Jason exclaims from behind me. Carter's eyes snap open, and he snatches his hand away like my face is on fire and I just burnt him. I start coughing and bend over, putting my hands on my knees, trying to bring oxygen back to my clearly not functioning brain. Word to the wise? Don't hold your breath after you just ran a marathon. "We'll be back in a bit," Jason continues, oblivious to my almost-death. I turn my head to see him and Aiden jump into the jeep and pull out of our driveway. How did Carter and I get back home so quickly? Must have teleported without my knowledge. I straighten back up and look at the boy in front of me. His fists are clenched and his whole body is rigid. I feel tears prickle in the corner of my eyes.

"Carter, what is it?" I almost whine. What is going on? Why is he acting so weirdly? Carter looks to the side where Aiden just stopped the jeep beside us.

"Nothing." Carter looks down, then back at the jeep, then back down before his eyes snap up again and they light up. "It's just that Reagan received her early admission letter to Starwood and is hell bent on starting this semester," he says suddenly with...triumph?

"Your sister is coming to campus?" Jason stage-whispers from behind me. I don't even have to turn around to see the joy on his face. I can hear it.

Oh. Oooooh.

"And you're worried..." I say, motioning my head in my brother's direction.

Carter nods. "How the hell am I supposed to keep the both of you out of trouble?"

"I can take care of myself!" I exclaim, aghast. As if I need a protector! I've got Jake, thank you very much!

"We need to get going," Aiden interrupts our little exchange. Okay... Thanks for the information, I guess? I look at him expectantly. Nothing.

"Aaand?"

"Err, do you want pizza or Chinese for dinner?" My brother asks. Are they freaking serious? I huff and stomp away towards the front door. "Jen!" Jason shouts after me. "Which one is it?"

"Whichever." I throw my hands up in the air.

"Must be that time of the month." I hear Jason's whiny voice. It takes everything in me not to run to him and punch a hole in his stupid face. Instead, like the class act that I am,

I turn around and put my hands on my hips, lifting my chin up.

"Carter is sexy," I shoot. Silence. Complete silence. Even the birds stop singing. Aiden's jaw is on the floor of the jeep; Jason goes wide-eyed. Only Carter is grinning at me, showing the full set of his perfectly straight, perfectly white teeth.

"Why, thank you." He nods in appreciation. "On that note, byee," he says, wiggling his fingers in the direction of the jeep. I shrug my shoulders at the confused expressions in the car and make my way inside the house. Carter better be a damn good unpacker.

"What the hell is this thing?" Carter exclaims from behind me as I drag Sully towards my room.

"Sully, the monster suitcase," I explain patiently. Some guys really are like twinkle stars...nice to look at, but not that bright. Not bright at all.

"You got that right," he mutters, taking Sully out of my hand and pulling it to my room. I let the muscle boy take over and look around, making a kissy sound. Nothing. I go on all fours and whistle. "Are you feeling okay?"

Getting up, I brush the invisible dust off of my knees. "Where's Jake?" I narrow my eyes.

"Oh, he's out for a walk with Hayley. They should be back soon—" As soon as the words leave his mouth, the front door opens and a bundle of fluff comes barrelling down the hall towards me. I drop to my knees and cuddle Jake to me. He yelps tiny yelps of happiness as I scratch behind his ear and give him kisses.

"Wow. I never get treated like that." Hayley smiles down at me. I get up to Jake's disapproval and give her a hug.

"Want me to scratch your ear and lick your face?" I ask.

She laughs, hugging me back. "No thanks, babe. God, I missed you."

"Missed you too!"

Carter clears his throat. "As much as I'm enjoying this, and as much as I have at least a thousand scenarios in my head of how this develops," he motions between Hayley and I, "I really need to get going."

Hayley stiffens and we break apart. Her cheeks are a bit red, and she nods once, curtly.

"But, what about Sully?" My whole world crumbles around me. "We had a deal! I was to tell everyone that I think you're sexy and you were going to help me unpack! I did that! I told them!"

Hayley bursts out laughing. "Ohmygod! You didn't!"

"Desperate times call for desperate measures. You know how much I hate unpacking." I pout, examining my cuticles.

Hayley wipes the tears of laughter from under her eyes. "Carter, if you need to go, go. I'll help Jenny," she says, then turns to me. "And you. Do you really need to stroke his ego even more? He's already convinced he's the Second Coming."

"Hayley, Hayley, Hayley...I am pretty incredible, but to compare me to Jesus? Well, I think I might just blush! The love! The devotion!" Carter interjects, giving me a hug goodbye while Hayley rolls her eyes. "I shall never forget this, sweet cheeks!" He turns to her with a flourish. "You shall always and forever remain in my heart as my number one fan." He places one hand on her cheek and the other on his forehead, whipping his head to the side dramatically. "But for now I must bid you goodbye, my little petal!"

With that, he turns and walks out of the house, leaving us in a stunned silence.

"Sweet cheeks? Petal?" I enquire when I finally get my voice back.

Hayley shakes her head. "Don't even ask."

"I'm not even sure if I want to know."

"Speaking of things you don't want, c'mon let's get you unpacked. You can tell me all about your holiday," she says, pulling me into my room.

"Fine," I sigh and walk towards the monster. Jake has settled himself on my bed already, so I give Sully a wide berth and go to him instead. Sitting down next to Jake, I stroke his soft fur as Hayley unzips my suitcase. This could work. "How was your break, anyway? Did you get any rest at all? Or did you work through the whole thing?"

"You know me." She smiles. "Work is my middle name. It felt like one really long shoot after another. With some promo parties thrown in between."

"Carter was in LA. Did you get to see him at all?" I yawn as Hayley starts taking out my clothes and folding them neatly.

"Bumped into him once in a bar. Speaking of Carter!" She suddenly grins. "Did you see that video of him singing 'The Wind Beneath My Wings' went viral?"

"What?" Does she mean the one I filmed during our road trip and posted on YouTube for shits and giggles?

"Yup," she nods. "It's got a million views so far."

"No way." I'm speechless. "Does he know?" God knows that would only feed his self-obsession.

"I think so." Hayley thinks for a second. "Listen, there's something else I've been meaning to talk to you about." Her face grows serious, and she looks up at me.

"What is it?" I get off the bed and walk towards her, picking up a Toblerone I just spotted in between my t-shirts. Score! Jake follows and looks at it greedily. Silly boy does not realize that the stuff is not good for him. I open the chocolate bar and break off a couple of pieces, handing one to Hayley. She shakes her head, so I pop both of them into my mouth. Bliss.

"Well, I'm sure it's nothing but, there are some rumours flying around campus..."

Chapter 32

Sociopath

Coffee doesn't ask questions. Coffee understands.
- Jenny

Cold sweat runs down the nape of my neck as I drive towards the dorms. I clench my hands tightly on the steering wheel, focusing on the road rather than the words I saw when I received the latest texts from Chloe.

"She replied," Jason startles me out of my thoughts. I all but forgot he was in the car with me. "We're good to go."

I nod and squeeze my eyes shut. How could I let this happen just as things with Jenny were so perfect?

"What the hell, dude? Open your eyes and watch where you're going!" Jason screams. I open them reluctantly and glance in his direction. "Eyes on the road, THE ROAD!" he panics. I focus back on the route I'm taking. The street is empty, but he's right, I've been careless with my driving lately. "That's better," Jason exhales, his shoulders relaxing a little.

I don't reply. There's nothing to say. Nothing to defend myself with. Everything, all the shit I'm in, is entirely my fault, my doing.

"She could be lying."

"What if she isn't? What then?" I ask. He doesn't answer for a long while.

"Look, she might be lying or she might be telling the truth. No point in sulking until we find out, is there?" Jason finally says.

We drive in silence the rest of the way. I've screwed up so badly, so Jason still standing by me and willing to help means everything to me. I knew ignoring Chloe was a gamble, but Jason assured me he'd keep her occupied. We were certain she was just trying to get to him, trying to get his attention by screwing with me. Then that text.

I didn't reply to her calls or texts in the last week, and they stopped almost completely. Until we landed, and my phone buzzed in my pocket. I wasn't sure what hit me when I took it out and read the messages in my inbox. There were two. One, which must have been sent just after we boarded the flight and I switched my phone off, and one received just before we landed. *I'M PREGNANT*, the first read. Enough to stop my heart.

Then, when I scrolled down, my whole world started collapsing.

Nameless people and their tired faces rushed past me like in a movie, and all I could see in clear focus was Jenny's confused expression as she sat on the bench waiting for Jason and me to collect our luggage. In that moment, I would have given anything to make that night with Chloe disappear. Where's the Devil when you're willing to sell your soul?

I must have read that last text a thousand times, trying to let it sink in, before Jason took the phone out of my hand and read it himself.

"Stop ignoring me, you're the father," he mutters, reading it out loud. "Well, shiiiit."

Shit is exactly what I was neck deep in. After that, he told me he'd help me find out the truth. He said not to worry. He texted Chloe that he'd like to see her, that he needed to see her as soon as possible.

We waited for her reply for ages and, in the meantime, Jason decided that it was best not to involve Jenny until the situation was resolved. It killed me not being able to talk to her, not being able to touch her, but I couldn't bring myself to deceive her like that. So I stayed distant. Every confused expression on her face, each tentative touch, was like a knife slicing my heart.

Chloe still hadn't replied to Jason's text when we got back home from the airport, and he made an executive decision to just go to her dorm and wait for her there if she wasn't in. "It's either that or you'll start sobbing on the floor any minute," he said. I agreed.

Anything to get me out of the house and as far away from kitten as possible. How could I look her in the eyes and not feel the shame and the disappointment? I was a jerk, a stupid jerk.

"So, the plan is we don't come in 'guns blazing'. She'll just fight back—"

"Why are you helping me?" I interrupt him as I put the car in park in front of the Starwood dorms.

Jason hangs his head. "Well, if she's lying, then I feel partially responsible. I promised I'd keep her occupied and off your back, but then...I have been ignoring her. She's been getting so whiney that I stopped replying in the past week, and I've got this feeling that she's trying to retaliate."

I fight the urge to give my best mate a hug in gratitude and just playfully punch him in the arm instead. He grunts and smiles. I can't stop the thought that the poor guy has nothing to apologise for. He wasn't the one who got hammered and then... What? Can't really call it an accident. You don't 'accidentally' fuck someone.

My mood instantly sours at the thought of that fateful night. How could I have done it and why did Jenny never let me explain properly? Why did I let her dismiss the subject?

Because I'm a coward, that's why. If only I had the guts to tell her the whole truth about that night...

The sky darkens, and it starts to drizzle as we walk with as much cheerfulness as a convicted murderer walking towards an electric chair the last few steps between the car and the entrance to the building.

Jason pulls open the large, glass door and guides me through the corridors. Too soon, he stops. The door is unassuming. Certainly, nothing gives the impression that behind this particular piece of wood is a person who holds my future, my happiness in the palm of their small hand. A small whiteboard hangs next to the door. I look closer 'Be the change you want to see -Gandhi' is written in neat handwriting.

Jason reads it out loud and snorts. "Can't believe how pretentious she is. Considering all the lies and manipulations she's put people through..."

I raise my hand and knock. "I'll be right back," Jason whispers before turning around and sprinting off. Shit. I guess I'm on my own then.

The door opens a crack, and Chloe's face pops out.

"Hi," I mumble.

"Hi." She looks around the corridor. I look as well. It's empty. How the hell did Jason disappear so quickly?

"May I come in?"

"Now is not a good time," she says, making the gap between the door narrower. I put my palm on the door to stop her from closing it completely.

"Chloe," I say with as much authority as I can muster. "Don't you think we need to talk?"

"Can it not wait?" she asks with irritation in her voice. What the hell? "I've got an appointment I can't be late to," she says, then looks up and down the corridor again. I thought Jason said she knew we were coming. Odd.

"I'd rather discuss the issue of you being pregnant with my child. Now," I say loudly, following a gut instinct.

Chloe jumps in her place, startled. "Shhh," she shushes me. "Fine, you can come in, but you've got to be quick." I push on the door. "Wait, a sec." She stops me then disappears from behind the crack only to reappear a few seconds later, opening the door for me and rushing me in. I recognise the pink room straight away. The room of my nightmares.

I turn around and see Chloe peering into the hallway one more time, then quickly closing the door.

"I thought you were rushing for an appointment." I gesture at her attire. She's wearing a short, almost see-through satin robe from under which you can clearly see a black corset and barely there panties. Chloe pulls the robe tighter.

"Yeah, well, I was just getting dressed. I was asleep. You woke me up." Right. And my name is Mother Teresa. Show me a girl who willingly sleeps in full makeup and a tight black corset, and I'll give you an island. I mean, not that it's not what guys' dreams are made of. We're just aware that our fantasies are not so close to the tank top and shorts truth.

I raise my eyebrows at her, making her scoff, then walk over to the chair by her desk and sit down.

"So?" Chloe asks, fluffing her hair impatiently.

"So."

"Spit it out, Aiden."

"Me?" What the hell? She's the one who's pregnant. I slowly look around the room, spotting a wine cooler with a Champagne bottle in it and two flutes standing next to it. I jump up to my feet. "What the hell is this?" I shout.

"What?" Chloe asks, looking around.

"This!" I point at the Champagne. "You're drinking? While pregnant? Are you out of your mind?"

"Oh, this... It's not even open!" She puts her hands on her hips, revealing the corset once again.

"Doesn't change the fact that you were going to poison our child."

"Stop saying that!"

"What? Our child? It is, though, isn't it? That's what you said in your text, I'm the father." Chloe's eyes dart around the room, averting mine. Has she been lying?

"No!" she shouts. "I mean, yes! But you can forget about it. You were ignoring me so I went...I went and got an abortion!" Oh. My. God. She is lying. I can smell the deceit hanging in the room, wrapped around in her sickly pink curtains. I narrow my eyes just as the door bursts open.

"Jasey, you came," Chloe purrs and launches herself at him. I want to puke.

"You're a liar," I grit through my teeth.

Jason pries Chloe's digits off his person and looks from me to her.

"What is Aiden doing here?" he asks her while gently cupping her chin. I look at him in confusion, then at Chloe, whose eyes are large and darting around the room in search of...an answer? I look at Jason again, and he winks at me, a barely visible wink, but I catch it.

"He came to borrow some notes!" Chloe exclaims while running to her desk. She picks a stack of papers and thrusts them at me. Is she honestly expecting me to go along with this?

I take the notes from her and flick through them absent-mindedly. Okay. I'll play along, Jason.

"Jason," I start. "I didn't know you were coming." A corner of Jason's mouth lifts upwards just a touch, and he nods slightly to me. Sly motherfucker!

"Aiden was just leaving," Chloe interrupts.

I look at her. "I thought you had an appointment to rush to."

Jason lifts his eyebrow and pouts. "But I thought we had plans." Jesus, he's a good actor.

Chloe is silent. I can see her thinking process, trying to find a way out of this situation. I decide to end the charade.

"Well, I'd better be going," I say.

"Yes, great, see you later." Chloe practically jumps at the opportunity to get rid of me. She runs to the door, reaching for the doorknob.

I laugh. "Are you serious? Do you really think I'm going to go before you tell me exactly what the hell is going on?" Her face falls.

"Aideeen, please," she pleads as the last resort, but I'm not budging. How the hell did I ever trust this girl?

Jason sits on the bed and reaches for the Champagne,

popping the cork with a loud 'pop' and pouring himself a glass. Looking at me, he says, "Aiden, want some? Chloe?"

"No, thanks," I reply. Chloe's shoulders sag as Jason takes a sip. "I'm driving, and Chloe is pregnant, or...not anymore? Which one is it Chloe?"

Jason spits out the mouthful of Champagne onto the pink rug under his feet. "Wait, what?" he exclaims. Bloody hell, this guy should be an actor. If I didn't know better, I'd totally believe that this is the first time he's hearing about it. His eyes are bulging and his gaze wavers between Chloe and I. He finally spits out, "Care to elaborate?"

"Chloe?" I look at her.

"I'm not pregnant," she says quietly.

"Because, in the last few hours, you had an abortion?" I cock my head to the side, willing her to just come out with the truth.

Jason gasps and covers his mouth with his hand. "What would Gandhi say?" I fight the urge to roll my eyes at him. Reel it in, Mad Dog.

Chloe hangs her head and sighs, not replying.

"Chloe," I say. "Were you pregnant with my child or not?" She looks up and stares at Jason, anxiousness in her features. She shakes her head. "You weren't." I exhale in relief.

"Aiden, I—"

"I can't believe you'd lie like that," I say in disgust.

"You slept with my best friend?" Jason shots up to his feet. Chloe's eyes go huge.

"Jason..." she begs, her voice whiney.

"I can't believe you'd sleep with my very best friend!" he exclaims. "I can't stand to look at you," he spits out, and I'm honestly not sure whether he's acting the part or not. Either way, he's very convincing. I'm trying to figure out what the main goal behind this outburst is. I mean, we know the truth now, she's not pregnant. Why antagonise her even further? Not that I'm not enjoying the horror painted on her lying face.

"Jason. I wouldn't! You know I love you!" She falls to her knees. My jaw drops.

"You wouldn't?" I say incredulously. Chloe's eyes are focused on Jason's face. It's like I'm not even here.

"Elaborate," he grits through his teeth.

"I love you. I never stopped loving you. Jasey, you're the one for me."

"No," he says coldly. "Elaborate on sleeping with my best friend."

"I didn't sleep with him," she pleads. "Please believe me."

"But you said—" I start.

"Well, I lied!" she interjects, snapping at me. I can't believe this shit. All this fucking heartache, and all because of the whim of some stupid, blonde bimbo who was trying to get at her ex.

"You're a sociopath," I state, blinking my eyes, trying to see if I can wake up from this nightmare.

"Jesus Christ, Chloe," Jason says, and his act finally breaks. He's staring at her like he can't recognise her. "What the fuck is wrong with you?"

Chloe sniffles, and a tear runs down her cheek. "I just wanted us back."

"There is no us!" Jason exclaims. "There never was. We dated for a month. We both agreed it was casual."

"That's not true," she whines.

Jason kneels by her and takes her hand. His voice is quiet, almost a whisper. "Yes it is, Chloe. Don't you remember?" He rubs her cheek with his other hand in a calming motion.

"But...I wanted so much more." Chloe's face scrunches up, and tears now fully spill down her cheeks.

"I'm sorry, Chloe," he soothes. "I can't give you more. I never could. Especially not after this."

I retract out of the dorm room and wait for Jason to finish the conversation privately. I still can't believe what just transpired. What a conniving little b—.

I can't even finish the thought before I realise, I haven't slept with Chloe. I never betrayed kitten!

I smile.

It's a full on grin.

I can't wait to get home and tell her that I didn't screw up. That I love her. That everything is going to be okay from now on. It's her and me against the world, and we're going to face whatever else life throws our way together. Jenny by my side and her palm in mine.

I grin again at the prospect of what's to come, at all the happiness ahead of me.

Boy, was I wrong. All hell was about to break loose.

Chapter 33

Hey, Beautiful

***I love asking kids what they want to be when
they grow up because I'm still looking for ideas.***
- Jason

"Well, I'm sure it's nothing, but there are some rumours floating around campus..." Hayley says.

"Oh?" I peer up at her. "Is it about that thing you can do with your legs? I swear I never told anyone!" Hayley laughs and shakes her head.

"I believe you, and no, it's not that. It's about Chloe, actually..."

"Wait, don't tell me! Did her spray tan get mixed up with acid like on Scream Queens? Has everyone found out she's got a tail? She has eleven toes, doesn't she? OH MY GOD, she finally grew horns! The Devil came to claim her!" I cover my mouth with my hands.

"You're funny today." Hayley shakes her head, laughing.

"How dare you! I'm always funny!" I gasp, aghast. "In fact, I often ponder the possibility of me being a love child between Kevin Hart and Tina Fey. That would explain my height, but not the pasty complexion."

Hayley stares at me blankly. "Riiiight." Picking at the invisible fluff on my jeans, I pretend I didn't hear her. She doesn't need to know that that last statement was too close to the truth. I mean, how do you end up a hobbit in a family of giants? Seriously! There must have been a mixup in the hospital.

If it wasn't for the fact that my face was the spitting image of my mother's, I'd be online now, trying to find my birth parents. Not that I'd ever leave my dad and brother behind. I'd just want to meet the suckers with such a fantastic gene pool. "Anyway," Hayley continues. "Are you done guessing? Shall I tell you?"

"Shoot."

"Well, apparently, Chloe is knocked up."

Whoa, whoa, whoa. "I thought her vagina had teeth! How did it even happen? Has some poor bastard gotten his penis chomped off in the process?"

"Probably." Hayley smirks. "Most likely, it's just gossip anyway with not even an ounce of truth to it, but I thought the possibility of Chloe getting fat and pimply would brighten your day up!"

"Oh it does, sister from another mister." I grin at her. And really, it does.

For the rest of the evening, I burst into fits of giggles every time I think of it. Hayley manages to unpack me, fold my clothes into neat squares, and put them away without batting an eyelid. She's a saint.

We chat for a while, making up for lost time. With all that

happened in London, I forgot how much I loved her company and lighthearted humor, and, by the time we finish exchanging stories, we're both yawning with exhaustion. Jake is happily snoring with his head on my lap, and I absentmindedly scratch behind his ear. The boys are still missing, and I'm surprised. I glance down at my watch and find out it's almost ten o'clock. There goes their promise of bringing back dinner, I guess.

Hayley leaves to get back to her dorm shortly after, and I make my way to the kitchen to forage for something to eat. Hunter-gatherer style, or at least a sneaky-style, since I fish out a tub of Pringles I hid behind a box of granola, knowing the guys would never reach for the 'healthy option' breakfast.

Munching my way through half a tub with the speed of a thousand gazelles, I check on Edward, amazed that it's absolutely fine and looking as fresh as a daisy. I snap a photo and post it on instagram, updating Edward's followers that the guy is still going strong.

Instantly, my account is flooded with likes and comments. Some of them, clearly the ones who placed a bet on him going green during Christmas, are quite rude, calling the whole thing a hoax. I decide to not get myself involved in that battle. In the wise words of TayTay 'Haters gonna hate'.

I close the cupboard, silently bidding Edward goodnight, and think back to the time when Dad told us for the first time we would be moving. It was here, in this kitchen. I was sitting on the counter, my legs swinging while Jason was sprawled on the floor, trying to find an insect or a rodent he could call his pet. Thankfully, he was unsuccessful. I remember feeling hopeless, upset, and so angry at dad for ripping us from the only place we felt safe in, and the only place that held all our memories connected with Mom and Grandma.

Funny how things turn out. Would we have ever met Aiden if we never moved to London? Would he still have come to Starwood to study? Would I want to go here or would I want to be as far away as possible, like so many kids that grew up in this town? Questions I'll never know the answers to.

Dropping the now empty Pringles tub in the bin, I head to my room and jump into a hot shower. No point waiting for the guys any longer. A girl could starve waiting on them!

When I come back out, Jake is sprawled out on my bed looking so cute that I don't have the heart to push him off. Instead, I towel dry my hair and change into a pair of shorts and a tank top and make my way out of the room, letting him sleep. The poor chap looked exhausted.

Yawning, I walk over to the sofa and flick through the TV channels for a good fifteen minutes before realizing there's nothing on, not that I'm paying any attention. I'm so tired my vision is blurry, and it's too hard to focus. I switch off the TV completely and yawn again. When I look at my watch it's eleven, time for bed. I hope Aiden and Jason are okay; they've been gone for a long time. Making my way back to the bedroom, I grab my phone to call them, only to see a text from Aiden.

AIDEN: *I'm so sorry, kitten. We got held up :(We'll be home as soon as we can. Love you :**

I smile at the text and hold the phone to my chest, blushing, then looking around, worried that someone saw. Yup, I'm *that* girl. The one that goes gooey because her boyfriend sent her a kiss via text. Thankfully, only Jake's in the room. Still on my bed. Farting.

I grimace and make a split second decision. Still holding

onto my phone and grinning like an idiot, I walk across the hall to my old room. Placing my phone on the nightstand, I slip under the covers and put my head on the pillow. Aiden's smell surrounds me like a cocoon, so I close my eyes and inhale.

It only takes a few seconds before I'm asleep.

A soft hand strokes my cheek and I groggily open my eyes.

"Hey, beautiful," he whispers from behind me in his deep voice, making my lips turn up in a smile. He places his face in the spot between my shoulder and my neck and inhales deeply. His hand snakes around my body and rests somewhere around my midsection. I shiver, instantly awake. More than awake. I'm suddenly aware of every cell in my body.

"Hey yourself." I smile into his cheek. "Where were you? Is everything alright?"

"More than alright. I had to deal with something. I'll tell you everything in the morning," he says into my neck, his voice causing electricity to charge through my veins.

I turn my body so that I'm on my back and reach around his neck, pulling his face towards mine and his body closer to me.

I can feel every single gorgeous muscle in his chest as he breathes steadily. His face is mere inches from mine. I move my hands from around his neck down to his waist and am pleased to discover he's only wearing a t-shirt and boxer shorts. Impatiently, I tug his shirt up. Placing my palms on his bare back and straining up, I connect my lips with his.

I'm rewarded with a groan, a groan that thrills my lady

parts. Seriously, they do a little happy dance; Cha-Cha or Macarena, I think. But honestly, I don't care which one, because, in that moment, Aiden pulls away from my mouth and places his gorgeous lips on my neck.

My body tingles, and desire spreads across my skin. I'm hyper aware of every single part of Aiden that touches me, but it's not enough. Too many layers. I want more of him, I want him closer. I want his skin on my skin.

I push him away from me. He obliges with no protest, and when I look at him, I can see the disappointment in his eyes. The boy is in for a big surprise if he thinks I'm wanting him to stop...

Climbing from under the thin cover, I join him on top. He sits up, looking at me, puzzled. I silently reach and pull his t-shirt up and off of his gorgeous body. As soon as his t-shirt is off and those magnificent abs are making an appearance, scouting for compliments, no doubt, my hands reach for him and connect with bare skin, stroking his chest.

Aiden's breath hitches, and I can see the desire in his eyes. My brain sings Hallelujah and I kiss him hard. He responds instantly with a heat I've never felt from him before. He yanks me closer to him, and I take the opportunity to explore his body further, my hands running up and down his chest, then finally going lower, down to the band of his boxer shorts. I skim the border gently with my fingertips.

Aiden moans into my mouth. A moan that I can feel right down to my tippy toes.

"You can't touch me like that and expect me to remain in control." A clear warning in his voice, and I know that he's on the verge of finally giving in to me. "If you do it again, I can't be held responsible for what happens," he croaks out.

"Good," I say and skim my fingers around the waistband again. His stomach muscles clench and his breath hitches. I smile, loving the effect my touch has on his body.

"God, kitten," he whispers, his eyes closed. "Please stop if you don't want this to go any further," he begs.

I place my lips on his and kiss him deeply, then move away. Aiden's eyes snap open and he breathes heavily. I sit up. "I want to go further," I say with conviction, then pull my tank top off. Aiden pulls his bottom lip in between his teeth, making a dimple appear in his left cheek as his gaze roams over my face, then down to my exposed flesh, stopping for not so brief a moment on my breasts.

My breath quickens, embarrassed under such scrutiny. Then Aiden's eyes meet mine, and he whispers, "You're so beautiful." I smile shyly and get one from him in return. "How did I get so lucky?" he muses. I could say the same, I think as my gaze roams around his gorgeous body.

"Touch me," I say with a shaky voice. He hesitates for a few unbearable seconds, then his right hand moves slowly towards my body, resting on my hip.

"Not there." I roll my eyes, making a corner of Aiden's lips turn up in a crooked smile. He doesn't move his hand, though. Instead, he looks at my breasts hungrily.

"I'm going to kiss you now." His voice is hoarse. I nod in agreement. At least I'll have his body touching mine. Maybe that will calm the fire that has started burning in my belly under his heated gaze.

He leans towards me, and I start moving up when his hand, the one on my hip, stops my movement. He gently pushes me back onto the bed until I'm flat on the mattress with my head resting on his pillow. Then, following close behind, his face hovers above mine for a few seconds. I close my eyes in anticipation, basking in the feel of his warm breath on my cheek. Any second now, his lips will touch mine.

Aiden shifts his weight, making the mattress dip a little, and his lips move from my face down my neck. I try to remember to breathe as goosebumps rise up where his breath connects with my skin the split second his lips touch my body I gasp, something between a cry and moan escaping my throat as I'm flooded with so much pleasure and desire I can barely think. His hand softly strokes the side of my body as he places gentle kisses on my collar bone, then lower and lower.

One thing is clear. There is no going back now. I'll be damned if I let him weasel his way out of this now.

Heat is pounding through my veins, my nerves on edge. With each flick of his tongue on my skin, a shiver runs down my body. Every cell inside me screams for more, and when he covers one of my nipples with his mouth, gently sucking it while his hand covers my other breast, I all but scream with pleasure.

Aiden is successfully turning me into a puddle. A puddle of nerves and desperate with desire. Everything he does seems to singe, marking me in some way.

"Aiden," I moan as his lips tread down to my hip, and then my inner thigh. He stops for a moment, holding my legs in his strong arms, and looks up at me.

"I can stop, kitten, if you want?" he croaks, placing a kiss on my thigh and moving upwards, his body covering mine. At the feel of his naked skin on mine, my legs instinctively open up for him, wrapping around him. The only thing between us is the flimsy material of our underwear.

"It's not that, I'm just nervous." The words escape me. "I don't know what to expect. Will it hurt?"

"It's okay if you're not ready. We can wait." He smiles a

gentle smile as he strokes my cheek with the back of his hand. "There's no hurry. We've got our entire lives in front of us. I'm not going anywhere." His words tug at my heart, and the fear starts dissipating.

"I want to make love to you," I whisper and move my body against his. His length presses against me, and I gasp at the same time he sharply inhales. Heat pools in my lower stomach at the feeling of him against me.

"Are you sure?" His eyes are questioning, and his concern pushes me over the edge.

"Yes," I say. Pulling him closer, I cover his mouth with mine, joining us in a deep kiss, and instantly move against him, my legs wrapping tighter around his middle. Aiden moans and pulls his mouth away from mine, pushing himself to his arms and away from me. His hips are still pressed against me, I gleefully note.

"Let me do this right," he says, his eyes dark and his voice hoarse. "Let me make sure you're ready. Let me love you," he pleads. I nod almost imperceptibly, but that's all the confirmation Aiden needs as he pulls himself away and starts trailing kisses down my collarbone, causing me to squirm from the pleasure that floods me. He takes his time exploring and probing my body with his lips, gently kissing and nipping, stopping every so often to make sure that I'm okay. By the time his lips make it back down to the thigh he left so abruptly earlier on, I am positively panting like a dog in heat.

His mouth hovers over my bare skin, then his tongue darts out as he gently caresses up my inner thigh towards my underwear. He presses his finger against my centre and strokes leisurely up and down. "Your panties are soaked." I blush. "Fuck, that's so sexy." His nose touches the same spot, and he inhales. "You smell so good." He licks my underwear. "I'm going to remove these now," he says, lifting the band of my panties. My body trembles as Aiden's skilful fingers trace the pattern of the material before gently pulling them down my legs and over my ankles. And just like that, I am completely naked.

Nerves are wreaking havoc in my brain, and I clutch my thighs tightly together. Aiden just strokes and kisses the sides of my legs, and then goes back to my breast, his glorious tongue flicking my nipples until I can't bear it any more.

Forgetting all about the nerves, I start moaning, and, before I know it, my legs are being gently spread by his big hands. He lowers himself back down, positioning his face right between them.

"I'm going to kiss you now," he says hoarsely, and before I have the time to think, to process, his tongue connects with my pussy. I cry out as my hips buck. What in the name of all that is holy is this magic? I can't control my moans as Aiden's tongue keeps licking and sucking at my clit, making circles and patterns I can't comprehend in my muddled brain.

My fist is clenched, and to stop myself from screaming in pleasure I pound it into the mattress without realizing.

Aiden hesitates. "Don't stop," I almost beg. He chuckles at my words and dives back in with renewed vigor. This time, he licks fervently, going from clit to lips, then back to clit. I moan when he pushes a finger into me, stroking me from the inside as his mouth devours me whole.

"Aiden," I plead as his finger picks up speed.

"You taste so good," he groans in reply. A groan that reverberates down my legs, making me push against his finger frantically. He slips a second finger into me and starts pumping. I can't control the sounds escaping my mouth as he sucks, then circles his tongue around my clit, over and over again. This feels like sensation overload, and I don't think I can take it much longer. Heat starts pulling in my brain, breasts, my legs. I can't take it anymore and as he growls into my pussy. With a loud moan, I go over the edge. My upper body lifts off the bed in a spasm as pleasure spreads all over my body. I try to push Aiden's head away from me, but he keeps continuing his actions, making me come for what feels like hours.

As my body calms down, Aiden's kisses get gentler and less frantic, as if he knows how it feels. I can't believe what just happened. And finally, I admit to myself that Aiden has me in the palm of his hand. If he can make me feel like this, I don't want to leave this bed, ever.

Why would people want to ever leave their beds? Go to work? No, thank you. Now, can you please go down on me again? Yup, that's my new motto.

Aiden lifts his head from between my legs and brings his glistening fingers to his lips, sucking at them as he closes his eyes with pleasure. I should feel embarrassed, but I don't. I feel sexy and empowered and ready for more.

"You're so fucking hot," he says, his eyes hooded with desire. "And you taste like goddamned strawberries." He shakes his head as I throw all shyness out the window and pull him in for a kiss.

He presses his body against me, and I can feel how hard he is. My body tightens at the sensation of him against me, and, once again, I start wanting to feel him inside me.

I pull at Aiden so that he rolls on his side, then push him onto his back so that I land on top of him. I sit up in all my naked glory, feeling his boxer shorts against my skin. Aiden's eyes roam over my naked body, and his hands reach out, gripping my hips as he moves against me in fluid motions that make my back arch.

"Fuck, kitten," he gasps. "You're driving me crazy. Your little moans...the way your body responds to me. You're just...so beautiful. So perfect." His voice is rough and full of desire, and I quirk a half smile before removing my hips from him.

I reach down and pull his boxers off, letting him finish the job by kicking them off with his legs.

"Mesmerizing," I mutter in awe, looking down at his penis. He is fully erect and ready. I reach with my hand and stroke him. Aiden gasps and moans at my touch but doesn't tell me to stop, so I continue in my exploration. He looks large, and I'm starting to get nervous about how the hell he is planning to fit himself into me.

Aiden moans loudly and pushes his hips up, and my fingers grasp around his length. He inhales loudly, then, with one quick movement of his body, he changes our position.

One moment, I was on top of him holding his smooth penis in my hand, next he's on top of me, his hand between my legs, his fingers parting my folds. I gasp and start moving against him, a new wave of desire making its way up and down my body.

"I'm going to make you come again and then..." His voice is hoarse, and I stop his words with a kiss. I'd rather not know what's coming. I don't want to get nervous again. I just want to feel, experience this. I just want him.

He rubs me with his fingers, making me writhe with pleasure with each stroke of his hand. Soon, he enters me with his finger and strokes. It's easier this time. I can feel how wet I am around him as he moves in and out while his thumb rubs at my clitoris. Soon, the second finger joins, and then the third. Aiden stretches me in the most pleasurable way possible as I move against his hand, anticipating the feeling that starts building in my core.

I climax so hard I thrash against the bed, moaning Aiden's name, praising him to God. His lips cover mine, muffling my screams of pleasure as I ride to bliss against his hand. His hand moves away when I finally stop coming, his lips still on mine, kissing me desperately as he reaches to the side of the bed. I hear foil rustling, and the lightbulb flashes in my head.

I deepen the kiss in anticipation as he lowers his body back onto me, and the tip of him presses against me. He stops kissing me and looks at me with deep emotions of concern. "This might hurt a little."

"Okay," I nod and press myself against his tip, wrapping my legs around him.

He goes slowly, stopping every few seconds to ask if I'm okay. Each time I nod, even though it hurts, and push him further in with my legs. Tears gather in my eyes. He is not even halfway in, and I don't think I'll be able to take anymore. He instantly pulls out and starts kissing my face, my eyes.

"I hurt you," he says. His voice is strained, and I can't imagine the self control he must possess to stop so abruptly when I could clearly see the pleasure on his face just a second ago.

"Just a little. It's okay though, it's bound to hurt."

"We can wait, next time maybe," he says, and, in that moment, I love him even more. All I want is for him to feel the pleasure he just gave me. Determined, I squirm from under him and straddle his hips, positioning myself just above him. His eyes grow large.

"This way, I can stop if it hurts. I'm in control," I say as I stroke his cheek. I don't let him respond. Instead, I lower myself down onto him slowly. This time it's easier, and when his tip is inside me and his eyes roll in pleasure, a shiver runs down my spine, causing a surge of bravery.

Without a thought, I slam down on him, taking him in fully, gasping as a sharp pain takes my breath away. Aiden moans as his body jerks upwards. "Fuuuuck." I can hear his whisper as he sits up and his mouth connects with my nipple.

Although it hurts, I move my legs so that they once more wrap around Aiden as his arms pull me into him. His lips frantically kiss my collarbone and neck. I move a little against him, causing him to curse again.

I'm getting used to the feeling of him inside me and gently start to rock against him. I'm not moving him in and out much. I think it's mostly the movement inside of me. Little circles and gentle back and forth with my hips, but he seems to respond, and, before long, he is breathing heavily, rocking against my movement.

It's easier now, and I allow deeper and faster movements. Aiden responds to the change with a loud grunt. I become bolder with my movements, and it doesn't go unnoticed. Aiden kisses me deeply and skillfully flips us over, landing on top of me. He starts moving in and out of me, faster and faster.

The sounds of our bodies almost makes me giggle. Almost, because, at some point, this became less funny and a whole lot more pleasurable. Don't get me wrong, it still hurt like hell, no small part to Aiden's monster dick, but I could understand how this could feel amazing.

The thing that gave me the most pleasure was seeing his face as he moved inside me, his eyes locked on mine, his lips parted.

"I love you," I mouth as his breathing gets ragged and movement becomes erratic.

Three simple, little words, but they seem to push him over the edge as his beautiful face contorts in pleasure. His movements stops, so I rock against him instinctively, letting him ride his wave of pleasure.

His lips seek mine out as he tries to catch his breath.

"Jenny," he gasps in between kisses. "I love you."

Chapter 34

So Fucking Much

I'm not bossy, I just know what you should be doing.
- Carter

The morning sun dances on my face, bringing me back to reality and making me sigh with contentment.

Last night, damn. Last night was just...perfect.

I stretch my body under the cover of Aiden's thin sheet, my eyes still closed. I should feel different. More mature, maybe, like a woman?

Is my life going to change now?

Apart from some soreness, which was to be expected, I feel exactly the same, giddy with love and excited at the prospects of what's to come.

The 'first time' that everyone talks about, the one in all the movies, the one in all the books where the couple makes love twenty times during the night and orgasms simultaneously, not very possible. At least, not in our case, since Aiden is rather on the largish side.

Even though he took care of me, treated me like a princess and handled me like a breakable egg, it hurt. A lot. The only thing that made it better was knowing that it was with him.

The man I gave my heart and soul to. Am I silly giving myself to someone so completely at such a young age? In my mind, I have no doubt that Aiden and I will still be together when we're old and gray, a thought that scares and excites me at the same time.

"Let me do this right, let me love you." His words from last night make my whole body tingle. The way he looked at me, the way he held me, the way he kissed me. The way his body felt against me, the way his cock felt inside me. Just the memory makes my insides swirl in anticipation.

Speaking of heat, I could really do with some food. My stomach grumbles in agreement, and I open my eyes reluctantly. My old room, Aiden's room, is quiet as the sunlight seeps in through the half-drawn curtains. I slowly turn to the side, wanting to look at him, touch him, but there's no one there. The realization jolts me awake, and I sit up in confusion.

Then I spot it, the little piece of paper with Aiden's handwriting on it. I snatch the note with the speed of the French, trying to outrun the guillotine and scan the words, my heart fluttering.

Kitten,
I went to get some breakfast for us, and will be back shortly.

Didn't want to wake you up, you looked so peaceful.
Last night...was the best night of my life, but I'll tell you all about how you made me feel when I get back.

I love you...so fucking much,
Aiden

P.S. If you're still in bed, naked, when I get back, I can't promise I'll be able to keep my hands to myself. Not after last night. Not ever.
P.P.S. I'll totally take advantage of you again.
P.P.P.S. And again.

I grin and fall back onto the bed, my head hitting the pillows. I inhale his scent like a desperate sniffer dog. I'm an addict.

An Aiden addict.

There are worse things I could be.

Like an elf in Santa's toy factory, all work and no play. Or the Devil. Ha! The She-Devil.

Ugh, Chloe.

My train of thought makes my morning seem a little gloomier, and I decide it's best if I have a quick shower before Aiden gets back.

I walk across the hall to my room and head into the bathroom. The shower is glorious, and I stand under the hot stream until the skin of my fingertips turns into something resembling prunes. When I'm finally done, I quickly get dressed, choosing black leggings and a loose jumper with a purple happy hippo drawn on the front, finishing this dazzling outfit off with a pair of purple converse.

I'm utterly sexy, I know. Pulling my wet hair into a messy bun, I check my reflection in the mirror then head back to Aiden's room. I make the bed and consider arranging myself into a sexy position on top of it, but decide against it. I'm still sore from last night. Plus, who am I kidding, my hippo jumper is a mood killer. My phone is still on the nightstand, so I pick it up, wanting to text Aiden, tell him to hurry back home, hurry back and kiss me senseless again.

Only.

It's not my phone.

It's definitely not my phone.

Because I don't remember receiving a message like this.

And the message I see breaks my heart into a thousand little pieces.

"*Stop ignoring me, you're the father,*" it says. Sender: Chloe.

Somewhere, in the back of my mind, the synapses are working overtime. They know. They know that the phone belongs to Aiden. I'm not as quick though, firstly trying to figure out how Jason's phone got into Aiden's room. Because it must be Jason's, what with Chloe being his ex and all. It takes me another whole minute to accept the truth.

The message was meant for Aiden, my boyfriend.

The phone slips from my hand, and when, like a zombie, I lean down to pick it up, I see my phone lying on the floor. It must have fallen down at some point during the night.

The night I slept with my boyfriend for the first time. The boyfriend who is going to have a baby with Chloe. The boyfriend who failed to tell me about it prior to sleeping together.

Oh God, what have I done?

For Crying Out Loud

I pick both the phones up and place Aiden's phone on his pillow, next to the note he wrote me earlier.

He's the father...

So the rumors must have been true. My head spins and my chest constricts. I need air, I need to think. I need to be alone and process this whole thing.

Why would Aiden lie to me? Why wouldn't he say anything?

Well, technically, he didn't lie. You told him you don't want to know what happened between him and Chloe. You told him it was all in the past, my inner voice scolds me.

It's true. I gave him a clean slate.

Stupid, stupid girl. But would knowing that they had sex change anything? Probably not much.

However, knowing that he's about to have a baby would... At least, until I figured out how to deal with that fact.

I make my way, blindly, through the hall and somehow I end up in Kitt, my hands gripping the steering wheel, driving around the town, trying to find somewhere where I can sit down and think.

But why wouldn't he tell me that Chloe is pregnant? Why wouldn't he confide in me? My brain is trying to process the information. My vision is blurry and I shake my head, trying to clear it of the fog. Why would he not tell me and then sleep with me? Surely he knows that's wrong... Bastard!

I drive around aimlessly for what feels like an hour before I park behind the dorms.

Hayley will know what to do.

She'll tell me I'm overreacting. It can't be as bad as it sounds. It's probably just another lie.

And why hasn't Aiden tried to call me yet?

My hand is gripping my phone, and the damned thing has not buzzed once since I left the house. Maybe he's still out, maybe he doesn't know I left. I guess he will soon. How will I talk to him then? How will I be able to trust him ever again? I'm not ready to be a stepmother. I'm only nineteen for god's sake!

I shove the silent torture devise, aka the phone, into my pocket and barge into the dorms. Taking the steps two at the time, I run up to Hayley's floor, stopping only when I'm in front of her room.

When I finally get there, seriously out of breath, I bang on her door, desperation making me panic again. She doesn't answer. She's either not there or she's a heavy sleeper. I know that it's not the latter. The girl gets woken up when a cricket makes a sound, so she must be out.

Resigned, I slide down the door. The tears I've been trying to hold back finally break out and I start crying.

Way to throw yourself a pity party, my inner voice snarls at me. You're better than that.

I know I am, but that doesn't change the fact that this whole situation sucks.

So you gave your heart to him, your virginity, your soul... And all the while, he knew he had a bun baking in someone else's oven. Big deal.

Well, actually it is a big deal!

Not if it's another one of Chloe's lies. A sliver of hope tugs at my heart.

It can't be... It's not possible for someone to be so evil.

You're right. You'll just have to get used to the fact that the love of your life will marry an Oompa-Lumpa.

Shut up! Shut up, shut up, shut up!

Tears start streaming down my cheeks again.

"Jenny? What's wrong?"

For Crying Out Loud

I lift my head up and am greeted by the sight of my best friend wrapped in a towel. Her wash bag in her hand. She kneels beside me, looking into my swollen eyes. "Jenny?"

"Hayley," I manage to say before the floodgates open again and I break into a full-on ugly cry.

Chapter 35

See Her Again

Life is like a box of chocolates, I need to get one.
- *Jenny*

There's nothing in the whole entire world that could wipe the grin I'm currently sporting off my face.
Nothing.
I even start humming. Humming!
Humming as I put the finishing touches on the breakfast tray I made for kitten, arranging the strawberries in a little heart.
There was never any question as to what I should get her for breakfast. Waffles, strawberries, and her favourite mocha latte from the Bean Stop a few blocks away.
Carefully, I make my way to the bedroom, passing Jason's door and silently thanking The Guy Upstairs for making sure Jason went to Carter's after we were finished wringing the truth out of Chloe. I can only imagine how big of a black eye I'd have had if he stayed here. Actually, I'd

probably have a couple of broken bones, too. What with kitten being so loud.

Just thinking about her screaming my name over and over makes my jeans tighten again. I push open the door to my room, expecting to see Jenny sprawled across my bed, but instead, I'm greeted with an empty room, the bed made, cushions arranged. I frown and put the tray down.

Maybe she's having a shower?

That wouldn't be too bad. I could join her then. Wash her back...and front. I strut to her room and into her bathroom. The mirror is fogged, but the bathroom is empty. Weird.

Where could she be hiding? Are we playing a game?

I go back to my room and sit on the bed, searching for clues. Maybe she didn't see my note? Maybe she thought I just left her alone? Shit! I'm so damn stupid, I should have woken her up. What if the note slipped onto the floor and she never found it?

But no, the note is lying on the pillow, neatly folded... right next to my phone.

What the hell could have happened? I hope she's okay. She would have called me or texted me if something was wrong, wouldn't she?

I reach for my phone, open it, and look at the screen.

All I can feel is dread.

Oh no. No, no, no, no, no.

You know when I said 'nothing could wipe that grin off my face'? Boy, was I wrong.

How could I let this happen?

The message from Chloe is the first thing I see. A dozen scenarios run through my mind, but my brain knows already. There's only one explanation.

Jenny has seen it.

Jenny has seen it and I haven't had a chance to explain anything to her yet. I was going to tell her everything today. I had a whole plan. Damn it!

I scroll through my contacts and dial her number. It goes straight to voicemail. Shit. I try her again and again.

And again.

Always the same result. Her cheerful voice instructs me to leave a message, the only thing that answers my call.

I call Jason. He doesn't answer either, so I try Carter.

"Hello," His groggy voice answers on the fifth ring.

"Kennedy, is Jenny with you?"

"What? What time is it?"

"Is she with you, man?" I almost shout.

"Jesus!" I hear rustling. "It's eight a.m! Are you trying to make my life a living hell?"

"Please, just tell me if she's there." My voice breaks. Carter must hear the desperation because it sounds like he's moving.

More rustling follows then a muffled, "What's your name sweetheart?" and, "I'll be back in a sec." I start pacing around my room, trying to calm down and stop myself from throwing my phone at the wall. "Unless her name is Katie, and she turned into a blonde, she's not here," Carter finally says, his voice hoarse from sleep but also alert. "Care to tell me what happened?"

"She saw the text..."

"What text?"

I fill Carter in on last night's events, minus the part about Jenny and me, and the way I found my room this morning. "Is Jason with you?" I ask hopefully, maybe she got in touch with him.

"He's left already. He slept on the couch. But it all makes sense now. He was quite traumatised last night, kept on murmuring to himself about crazy eyes. Must have been after his conversation with Chloe."

"I'll try calling her again," I say, interrupting his musings.

"Okay, I'll do the same."

"No, I need to talk to her. I need to explain. She deserves to hear everything from me."

Carter reluctantly agrees, and I finish the phone call, dialing Jenny's number straight away.

Voicemail.

I hate voicemail with a passion right now.

My skin crawls and I'm itching to do something. I can't stay in the house, not while she's alone, thinking I've done God knows what.

I text Jenny. "Please call me" and "I need to explain", then "It was all a lie." But before I spam her inbox, I decide to go look for her. Kitt wasn't parked up front, and it finally clicked that she must have taken her car and gone somewhere, maybe for a drive?

First things first, though. I head down to the campus, hoping that she'd have gone straight to Hayley. Disappointment fills my veins as my heart sinks at the sight of a nearly empty parking lot outside of the dorms, Kitt nowhere in sight.

At least I know where she is not. Not at home, Carter's, or Hayley's, so maybe she went for a drive. Trying to clear her head. Maybe she's driving around now and I'm sitting here like an idiot, waiting for a miracle to happen.

Pulling out of the parking lot and heading in the direction of the city centre, I notice my hands are shaking slightly. I'm agitated. No, I'm worried. Worried that something happened to her, that I'll never have a chance to explain.

The worst-case scenarios are flooding my mind when the phone rings in my pocket. I quickly undo my seatbelt and pull it out, hitting the answer button without even looking at the caller ID and putting it on speaker.

"Hello? Jenny?" I say, slowing down to the speed limit.

"Nope. Only me, your favourite future brother-in-law." Jason's cheerful voice is a stark opposite of my gloomy mood.

"Are you home? Is Jenny there?"

"Yup, aaaand nope! Where are you guys? I thought you'd be here."

"Shiiit," I swear.

"What's wrong?"

"She saw the text from Chloe before I got to tell her anything. And now...and now she's gone. Fuck Jason, what if I messed it up? What if she never forgives me for lying to her, not telling her everything straight away?" My eyes burn.

"Jesus, calm down, Aiden! She loves you. You just need to talk to her. She'll understand. She probably just needed a breather." I need to find her first, I think as I speed down the road and through an amber light, barely making it before it turns to red. I make a conscious effort to slow down again, meandering through the streets of Starwood.

"I've got to go. I need to find her."

"Okay, well...let me know if I can do anything to help?" I don't reply, instead I switch off and try Jenny again.

"Hi, you've reached the phone of a megageek," her cheerful voice greets me again. I sigh. "You know what to do after the beep."

"Jenny..." I say after a pause. "I think you saw the text message from Chloe. I'm sorry I haven't had a chance to explain earlier. Aaahh, I want you to know that the whole thing with Chloe...it was all a lie. She lied about everything. Being pregnant, sleeping with me... It was all a ploy to get Jason back. I should have told you everything straight away. I was going to. I'm so sorry. I love you. I love you so mu—" my voice breaks, and I press the gas pedal harder.

I think I just saw her car. To catch up to her, I speed through the intersection like a maniac, running a red light.

As the blue truck hits the side of my jeep, I realise I forgot to put my fucking seat belt back on. Jenny will be so mad. She hates it when I speed. She hates it when I don't wear the seatbelt. She always says it's dangerous and stupid...

Jenny.

The force of the collision throws me against the wind shield, breaking it in the process. As I tumble through the air above the hood of my jeep, I don't feel any pain, at least not the physical kind.

My heart hurts.

I need to see her again.

Chapter 36

One Voicemail

I'm not arguing. I'm simply explaining why I'm right.
- Jason

"Wow," Hayley says after I fill her in on the events from last night and this morning.

"That's one way to put it," I grumble.

"You know, maybe you should talk to Aiden. Let him explain."

"I know, I'm going to. I just needed some space." I sigh. "To be honest, I thought he'd call by now."

"He hasn't?"

I shake my head, frowning as I pull my phone out of my hippo mouth pocket. The screen is black.

I swipe at it a couple of times before Hayley tsks at me, pulls it out of my hand, and plugs it in to charge. We both look at it silently, as it takes its sweet ass time to switch back on.

"No battery. Classic," I sigh with relief. For a moment, I thought Aiden really didn't care about where I was or what happened.

When the screen finally flashes back to life, I grab my phone and stare at it intently. Fifty missed calls, fourteen text messages, one voicemail. I scroll through my texts, first reading, scanning through the names, and going straight for the ones from Aiden. I sigh with relief when I see that the whole thing was a lie.

There's a story he can explain. He's not a dad. Phew. That was a close call. I'm seriously too young and too pretty to be an evil stepmother. Although... No. Too young and too pretty. Fact.

Next, I read messages from Cart and Jason. *Where are you?* and, *Call Aiden!* seem to be repeating themselves. Then, the last message from Jason chills my bones. There's something wrong. Breathless, I re-read the message over and over again. *Jennifer, call me NOW*, it says. *It's urgent.*

Jason never calls me Jennifer. Ever. Unless it's a life and death situation. Last time he did was when Grandma passed away.

I'm about to hit the call button when I hear Hayley's voice. "Shit, my phone was on silent all this time." Her phone starts buzzing in her hand, and she picks it up instantly.

"Yes?" she answers. "She's here. What's going on? I only just saw the texts." Terror flashes in her eyes, and I know something is horribly, horribly wrong. I look at my phone, then at her. Her eyes are wide. She picks up a pair of jeans lying on the floor and starts pulling them on. "We'll be there as soon as we can, which hospital?" My heart stops beating. "Okay, see you shortly." She finishes her call.

She quickly pulls a t-shirt on and a pair of shoes, then

looks at me. "Give me your car keys," she says steadily. I point to her bed where I threw the keys. She grabs them, then reaches for my hand. "Breathe." I nod and let my lungs fill with air. Before I know it, Hayley is pulling me out of the room, down the stairs, and into the parking lot.

I must have had an out of body experience because, before I notice what's going on, I'm sitting in the passenger seat. I don't remember going across the lot or getting into Kitt though. Hayley turns the ignition on, straps my seatbelt on, and pulls out of the lot quickly. I feel like a child that doesn't know what's going on but knows that something bad has happened.

"That was Jason on the phone," she says. I nod. This much I figured out. I also know that whatever is going to follow is not going to be good. No 'We just won the lottery'. I can put two and two together.

'Hospital'. 'We'll be there as soon as we can', she said. She needed me with her, in the car, before she said that Jason was the one who called. That means whatever has happened involves me, or that I would break down as soon as she filled me in. Jesus, what could have happened? I need to be strong. Breathe Jenny.

"Jenny," Hayley speaks again after a pause. I turn my head to look at her, hoping, wishing, that whatever comes next has nothing to do with A— "Aiden was in an accident; he's in the hospital."

Just like that, the ground slips from under me. The universe sure has a funny way of throwing things at you. I thought that text was bad; I guess it wasn't bad enough. Here, have some more tragedy, Jenny. My vision blurs, my cheeks are wet.

"Jenny?" Hayley asks.

I don't reply. Instead, I look down at my blurry phone,

at the voicemail he left me, and press the button to play it, putting the phone to my ear.

It's quiet for a few seconds then "Jenny..." Aiden's beautiful voice says my name. If I close my eyes, I can pretend he's next to me, his mouth by my ear. "I think you saw the text message from Chloe. I'm sorry I haven't had a chance to explain earlier." He pauses, inhaling loudly. My free hand flies to the middle of my chest, pressing my palm against my aching heart. "Aah," he continues. "I want you to know that whole thing with Chloe...it was all a lie. She lied about everything. Being pregnant, sleeping with me..." *I know, Aiden, I know.* I want to tell him, but he continues without waiting for my reply. "It was all a ploy to get Jason back. I should have told you everything straight away." *It's okay. I know it must have been hard. I didn't give you a chance to explain.* Tears are running down my face as I clutch the phone harder to my ear. "I was going to." *I believe you.* "I'm so sorry." *Don't be. I'm the one who should be sorry.* "I love you." His voice cracks. *I love you too.* "I love you so mu—"

He doesn't finish. Instead, I hear the engine gather speed, then a loud bang.

And an ear shattering scream.

The scream is mine.

Chapter 37

Beep

J*enny...*
"I love you."
I love you too, kitten.
"Please come back to me."
I'm here.
"You promised. You promised me we'll be together. Until we get old."
I'm here. We will...
"Don't break your promise."
I wouldn't, not ever.
"I love you."
I love you too. Why do you sound so sad?
"Come back to me, please."
Jenny... I'm here.
"You promised me forever."
You are my forever.

Beeeeeeeeeeeeep.

. . .

Jenny? What's this sound?

"Nurse! Nurse!"

Chapter 38

Family

They say you are what you eat. Funny, I don't remember eating 'sexy' this morning.
- Aiden

I give myself five minutes.

Five minutes for a full on breakdown.

Five minutes is too much.

Five minutes is not enough...

Five minutes is exactly how long it takes us to get to the hospital.

As Hayley parks the car, I shake myself out of the despair I'm feeling, knowing that it's time to put on my big girl pants and be strong.

Be strong for him.

I run from the car, through the parking lot, narrowly missing being hit by an unassuming, blue Jetta. The driver shouts after me, but I can't hear him. All I see is the glass door entrance to the hospital as it gets closer and closer until, finally, it automatically opens in front of me. I stop, and tentatively walk through and to the information desk. A middle-aged, tired-looking nurse wearing flowery scrubs and large, red rimmed glasses looks up at me expectantly.

"Aiden. Aiden Vaughn," I gasp out, trying to catch my breath. She just keeps on looking at me, so I clear my throat and start again. "Can you tell me where Aiden Vaughn is, please? He was...in an ac-cident." My voice breaks on the last word, and I fight back the tears. In my head, the last bit from the voicemail, the crash, is playing on repeat. The screeching tires, breaking glass, screams of passers by... Then, silence as the message ends.

I need to be strong.

The nurse types something on her computer, then looks up at me.

"He's in surgery, but only family is allowed in the waiting room."

"I-I'm—" Tears threaten to break free again when a familiar voice says behind me,

"She's his sister."

I nod.

"And you are?"

"I'm their step-sister," Hayley says. Quick thinking. I'd have never thought of that. I nod again, this time with more conviction. The nurse looks at the both of us, narrowing her eyes, then back at the screen, muttering something to herself, shaking her head.

It seems Hayley's white lie has worked, because, soon, we are walking through winding corridors until we reach a small waiting room with a few plastic chairs and a dying ficus plant in the corner.

Two figures stand up and rush toward us when we arrive.

"Grasshopper." Carter pulls me into a hug. The world blurs as fresh tears stream down my cheeks and onto his shirt. I allow myself a minute of being weak, then take a deep breath and step out of Carter's warm embrace.

I wipe my cheeks with the sleeve of my jumper and look around. "Tell me everything."

"We don't know much," Carter hesitates.

"Then tell me what you know."

"Jen..." Jason interrupts. I whirl around to face him just as the double doors open.

"Nurse Riley." Carter beams at her. She shakes her head and arches her brow, looking around at us with disbelief.

"I see Aiden's family is ever growing," she mutters to herself.

"I'm his sister," I burst out.

Jason snorts quietly. "That's just wrong. So wrong."

"Step-sister," Hayley chimes in, putting her hand up like we're in class and she's just been called upon.

"Ooooh, we're doing the introductions?" Carter says in a husky voice. "This is Aiden's cousin, no one important, really." He points to Jason before putting his palm on his chest and taking a step toward the very pretty nurse, who looks unimpressed. "And I am Aiden's better looking brother, but you may have noticed that already." He winks at her.

Nurse Riley takes a deep breath and turns to leave.

"Ma'am." I run to her. "Can you tell me how he is? Please?"

"It's Riley. My mom is a Ma'am," she says gently. "His sister, huh?" I nod, my eyes pleading. She puts her hand on my shoulder, and I swear it weighs a ton. Please let him be okay. "What's your name, hon?"

"Carter!" Carter shouts from the corner. "But you can call me sugar plum," he finishes in a stage-whisper. I shot him a look that could shrivel his nuts if I had the magical powers of Hermione. But I don't, so I just turn back to the kind nurse.

"Jenny."

"Well, Jenny, your 'step-brother' is in the best possible hands he could be. He is currently in surgery and we are doing the best we can..."

"How long will he be in surgery for?"

"I can't tell you that, but there's a lot of damage and internal bleeding."

"Could you—?"

"Yes," she reads my mind. "I'll come back every so often to let you know how it's going. For now, rest assured that the surgeon is doing everything he can to keep him alive."

"Thank you," I whisper and hug her. She strokes my hair and unwraps my arms from around her. She smiles a small smile, then turns to leave. Carter runs after her, hot on her heels.

"Seriously, does he ever stop?" Hayley grimaces.

"Give him a break," Jason says. "It's his coping mechanism. When things get tough, or awkward, or scary, or are normal...he flirts."

Hayley grunts, then flops on one of the plastic chairs. I walk over and sit next to her, glancing at the white clock on the wall, at my shoes, the clock, my nails, the clock again.

The clock is definitely broken.

I get up, pace around the room, sit down again, and flick through a magazine, look up at the clock again...

How the hell has it only been five minutes?

"I'm going to grab a coffee. Anyone want a coffee?" I

jump up from my seat, my fists clenched. The need to do something, keep busy, is overpowering.

No one replies, so I just leave in search of the cafeteria. It takes me half an hour to find it, get coffees for everyone, then make my way back to the rest of the group.

As I near the door, balancing the styrofoam cups filled with the magical liquid, the nurse from earlier walks into the corridor. She looks at me and smiles. My heart flutters in hope. She reaches me and opens the door to the waiting room for me. Her eyes are tired and sad, and I nearly drop the coffee cups when I realize she's coming with the news I was hoping for.

A tear trickles down my cheek as I put the coffees on the table and turn to face her.

"The surgery is finished," the nurse says, then takes a deep breath. "It was very difficult. A lot of internal bleeding." I feel Carter and Jason step behind me in a protective manner as the nurse continues, unaware of the fact that each word she utters stabs my soul. I hang my head. "Jenny," she places a hand on my shoulder and gently squeezes. "We fixed what we could but," I see a water droplet on the floor. I stare at it intently as another one drops from my eye and joins it, making it a tiny bit bigger. "He's in a coma," she finishes.

My head whips up. "He's alive?" Please say yes, please say yes.

She grimaces. "Yes, but the next few days are touch and go." All I hear is that Aiden is alive. He's alive! A rush of emotion overwhelms me. Alive!

"Can I see him?" I plead, barely able to choke out the question as the lump of relief grows in my throat. She's silent for a while, studying my features, then nods, almost imperceptibly.

"Give me a minute."

"Thank you," I whisper.

Nurse Riley is back within an hour and leads us to another waiting area near where we were.

"Just one of you, okay?" She looks at us as we stand in a perfect row and nod in unison. She opens the wooden door, and I unsteadily step into the room.

It smells clean, sterile.

I look around and take in the large window, the bathroom door to my right. To my left, a TV is mounted on the wall, and there's a large wardrobe unit next to it. I look at the one place my eyes have been avoiding thus far.

The bed.

The bed and the person in it.

Aiden is lying on his back, under a thin, white sheet. Is he cold? I take a step toward him and take him in. His eyes are closed and his face is bruised with little cuts all over. There are wires attached to his body and a large tube coming out of his mouth, keeping him alive. That's all I need to see in order to get my wits back.

I rush to him.

His chest and left arm are covered in a cast, as is one of his legs. There are bruises and cuts everywhere, and half of his head is shaved, revealing a big bandage. I shiver, then take a hold of his hand and squeeze it. Hoping, praying for a squeeze back.

Nothing happens, and I close my eyes.

"Aiden," I whisper, my voice cracking. "I love you." I open my eyes and drink in his face, wishing for it not to be the last time. "Please come back to me," I croak out and squeeze his hand again.

I lay my head next to his arm, his hand still in mine, and breathe in his scent. He doesn't smell like Aiden, he smells like a hospital, like surgery, like medication. Tears threaten to break free yet again, so I take a big breath and sit up. "You have to live," I say with conviction. "You promised. You promised me we'll be together," I say to him. "Until we get old."

I pull his hand to my cheek, then gently move it to my lips and place a small kiss on his fingertips. "Don't break your promise."

The large lump in my throat stops me from speaking. I stroke his face and start praying. I've never prayed before in my life, but I don't find it awkward. Instead, it feels comforting. I have this feeling, this belief that someone is listening.

"I love you," I whisper again to Aiden. "Come back to me," I tell him. I'm not giving him the option not to.

The beeping of the heart monitor is steady, and I take a deep breath, knowing that I'll need to get out soon. I place a kiss on his forehead and whisper. "You promised me forever."

A simple reminder, but maybe he'll listen. I hold on to his hand for a while longer, then unwrap my fingers and gently place it by his side. I take a deep breath, then get up and start walking toward the door. I'm not going to look back. Looking back would mean I'll never see him again. So I'll be strong.

My gaze fixed on the door, I take wobbly steps. As my hand reaches for the door handle, the sound I've been dreading fills the room. One singular, long beep. I pull open the door and shout for the nurse.

Doctors and nurses rush in, and the guys and I are left alone again. Hoping. Anticipating.

Was it my fault?

I fall to the floor and my head drops into my hands. I don't want to be strong anymore. Can someone else please be strong for me? My heart breaks over and over with every second the doctors don't come out. Then again, every second they are gone means that they are still trying, doesn't it? I hope they never come out!

After what feels like a million years, they do. Their faces grim.

I stand up and look into the room through the gap between the door, and I nearly cry out as I hear the steady beep of his heart monitor.

The rest of the day is a blur. We're told to go home, but we all refuse and, finally, they let us back in to see Aiden. I stay by his side, holding his hand, worrying that if I let go again, he'll get worse...again. I sleep by his bed that night.

When I wake up the next morning, Aiden is still alive and still in a coma. I keep talking to him, telling him about anything I can think of. I recite poems, I tell him stories, I read, I teach him all about biochemical techniques and systems used to analyze data. I'm hoping that he'll get so bored with my aimless babbling that he'll wake up.

By noon, I really need the toilet and I call Carter in, making him swear to hold Aiden's hand until I come back. He shakes his head begrudgingly but complies nonetheless while muttering that King Carter should be left out of it. I'd called Aiden's parents in; they arrived late last night. But they left to check into a hotel. They were not impressed with having their family expanded by four new kids, but they didn't blow our cover. I think they were just relieved that Aiden was not on his own.

In the bathroom, I wash my face with cold water. My eyes are red and puffy, but I don't care. All I care about is Aiden.

When I come back out, Jason intercepts me, dragging me to the cafeteria and making me drink a cup of hot coffee and eat a stale sandwich. I break all kinds of records with the speed I ingest the food. I've been gone for over half an hour. So, once I finish, instead of walking, I run, not wanting to be gone from him any longer.

I run as fast as my feet allow, dodging doctors and wheelchairs, forgetting all about the fact that I hate running. I run until I don't.

Until I see Carter outside of Aiden's door.

I come to a full stop.

What is he doing outside? He promised! He promised not to let go!

Unless...

The sandwich threatens to come back up as I take the last few steps towards Carter.

Then I see his face.

He's beaming.

And just like that, I start crying again. I cry with relief. I let the happy tears fall down my cheeks as my chest fills with air; light, fluffy air. I can breathe again. I wipe my cheeks and fold myself into Carter.

"He's out of the coma, grasshopper." I nod into his neck in understanding. "They're still inside, unhooking him from the tubes, you know?"

I nod again and step away, a smile breaking my face for

the first time in what feels like forever. "He's alive and awake," I whisper in amazement.

My Aiden.

He's alive.

He's awake.

Nothing could make me happier.

"Listen, there's something you should know," Carter says grimly. I look up at him expectantly. "After the coma, he might not remember you."

My jaw drops just as the door opens, and a young doctor comes out smiling at us. Nurse Riley is right behind him. She stops in front of me.

"It seems to me that you all have lost your British accents," she says, mirth in her eyes. Busted. We managed to keep her away from Aiden's parents all through the night, but I guess our cover was blown as soon as Aiden woke up and was able to speak.

Carter pushes me toward the door and whispers, "You go see him. I'll take care of this."

I walk into the room.

Aiden is on the bed; his eyes are closed.

"Aiden." I rush to his side, taking his hand. His eyes flutter open and he looks at me. "It's me. Jenny," I say, keeping my voice light. "You might not remember me but... well...you love me and...I love you too," I rush the words.

Aiden smiles. "How could I ever forget you?" His voice is hoarse, barely audible, and he squeezes my hand, making my heart jump. "I mean, I tried," he continues. "For six years, I tried to forget you to no avail. I guess you should just count yourself stuck with me."

I smile at him, squeezing his hand back. "Sorry, Carter said—"

"In my defence, I watched 'The Vow' last night. That

shit was a true story, so there." Carter walks into the room, Jason and Hayley behind him. They all gather around Aiden's bed.

"You scared us, man," Jason says, smiling. "For a minute, I thought I'd have to find another roommate, and you know what a hassle that can be. There are some proper British weirdos out there."

"Shut up." I laugh. "I think what Jason is trying to say is that we're all happy that you're okay." I lean over him and place a gentle kiss on his lips.

"Incest!" Carter shouts.

Aiden looks confused. "Let's just say that, for the time being, I'm your sister," I say in a terrible British accent.

"Oh yeah, we're all one big, happy family," Carter confirms in his version of British, wrapping his arms around Hayley and Jason. Jason follows, putting his arm around me.

We are.

Happy.

Family.

Chapter 39

The End

I'm not half as crazy as I look. I'm twice as crazy.
- Carter

Being in a car accident is not a cakewalk. Everything hurts, add to that all the tubes sticking out of your body; the incessant itching under the casts, of which I have too many; and you have yourself one very itchy, very annoyed British guy.

Or, at least you would, if it wasn't for one little ray of sunshine in this whole awful scenario.

Jenny.

She hasn't left my side since I woke up after the surgery, and while some people might find that a bit too much, for me, it's a breath of fresh air. It's exactly what I need. Her. I need her.

Having her here with me, by my side, makes it all easier to deal with. Especially when she puts on that god awful

British accent whenever any of the staff comes into the room. She cracks me up, making me forget all about the pain.

She doesn't have to, though. Her presence alone makes the pain go away. Her smile... Her smile makes me forget that anything was ever wrong. And she seems to be the only thing that calms my overachieving parents down. Thankfully, as soon as I woke up from the coma, they decided that they should go back to London, since I was 'just fine'. Otherwise, I would have lost it a million times with them.

"You ready?" Her eyes, full of wonder and relief, lock with mine, and her lips twitch into a smile, making my heart jump in my chest. I nod and place my hands on the armrests of the wheelchair they insisted on. I could limp with one leg in the cast. No problem. But, apparently, there are protocols when it comes to 'early discharge'. Not that it was that early.

It felt like I've been cooped up in the hospital for far too long when, in reality, it's only been three weeks. I was ready to face the world last week if you asked me, especially since classes started back up.

Kitten wheels me outside straight to her car, parked right up front.

Oh yeah, I forgot my car—which would have been so much more appropriate for transporting me back home—was totaled in the crash.

The crash, which was a bit more sinister than we initially thought. After I woke up, we had a visit from the police. The blue truck that hit my car belonged to none other than Benny's cousin. Apparently, Diego was watching our house, trying to figure out where Benny was. Somehow, he knew I was Benny's Big Brother and was trying to send a message. What sort of a message, I don't know. I'm just happy that I was the only one who got hurt and that Diego ended up with an extended sentence and no prospects for parole anytime soon. Most importantly, he never got to Benny, who was back at his mum's.

Jenny and I talked for hours about everything that went down as soon as I was able to stay awake long enough to hold a conversation. I couldn't shake the feeling that she felt guilty, somehow responsible, for what had happened. When, in fact, I knew it was my stupid brain and the fact that I decided to keep shit to myself that caused all of this mess. It seemed like neither one of us wanted to back down, though, so we agreed to disagree, especially when Jenny promised to make it up to me 'when I was well enough'. I could get down with that. Literally.

I smile as Jenny gently buckles me up in the backseat, propping blankets around me.

"I'll drive carefully." She kisses my lips, and I pull her in closer, deepening the kiss. The last three weeks drove me crazy. Having her near but not being able to hold her in my arms, kiss her like I wanted to kiss her, was my personal hell.

Jenny pulls away, and my eyes zero in on her swollen lips, making me think of all the things I will be able to do to her once we're back home.

"We're still here, you guys." Jason clears his throat. "And I'm still finding this very, very wrong."

"Oh well." Kitten beams up at him, her voice a bit hoarse. "Meet you at the house?"

"Yeah," Jason hesitates. "We'll drive slow. Really, really slow in fact. Take back roads and all. Maybe go for food." I grin at him as he shakes his head in disgust. "Maybe...I'll stay over at Carter's tonight. Don't think I'll be able to handle you two." He makes a gagging noise.

"Agreed," Carter says. He's not looking at me. He's staring at his hands, glancing up at Jenny every so often. His eyes are sad, and I feel a ping in my chest. My best friend is hurting, and I have a good idea why. He needs a distraction.

"Suit yourselves." Jenny laughs, then hops into the driver's seat, waving goodbye at our friends.

She drives carefully, glancing into the back mirror every minute, checking if I'm okay. This is the first time in three weeks her back is to me and, even though she is still very close, only a few feet away, her seat between us, my body aches for her touch. My skin is crackling with anticipation of her being near again.

When we arrive at the house, she takes great care in helping me out of the car and into my room.

"Kitten, I'm not made of glass. I won't break," I tease.

She gazes at me, searching my eyes, then sits next to me on the bed. "You nearly did. You nearly didn't come back... to me." Her voice breaks, and something in her words tugs at my soul. It's like I've heard her say this before...

I frown, concentrating. "I'll always come back to you."

"Good, because you promised." She nods, giving me a small smile. "You promised me forever and I will hold you to that."

Her words play on repeat in my head until I find what I was trying to grasp at. I remember. I remember her words, the only thing that kept me grounded while I was in the comma. I thought I imagined it all, but could she have actually spoken them to me?

"You said that before," I hesitate. "I remember..." She looks confused. "I heard you." Words rush out of my mouth. "I heard your voice. You said to come back to you, you said I promised. I promised you forever."

"You heard that?" Tears start rolling down her cheeks as I nod, pulling her to my chest. "Kitten, you're the only thing that kept me alive. Your voice, your touch, they gave me hope. They reminded me that I've got something to live for," I whisper into her hair.

She hugs me tighter, and I wince in pain but don't say a word, revelling in her proximity.

"I love you," she mumbles.

"I've always loved you."

"Bull poop," she sniffles, laughing.

"You don't believe me, huh?"

"Nope. I have it on good authority that you hated me."

"Now that is a lie. I managed to convince myself that it was true for a short period of time, but deep down inside, it has always been you. As soon as you sauntered back into my life, wiggling that amazing butt of yours at me, I was a goner."

"Ah-ha! So you only like me for my butt! I knew it!" She laughs.

"Kitten, kitten, kitten... I don't like you. I love you. And I sure as hell love your butt. Now, do me a favour and reach into my nightstand." I arch my brow at her suggestively.

Her eyes go huge, and I have to stop myself from laughing.

"Okay." She opens the little door and looks confused. "They're just books..."

"You have a dirty mind." I smirk. "And I like where it's gone. I promise, we'll get to that in a second. Now, take the books out."

She obliges, pulling the stack of paperbacks. She scans through the titles, when finally, she notices. Her lips part as her hand reaches her mouth, and all books but one topple down to the ground. I smile.

"You kept it all this time?"

"Must have read it a thousand times by now." She gently strokes the cover of the book she gave me so long ago.

"But it's been forever."

"Jenny." I tsk. "When will you learn that you are my forever?

I take the copy of *Life of Pie* out of her hand and pull her to me, placing a kiss on her lips and gently prying her lips open with my tongue, tasting her. She moans into my lips and runs her fingers through my hair.

"You're home," she whispers. "I have finally found my home."

Epilogue

6 years later

"This bloody thing won't close!" I exclaim, exasperated. You'd think that after all this time, the monster would give out and die on me. But noooo... He just keeps on living his best life, mocking me every time I travel anywhere.

"Awww, kitten, you want me to close Sully for you?" Aiden comes up behind me and kisses the nape of my neck. I turn around and wrap my arms around him, the suitcase all but forgotten. "Yes, please, Mr. Vaughn." I pull his head close to mine and land a big smoocher on his stubbly face. He has not shaved in over two weeks, and I have to say I'm digging the stubble, especially in the bedroom...

"At your service." He winks at me.

Aiden, ever the seducer, trails his fingers down my side, lifting me up and wrapping my legs around him. "Mmmm, I will never get tired of this." He nuzzles my neck, the scruff of his beard rubbing against my sensitive skin.

"Good thing I'm keeping you." I smile into his hair, then sigh. Aiden strokes my face once, twice, then gently drops me to my feet and turns to face Sully. With minimal effort, he closes that fucker and zips him up. How the hell? This hunk of a man never fails to impress me. We've been together for over six years and, with a hand on my heart, I can honestly say I have never been happier. He is the key.

I used to be terrified at the prospect of moving to new places, at having to start over. With Aiden, that fear is gone. He is my anchor, my constant, my everything. It doesn't matter that straight after college we moved back to London. Aiden set up a charity practice where he helps those in need of legal services but without the means to pay for it. I'm so proud of him. It took a lot of convincing and shouting, but his dad finally came on board when Aiden signed the paperwork to be a silent partner in the Vaughn Industries conglomerate. I think his dad just really wanted it to stay in the family. I get that. The money doesn't hurt either. Apparently, being a silent partner brings with it some nice dividends, which means Aiden can truly focus on his passion for helping underprivileged kids.

I'm sure you're wondering what has happened to little, old me. Straight after we moved to London, I snagged a job with Cancer Research UK. No, no... I haven't found a cure yet, but I'm working on it. The best thing about my job is that I can continue my education while doing research and lab work, so basically a dream for a nerd like me!

"We really should be checking out," Aiden groans from behind me. I dive onto the bed and bounce a couple of times, spread like an eagle.

"I'm gonna miss you, bed. You've given me some fantastic memories and nights full of blissful slumber."

"Er-hmm," Aiden harrumphs behind me. "I think you'll find I was the one who gave you all the blissful memories." He was, but the guy already has an enormous ego, so I try not to indulge it too often. I nuzzle the pillow and consider if stuffing it under my dress could fool anyone into thinking I'm pregnant. Probably not, as the staff here came to know us by name in the last two weeks. Imagine if, on the last day, I'd come out looking ready to pop. Nothing to see here, peeps, supernatural pregnancy here. You know, like Bella Swan. Duh, all I needed was two weeks. But honestly, both the pillows and the mattress were so comfy I'd happily stuff them in Sully to take them home. "C'mon, kitten, let's get going. They'll come and pick up our bags for us while we check out." I huff and get off the bed. I'll miss this, the sunshine, the holiday mode, the constant free drinks, all the food you can eat, the pool... "We'll come back next year, if you want." The wonderful mind reader takes my hand. I knew I loved him for a reason.

"I hope you enjoyed your honeymoon, Mr. And Mrs. Vaughn," The lady in reception says as Aiden hands her his credit card. Oh, did I forget to mention this tidbit? YES! We totally got hitched! He liked it and he put a ring on it!

It was a small ceremony with just our families, and Carter, obviously. That boy would not miss a party if his life depended on it. But it was perfect. Aiden's dad wasn't too happy that he couldn't throw a big wedding party to invite all his business contacts, but Aiden and I wanted it to be just us, so we promised him that once we get back from our honeymoon, he can host a business party to celebrate our nuptials. I don't mind. In the end, I had my perfect wedding with all my important people, and my perfect Aiden.

Honestly, to this day I think he'll turn around at any moment and ask himself 'What am I doing with this crazy woman?', but he hasn't yet, and I'm keeping my fingers crossed that it'll take him at least 60 years to figure out he married a total nutcase. By that time, he'll be too old to get rid of me. Oh, who am I kidding? He'll probably be a GILF.

"It was amazing," Aiden replies. "In fact, I think we'll be coming back for our anniversary."

"Oh, that's wonderful!" She hands Aiden a bill to sign. "As requested, we contacted our supplier and the new mattress and bedding should be delivered to London in the next week."

My jaw hits the floor. "You didn't!" Aiden's dimples flash my way, those damned dimples... "You little rascal."

"What can I say? What my wife wants, my wife gets." A hundred orgasms, stat. No. I'm joking. Seriously joking, I'd die after the tenth one. Nine is how many Aiden got out of me in one go. He's a wizard, just like Harry Potter. But seriously, when that eighth one happened, I was ready to keel over and die, but the devil himself possesses Aiden each time we are in bed, and he makes it his personal goal to coax as many as he can. Every. Single. Time. I'm not complaining. I'm not! But when tears are streaming down my face, snot out of my nose, and my whole body is shaking...you gotta give a girl a small break, you know what I mean? Otherwise, I'll end up in that book, 'Unusual ways to die'. That's a book that'll take you down a dark, dark rabbit hole. I digress.

"I'm definitely keeping you." I smile up at my hunky husband adoringly. "You, mister, are stuck with this." I gesture up and down my body.

"Thank fuck for that," he mutters as he takes my hand

and guides me outside to the taxi. The driver jumps out and opens the car door for us. I'll miss being a honeymooner, where everyone waits on you...

At the airport, we spend a short amount of time browsing for last minute gifts, then, before I know it, it's time to board. I miss home. I miss Jake and Buke. Buke is the only one of Aiden's dogs that's still with us, and her and Jake are inseparable. Dad also lives in London with his girlfriend, Lisa, whom he apparently met the year I moved to Starwood. Talk about when the cat's away.... But, of course, I'm happy for him. Lisa is wonderful and Dad finally put down roots in one place. As I settle into our comfy first class seats, wondering if ten in the morning is too early for champagne, Aiden squeezes my hand.

"You okay, love?" he asks with concern in his voice. Fuck. I always forget. I should really tattoo this on my hand for situations like that. 'Aiden thinks you're afraid of flying'. I take in a shaky breath, ready to start the performance of a lifetime, then I exhale. I mean, the dude married me. Divorces aren't easy so, maybe it's time to fess up?

"Aiden..." A corner of his mouth lifts up, and a small dimple makes an appearance. "There's something you should know..." He raises his eyebrow. I take a deep breath and prepare for what surely will be the start of a divorce conversation. You lie to somebody for six years, shit is bound to come back and bite you in the ass. But maybe I'll manage to convince him to forgive me before he signs on the dotted line?

"You're not afraid of flying," he says matter-of-factly. What the hell?

"You know?"

"I've known for a while. Since our first flight back from London, actually." I hang my head. "Why didn't you ever tell me?"

"I dunno," I mumble. "I was embarrassed at first, cause I was so into you, and then... It just became a thing. I'm sorry."

"I forgive you," he says, stroking my cheek. "In fact, I know just the way you can make it up to me." He does? Naughty thoughts start swirling in my head. As much as he always says he doesn't, he wants the membership card to the Mile High Club, I just know it!

"Oh, yeah?" I look up at him from beneath my lashes, with what I hope is a seductive way.

"Yeah," he blushes. Aiden blushes! This must be some kinky stuff he is thinking of. "I was thinking..." He takes a deep breath, takes my hand and looks into my eyes. He seems terrified, but also kinda hopeful. "Now that we're married... That maybe... You know, only if you think you're ready," he blurts out, and my heart begins to race as if it's knowing where this is going, even if my head is still not quite there. "That maybe we could start trying."

I draw a blank. "Start trying what?"

And, as Aiden squeezes my hand again, my brain catches up.

"For a family." He smiles a small smile. My eyes well up and a tear escapes. "Oh, Jenny! It's okay if you're not ready. There's no rush. I just thought I'd bring it up in case you are."

"N-o," I manage to say. Aiden's face falls. "No. No. I mean, no. Shit, I'm not doing this right. Aiden," I slip my hand from his and cup his face. "It's everything I wanted.

Yes, I want to start a family. Yes, I want to start it with you. God, I can't think of anything else I want more right now!"

His crumpled face rearranges into a bright smile. "Yes?"

"Yes."

Want more of Jenny and Aiden?

Scan or click the QR code to receive two deleted scenes straight to your inbox

Read on for a preview of Carter's story in For What It's Worth

For What It's Worth

Prologue

Christmas Day - One year ago

Fucking Christmas spirit, my ass. Who's to say Christmas is supposed to be the time of happiness and tinsel shit, anyway? Not this guy. How can you live through the happiest time of the year when your heart has been stomped on? How the fuck are you supposed to be smiling through presents, food, and family stuff when the person you're in love with is all loved up... With someone else. Yup, I'm that sucker. The guy who falls for his best friend then watches her fall in love with another dude.

It didn't happen instantly. Don't get me wrong, Jenny, or as I like to call her, Grasshopper, is gorgeous and clever and out of this world funny, but I have my qualities too. And my qualities, well...they bring all the girls to the yard, and this yard ain't discriminating. So it took me a while to get my head out of my ass and realize that the girl I'm crazy about was worth fighting for. Needless to say, I was a little too late, and Grasshopper was currently loved up in London with my other best friend. Fucking cliche.

What can a guy do in a situation like this but get himself out of this world drunk? Nothing.

"One more shot!" Hayley shouts, pouring the whiskey into our shot glasses as Frank Sinatra sings '*Jingle Bells*' over the speakers.

It's funny how small the world is. One minute you think you're drowning your sorrows all by yourself, the next a friend from college, located three hundred and sixty miles away, sits down next to you and demands you celebrate Christmas in style. Hayley, Grasshopper's best friend, is in L.A. for a modeling gig or something, and they chose tonight to come out on the town. To the same bar I always go to when I visit home. When all I wanted to do was be alone and mope. Call it fate. Call it shit luck. Call it whatever. I'm done caring.

"To misery." I raise my shot glass, liquid sloshing over the rim. Hayley narrows her eyes at me but lifts her glass to mine.

"To freedom." Sydney, the girl sitting with us, clinks her glass with mine and, without thinking, downs the whiskey in one go. I follow suit, not wanting to be left behind. That will make it...six shots? Maybe. Maybe eight. Hayley gets up and makes her way towards the bar. She's steady on her feet, which I find impressive. You have to admire a chick that can hold her liquor. As she leans over the bar and starts chatting to the bartender, I turn my head and face Sydney.

"Why freedom? Aren't we all free? Isn't that what America stands for? Land of freedom?" I ask, pouring another shot. She cocks her head and picks up her glass.

"I'm English. Why misery?" She deadpans, then downs her shot.

"English-shminglish, you're in America, babe. Did you just get out of prison?"

"No, and you're changing the subject."

"Who cares, anyway? I'm miserable, and I'll drink to that." I lift my shot glass to my lips. Her gaze doesn't waver, so I sigh and put the shot down. "I seem to be suffering from a serious disease called badassery." She doesn't bite, so I lift the shot again and throw it back. Slamming it down on the table, I smile. "I'm the jackass who's in love with his best friend."

"I assume it's not reciprocated?" She pours two more shots. Good girl.

"Would I be drinking myself into a stupor if it was?" I pluck one of the shot glasses from her hand and, as our fingers touch, an electric shock runs through me. My eyes meet her blue ones as, simultaneously, we down the shot. I'm probably not going to remember much tomorrow, but I sure as hell hope I'll remember her. She's fucking beautiful. Like, should be on the covers of magazines type of beautiful. Who am I kidding? Given her employment, she probably *is* on the covers of all the magazines. Her hand brushes my leg, interrupting my thoughts.

"You know, the best way to get over someone is to get under someone else." She winks at me. I fucking knew it. God must have been giving out lottery tickets today, and yours truly has hit the jackpot. I'll be sure to say a couple of Hail Mary's in thanks for this miracle.

"Oh, yeah?" I reach for the bottle, but her hand gets there first, and as she lifts the whiskey to her lips, her gaze not leaving mine, my dick stirs in anticipation of what's to come. I smile at her then take the bottle out of her hands. She lifts her eyebrow and, not breaking my gaze from her, I take a long swig. "Want to go somewhere where they're not trying to brainwash us with Jingle Bells' subliminal message?" I ask.

When she nods, I stand up and reach for her hand. She takes it without hesitation. As we weave through the crowded bar, I look over at Hayley to wave goodbye. She's busy kissing the bartender, so I don't bother interrupting.

"I don't do relationships," I say once we're in an Uber. I want to get this out of the way before we get any further.

"I didn't ask for one. I just want to fuck." The driver's mouth opens. Yes, dude, I'm the master of the universe. This hot as fuck woman wants to have sex with moi!

"Lovely." I lean in and nuzzle her throat. She smells floral and fucking arousing. I lick at the spot on her neck where her vein pulses and am rewarded with a gasp.

"That, that there, now go lower," she whispers. The whiskey starts hitting me, so I wrap my fingers around her short, sunshine-colored hair and pull it.

"Patience, Sunshine." I nip at her earlobe as the Uber pulls up in front of her hotel.

Drunkenly, we make our way to the room. It's not pretty, but who the fuck cares? Carter *is going to get some*. When the key card clicks and the door opens, we tumble to the floor. My hands are all over her, rough and exploring. She tears at my clothes, ripping my t-shirt in half.

Fucking hot.

"Mmmm, nice, just what I was hoping for," she mumbles, stroking my chest up and down. That's all the invitation I need. In one swift motion, I lift her up and stumble to the bed, dropping her on it unceremoniously. The world is spinning full force now, but I'm a man on a mission. A mission to get my dick wet. Sunshine lifts on her elbows, her crop top riding up, and I am graced with a sight of glorious underboob. The view is so incredible I lick my lips, already imagining my mouth on them. Clumsily, I lean over her and pull her top up, exposing her pert nipples. As I circle my tongue around one, then suck it into my mouth, I lose my balance and fall to the side, catching my face on her shoulder.

"Fuck!" she yelps.

"You okay?" I slur.

"Yeah, I think so, You?" My eye is throbbing something fierce from the impact, but that's not going to stop me.

"Yeah."

"Great, now take off your jeans," she commands drunkenly. "We're breaking my dry spell."

Fuck yeah, we are. I stand up and unzip my jeans, but the fucking zipper catches on my boxers, so it takes some serious pulling for the fucker to go down. With a little force, I manage to unzip them. There's a hole in my Calvin Kleins', but I don't need them right now anyway. Eagerly, I pull my jeans and underwear down at the same time, and it's the wrong fucking move. I'm such an idiot. I stumble and—unable to catch my balance with my legs caught in this self-made denim trap—fall on my ass, banging my head on the leg of a chair in the process.

I think I'm dying.

I'm pretty sure I am, or at least I'm bleeding out.

Possibly, it might just be a big bruise, but it hurts like a motherfucker.

Sunshine's head peeps over the edge of the bed. Her eyes zero in on my cock, which is standing to attention despite the amount of whiskey I have running through my veins and injuries I have sustained. She licks her lips and slides off the bed, pulling her skirt down and lifting her top over her head, leaving her in just her panties. She goes to her knees, runs her hand up my leg, and all thoughts of bleeding out are instantly forgotten. When her fingers graze my balls, I nearly die. It feels like it has been forever since anyone touched me, and it has been. Truthfully, I haven't been with anyone since I kissed my best friend and realized I might have feelings for her. My stomach tightens. I close my eyes, trying not to think about Grasshopper, but it's the wrong move. The world just won't stop spinning. I'm half-aware of Sydney's hand wrapping around my cock, but the asshole is not cooperating, probably enjoying his time on the carousel much more than I am.

I open my eyes. Sydney is above me, my dick still in her hand. One look at her, her body, her face, her hair is all it takes to get me ready. I flip us around, Sydney landing underneath me. "Condom," she demands, wriggling down her panties. I couldn't be more on board with that demand. I reach down to my ankles, where my jeans still are, and pull a condom out. Sydney's eyes are half-closed, her lips parted as I pull it on.

I lean down to kiss her. The moment our lips connect, an electric current goes through me. Her arms wrap around my neck as she molds into me. The kiss is slow and deep, unhurried. She tastes like whiskey and mint, and her lips move against mine like they were made for each other. At the back of my head, I have a nagging thought, but I can't quite grasp it. When I pull away, her eyes are closed, lips tilted up in a small smile, a smile that spreads warmth around my body. I trail kisses down her jaw and neck before coming back up to nibble on her earlobe. As much as I want to fuck her, something urges me to make it last, make it count. My dick has other ideas and, as it brushes against the inside of her thighs, I can't help myself. Her legs open even more for me as I position myself against her heat. I push, no, slide into her in one go. She's so wet, so fucking wet. And tight and so fucking warm. The thought keeps coming almost within my reach, but I still can't quite grasp at it. I slide back out and push again. God, she feels so good. So fucking good. Like she was made just for me. I lift my head to look into her face and freeze. Sydney's eyes are closed, mouth parted. Her breaths are steady and deep.

A little snore escapes her.

The fuck?

She snores again, and I instantly pull out. What. The. Fuck? Did she just fall asleep while my dick was in her? I'm not being funny, but it's not like Carter Junior is a small guy. One does not simply fall asleep while my dick is inside them!

Sydney makes a content sigh and tries to turn to her side. I slide off her. Who is this devil? I lift her up and put her on the bed, then I go to the bathroom to discard the condom. How did this go from me putting the fucking thing in to her asleep in the next five seconds? I splash some cold water on my face, trying to get the world to stop spinning, but the world's not cooperating, so I go back into the room and slide in beside Sydney. Wrapping my arms around her, I nuzzle her hair and close my eyes. *Mine,* crosses my mind. Huh? *It's her, it's always been her.* I shrug the thoughts off and fall asleep.

When the sun wakes me up in the morning, I have a black eye, the room is empty, and Sydney is gone.

For What It's Worth

1. I'll Owe You Big Time

One year later

Your life can change drastically from one day to the next, trust me. I'm a prime example of that. Last year my best friend shared a video of me singing, and the thing blew up. I went from your average heartthrob next door type of guy to...not so average. Huh. Joking aside, I never lacked attention from women; they'd just fall into my lap, and things would go from there, usually ending up in a sweaty but satisfying finish. I like my women well sated and thoroughly fucked before I send them on their way. So what the hell has been fucking with my mojo this past year? For I, Carter Kennedy—also known as Casanova, as my best friend likes to call me—have not had sex in almost a whole year. Three hundred and fifty-two days, to be exact. It's absolutely unheard of for me. After the failed one night stand with Hayley's friend, Sydney, I tried again. I really did.

We were having a great time, we drank, we talked. There was chemistry between us, so we went back to my place. Katie was great. She had a dirty mouth and a banging body, and as soon as we got back to my place, she undressed herself and went down on her knees, unzipping my fly. A true sign of a keeper, that's a no brainer, right? So why, when I went to brush her brown hair out of her face so I could watch her lips wrap around my dick, did it go flaccid? For the rest of the night, I couldn't get it up, and trust me when I say it has *never* happened before. Never.

It was the worst night of my life. Katie didn't get anything out of it either. I tried, I really did, but she was... wrong, just wrong. I can't explain it. Maybe it was the Grasshopper thing, perhaps it was something else, but it allowed me to take a good, hard look at myself and realize that fucking my way through college might not be the best career choice. So after that, I did what I thought was best. I pretended I didn't have feelings for Jenny and poured all my emotions into writing songs. Songs which I then recorded and posted online. Songs that got me where I am today. It didn't hurt that I already knew how to play a guitar and string together some chords. Who am I kidding? When I was fourteen, it was my dream to be a singer songwriter, a dream which would have been a reality had it not been for the stage fright I experienced at a talent show I entered. Yes. Yes, I did. No, seriously, I did! I puked my guts out, ran away, and never looked back, I swear. I know it's hard to believe, but it's true. Yours truly has a weakness. Unfortunately, that weakness proved stronger than my desire to sing. Until last year, when that fire was lit again. A fire that was now burning stronger than ever, and it didn't hurt that, this time around, all I had to do was sing in front of the camera. No audience, no drama. But that was all about to change.

"Are you excited?" Jenny asks, plopping down in my chair as I stuff a t-shirt into my bag.

"Sure." I rub my temple. I'm not. I'm terrified, but I just need to man up and face my fears. That's exactly the reason why I'm taking this trip. I'll drive home from Starwood with a few stops on the way. The trip that would typically take me no longer than five and a half hours will take about a week.

"Itinerary is sorted?"

"Yes."

"How many stops are you making again?"

"Just a few. It all depends." I grit my teeth. Talking about this does not help my nerves. At all.

"You'll be fine, Carter. You were born for this, and I'll see you on New Year's Eve." Grasshopper grins at me. "Stop stressing, you nutter. You'll be amazing. I've watched every single one of your videos. Hell, I recorded some. And you, Mr. Miyagi, you rock!"

She's right. I need to stop getting stressed about this. This is just the test run. If I can't do it? No biggie. I'll just need to figure out something else to do with my life. I might go back to fucking my way through college. Sighing, I hug her.

"Thanks, Grasshopper. You're right, I'll be fine. Now go and make us some popcorn." She walks out of the room, and I shout after her. "Two bags, please. I would actually like to eat some this time!"

When the credits roll, Grasshopper is asleep, breathing softly, her head resting on my shoulder. I turn my face to her hair and breathe in her strawberry scent. It still hurts, watching her relationship with Aiden blossom and having to keep my feelings to myself.

"Is she asleep?" Aiden whispers from the doorway. I nod, embarrassed, pretending I wasn't just sniffing his girlfriend's hair. "You okay, mate?" I nod again. He knows I'm not, but he's not going to press. What could he say to a guy who's fallen for his girl? "I'll take her home." He walks over and lifts Jenny up. Her arms wrap around his neck on instinct, and she nuzzles his throat. Jealousy eats me up inside. I want to be him so badly, to have that sort of connection with her...with someone.

It doesn't take a genius to notice that I haven't been myself this past year. I don't know if it was Jenny, Sydney, Katie, or the combination of the three. I feel like I've just been going through the motions, smiling and talking where appropriate, but not really feeling anything. Except when I'm writing, then my emotions pour out and things are more clear. But it leaves me drained and in a zombie-like state. The whole process is a vicious circle.

I stand up and walk Aiden to the door, watching him put Jenny gently into the passenger seat and clip the seatbelt in. After his car accident last year, he became a stickler for rules, never going past the speed limit, always making sure everyone was buckled in. I don't blame him. I wave him off and walk back to the living room to tidy up, then to my bedroom. My phone is on my nightstand and, like every night, I battle with myself. I want to scroll through my contacts and call one of my sure things to end this miserable dry spell. But, like every night, I don't. It's not about fucking anymore. I'm missing that *something, that spark, that magic.* As much as it sucks, I want to find it.

I grab my phone and walk over to the bathroom to brush my teeth when I see a message notification.

Hayley: *Friend emergency. I have a huuuge favor. Please say yes.*

Me: *The answer is maybe. What's up, cutie?*

Hayley: *Friends' car broke down and they need a ride to LA. Can you please, please help?*

I hesitate. This trip was meant to be soul searching, in part. I don't know if I want a tag along.

Hayley: *They're quiet as a mouse, you won't even notice they're there.*

Hayley: *Pleeeeaaaase. I'll owe you big time.*

I sigh. Fuck it.

Me: *Tell them to be at mine at 10 am. If they're late, I'm leaving by myself.*

Hayley: *OMG thank you! You're the best! I shall be forever grateful.*

I get into bed, take a snap, and post it on my Instagram, wishing my followers a good night.

I close my eyes and take a deep breath. I hope I won't regret this.

J. Preston

WANT MORE
FOR WHAT IT'S WORTH?

READ NOW
just scan or click the QR code

About The Author

Jo Preston writes fun and sexy romance books.

She lives with her husband, son and a dog (that doubles as a teddy bear) in the UK, where she wraps up in warm clothes and hang out under umbrellas, dreaming of warm destinations.

When she's not writing, she enjoys a glass of wine (or two) with a good book or a favourite Netflix show and coming up with terms like #SmutCom.

Want to be a part of an exclusive smut loving community?

Become a member of the smut tribe

Scan or click the QR code

- facebook.com/authorjpreston
- instagram.com/authorjpreston
- goodreads.com/jpreston
- bookbub.com/authors/j-preston

Acknowledgements

Gosh, these are so much pressure! Bear with me since I'm doing it for the first time! There are so many people I need to thank. If I forget to name anyone, I'm truly sorry but please know I still very much appreciate you! Thanks for being the reason this book exists!

My beta team: Kirty, Carissa, Marcie, Chelsea, Bri, Channin, Jessica, Kyra, AmyLynn, Ashley, Dakota, Sami, Elizabeth, Brooke and Jenny. Each and every one of you has been invaluable in making this book into what it is today. Thank you for believing in Jenny and Aide, for answering my random questions at various hours and for inspiring me. Now onto Carter's story! Who's with me?

Special thanks to Carissa, thank you for doing the graphics and helping me out in the minefield that is trying to get your book out there! You're an absolute gem.

To all my author friends, you guys rock, especially my Motivational Arse Kicking Group. Your support and belief in me means the world to me. Love you all!

To my editor Addie. Thank you for putting up with me reformatting things half way through edits! Again sorry! I swear, I won't do it again :D But most of all thank you for helping me, you're never getting rid of me.

ARC team - thank you for giving me your notes and spotting last minute edits!

Thank you Rich, for being so patient and supportive each time I said I needed to write or edit. I love you to the moon and back, monkeypants.

And most importantly, thank YOU for picking up this book, and making my dream a reality. I hope you had a good laugh, maybe got a bit sad, but most of all enjoyed yourself while reading this book.

THE FALSE STARTS SERIES

For Crying Out Loud

For What It's Worth

Forever and a Day

For Heaven's Sake

THE HOLIDATES SERIES/ THE FALSE STARTS CROSSOVER

The Sexiest Nerd Alive

HEART OF A WOUNDED HERO/ THE FALSE STARTS CROSSOVER

Nothing Left To Lose

CURVES FOR CHRISTMAS/ THE FALSE STARTS CROSSOVER

Frost My Cookie

Printed in Great Britain
by Amazon